HIDDEN TREASURE

At the bottom of the suitcase was a blue velvet bag. Lily undid the drawstring and tipped out a strand of magnificent, fat, glowing pearls. She gasped as she fingered them, but what caught her attention was the strangely carved mother-of-pearl pendant that hung from the center. On it were carved parallel lines, a circle with smaller circles in it, and an X.

Impulsively she draped the rope of pearls around her neck. It felt smooth and cool and Lily shut her eyes as a wonderful feeling swept over her.

Other books by Di Morrissey

Heart of the Dreaming
The Last Rose of Summer
Follow the Morning Star
The Last Mile Home
When the Singing Stops
The Songmaster

HarperChoice

DI MORRISSEY

TEARS OF THE MOON

HarperPaperbacks

A Division of HarperCollinsPublishers

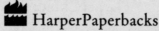
HarperPaperbacks
A Division of HarperCollins*Publishers*
10 East 53rd Street, New York, N.Y. 10022-5299

This is a work of fiction. The characters, incidents, and
dialogues are products of the author's imagination and are not to
be construed as real. Any resemblance to actual events or
persons, living or dead, is entirely coincidental.

ISBN 0-06-101314-5

HarperCollins®, ®, and HarperPaperbacks™
are trademarks of HarperCollins*Publishers* Inc.

The original paperback edition of this book was published in
1996 in Australia by Pan Macmillan Australia Pty Limited

Cover photo © 1997 by Photonica

First HarperPaperbacks printing: March 1998

Printed in the United States of America

Visit HarperPaperbacks on the World Wide Web at
http://www.harpercollins.com

10 9 8 7 6 5 4 3 2 1

ACKNOWLEDGMENTS

The Continental Hotel, Broome
Val Burton, Broome Historical Society
Broome Tourist Board, Bill Reed,
Linneys Pearls;
Broome; Peter and Jean Haynes,
ex-Broome; Brenda Anderson, Byron Bay, for
checking the manuscript, Ted Johnston for
proofreading
Selwa Anthony
Les Johnson, Albany (war historian)
And to **all** the staff of
Pan Macmillan throughout Australia
especially James Fraser, Nikki Christer,
Madonna Duffy, Roxanne Burns, Peter
Phillips, Jeannine Fowler, and
Lyndal (Charlie) Charles.

SPECIAL THANKS TO . . .

The man I love, who makes me joyful and suggested the idea for this book.

Jim Revitt for his critical and creative input—which goes back to showing a very young niece the magic of writing.

My children, Gabrielle and Nicolas, who are my best friends, best critics, and with whom I share unconditional love.

My mother, all my dear family and those who count as family.

And Uncle Ron Revitt for his terrific illustrations.

In memory of all those claimed by the sea . . .

According to Indian mythology it is believed
that pearls are formed by the tears of the moon
dropping into the sea . . .

WESTERN AUSTRALIA IN THE 1800s

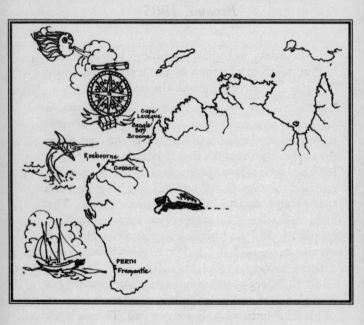

PROLOGUE
Broome, 1905

The deep-sea diver moved in slow motion, a heavy weighted boot kicking up small clouds of gray sand. All he could hear was the hiss of air down the hose and his own rhythmic breathing as he was towed above the sea bed by the lugger. He exhaled, a cluster of bubbles pushing upward toward the surface, thirty fathoms above. The clear capsules of trapped hot breath smelling faintly of chili and black sauce, eventually burst on the surface of the Indian Ocean close to the drifting lugger.

To the sleepy-eyed tender, vigilant despite his slumped and somnolent pose, the steady cluster of bubbles indicated all was normal. Through his fingers ran the coir signal rope and life line which acted as umbilical cord between the two men of two worlds. Ignoring the clatter of the hand pumps, the noise and chatter of the shell opener, the tender followed the footsteps of the diver, guiding the drift and direction of the lugger as the diver explored below.

The Japanese diver worked alone, secure in his

1

ability to stay deep, keep steady and "see" shell. He trudged across the sea bed, his rope basket almost filled with the broad, flat gray shells that were for some so difficult to spot. For nearly an hour he stayed in a world of intense strangeness and beauty, unaffected by the secrets and magic that unfolded about him. The novelty of the underwater world had waned early in his career. Inattention could result in missed opportunities or an accident.

The hiss of air was a constant noise in his head. Like a creature from some other planet, the bulbous form with the glass-windowed copper helmet made his way through water space, a stranger in an alien world.

He had been indentured for five years on Thursday Island, contracted for a further three here in Broome. He was a number one diver, one of the kings of Sheba Lane. The men who walked in the sea. The men who could stay deeper, work longer, find more shell than white, Malay or Aborigine. He had sold his share of snide pearls, done deals and profited from pearl finds and the shell take. But this was his last season. At lay up he would return to Wakayama Prefecture and Akiko san.

Was it the thought of the woman that distracted him? Was his ever-alert peripheral vision clouded for an instant with the rush of memory of the warm body, soft hair and sweet voice? Or had the gods decided this day, this moment, was his time? The small whale-bone charm nestling beneath the layers of flannel, rubber and canvas could not protect against the events that swiftly followed.

Out of the corner of his eye, he sensed a sudden movement, a glimpse of something large gliding close to him. Inadvertently, he expelled a rush of air, the burst of bubbles startling the silver shape. The huge swordfish angled away, its lethal broad sword slashing ahead of it. In its path were the dangling air hose and safety rope looping above the diver, but the monstrous fish barrelled on regardless.

The red rubber artery snaking above the diver was partially severed, the escaping air churning the water to a boiling cloud around him. He was dragged off balance by the force of the encounter, fumbling frantically to close his air escape valve and trap the remaining air in his suit, long enough to see him to the surface.

The tender was aware of some disaster, having felt the sudden drag and slackening of the air hose before the frantic signal from the diver to bring him up.

Normally the diver would be staged, resting at intervals to allow his body to adjust and prevent the build up of nitrogen in the blood. But the tender could tell from the wild signals of the desperate diver that he was losing air. Although the risk of paralysis would be high, he decided to bring him straight up.

Shouts aboard the lugger alerted the crew, and the men on the hand pump worked feverishly trying to force air down the hose and past the gaping leak so some breath of life reached the diver's helmet.

The diver felt the pressure mount. Burning pain seared through his joints as he swung like a puppet upward through the water, his body compressed and squeezed as he was dragged too quickly toward life-giving air.

In his last moments of consciousness he hoped they could swiftly patch the air leak and drop him back to a depth where he could be suspended for several hours while his body readjusted.

There are some miraculous stories of survival and just as many of the horrific fates met by divers of the deep. It was either death in the sea, by currents, whirlpools or hidden craters that simply sucked a diver into oblivion, or by unfortunate encounters with devil rays, swordfish, sharks or whales. Above the water, beri beri, cyclones, shipwrecks and mutinous crews could kill just as quickly. A diver might survive, only to be sentenced to a life ashore as a blinded, twisted cripple. The streets of Broome were haunted by the relics of men who'd wished they'd died a diver instead of living as one of the "bad luck ones."

They knew the dangers, but they took the risks.

The lugger lurched as all hands leaned over the side. The dripping diver was heaved on to the deck, his metal boots and helmet crashing on the planks.

The men shook their heads at the glimpse of the black skin through the glass. The helmet was unscrewed and the awful face greeted them ... eyes bulging, one eyeball popped on to a cheek, blood pouring from ears, nose and mouth. Where some bodies have been squeezed up into the corselet and helmet and had to be cut free, this diver could have some life left yet. They reattached the helmet, bound the air hose and slid him back into the sea while there was still a chance of saving him.

The number two diver went with him and waited, floating in the eerie silence of the tomb-like sea. He adjusted the air pressure in the suit and helmet in the hope the blackness would fade to pink skin, that the damaged head might lift within its metal casing.

The two divers hovered, side by side, as an hour passed. Finally the number two diver signalled to ascend. He hoped should his time come beneath the sea, that his own death would be swift.

The body was hauled from the suit, and as the lugger left the fleet to return to Broome, the shell openers returned to their work on the deck.

The first shell opened from the dead diver's basket showed a perfect roseate round. Its beauty would grace some privileged woman in a distant city, but it had come at a high price.

CHAPTER ONE
Sydney 1995

Lily sat on the floor of her mother's bedroom, feeling like an invader. Drawers of underwear, personal papers, jewelry, and two hat boxes filled with travel souvenirs and memorabilia were scattered around her. Piles of clothes and shoes buried the bed. Her mother's perfume, "Blue Grass," hung in the air and Lily wished she could cry.

She had put off the sorting of her mother's belongings for as long as possible. But now the apartment was on the market and several weeks had passed since the funeral, so she could delay no longer.

Lily noticed that dusk was settling in so she got up, switched on the light and went to pour herself a glass of wine.

How had it happened that she'd never been really close to her own mother and never noticed she had no family? She'd loved her mother, she was different to other mothers it seemed, and now Lily wished with all her heart she'd known her better. Truly known her—what important things had happened in her life that had hurt her, thrilled her. What dreams had never been fulfilled. How she'd felt when Lily was born. They'd never talked of such things. She'd never asked her mother and her mother had never asked her. And now it was too late. The hollow despair of this knowledge caused Lily feelings of guilt, failure and disappointment. Grief was a catalyst for many things and now Lily found the ground beneath her feet distinctly wobbly. Georgiana, her madcap, restless mother, had filled their life with travel and drama and told her how lucky they were to not be tied down by family strings. Just the two of them against the world. And Lily had believed her—until she had wanted a family of her own and the certainty of being in one place for the years ahead.

Lily wished she had known her mother's family and also her father, or his family. Georgiana had discarded several husbands, including Lily's father. They had met during the war. He was a charming American serviceman and she was young and ready for adventure. There was a swift courtship and what her mother dismissed as a "low-key wedding" before boarding one of the war-bride ships.

Lily had been born in 1947 but apparently life in Torrance, California, was not the life Georgiana had been led to expect after a diet of American movies. Georgiana divorced when Lily was a toddler and saw no reason to maintain any contact with her ex-husband. She gave Lily the impression that he'd never shown any interest in a child he had barely known. And as for in-laws, Georgiana had shuddered and stressed again how they were the lucky ones, to be as free as birds and able to choose their friends instead of being burdened with unpleasant relatives.

Lily's memories of her youth were of boarding schools and holidays in exotic places with her mother. These were treasured times with just the two of them. Georgiana never inflicted ex-step-fathers on Lily and Lily was always broken-hearted at leaving her fun-loving mother at the end of the holidays to return to school.

Georgiana made no secret of the fact she had been a difficult and rebellious child and had given her mother hell.

"I was happier in boarding school than stuck over in the west. You'll thank me one day for sending you to good boarding schools," she told Lily.

Georgiana refused to discuss "family," except for flippant remarks and anecdotes that were generally unflattering. She did once say she'd had to keep her family background "a bit quiet" when she went to America as a war bride. "Not that it mattered as it turned out. His lot were Orange County hicks."

So Lily's childhood had been spent in the care of other people, punctuated by periods of travel, with pauses in pensions and tropical Somerset Maugham hotels. Within minutes of arrival anywhere Georgiana had admirers, help from all quarters and entertaining company.

The only reference Georgiana made about her own parents was that her father had died in France during the First World War before she was born and that her mother had lived in the west, a place Georgiana hated. Georgiana caused everyone such trouble that she forced them to put her in boarding school, in Perth, which she far preferred. As soon as she could she moved to Sydney, worked as a secretary and met her American husband-to-be.

That was the sole extent of Lily's knowledge of her family. She had only vague memories of one occasion when they visited an old lady, her great grandmother in Perth. She recalled being in a beautiful garden with a sweet and loving lady. She had always wanted to go back there but it never seemed to fit in with Georgiana's plans and then Lily had been sent to an expensive private girls' school in Sydney and had never seen her relative again, Georgiana declaring the west to be even more behind the world than the rest of Australia.

With the self-centeredness of children, Lily had never questioned her mother about their family. When pregnant with her own daughter, Samantha, Lily wrote to Georgiana asking if she knew of any possibly inherited medical problems. Georgiana dismissed Lily's fears by pointing out she knew next to nothing about Lily's father's medical history and was not about to try and make contact with his family even if she knew where they were. In her letter Georgiana had written:

Life starts at birth. Forget all the baggage because there isn't a damn thing you can do about it anyway. I tried to let you be free. You find out what you need to know, when you need to know. Sometimes knowing too much can be painful.

Lily wasn't sure what to make of this remark but realized she wasn't going to get anything further from her mother. Her then-husband Stephen told her not to worry about it. He was relieved that his erratic and volatile mother-in-law kept to her own path in life. He regarded her with long-suffering patience that didn't endear him to Georgiana. When Stephen and Lily divorced, Georgiana was delighted. When she visited she could now have the attention of Lily and Sami without the "interruptions and interference of *that* man."

Lily was adamant that Stephen continue to be involved with Sami's life. "I didn't have a male role model and a girl needs a dad."

Her academic ex-husband, vague about the nitty-gritty of life, nonetheless was a devoted if distant father—distant due to them being in different cities.

Lily sighed. How she wished she had sat down with Georgiana and insisted she tell her all she knew about her family. She had a thirst to know about her mother's background and now it was too late. Too late to understand her rebellious, flighty, independent mother who had lived life at full speed. She'd never even called her "Mother," Georgiana had said it made her feel "old." Even in her later years, Georgiana continued to flirt, to look years younger than she was. When she visited Lily she told her granddaughter Sami to call her Georgie, not Granny.

Lily and Sami had thought it amusing at the time, but now Lily found her mother's dedicated zest a pathetic attention-grabbing tactic.

When Lily was growing up, her friends had envied her such a glamorous, funny and slightly eccentric mother. In reality, Georgiana had been selfish and self-centered, and now Lily resented the loss of family this had caused.

While wallowing in her personal loss it suddenly occurred to Lily that she was doing what Georgiana always did—excluding everyone else. She had gently broken the news to Sami of her grandmother's death. Her daughter had then flown from Melbourne for the simple funeral, but with impending university exams Lily had encouraged her to go straight back to Melbourne.

Now she wondered how her daughter was dealing with this first, unexpected, death in their small family unit. They should be sharing this. It didn't seem sensible that in this society mourning was a private affair. Where was the ritual, the wailing, the sharing, the support and continuum of death shown by other cultures? Was this why she was finding it so hard to let go of her mother?

A twinge of bitterness hit Lily as she stretched and went to the wardrobe. Apart from the satin-covered hangers it was empty except for an old leather suitcase that Lily knew held the core of

Georgiana's life. She had once pointed it out to Lily and told her, "When I die you'll find my life in there."

Lily had never looked in the suitcase but had persuaded her mother to take out her will, share certificates and deed to the unit and put them in the bank.

Lily dragged the suitcase out to the middle of the floor, took a sip of wine and unbuckled the old-fashioned catches. It smelled faintly of mothballs and she lifted the tissue paper off the top to reveal a disorderly stack of photographs and letters. She randomly leafed through several letters from one pile. There were love letters between Georgiana and the numerous men in her life. Others were from people she'd met in her travels whom she'd written to for some time until lack of contact and interest had seen the correspondence fizzle out.

Familiar, though childish, writing in another pile caught her eye. Lily was touched to find all the letters she had written to her mother while at school were carefully bundled together. Georgiana hadn't been such a diligent correspondent, preferring to telephone. Lily always had a sneaking suspicion the letters her mother did write to her were written for public approval, to be read to others and admired. Dramatic and detailed descriptions of exotic places interspersed with funny anecdotes, outrageously exaggerated, written on thick hotel stationery in a large, free-flowing hand.

The suitcase also contained dozens of photographs of Georgiana with friends and on her travels. She noticed one photograph was wrapped in tissue paper. Curious, she folded back the yellowed paper to reveal a sepia-tinted photo set in a small silver frame. Staring out at her was a handsome man in a white uniform, wearing a nautical hat set at a jaunty angle. Despite the formal pose there was a hint of a suppressed smile about the mouth and merry eyes. She'd never seen this man before and wondered for a moment if it was her father, then remembered that he'd been in the army. She opened the back of the frame and read in spidery writing on the back of the photo, *"Broome, 1910."* He was too old to be an amour of her mother and, knowing Georgiana's family had come from the west, there must obviously be a connection.

There were other photos taken at balls and dinners, and in gardens of unknown houses. There was one of a man in uniform who appeared in several photos which, judging by the car, she took to be in America. There were photos taken around the world, which featured Georgiana center stage with elephants and castles, alongside laughing companions. There were photos of Lily taken on their holiday trips and some of her as a small child playing with a sailboat, on a merry-go-round or dressed to kill in bonnet, bows and Mary Janes—what Georgie called her "Shirley Temple shoes."

But it was a record of Georgiana's life only after she had left Australia. There was nothing that connected her to her own family, her childhood or her country. Nothing, except for this mysterious framed photograph of the man in Broome.

Lily had reached the bottom of the suitcase now and found a parcel. Inside was a letter and a cloth-wrapped package. She opened the letter, addressed to her in her mother's writing, with trembling hands.

> *Lily dear,*
>
> *I always intended to give you these but could never find the right time. I held back as I knew you would ask questions and I don't have all the answers.*
>
> *I had such an unsettled youth, I felt no interest in my past. And I preferred to stick to the old adage that what you don't know won't hurt you. Ever since the war, I suppose my philosophy has been to live for today.*
>
> *Now these are yours, for they have been passed on to the women in our family for so very long. When my grandmother gave them to me she said, "Keep them close to your heart as I have done. If they are not cherished and cared for, like love they will turn to dust."*
>
> *Just know you have been my life and in my way I did my best for you. I didn't need any family but you.*
>
> *My love,*
> *Mother*

Lily wept as she read her mother's words. It was the first time she could remember Georgie calling herself "Mother."

"Why didn't you tell me this before! You were all I had, Georgie. My mother, yes, but I needed more."

Lily sobbed with the pain of loss, for her mother and for the family she never knew, and for the woman she was and didn't understand and for her own daughter to whom she could pass on so little of her past.

When she eventually stopped crying, but still shaking with emotion, she unwrapped the lumpy, cylindrical parcel.

In it was a blue velvet bag. She undid the draw string and tipped out a strand of magnificent fat, glowing pearls. Lily gasped as she fingered them, but what caught her attention was the strangely carved mother-of-pearl pendant that hung from the center of the pearl necklace. On it were carved parallel lines, a circle with smaller circles in it, and an X.

Impulsively she draped the rope of pearls around her neck and pressed her hands over the pendant. It felt smooth and cool and Lily shut her eyes as a wonderful feeling swept over her.

And then, faintly, like looking through a misty screen, she remembered. She had seen this wonderful necklace before. It had shone against the navy silk of a dress worn by—the lady in the flower garden. Other small details came back to her. They had been walking among the flowers, holding hands. Her great-grandmother had been telling her the names of the flowers. Once when she turned to smile down at Lily, the little girl had reached out and touched the swinging pendant.

Great-grandmother let her wear it saying, "One day this will come to you, Lily." Then Georgie had come along and said the necklace looked silly swinging down near her knees and had taken it off and handed it back saying, "She might break it."

Lily had forgotten the incident but now it was vividly recalled. It was on that one trip they'd made to see her great-grandmother in Perth. She wondered why she had never seen her mother wear this family necklace. It was obviously old and valuable. But what made it most precious was the knowledge it was a family heirloom. She felt it was the only link she had with her past and her unknown family.

Uncurling her cramped legs, she swallowed the last of her wine and began to pace about her mother's flat wearing the magnificent pearl necklace and pendant.

Lily wanted to lift the phone and call her daughter but she held back, not wanting to dump her confusion and misery on a young woman busy with university finals. Her thoughts then moved to the man in her life. She knew Tony would be sweet to her if she called, but it was the sort of conversation where they needed to be physically close, where she could have his full attention, cry and be held. Distance and private lives separated them.

Suddenly, Lily felt incredibly lonely.

For the next few weeks she went through the motions of settling her mother's affairs; selling possessions, giving things away, putting the flat up for sale. But she couldn't shake her feelings of dislocation, of loss and a gnawing sense of wanting to resolve the gaps in her past. So much emotion had been triggered by the discovery of the pearl necklace. She found herself staring at herself in the bathroom mirror, studying her features, searching for clues from the unknown ranks of ghostly relatives who swam through her past— who had formed this person called Lily. Where had she come from . . . what genes had she passed on to her own daughter?

As if hearing her silent call, Samantha rang her. "I've been thinking about you, Mum. It must be hard, sorting out Georgie's stuff and everything. I wish I'd come and helped. I think it would have been easier—to know she's really gone—if I had been there with you."

"Yes, I wish you had, too. But you had exams, Sami . . . It's certainly been . . . strange."

Sami heard the vulnerable tremor in her mother's voice. "Dad asked how you were getting on. Said he didn't want to intrude but hoped you were coping all right."

"I *am* coping all right. You know me. It's just . . . " and her voice trailed off.

"What, Mum? You don't miss her do you? I mean, it's not as if she was around a lot."

"But she was my mother, Sami . . . and I can't help wondering. About her and her life."

"We don't know much do we?" Sami's voice was hard. "I think it was *so* unfair of her, to keep everything to herself. She never told us anything. Whenever I asked about her side of the family, she said I didn't need to know that stuff. But I do, Mum!" Now Sami's voice was trembling. "It's all part of us. It's like she took away our family, wiped them all out. And now there's only you and me and a bunch of letters and photographs of people we know nothing about. What am I supposed to tell *my* daughter when I have one?"

"Calm down, Sami. Don't be melodramatic. But you're right, darling. That's why I'm feeling so sad, for just those reasons. I feel I've let you down, too . . ."

"Oh no, Mum. You haven't. Maybe we can piece it all together and trace our family tree when we have time. Please don't feel badly. Do you want me to fly up?"

"No, sweetheart. It's only a few months till the holidays. You keep your head down and study hard. Maybe we'll do something special, go somewhere nice—if you don't have plans that is."

"I'd love that. Let's make it a date. I love you, Mum."

"Love you too. Take care, Sami."

Lily hung up, grateful to her daughter for her thoughtfulness, but feeling worse than before. She felt history was repeating itself. Deep in thought, Lily packed the photos and letters back in the leather suitcase but kept out the silver-framed photo of the man from Broome. She kept the necklace on and that night slept naked, wearing just the pearls. They felt alive and warm

19

against her skin and once, waking in the moon-light, she looked at them and thought it was like they'd come to life, for their luster had an almost luminous glow.

By morning, she'd made up her mind. She'd take three months' leave from the medical clinic where she worked as a research technician, for she was owed long service leave. She would go to Broome and start the search for her mother's family there. She owed it to herself and to her daughter.

The more she thought about Georgiana's atti-tude, the more convinced Lily was that there were secrets that perhaps her mother felt best buried and forgotten.

It surprised her how easily one could make things happen. In a matter of weeks she had rearranged her life.

Tony, her lover, good friend and part-time com-panion, was initially surprised and asked why she was undertaking this search now. "Why didn't you do this years ago? You said you felt strongly about it when you were pregnant with Sami. Why do this now? What's it going to achieve?"

His gentle questioning made her try to find the answers in her heart. Several times in her life she had felt the need to trace her family. Being preg-nant had made her wonder about hereditary traits and genes but she had enough to deal with at the time and never followed it up. She always intended to sit her mother down with a bottle of wine and ask all the questions. But she never got around to it. And at boarding school, when girls talked about family stuff and shared secrets, Lily had little to offer and let them think she was holding something back rather than tell them how little she knew about her family. Dear God, had Sami faced that same questioning and, like herself, had no answers?

Maybe it was shock, grief, the emotional rocking of her life, the realization that she owed her daughter something. But Lily knew the time had come to look at her life—the past and the future.

Strangely, she felt invigorated and renewed and she spoke aloud, "I hope you're at peace at last, Georgie, but I have unfinished business. Family business. I'm going west."

Lily lifted up the pearls and kissed the pendant and for the first time in many weeks, laughed aloud.

Lily was sitting in the forward section next to the window, her face obscured by the pages of the *Australian* newspaper. Her concentration was interrupted by the flight attendant unlatching the small table and placing a tray of food in front of her.

Lily started, and then smiled over the top of the paper. "Sorry, I was reading."

The young woman in the Ansett uniform smiled back. "Tea or coffee?"

"Tea, please."

As she began pouring the steaming tea the stewardess gave this attractive woman a friendly glance. "Going to Darwin on a holiday?"

The cabin crew had been eyeing this pretty forty-ish woman in the beige linen slacks and cream silk shirt, her thick dark hair coiled on her head, a minimum of tasteful gold jewelry. "Classy" was the word they'd decided suited her. She had olive skin and large dark eyes. Her mouth was wide and generous. She was one of those beautiful women whose looks crept up on you, feature by feature.

Lily answered in her soft husky voice. "I'm actually going on to Broome."

"Oh, that's a great place for a holiday."

"I'm going there on business. Family business. How long do I have in Darwin?"

"Five hours, I'm afraid. You have to change planes."

The attendant smiled and moved on to the next row.

When she returned later to offer a refill, Lily was lying back with her eyes closed and a wistful expression on her face that didn't invite disturbance.

Lily was not asleep. But she was tired, emotionally tired as well as physically. She had finalized the storage, sale and charity donations of Georgiana's belongings. The apartment was clean and empty and in the hands of a real estate agent. She'd had a late night packing and leaving things in order for the housekeeper she had hired for the time she was away. She had been up early, phoning

Sami to say she was on her way, and that she would be staying at the Continental Hotel in Broome. She promised to call regularly.

Lily now regarded this trip as something of a turning point in her life. She realized she had been treading water for some time and could not go forward until she had settled the past. It seemed strange to think she had reached her forties before "finding herself," but maybe certain things came along at certain times in your life.

Her marriage to Sami's father had been conventional. As time went on, it became stale and they began to drift into separate worlds. He into the cave-like world of academia as a university lecturer, while she had begun to widen her horizons, looking for something else in her life.

Four years after her divorce she'd met Anthony Jamieson—Tony—a widower whose wife had died two years before. Her death had led him to withdraw emotionally and, despite his worldliness and professionalism in his job, he was a vulnerable man. At fifty-two he'd had no intention of becoming seriously involved with a woman. He had a demanding job and a grown family which included grandchildren. But Lily had crept under his guard and into his heart and, he'd confessed, taken up residence in his soul. It had come as something of a wonderful surprise to both of them to discover sexual and emotional passion they'd never experienced before. They thought they had the best of both worlds, for living apart kept the romance and passion burning brightly.

23

She knew in the beginning he didn't want the responsibility of another person's happiness. In her time alone after her divorce, she'd learned the valuable lesson of enjoying her own company, finding her own strengths and taking full responsibility for her own life.

It had been a bumpy road, tears of self-pity and loneliness welling often and unexpectedly, but she'd weathered it and become strong, self-reliant, yet gentle and calm. Tony often wondered at the depth of her understanding, warmth and tolerance. She'd become a giver rather than a taker without realizing it. But the threads that bind two people to each other are not made of inflexible steel, but stretch and quiver and snap like elastic, and nothing stays the same. Life was a matter of constant little adjustments, tightening and loosening those ties where necessary. But some issues weren't addressed and now Lily had the space to reassess many factors in her life. And while she mightn't find what she was looking for, or like the answers she may find, for the first time in a long time she had a purpose in life.

Lily stirred, feeling the plane begin its descent into Darwin. Stepping from the cool interior of the plane, the blanket of wet warm air enveloped her body and made her think of Asia. The straggly palms, the blindingly bright sunshine, and the smiling man in shorts, long socks and crisp short-sleeved white shirt told her she was in the north.

She smiled back at him. "You'll find your bags over on the left," he told her.

"I hope not," grinned Lily. "They're supposed to go on to Broome."

"Never know your luck, luv. They might, too."

She rechecked her flight departure time then picked up a taxi and asked for the museum.

"Great exhibition there. Nice building, too. You'll like it. The bureaucrats got it right this time. For a change," the driver commented with some cynicism.

He dropped her at a building embraced by shrubs and greenery on a headland near Mindil Beach. As soon as she walked through the glass doors a big display of Aboriginal wood carvings from islands north of Darwin and Arnhem Land attracted her attention and she found herself instantly captivated by the mysterious yet exciting cultural experience. There was something very spiritual about the carvings and the ochre-colored designs.

Nearby was a huge exhibition of Aboriginal art from many parts of north Australia, works on bark and canvas in styles that owed nothing to Western art but much to an ancient culture and an almost incomprehensible spiritual world called the Dreamtime. As she wandered through the gallery, she felt a curious and exciting empathy with the work, although she didn't actually understand it.

An arrow and a sign reading "Maritime Museum" caught her eye and broke the trance-like state that she found herself in as she wandered through the

Aboriginal display. She quickened her step and soon found herself in a gallery overlooking a collection of sailing craft unlike any she had seen in her life. There were the dugout and bark canoes of the Aborigines, tiny boats with odd-shaped sails and huge trading *praus* from the islands of Indonesia, a Vietnamese refugee boat, and outrigger canoes from Papua New Guinea. But what dominated the exhibition took her breath away.

It was a sparkling white pearling lugger with all sails rigged. Beside it was a display of an old pearl-diver's suit with bulbous metal helmet. Suddenly she found herself thinking of the dashing seafarer whose photo she'd brought with her from her mother's bag. She could just see him beside the helm of the lugger and the imagery brought a soft smile to her face. For several minutes she took in every detail of the boat and ran her hands along the curving lines of the hull.

"Beautiful," she whispered, "just beautiful."

From other exhibitions she learned that for centuries foreign ships had been visiting the northern waters and shores of Australia, long before Englishman, Captain James Cook, had laid eyes on the east coast of Australia. Golden-skinned men from Macassar had made this journey each December, sailing their *praus* on the north-west monsoon to trade cloth, metal tools, tobacco and rice for trepang and turtle shell. The dried trepang, sometimes called bêche-de-mer or sea slugs, were sold for a great profit to Chinese merchants for use in medicines as well as being a delicacy.

For several months these archipelago men lived, labored and traded with the local tribes before returning when the south-east winds began.

The traders and seafarers who sailed with the monsoon winds were not settlers or imperialists. They were simple traders from the Spice Islands of the archipelago across the Timor Sea. So long as they observed the long-established cultural and trading customs, they were welcome visitors. Less welcome were the occasional off-course Portuguese and Dutch mariners cursing their navigational error of coming too far east from the Cape of Good Hope before turning north to their fortressed trading posts throughout the Malay world. If, through misfortune or need for fresh water and food they did go ashore, they usually fought with the local tribes and there was much loss of life on both sides.

Lily looked at her watch, took one last look at the lugger, then strode quickly to the reception desk to ask where she could find out more about pearling. An obliging young woman telephoned for a taxi after explaining Lily should visit the pearling museum in the wharf precinct in the center of the city.

This time the taxi deposited her outside an old shed on the harbor below the steep bluff on which the city heart of Darwin had been built. She paid her five dollars and walked into what seemed to be a small dark cinema.

Fluorescent blue lights shone through large

aquariums, the hissing and gushing of air inhaled and expelled with a gurgle of bubbles through an air hose came over the PA system. A small walk-in cave shaped like a half section of a diving helmet housed more exhibits and the glass viewing panel looked into a video screen showing underwater scenes of old-style pearl diving. A video played on a large screen telling the story of modern pearl farming. Panels of spotlit colored photos showed needles being slipped into the muscle of oysters, followed by open shells exposing their wet and glistening pearls and finally, the fabulous pieces of princely priced pearl jewelry which could be seen in international jewelry stores.

Lily was more interested in the early pearling days and stared at the sepia photos, the newspaper cuttings and the bits of diving equipment, the tools of the pearl "peeler" and a selection of graded pearls displayed in a glass case. Then, in a dim corner, she saw part of the hull of a small lugger. Though it had no rigging, it showed the neat construction.

Photos of this and similar luggers showed decks heaped with mother-of-pearl shell, dark-skinned crews and the Japanese divers, smiling over the brass-ringed neck of their bulky canvas diving suits and cradling their big metal helmets. Lily could almost smell the coir rope, tar and saltiness of the sea.

A voice beside her and a strong smell of tobacco caused her to turn and confront a burly man in a navy shirt with a badge on the pocket which read "Dave."

"You interested in all this?" he asked genially.

"Yes, I am. Do you work here?"

"Yep. Ask me anything you want."

Lily smiled and wondered what he'd say if she asked, "Tell me who my family are," but instead she said, "I'm on my way to Broome, so thought I'd do a bit of homework."

"You on the three o'clock flight, eh? Well, this is a good place to pass the time. So you're off to Broome? I lived there for a bit, worked for a shipwright, did a bit of this and that, then went to one of the big pearl farms. All different now compared to the old days." He paused to reflect on some of the photographs. "Tough life then. A lot of the romance has gone out of pearling now, it's just another business. Mind you, there's still some intrigue and infighting. Someone gets a new process and then they're all on to it. Gangs raid the remote pearl farms at night. Those big Broome pearls fetch unbelievable prices overseas. Hundred thousand dollars a strand, some of them. So, who's your family? Small place, Broome, I might know them."

"I doubt it, they're all gone now. Dead and gone." Lily changed the subject. "Is there much history of the old days still left in Broome?"

"Thanks to Lord McAlpine, some of the old buildings—Chinatown, the open air cinema— have been saved. Too bad other developers and outsiders who move in on a small town don't have the same attitude. If you want to find old Broome, all you got to do is smell the mangroves, walk on broken shells and look at the wrecks of the old flying boats when the tide is out. Wander round the shore and you're right back in the old days. But take a good look at this lugger . . . none of them around any more."

Lily was starting to feel claustrophobic in the small dark museum where the amplified sound of air bubbles was making her feel light-headed.

"Thanks for your help, Dave, I think I'll go down to a hotel and have a sandwich before heading back to the airport."

"Try the Hotel Darwin," he suggested with enthusiasm. "My favorite watering hole and, like this old boat, a blast from the past."

Lily laughed. "Thanks for the tip," and she turned to leave.

Dave escorted her to the door gushing with advice all the way. It was with relief that she stepped out into the glare and heat of the midday sun. She put on her sunglasses and walked slowly to the steps that wound up the bluff to the business district, all the way longing for a cold lager and a sandwich in the coolness of the old-style hotel.

CHAPTER TWO

It was dusk when the plane landed at Broome, and as she walked across the tarmac, Lily felt the last of the day's warmth beginning to fade into the tropical evening coolness.

The little courtesy bus was driven by an affable young man who doubled as bartender and receptionist at the Continental Hotel. In the brief research she'd done on Broome she recalled photographs of the grand old "Conti" in its heyday in the early 1900s. But as they turned into the entrance, Lily thought that the long, low buildings looked more sixties motel than colonial splendor. The Raffles it wasn't, but what it lacked in grandness it made up for with friendly smiles and immediate chatty intimacy. Her room was plain but comfortable, and she turned on the fan rather than the air-conditioning. Lily was glad the room opened on to a private bougainvillea screened garden with a small table and chair.

Lily let down her long, thick dark hair, brushed it, touched up her lipstick and headed for the

Lugger Bar. Another blast from the past, she thought with a grin.

But there was no Long Bar and not a Gin Sling in sight here. It was RSL decor, practical and familiar to every drinker in Australia. However it was quiet, with few customers, and she felt no qualms at being the only woman in the room. She ordered a glass of wine and wandered around looking at the large framed photographs on the walls. This was old Broome—luggers lined up alongside the long jetty, lying on their side in the low tide mud; Japanese divers in balloon-like suits, metal helmet held under an arm; Asian laborers sitting beside great mounds of mother-of-pearl, shelling and sorting.

Lily had an overwhelming longing to be a part of that romantic era. How she wished the Ansett flight had whisked her to the Broome of the early 1900s. Even though she'd seen nothing of the place, Lily felt a tug at her emotions simply by being here and hoped she wasn't going to be disappointed by finding the past had been erased and that her private quest would reach a dead end.

A sun-shriveled, gray-headed, nuggetty little man in a faded T-shirt commemorating a decade past "Fun Run," swung around on his bar stool and addressed her. "Them were the days, girlie. This was a wild town in the twenties."

Lily smiled slightly at being called "girlie." Political correctness obviously didn't have much currency in Broome. "I bet you're a local," she said sweetly.

"Yeah, I guess I sorta qualify now." His face fractured into a hundred wrinkles as he smiled at her.

"Have you been here a long time?" Lily walked to the bar past the empty mock Tudor-style tables and joined the old man.

"Too long. Everyone comes to Broome for a season or two, they say, then never leave. I always planned to move on after I'd made enough moolah. Never did. Ended up retiring to a home in Perth a few years back. Couldn't hack it. Rather live in a shack here. So, you on holidays?"

"In a way. I'm doing a bit of research, looking back at the old days, the old families."

"Go on!" he said with genuine surprise. "What for?"

Lily sipped her wine while she thought of an answer. "I might write something. Or uncover a family tree."

"More likely find a skeleton or two in the closet round these parts," winked the old-timer. "So where're you going to start?"

"I'm not sure. Where would you suggest?"

"You'd be best going to the hysterical society. It's just down the road. Never been there meself."

Lily laughed. "Is it a big historical society?"

"It's in the old Customs House. Only a small joint, but they might have stuff you're after. There ain't anywhere else," said the man finishing his drink and looking expectantly at Lily.

She took the hint and ordered a round. "I'm Lily Barton."

They shook hands.

"Clancy. Well, me real name is Howard. But I like poetry, hence the moniker."

"You read poetry?"

"Sometimes." He shrugged, then added with obvious enthusiasm, "The stuff I make up is better."

Lily spoke quickly to divert an offer to quote his original works. "So tell me, are there any old-timers around I could talk to, divers or some of the old families?"

"What's wrong with me?" grinned Clancy. "Listen, there are some old-time families around, most of them are gettin' on and they keep to themselves. They're a mixed bunch. Mrs. Fong might yarn to you, her old man was a diver. She used ta clean houses for the rich white ladies when she was young. The Fongs are pretty successful business folk now. The working pearl people here are fairly new. I mean it depends a lot on what you're lookin' for."

Lily fished in her shoulder bag for the old photograph of the man in white and showed it to Clancy. The bar man and the other drinkers gathered around. "He's part of my past but I don't know anything about him."

They studied the picture.

"Well it's not the Prime Minister," said Clancy with a grin. "Dunno who it could be. Before my time."

The others nodded agreement and Lily put the photograph back in her bag.

The conversation rambled on with the other barflies joining in, entertaining Lily with some highly improbable stories of the past which she enjoyed immensely. Hunger and tiredness eventually forced her to bid them good night.

"My day has been three hours longer than yours, thanks to time zones," she explained to stop yet another round of drinks being ordered. "You've all been great company. I'm sure we'll have a chance to chat again."

"Yeah, that'd be great. Can always find us around the bar here most evenings," said Clancy warmly.

The men watched appreciatively as the slim figure disappeared across the darkened lawns.

"Good lookin' bird. What do you 'spose she's after?" pondered Clancy aloud.

"Hard to say," replied the bar man. "She's booked in for a couple of weeks, though."

The next morning, Lily ate breakfast on her little patio hung with brilliant bougainvillea. A note apologized that there were no croissants, so muffins were substituted and the *Australian* newspaper wouldn't arrive until the late morning flight. An array of brochures of "Things To Do in Broome and the Kimberleys" had been provided instead. She fiddled with the bedside radio to find a news bulletin but gave up and drank her tea before it got cold.

Later, dressed in jeans and a shirt, Lily asked at the front desk for directions to the Historical Society, but the girl looked blank.

"It's in the old Customs House, I think," said Lily.

"Oh, that's in the Seaview Shopping Center, two blocks down the road," she pointed.

Lily stepped into warm air and a caressing breeze. She stopped and caught her breath as she gazed across the road at the expanse of Roebuck Bay. The water lapped at the edge of stubby mangroves where a few rusty rocks jutted from the extraordinary turquoise sea. She stood, transfixed, wondering how long it would take to get used to this amazing color. Milky patches gave the water a solid appearance and in contrast the clearness of the blue sky appeared translucent.

She walked on and found herself stopping and staring once again as she looked at a remnant of the past. This time she couldn't immediately understand what had so grabbed her attention. It was merely a closed small store that faced the sea. Its rusting tin was the blood red of the rocks, its walls were thin and full of holes and through gaps and windows could be seen piles of rotting oyster baskets, nets and ropes. She walked around the small lonely building and took a photo, unsure of why the place intrigued her so.

The little white wooden building that now housed the Historical Society bore a neat little plaque which gave details of its past life as the Customs House. Diving gear, pumps from luggers and pioneer household items were scattered in the small front garden. Along the small verandah were glass-topped display cases, locked, but trustingly left to public view.

Lily went to the front door with its large sign, AIR-CONDITIONED. ENTER, then she saw a smaller handwritten note, CLOSED. RE-OPEN IN A COUPLE OF DAYS. Lily was faintly bemused, wondering how long the sign had been there and how she could get access to the museum despite the sign. She walked back to the Continental and rang the car rental place they had recommended.

In a short time a cheerful woman arrived in a small light four-wheel drive. They drove back to the tin shed that served as an office, the woman telling Lily her life story and how her marriage had improved immeasurably since moving from the east coast to Broome. Lily pondered on the possible influence of geography on marriage.

Soon after a waving of her credit card, Lily found herself driving out on a dusty road, cruising past small bungalows shrouded in tropical plants. She stopped at the Tourist Information Center. Inside, she asked about other sources of information on the old days, pointing out that the Historical Society was closed.

"Oh yes, the woman who runs it has family problems and the other volunteer lady is away. What sort of stuff do you want to know about?" asked the helpful girl behind the desk.

Lily had her story down pat. When she threw in a reference to the intriguing history of the first traders to the coast and her fascination with the very early days, the tourism director snapped her fingers. "Hey. If you can get up the coast, you might find this place interesting. Your team'll need a four-wheel drive, but it's dry and a quiet time of year—you shouldn't have any trouble." She fished around for a map.

"Where's that?" asked Lily.

"Cape Leveque. The old missions might answer some of your questions. All quiet now, but if you want to go backward that's the place you guys should start."

Lily left with maps and a colorful collection of brochures for her "team." She guessed the woman was used to dealing with journalists, documentary crews and travel writers who came with an entourage. Maybe she'd given the impression she was looking for something more than a family history. A cursory glance showed that Cape Leveque was a long drive and fairly remote.

She drove through town and parked in Napier Terrace. Again the strange sensation of *déjà vu* swept over her as she walked past the old pearling sheds, the long jetty where the tide had exposed the mudflats, stranding mangroves in the tidal channels.

She stood at Streeter's Jetty which stretched out into the slate mud. In its heyday before the First World War, 400 luggers struggled to find space to berth by the jetty, along the fore shore and in the creeks that were flooded by the ten-meter tides. Now with the disappearance of the luggers, the mangroves had spread over the mudflats, split by a narrow maze of channels. The area was deserted, the heat of the dry season morning warmed the old planks of the jetty.

Images of this jetty and the fore shore lined with luggers afloat at full tide or lying in the mud on the ebb tide were synonymous with Broome. Lily tried to imagine it in the old days with the men working on the luggers, repairing gear, the activity in the sorting sheds, the babble of languages, the shouted orders of the pearling masters, the rattle of shells being stacked in bags, the tinkle of bicycle bells.

She could almost smell the spicy Asian food, the sweetness of Indonesian tobacco, the marine tang of the pearl shells, the tar on boats. But all she could really smell was the saltiness of the air and dankness of the mangroves.

Lily walked back behind an old pearling master's office which had been freshly painted and was being used once again as headquarters for a pearl export company. Looking further up the creek she saw a stretch of exposed sand bank that faced the tidal creek. A solid black lump of a figure was sitting on the sand, legs stretched out in front, hat pulled low, holding a fishing line.

Lily jumped down from the low sea wall and trudged along the sand to discover the figure was that of an elderly Aboriginal woman. She smiled and walked past her to the end of the little sand spit where a small yacht was moored in the shallow water. The channels ran between low and bushy mangroves in several directions. About two kilometers away was the open water of the bay. But in here, the narrow channels of the creeks which all looked alike, presented a maze that would be a nightmare to navigate. She turned back and stood beside the old woman as she pulled in her coarse line and inspected the bait.

"No luck, eh?" Lily commented.

The woman adjusted the chunk of meat and swung the line in a powerful whirl above her head and watched it plop into the channel.

"Are there many fish out there?" A plastic bag floated past.

"Them're fish there. Not so good fish now, but."

"What sort of fish?"

"Catfish. Sometime mullet. Used t'be good fish. Too much rubbish now."

"You lived here a long time?"

"All my family worked round here."

"What work did you do?"

"Clean and wash everyt'ing." She flashed a gap-toothed grin. "Work for the white ladies. My great-granny, granny and mummy all for same family. Too old t'work no more."

Her hands were gnarled like a man's, veins and bumps stood out along her thin legs, but her body was heavy and a cotton hat hid what remained of her wispy gray hair.

"My name's Lily." She sat down on the sand beside her.

"Me is Biddy. I got me little house down back of the creek there." She nodded over her shoulder. "Dat's some of me mob over there." Another tilt of the head was aimed toward half a dozen men sitting in the shade by one of the old sheds, a pile of empty beer bottles and the glint of silver bellies of wine casks testament to weeks of drinking.

"Lazy buggers, some of 'em," she continued. "Men worked hard in the old days but. Plenty work round then."

"Tell me about the old days, Biddy. What was it like?"

Biddy tested the line draped over her finger then settled back and started to reminisce—colorful stories punctuated by frequent cackles. She talked about the big bungalows, the fancy furniture. "Some of 'em even got pearl and gold made into chairs and what-not." She described the ornate embroidered dresses, the men's uniforms, the parties.

"That washin' was somethin'. Them Masters change their whites many times a day."

"Their whites?" Lily was thinking of the photo of the smiling man in the starched white suit.

"An' their shoes. Fifteen pairs of shoes I hadta white up for the boss . . . But they were good people, good people."

Lily listened, asking a question now and then, starting to see color flow onto her black and white image of old Broome.

Biddy told of how she'd stayed with one family most of her life till the war came. "Everyt'ing in Broome go upside down. T'ings come good in last coupla years but. Never be same as old days for many fellas, but for Biddy, it's okay. My granddaughter doin' really good."

Lily felt herself warming to Biddy—to her

strong sense of humor and her keen observations of life.

"Did they treat you right in the old days, Biddy?"

"Yeah, all right with my one white family. We like family. All my family come t' Broome. Even bush aunties and uncles. Now only us left."

"Were there bad times?" asked Lily.

The old woman shrugged. "Sometimes. Old Biddy now always here fishin', good times 'n' bad times. Not much else yer can do, eh?"

Lily smiled. That was one way to deal with life, go fishing. She'd always liked fishing. Quiet fishing, from a boat with a hand line. It gave you an excuse just to sit and think, or to let the mind drift. You weren't doing nothing, you were fishing.

"Tide's comin' in," remarked Biddy. "Wash everyt'ing fresh agin."

The tide now ran swiftly and started licking at Biddy's torn sand shoes. She started rolling in her lines. One was around a big plastic reel, another on a cork and one around a lemonade bottle.

Lily picked up the bottle. "Can I help?"

"You feel 'im run, you jag 'im quick," instructed Biddy.

"Don't worry, Biddy, I've fished for my supper before today."

But it was Biddy who had the strike and landed a fat catfish which she expertly dispatched, avoiding its cruel spines.

"You holiday in Broome?" Biddy asked as they packed up.

"Sort of."

Biddy looked at Lily with some intensity. "Broome a good place. You look aroun'."

"I intend to, Biddy."

Lily walked back to where the pearl shops housed in old shell sheds began. She swung down an alley and found herself in the remains of Chinatown, the crooked alleyways, renovated dark and narrow shops and eateries, all hinting of a shady past. She headed back past the Roebuck Hotel. The pub was quiet, a group of Aborigines squatting in some shade by the entrance. Despite the bright touristy coat of paint on the town, the past was still visible and Lily found herself soaking up the atmosphere.

That evening she decided to walk up the road to the Mangrove Hotel which overlooked Roebuck Bay, have a drink and watch the sunset before finding a restaurant for dinner.

She walked across Bedford Park, past the rusting horse-drawn train carriage which used to run down to Streeter's Jetty, and past the replica of Dampier's sea chest. Lily paused to read the inscription to the intrepid English pirate turned explorer who landed on the northern coast of "New Holland" in the *Cygnet* in 1688. She then crossed the deserted sea front road to where a spacious old-style bungalow crouched beneath its sloping hat roof, surrounded by heavily drooping trees. Lattice screened the wide verandah on three sides, a wind chute punctuated the roof and on the white wooden fence a painted sign said GALLERY.

Lily paused, noting the doors along the verandah stood open. She walked through the sandy leaf-littered garden, stepping up onto the wooden verandah. The section leading to private quarters was screened off by Indonesian carved wooden screens. She turned and wandered through the open doors she had noticed. Inside was a large, high-ceilinged room which Lily assumed must be the main gallery space. Fans hung from the exposed, white-painted wooden beams. Contemporary Aboriginal acrylic canvases, watercolors of local land and seascapes along with fantasy underwater scenes hung on the walls. Freestanding panels held a display of exquisite small botanical and reptile etchings executed in fine miniature detail.

A breeze blew in from the bay and for a moment Lily thought she was alone, but a short slim woman with a flurry of auburn curls and pale skin came in carrying lengths of hand-painted silk. She wore a sarong topped with a cotton camisole and leather sandals. "Hi," she said brightly. "You left your browsing late in the day, I was about to close."

"I'm sorry," apologized Lily. "I was just passing when I saw the sign and the door open . . . if it's inconvenient . . ."

"Good Lord, no," the woman interrupted, throwing silks over a display stand. "Take your time. This is all the work of local artists by the way."

Lily looked around. "You have some wonderful work here. This is a great space for it. The house is obviously old—was it a home originally?"

"Yes, and a place called Imata's Store. These old houses are wonderful to live in. The new places don't suit the climate. Too many people come up here and box themselves in with air-conditioners. They aren't really part of the place. You don't need AC's if you build properly."

Lily looked through the open double French doors to the bay where the sun was beginning to sink. "How peaceful it is."

The woman stood beside Lily and gazed at the vista. "Yes. I never regret moving up here." She gave Lily a shrewd look. "A lot of divorced women like me come here. Very healing."

Lily studied the gallery owner who looked to be in her mid- to late thirties and who exuded a calm confidence. "You don't get lonely?"

The woman gave a soft laugh. "Not at all. Like my friends, I remarried. To a younger man. You on your own?"

"Yes."

"Where are you staying?"

"Across the road at the Conti. I was heading up to the Mangrove to watch the sunset."

"Would you like to join me for a glass of wine on the verandah? We have a splendid sunset viewing spot. My man and my daughter are out at a music lesson. I was looking for an excuse. I'm Deidre, by the way."

They pulled up Moses chairs made of polished

45

twisted branches bound with vine and seats of braided leather. Deidre poured wine into two heavy glass goblets and stood the bottle on the railing. Leaning back in her chair she put her feet up beside the bottle. "So why are you here? You don't look like a tourist. In fact, you almost look like a local." She was referring to the frangipani blooms Lily had tucked in her long hair and the loose white Hawaiian-style dress she was wearing.

Lily sipped her wine. "I've started asking a few questions about myself and some of the answers are probably here in Broome, not that I've got very far yet." Lily paused briefly. "I'm sorry if that sounds a little enigmatic."

"It sounds like a divorce."

"Not really. But my mother died a little while ago. That started me searching. For myself, for her, for my family, where I'm going in my own life . . . all that kind of thing."

"Most of us get to that point in life at some stage. Some ignore it and go on as before, some of us make a wild and dramatic move, or do what you've done and start looking."

"I've done all three," Lily admitted.

"But that's good. It's a process that can be painful, but you come out of it feeling renewed and more focused. It gives you a stronger sense of yourself and then good things happen." Deidre topped up their glasses. "Let it unfold, don't go chasing butterflies in circles. Up here, in this kind of crazy place, things have a strange way of falling into place."

The sun had now slipped into the wine bottle, its fat gold shape glowing through the green glass. The two women were comfortable and at ease together in the way that women often make instant contact. Men find the immediate self-revelation of women unfathomable, but women understand its natural and intrinsic value.

Lily finished her wine and rose from her seat. "Thanks for the sundowner. It was really very kind of you. I think I'll head into town and treat myself to a seafood meal. Where's a good place to eat?"

"Noshi's. Next to the Pearl Palace," Deidre suggested. "By the way I'm arranging an art exhibition at the Cable Beach Club on Thursday night. Would you like to come?"

"I'd love to. Whose work is it?"

"Rosie Wallangou. I'll drop an invitation to you at the Conti. What's your last name?"

"Barton. Lily Barton." She slipped into her sandals and went down the steps.

Deidre called after her, "Take the dirt road around the back of town, it's quicker. You'll see the track past Captain Tyndall's house."

Lily turned around. "Where's that?" she asked.

"Just up the road there on the bluff. Great old house. Enjoy your dinner."

Lily stood in the twilight staring at the beautiful old bungalow that faced across the bay. It was surrounded by spacious verandahs, and embraced by huge frangipani and rioting bougainvillea. "Well, Captain Tyndall," she thought, "you certainly knew how to pick a place and make a great

47

house." She was entranced by the romance of the setting. The view was breathtaking and she wondered if Captain Tyndall, whoever he was, had sat on the verandah enjoying the tranquil panorama of the mangroves, creeks and brilliant waters of Roebuck Bay.

In the distance, she watched a lone sail boat inch its way across the water.

Lily continued her walk into town and found a trattoria-style restaurant and ate in the open air garden by flickering flame torches. Lily had long adjusted to being a woman alone in a restaurant and treated herself to a three course meal, chatting with the young waitress who was over from Denmark on a working holiday. Then, feeling pleasantly satisfied, she strolled back to the hotel in the cool evening air.

There was a message from Tony waiting for her—he was off to New York and would call when he could and sent his love. Lily felt the flush of love she always did when she thought of him, and tucked the message away . . .

In the bright morning, she pushed her breakfast tray to one side—still no croissants or newspaper—and studied the basic map of the country north of Broome. She packed a bag of mandarins and two liters of bottled water in a holdall and set off in the four-wheel drive. In a few minutes she had reached open road and within half an hour the bitumen had given way to a long stretch of orange dirt road. The lightweight four-wheel drive was difficult to control in the loose dust and she forced herself to slow down.

Lily drove in silence as there was no radio reception and no tape deck. Through her sunglasses the road looked deep sienna and it was obvious that no vehicle had passed this way for some time. She was glad she'd taken the precaution of telling the girl at the reception desk she was making this trip and if she wasn't back by 8.00 P.M., to let the police know.

The driving now required intense concentration as the wheels were wandering in deep powdery red dust. She tried to drive in the center of the road, hopeful of finding a firmer surface. But in a moment, before she was aware of what happened, the little vehicle slewed and spun across the road toward a great red bank. Lily struggled with the car, praying it wouldn't tip over, but instead it turned around and came to a stop against the crumbling bank.

Shaking, she stepped out and sank into talcum powder dust that reached halfway up her calves. The car was in well over its axles. She looked around in the glare hoping to find a paperbark tree or branches that could be put under the wheels for traction. All around her there was nothing but open desert country and one tall spindly tree by the road which barely offered any shade from its frail sprays of leaves.

She searched the immaculate new car. There was nothing in the way of tools other than a shiny jack. She tried scooping away the dirt from the wheels, but when she attempted to move the car, it just settled deeper into the drift as the tires spun uselessly. Cursing, she sat by the car and ate a mandarin.

The sun inched higher into the sky and with it the temperature. It was well over thirty degrees and Lily could feel heat radiating off the metal. She knew to stay by the vehicle—where would she go out here anyway?

By late afternoon she had eaten all the fruit and drunk one of the bottles of water. She was now resigned to the probability that no one would be traveling this road so late in the day, if at all, and she'd have to spend the night in the car. By the time the girl at the desk raised the alarm it would be late and she doubted anyone would come looking till daylight. She wasn't frightened, just irritated at getting herself into this predicament. They'd told her it was an adequate road so long as you had a four-wheel drive. But she could see she needed a solid, hefty vehicle, not the zippy little number from the rental company which was best suited to beach roads.

Lily dozed and stirred at sunset when she thought she heard something—a strange animal sound. She stood in the middle of the road gazing in both directions at the endless strip of bronze ribbon.

"COOEE!" she sang out to the emptiness.

Two Aboriginal men appeared behind her out of the scrubby desert causing her to jump. On their horses they loomed large and for a moment she felt threatened and helpless. But then she noticed they seemed as surprised as she was.

"You broke down, lady?"

"Nah, accident, lookit the car," declared the other before Lily could answer.

They dismounted and inspected the car.

"How long ya bin 'ere?"

"Since this morning. Do you think you could help get me out?"

"Ya by yourself?"

Lily nodded. The men looked at each other without expression. They dropped the reins of their horses and walked around the car again.

"Where ya going?"

"I was heading for Cape Leveque."

"Road no good for this sorta car."

"I can see that. It was all I could rent. If you can get me out I'll head back to Broome."

The two men pushed and bounced the car and finally got her back to the middle of the road. "Oh, thanks so much. I'm so glad you came along. What are you doing way out here?" she asked.

"We're ringers. Run cattle on the mission here."

"Where's the mission?"

"Beagle Bay. Not far back. You passed a turn-off to the right. Ya'd be better off staying there till tomorrow. Dark soon."

"Yes, I don't fancy trying to drive back in the dark." Lily looked at the last streaks of the sun heralding the night.

The men returned to their horses.

"Where are you going now?" she asked.

"Campin' a little bit on. Got stock at a waterhole," explained one of the ringers.

"Well, thanks again for your help," said Lily as she put out her hand. The two shook hands with her and Lily was surprised at the lightness of their grip.

"No worries," grinned the younger and they both swung into their saddles with a fluidity of movement that struck Lily with its almost gymnastic grace.

She drove cautiously and eventually the headlights showed a break in the edge of the road marked by a leaning post. She got out and found a faded sign lying on the ground. In the beam of the headlights she read—BEAGLE BAY 8 KMS.

The road was appalling, corrugated and narrow, so she drove with even more care, much of the time in second gear. It was very dark by the time she reached the settlement, which seemed to be deserted. She glimpsed a few shadowy figures beside box-like houses, the occasional lamp or campfire in a yard. Continuing along the sandy track she passed a small fenced-off graveyard and stopped suddenly, spellbound by the luminous vision in front of her.

The moon was high and full and a whitewashed church glowed in its light like the Taj Mahal. She switched off the motor and stepped out to fully appreciate the scene. Noticing that the old arched wooden door was ajar she walked over and stepped gingerly inside.

For a moment she blinked, wondering what strange and wonderful world she'd walked into. The whole interior shimmered and gleamed in the milky light that shone through the stained glass windows. Seeing a small table with candles and a box of matches she lit a candle and moved it in an arc.

The glittery silver light came from pearl shells. Thousands of them lined the walls and ceiling, cut into geometric patterns around windows and every available surface. Paintings and murals were framed in the painstaking mosaic of pearl shell. Lily smiled with delight. "How beautiful!" she exclaimed to herself.

The church felt safe, comforting and peaceful. She blew out the candle and returned to the car, drove it close to the side of the little church. Curling up on the back seat she promptly fell asleep.

CHAPTER THREE

The sun began to warm the interior of the car and Lily stirred uncomfortably. At a tap on the window her eyes snapped open and she sat upright.

A man's head and shoulders were outlined against the early bright light. He rapped insistently again. Lily unrolled the window a little way.

"*Guten Morgen,*" he said cheerfully. He was an older man, with badly cropped gray hair sticking up in tufts.

"Er, good morning," said Lily hesitantly.

"You were sleeping."

"Yes, I was."

He prodded a spotty banana through the window. "Would you like to share my breakfast?"

Lily gratefully took the banana, unlocked and opened the car door. "I had a bit of an accident and got stuck. This was as far as I got. My name is Lily."

"I am Brother William. So you have come to visit us?"

"I was trying to get further north but figured it was safer to spend the night here than drive back to Broome."

"I always took the boat to Broome. I don't drive no more. My eyes. No good." He tapped his face.

"You went by boat to Broome from here?"

"Ya, and from Lombadina—'bout 150 kilometers."

Lily sat beside him on the stone step outside the church and ate the banana while he talked.

"One time I come back from Broome. So rough, sea like mountains, up and down, took almost one week in the gale. We get to Beagle Bay, but the seas so bad we can't come in. I get in the lifeboat with three men to row over the surf, almost two kilometers to the shore. But we capsize, go upside down and so we have to swim. The tide comes in at eight nautical miles an hour, it makes the water rise twelve meters or more along this coast. I pray and swim, pray and swim and we make it."

He grinned at Lily who had been thinking a boat trip to Broome might be easier than the drive. She changed her mind—the sea was undoubtedly just as treacherous. She shook her head in admiration as he finished telling the story.

Looking at the deepness of the wrinkles in his face, Lily realized Brother William was older than she'd first thought. He wore a blue, short-sleeved shirt and loose gray pants held up by a well-worn belt. He looked fit and his eyes, though watery with age, were a vivid blue. His German accent was unmistakable. "Do you live here at the mission?"

"Yah, yah. I live here long time now. This is my church." He waved proudly at the little building. "You like it?"

Lily beamed. "Oh yes. It's wonderful. Tell me about the pearl shells. They looked so lovely in the moonlight."

The Brother nodded happily. "Ya. And in the sunshine. See up there." He pointed to the steeple.

Lily gazed up at the tower to where the steeple was fitted with a copper ball on which a cross was mounted. The mother-of-pearl inlay sparkled in the sun.

"Now, you come inside and see."

It took a moment for their eyes to adjust to the dimness. The mother-of-pearl glowed softly, seeming to have its own inner light. The pearl stars set in the blue ceiling of the sanctuary glittered in shafts of light that angled through the thick stained-glass windows.

"Bishop Gibney and the Trappist Brothers started here in the early 1890s, in a primitive bush dwelling. This church was built during the First World War. The mud bricks were made here but there was no mortar so the missionaries and the blacks brought shells from the beach in billy carts and burned them with layers of wood to make a white lime. Brother Droste did the decoration with mother-of-pearl and sea shells. See, there at the top of the main altar is the big mother-of-pearl star. Fit for any cathedral," said Brother William proudly. He'd told the story to visitors so many times before that the telling now sounded almost like a recording.

"What are the blue stones in the pattern?" asked Lily.

"That's operculum, a little lid or cover which comes from shellfish. And here, set into the pillars are broken shells. They look like opal shining with all the colors of the rainbow, eh?"

"This must have seemed a long way from the war," said Lily. "It's still a remote area."

"It was more active in the old days. We sold timber to build the luggers. And it took a lot of effort to persuade the Aborigines to come in from the wilderness and to get their children to attend the school. Soon enough there was a good cattle farm. Now they run it all themselves." Brother William looked nostalgic. "The first Pallottine priests and brothers had much to do. I have little to do now. I am seeing out my days, observing Sunday services, talking to the visitors who sometimes come."

"Where is your home, don't you want to go home?"

"I have no family left in Munich. I will be buried here. Some brothers returned but some are buried here also. They didn't all die of old age— there were some accidents," he said wryly. He gave Lily a look, then asked, "You are interested?"

"Yes. I am."

"I have a book. It is a journal that one of the

Brothers wrote about the early days of the mission. It was added to over the years and printed by some later Brothers. Perhaps you will find it of interest."

Lily waited outside in the morning sun while Brother William rummaged in a suitcase under his bed in the simple room he called home that was attached to the community kitchen and social room. She could hear a woman cooking and admonishing two small children. One of the children came outside letting the screen door bang behind him, but stopped shyly when he saw Lily.

"Hello. How are you, young man?"

"Orright," he said with a flash of white teeth against dark skin, then fled inside, giggling. His mother appeared at the screen door and smiled at the strange woman.

"You need something?" she asked. "There's a store over the way, they should be open by now."

"No, it's all right thanks, I'm waiting for Brother William. He's getting something for me."

"I'm making his breakfast, tell him it's nearly ready. Would you like some? You must've started out early."

"I'd love some," Lily said and followed her inside.

Over their toast smothered in mashed tinned herrings, Brother William told Lily how life at the mission had changed. In the early days it had been like a small European village with over forty buildings including a convent for the sisters, separate schools, dormitories and dining rooms for boys and girls, a bakehouse and slaughterhouse, laundry, sheds, a stable for the goats, storehouse, a tannery, and dwellings for the missionaries, stockmen, servants and the Aboriginal families who all worked about the mission. On the outskirts was a camp of "bush blacks" near to where the road to Broome was hacked out of the scrub and sandy soil by Brother Droste in 1921.

Across the table he showed her faded photographs of barefoot children dressed in simple smocks, pants and shirts. Soft but wary eyes stared from scrubbed faces as they stood obediently by the formally attired Pallottine priests.

"They were good children. Did lovely needle-work, worked in the gardens, did their lessons, sang to God with all their hearts. For a long time it was as the Bishop dreamed, but. . . ." He shrugged. "Eventually they went back to their old ways."

"And now?"

"It's different. A little of both worlds," he said diplomatically. He then handed Lily a mold-spotted book. "I am afraid it is not healthy. The pages are sticking. But the writing is still clear."

Carefully Lily turned the amateurishly printed pages, pausing to read short extracts. "Brother William, this is fascinating, I'd love to read it all, but this should be kept under better conditions. And available for research."

"Oh, there is a copy or two back in Europe. I was thinking this copy should be in Broome."

"Like in the Historical Society perhaps. I'm about to go there."

"You take it. You give to them. I have another copy. Maybe the air-con will keep it safe."

"Are you sure? It does seem a sensible idea." Lily separated two pages seamed by humidity. "I'd love to read all of this. I'll do it at the Historical Society."

"Ya. Is a good story. Like a book," grinned Brother William. "It tells many things of this place."

"I'm glad your fellow brothers were diligent and wrote down their observations. Times change so quickly."

"Not in the Kimberley. But ya, it is good our work is not forgotten." He looked momentarily wistful and Lily wondered if the work of Brother William would be commemorated in some way other than in the affection of the small flock in his care. While the intentions of missionaries like Brother William had been to better the lives of the Aborigines, Lily knew that, in the light of modern knowledge, it had not been in their best interests. But Lily wasn't going to raise such issues with the old Brother.

After a few more pleasantries Lily said she should be on her way. "Thank you again, Brother William, it's been fascinating to talk to you. I promise to deliver this safely to the Historical Society and good luck to you . . ." She shook the Brother's hand.

"Bless you, young lady. Look around before you go." He grinned. "The ghosts are benevolent."

She took his advice and drove around the sprawling mission, looking at the scattered remnants of its distant better days—deserted buildings, the shell of a well, broken drays and farm equipment, though the stockyards were repaired and a shed held gear and feed. But then she walked into the community store and time leapt forward to a world of frozen food, magazines, junk food, a video game machine and city-style homewares. Lily restocked with bottled water and a couple of chocolate bars for the drive back.

As she passed by the white church again she noticed a small graveyard a little distance away. She stopped to look through it. Once it must have been hidden by bush, a remote repose for a French Trappist brother, several Pallottine priests, two sisters, some infants and many adult Aborigines. The blacks rested under Christian headstones and Lily wondered if the converts would have preferred to have been put to rest in a traditional tree grave. She was about to leave when an unusual headstone caught her eye. It was a simple bush rock with an inset of mother-of-pearl shell glinting in the sun. What made Lily catch her breath as she studied the shells was the delicate pattern carved into the biggest shell.

Trembling, she crouched down and traced over the design with her fingertips. The lines and small circles within a large circle were entwined just as they were on the circular pendant that hung from her mother's pearl necklace. Lily went back to the car, got her camera and took a photo of the headstone and a close-up of the shell. It was some kind of tribal marking she decided.

Who was buried there?

She walked back over to the church looking for Brother William to ask what he knew of the strange old grave that she felt might be linked to her own family's past. But the Brother had retreated to his room and the lady who had cooked them breakfast and was now sweeping around the church steps said he was praying and didn't like to be disturbed for at least an hour.

Lily was disappointed for a moment, then remembered the book in which the Brothers had told the story of the mission. She felt sure she'd find some answers in it. A twinge of excitement and anticipation gnawed in the pit of her stomach as she drove away.

It was afternoon when Lily, dusty, tired, hot and thirty-six hours late, strode up to the reception desk and announced brightly, "I'm back!"

A strange girl stared at her blankly. "You been somewhere?"

"Where's the girl who's normally here, with the short dark curls?"

"Oh, Bridget. She took a couple of flexi days. Can I help you?"

"Never mind, thanks anyway," muttered Lily, heading for her room.

Lily showered and lay on her bed to siesta and think about the old mission. While she admired the early missionaries' fortitude and dedication, she found their original aims misguided. What had they achieved? A handful of converts, an education for a few who managed some modest success in the world of the whites. At the most, a sanctuary from the onslaught of white settlement that probably would have totally exterminated them in time. But, Lily suspected, the price had been high. So much culture had been lost, for most of the Christian sanctuaries had not been tolerant of native language and customs, which, in ignorance, were deemed primitive and heathen.

She opened her eyes and felt herself become half-hypnotized by the slowly turning ceiling fan and began reflecting on her own attitudes to the Aborigines. Over many a candlelit dinner with friends in Sydney she had argued intensely in support of government-sponsored moves toward reconciliation with the Aborigines, supported the general concept of land rights, and was quite passionate about the need to lift their health and housing standards. But until she had come to Broome she had never met an Aborigine, let alone discovered or experienced firsthand something even remotely related to their ancient culture.

A politically correct urban trendy, that's what I am, she thought. Biddy—the old black woman fishing on the sand spit—was the first Aborigine she'd met. Funny, it hadn't struck Lily at the time that she was the first. It seemed no big deal, they'd simply accepted each other. But in retrospect it had been a significant event. She'd had a yarn with someone with links to probably forty thousand years of culture. God, forty thousand years of fishing. And those stockmen . . . they came out of the land as if they were organic to it, and disappeared back into it just as naturally. And she realized she'd felt so comfortable with them . . . and the old woman. Yet they had nothing in common.

Her eyes fluttered shut and the imagined melodic throbbing hum of a distant didgeridoo began to impose itself on her consciousness. She felt herself drifting into another world . . . the world of the mind . . . then the phone rang.

It was Deidre reminding her about the art exhibition at the Cable Beach Club and offering her a lift if she needed one. Lily accepted with gratitude and they arranged to meet at the Mangrove Hotel. Perched on the cliff top, the renovated Mangrove Hotel had a choice view over mangroves, the sweeping rush of tide across the bay and the novelty—for an easterner—of watching the sun set into the sea.

Lily sat in the hotel garden sipping a glass of wine with her back to the crush of jovial tourists, locals and a Perth convention group in the bar and on the verandah terrace. When she'd finished her wine she walked to the edge of the garden to peer at the skeleton of a boat in the mangroves, its hollow ribs filling with the tide.

"Can I offer you another glass of wine?"

Lily turned at the friendly voice to see an attractive man smiling at her.

"Ken Fitzgerald. I'm the manager. You staying with us? Haven't seen you around."

They chatted briefly and it didn't surprise Lily to discover he was a former grazier. He had an open and affable country manner.

"Bit of a change coming from the land to the hospitality industry," remarked Lily.

"Not really, people or cattle, they all have to be fed and watered," he chuckled. "Was hard to leave our property but this is a big challenge; my wife, Lola, is in the office side of things. But Broome is going to go through the roof with tourism in the next few years."

He told her of his own plans and those of the town. Lily listened with some sadness.

"I hope the town hangs on to its heritage as much as it can," she said.

"Don't worry about that. Broome is still a bit wild and woolly, the past is close on your heels here."

Lily arrived at the Cable Beach Club with Deidre and her handsome young husband. There, she found little that recalled the old days. Walking through the lush landscaped grounds and over tiny bridges they passed oriental-inspired bungalows containing suites decorated with fine antiques and *objets d'art*. The main building maintained a tasteful style despite its brilliant lacquer red and gold trimmings. Soft lights, citronella flame torches, candles and a caressing breeze that carried the sweetness of flowers followed her echoing steps along the wide wooden verandah to the reception room and art show.

Early arrivals from Broome's eclectic social set milled about the spacious room, sipping champagne and talking to each other. While Deidre saw to selling catalogues and introducing invited hotel guests to local identities, Lily strolled about the room. Spectacular framed prints, painted canvases, cloth and bark hangings of contemporary Aboriginal art were well displayed. Lily thought the work wonderful, full of energy and mystery.

Deidre was suddenly beside her, tapping her arm and saying, "Lily, meet our artist, Rosie Wallangou."

Lily reluctantly dragged her gaze away from the paintings to congratulate the artist, expecting to meet some wise old lady, but was taken aback to see an attractive Aboriginal woman about her own age. She was dressed in a dramatic Aboriginal print silk long dress and wore unusual wood and stone jewelry. Her wild curly hair tumbled about her shoulders, and was caught to one side by a shell comb. The impact of her looks, her wide smile, deep eyes and charismatic presence was stunning.

"I really love your work, I don't know what to say. It's just magic," said Lily, trying to find the right words to convey the impact the pictures had on her.

"Magic," repeated Rosie thoughtfully, looking Lily in the eye, then added softly, "Yes, there's magic in them all right."

"They're not easily understood, even after

reading the notes you've put with each painting," said Lily. "But there's something about them that keeps me looking, even if I'm not sure what they mean."

Rosie chuckled. "Well, maybe that's part of the magic. You've got to study them a bit . . . sort of discover things for yourself. They're not all Dreamtime stories you know."

"Rosie has just had a big show in New York. They're wild about her work over there," broke in Deidre.

"That's wonderful," said Lily, who was impressed but not surprised. The work was powerful and she knew how collectible high quality Aboriginal art had become.

Rosie shrugged. "New York is a faddy place. What's hot today can be cold tomorrow." She gave a hearty laugh and Lily couldn't tell if Rosie wasn't bothered about being a big deal in New York or was confident she'd remain "hot." There was no doubt her work—drawn from her own roots and knowledge and interpreted with artistic skill— would last.

Deidre excused herself to greet the former premier and Rosie took Lily by the arm. "Come and I'll give you a conducted tour of my favorite pieces in this show."

Lily was absorbed and fascinated as she listened to Rosie explain the inspiration behind each painting. Slowly, as if a curtain had lifted, she began to see something of the story and message in each painting. She tried to explain this awakening to

Rosie but ended up by saying shyly, "I feel so clumsy trying to express myself."

"No, you're just starting to learn the language," laughed Rosie. "The more you look at them, you either start to 'read' them and go into them or they just stay pictures on a wall."

Deidre plucked Rosie away for official introductions and Lily thanked her for taking the time to talk to her.

Rosie gave her a friendly smile. "I'm sure we'll meet again. By the way, there's a couple of works over there you might be interested in," she said, nodding toward the far corner of the room.

Lily lifted a fresh glass of champagne off a tray and wandered over to the last few pictures she hadn't seen. But as she approached, the largest one caught her eye and her legs began to tremble. In a beautiful, subtle rendering of the burning colors of the earth around the north-west, Rosie had painted in traditional style a pattern that Lily instantly recognized—small white circles within a large white circle surrounded by the parallel lines and large X. She spun around, her hand shaking so much she spilled her champagne. But the official launch of the art show was now in progress. Lily edged around the back of the crowd to the small table where a girl was selling catalogues and taking sales orders.

Lily leaned down and whispered, "Please put a red sticker on number nineteen, I must have it."

The girl checked the catalogue and shook her head. "I'm sorry, that's not for sale."

Lily swallowed, mumbled her thanks and waited impatiently for the speeches to end.

There was no opportunity to speak to Rosie alone, so she excused herself and intruded on the small group clustered around the artist. "Rosie, I *so* wanted to buy one of your paintings, but the one I want isn't for sale. I was hoping I could change your mind."

Rosie heard the note of urgency in Lily's voice and the group fell silent. "Which one do you want?"

Lily pointed and saw the swift expression pass across Rosie's face before she said, "I include that picture in every exhibition. I will never part with it. It's special."

"What does it mean?" Lily persisted. "It's very important to me to know."

Rosie looked directly at Lily for a few seconds without speaking. "Well, it's one of those paintings where you must discover its meaning for yourself." The cluster of people looked at Lily expectantly. To soften her words Rosie added kindly, "Perhaps one day you'll come to read its true meaning. Here's my card."

As Lily turned away feeling close to tears, fumbling to put the small white card in her handbag, Rosie called after her, "I can tell you this much— remember that the picture is called 'Tears of the Moon'."

At ten the next morning Lily stepped into the air-conditioned Historical Society building. A bustling lady, casually dressed in slacks and a blouse, her permed brown hair in perfect order, glasses hanging on a beaded gold chain, was carrying a pile of labeled binders of photos, letters and newspaper cuttings, which she placed in order on a shelf beside the others she'd completed. She spotted Lily and went to the little reception desk to take her entrance fee.

"Just looking in general are you, dear?" She put her glasses on her nose.

"Yes and no," began Lily.

The lady gave her a quizzical look.

"Yes I'm here to look at everything, and I also want to do some research. My name is Lily Barton. Oh, and by the way, I visited Beagle Bay and Brother William suggested you might like to keep this here for safekeeping." She took the old journal from her bag. "However, I would like to read it first if that's all right."

"Goodness, yes. Well that was nice of him. I'd heard about this." She thumbed through it and handed it back to Lily. "I'm Muriel McGrath. How can I help?"

"I'm not sure, perhaps I should just look around first and when you've got a minute I'll ask you some questions."

"Righto, dear. I'll put the kettle on. Tea or coffee? Only instant, I'm afraid."

"Coffee would be fine, thank you."

"This is the main room—there's some memorabilia in here and in those shelves are files, books, newspapers, letters, photos, you name it.

We have a lot from the old families, rescued in the nick of time most of it was, too." She waved toward the rear of the room, which opened on to a small garden. "Back there are two other rooms, a display and exhibition room and along the back verandah is a general history area and bigger pieces on show. Decompression chamber, stuff like that." Muriel disappeared to a small area that served as kitchen and private office.

Lily looked around the main room first, dipping into files, flipping through cutting books, studying photos which gave an immediate picture of life in the early days. There was the story of the Japanese cemetery where so many divers ended their days, pictures of Chinatown with its dim shops and seedy opium dens, a famous Indian pearl cleaner who was known for his precise skill in stripping away the rough outer layers of valuable pearls, the horse-drawn train that ran along the wharf, the shanty township with beached luggers on the foreshore at Dampier Creek. A photo by the sorting sheds in 1914 showed small mountains of pearl shell harvested that year—sixteen hundred tons according to the caption.

Lily moved into the first exhibit room. It was divided into two sections, one dominated by a full-scale diving suit, an iron lung used for decompression for the deadly bends, and a variety of tools and instruments used in pearling and sailing, a Chinese abacus, Japanese paper models used in festivals and some household artifacts.

She walked around an ornate Chinese screen and found herself in the display room—a mock-up of an Edwardian living room complete with a life-size family of wax figures. It was meant to represent a well-off European household with its heavy pieces of Victorian furniture. The lady of the house, in bustle and beaded dress with a rope of pearls, held the hand of a small boy with long curls, lace collar and starched sailor suit. Placed modestly behind was the figure of an Aboriginal woman domestic in uniform of white starched apron over black dress.

Lily found the room uncannily realistic with its planters, settler's chair, kitsch mother-of-pearl ashtrays and inlaid card table. Strangely the furniture all seemed to go together and wasn't the usual assorted accumulation from donations or rescued from household turnouts.

She fingered the crochet antimacassar cloth square on the back of the chair, then lifted her eyes to the walls where portraits, paintings and photographs hung in ornate frames. Her eyes went from picture to picture and then she caught her breath. Surrounded by photos of luggers was a large picture of a dashing man in a white uniform—the same as the one in Georgiana's silver frame.

For a moment she stood in shock—the over-sized picture seemed life-like, the amusement in the twinkling eyes faintly mocking. Finally, she turned away, her legs quivering and called loudly, "Muriel! Could I ask you something?"

"I'm right here, just made the coffee." Muriel was carrying a tray which she set down carefully on the small inlaid table by the chaise longue. "What's up, dear?" She looked curiously at Lily's drained and pale face.

"Who is that?" asked Lily in a hoarse whisper, pointing to the picture.

Muriel sighed. "Isn't he handsome? That's Captain John Tyndall, probably the greatest of the pearling masters. Such a character."

"What do you know about him?"

"Are you all right, luv?" Muriel looked at her closely. "We know a lot about him, are you interested?"

Lily nodded. "That photo was among my late mother's things. I didn't know who he was."

"Come and sit down on the chaise here and have your coffee." She handed Lily a mug and watched her take a fast gulp. Pulling up a chair, Muriel pressed on. "We know a lot about him. He was one of the colorful characters back at the turn of the century and especially through the 1920s and later. Are you interested in finding out his personal history?"

"Oh, I am. I think we must be related." Excitement was now replacing Lily's shock.

"Well, I never. And your mum and dad never told you about him. Is he a close relative?" Muriel was interested. This was living history.

"I don't know much. I never knew my father and my mother was a bit of a loner. Never talked about family. So when she died and I found the picture which had Broome written on the back, I thought I'd see if I could find a clue which might answer the questions I never asked when my mother was alive," said Lily, dismayed to find her voice was choking up.

Muriel passed her a plate of homemade Anzac biscuits. "I've read about a lot of strange family histories since I've been running this place I can tell you. Nothing would surprise me. Skeletons fall out of cupboards all over the place." She gave a chuckle. "Some families haven't been too thrilled to find out about the shenanigans of their antecedents. This was a bit of a free and easy place back then."

Lily gave a small smile. "But at least having the pieces of the puzzle is a help."

Muriel took Lily's mug and bent over to pick up the tray. "I think I might have more than that for you. If indeed Captain Tyndall is a relative." She smiled mysteriously and left the little room.

Lily went and gazed up at the portrait once more. "So just who are you?" She suddenly grinned back at the man whose face was becoming very familiar to her. "And what do you know about 'Tears of the Moon', eh?" she said out loud.

Muriel spoke to her back. "I know what that means . . . I read it in some of the pearling material."

Lily spun around. "What, 'Tears of the Moon'?"

"Yes. It comes from some old Indian saying, you know all those Hindu myths and stuff. It's what they believed pearls to be . . . the tears of the moon that drop into the sea and become pearls. It's why some people think pearls are unlucky. But this is what you should be interested in." She placed four fat leather-bound journals on the table with a grunt. "Whew. A lot of reading in there. These are Olivia's diaries. There are a lot of photos, too. I can't let you take them away but come as often as you like. You can camp in here while you read. Did you know all this furniture came from Captain Tyndall's house?" She pointed to a straight-backed worn leather chair. "I can just see him sitting in that chair with a gin and tonic." She chuckled at the thought.

Lily was trying to take all this in. "Who was Olivia? Was she his wife?"

"Ah, it's a long, involved story from what I gather. You start at the beginning. Make yourself comfortable and yell for coffee at any time. The odd visitor wanders around now and then but they shouldn't disturb you. We don't get coachloads of tourists in here!" She chuckled again and gave Lily a warm smile. "I hope you find what you're looking for."

"Thank you, Muriel." Lily swallowed hard. It had all happened so swiftly. In learning about Captain John Tyndall's life was she also going to find her own story?

She picked up the first of the heavy books and ran her hands over it. The leather was soft and the book seemed alive, as if the covers were forcibly pinning down the living characters who peopled its pages. Her heart was beating and Lily knew that as simply and as easily as this her family had been placed in her hands.

She turned to the first entry—thin flowing writing on a thick ivory page.

CHAPTER FOUR
The north-west coast of Nickol Bay, 1893

In the faint water-light of the moon, the sturdy schooner, *Lady Charlotte,* heaved as it moved slowly through the great breasts of waves, white crested and surging in a thick sea mist. When they reached the lee of a deep cove, the breaking of the waves on the reef was regular and rhythmic, like the hoarse breathing of some sea monster.

The dawn gave way to morning light and the gray clouds lifted as the ship's lifeboat ploughed gamely through the narrow channel now visible between the arms of the reef. The passage was safe and the crew pulling at the long oars kept a steady course, but Olivia Hennessy was too aware of the danger that lay on either side. Her arms were folded across her swollen belly and she held onto her shawl as if it were her salvation. Conrad Hennessy glanced at his pregnant wife in the stern surrounded by their possessions. He tried to give her a comforting smile, but her gaze was fixed on the desolate shore.

It had been a carefully reasoned decision to be

put ashore here. Conrad had explained to Olivia that the captain could not put in at nearby Cossack due to the fast-rising wind and sea and, as he was already behind schedule, he wanted to continue north to Broome as fast as possible. The cargo he was carrying was due for shipment to Singapore. They could either have gone on to Broome and made a long journey back to the land they intended to take up south of Cossack or, judging from the rudimentary map of this largely uncharted area, they could land here, which seemed to be in a direct line to their holding.

Olivia, cumbersome and heavy with her first child, had suffered greatly throughout this journey from Fremantle with seasickness and wished fervently for dry land beneath her feet.

Conrad asked the captain if they and some of their goods could be ferried to shore where he would make what he estimated to be a day's walk into Cossack to fetch a dray or wagon to take them overland.

The captain had been doubtful, but as both husband and wife seemed convinced this was a preferable arrangement, so, eager to push on ahead of a threatening storm, he agreed to the plan.

Eventually there was a grinding and a slight shudder passed through the boat as the hull scraped across the rocky shore. Two men leapt over the side and pushed and guided the boat on to the gray pebbled beach.

Low scrub and spindly trees fringed the edge of

the dunes with denser bush behind. Olivia, supported by the two sailors, was carried to the shore. She sat on the damp sand, her thick woven skirt and petticoats spread around her, watching Conrad direct and assist the men ferrying their goods to shore.

This was not how she'd imagined her arrival in a new land to start a new life. When she and Conrad had left London for Fremantle they saw themselves setting out on a grand adventure. They would found a dynasty and after diligence and hard work would oversee a fine spread of an estate. They planned to take up land south and inland of the coastal town of Cossack in the northwest of the state of Western Australia. Conrad had been as thorough as was possible in his investigations into opportunities in the colony. He had been spurred on by Olivia, who was determined to make a fresh start following the death of her widowed father. She had inherited enough from the sale of the small family emporium and could see the possibilities for her and her accountant husband would be greater in the colonies.

Together Olivia and Conrad had done some research and, despite the vagueness and sometimes conflicting reports about Australia, they saw the chance to make a better life. They invested in farm equipment and household supplies of every description and enough basic necessities to see them through their first year. They had sought advice in Fremantle and despite wild stories of the cannibalistic Aborigines, desperadoes on the high seas, unsavory characters in the small coastal towns and a rough lifestyle, they remained undaunted. All had agreed that fortunes could be made in the northwest.

The captain gave them canvas, ropes, food and two barrels of rainwater to make a temporary camp and, wishing them well, sent the newlyweds to shore, watched by the crew and passengers who were glad it was not them. The captain never ceased to be amazed at the determination and enthusiasm with which these pioneers ventured into isolation and the unknown.

As the schooner sailed away to the north into a rising wind and falling barometer, the couple standing alone on the beach looked abandoned and forlorn. Olivia slipped her hand into Conrad's.

He squared his shoulders and turned to eye the scrubland. "Let's find a place to make camp."

By nightfall they had made a rough shelter with firm saplings dug in as corner posts with brush and the canvas spread over it to form walls and a roof. They used their boxes and trunks as a barricade and settled down to sleep as best they could. The surf, strange bush noises and insects disturbed them. Although Olivia was fearful, she far preferred to be on dry land than in the heaving darkness she'd suffered below deck in the ship.

They huddled together and Conrad made an attempt to speak light-heartedly. "My dear wife, I promised you a better life and here we are, no better than the natives."

Olivia couldn't respond with any levity and her voice trembled. "I hope you won't be gone too long—I'm afraid . . . the natives, this place, the baby due so soon . . ."

"I would run all the way if I could. But you must be strong, my dear. You have the revolver—all will be well. We knew it would take great faith and courage to do this."

Olivia didn't answer. She'd known courage would be called for, but she didn't expect to be tested quite so harshly or quite so soon.

Conrad set off toward Cossack the next morning, boots firmly laced, water bag and rifle slung on his back and panama hat shading his fair English skin from the sun. With his coppery hair and pale gray eyes, he did not quite fit the image of an intrepid adventurer.

He had shown Olivia once again how to use the gun and urged her to keep the small fire burning and to stay out of the harsh sunlight. As she watched his slight figure disappear through the sandy scrubland, resolutely walking to the arrow of his compass, Olivia broke down and wept. She cried out of loneliness and fear, for him, herself, their child, and the unknown life they faced.

They had both grown up in south London but had met when Conrad came to work at her father's emporium as the bookkeeper and accountant. He had become smitten with the pretty and very bright young woman who had shown a keenness and aptitude for learning bookkeeping as well as serving behind the counter. Conrad had successfully courted her and Olivia's father was relieved his only child had chosen a suitable husband. He increased Conrad's responsibility and salary.

A year later he had died and, after long talks with Conrad, Olivia, as sole inheritor of her father's estate, sold the shop and used the capital to finance their plan to make a life in Australia. While they knew little of the land, they were told skilled farmhands were available for those taking up leases.

Conrad was a good, kind man but seeing him in this new and forbidding place, Olivia wondered how well she really knew him and how he would manage.

Her thoughts drifted back to her own situation. At first she had cowered close to the shelter, but then sparkling water, the call and dart of sea and shore birds called to her. Hesitantly Olivia walked to the water's edge and stood gazing at the wavering line of the horizon which was marked by a long dark line of clouds. She looked down at her feet. Shells, pebbles and broken chunks of coral were embedded like jewels in the sand. Impulsively she sat and pulled off her boots and thick cotton stockings and set off along the beach toward a distant headland.

When she returned, her feet were sore—she had never walked so far without shoes. Her bonnet trailed by its ribbons behind her, the combs from her hair were in her pocket and her thick russet curls were tickled by a faint breeze from the sea. It was liberating and invigorating and she felt the child within her stir with what she believed must have been pleasure.

She ate some bread and pickled meat, drank a little water and settled to a peaceful sleep, though she could still feel the motion of the ship after so long at sea.

That night the peace was shattered. The great storm which had been building up over the Indian Ocean smashed its way to land. Lashing rain and whipping winds screamed around Olivia as she huddled terrified, while it seemed the earth and heavens were caught in some exploding climatic war. The shelter was shredded, boxes and baskets turned over and rolled along the beach, the fire drowned in moments. Olivia inched back into the denser bush, tripping and slipping, picking her way by the flashes of lightning, then clung to a tree and prayed that she would survive this night. She also prayed for her husband, hoping that he had reached the township before this nightmare began.

In the calm of the following morning she picked her way back to her shelter. Debris littered the beach and her little camp. Laboriously she set about putting her shelter back together as best she could. She tied the remains of the canvas back in place, upended a sodden wicker basket, spreading her clothes about bushes to dry. Food and water were intact but her fire was drenched and the small tin of matches had disappeared. As she worked, hampered by the bulge of her straining belly, she felt as if she was being watched, but no sound, no movement gave any clue that anyone was near. She kept the revolver close at hand.

After resting in the middle of the day, Olivia decided to walk along the beach to see what the storm had washed up. She walked north, in the opposite direction to the previous day. Soon she came to a small headland. Climbing awkwardly over the rocks, she was unprepared for the sight that lay before her. Strewn along the beach as far as she could see was a mass of shattered wood, personal effects, and shipboard paraphernalia. Her heart went cold with the awful knowledge that this was the flotsam of a shipwreck, most likely the *Lady Charlotte* which she had just left.

She couldn't bring herself to inspect the debris too closely and she hurriedly retraced her steps, feeling vulnerable and inconsequential in the face of this mysterious land that overwhelmed with its immensity and the force of its elements. She concluded it was a country not to be trusted, its beauty could turn to destruction with what seemed unpredictable ferocity.

Olivia trudged despondently back along the

beach, the bulk of her distended womb weighing heavily. She saw some pretty shells underfoot but the strain of bending to collect them dissuaded her from making the effort.

Lifting her gaze as "her" strip of shoreline came into view, she stopped, looked again, felt faint and began to tremble. Her worst fears had come to pass—naked black men like silhouette figures were moving around her camp. Her initial impression was of their slight build and thick clumps of hair. Their curiosity was apparent as they peered, dipped and prodded spears into her belongings like a bevy of inquisitive birds. This intrusion into the little haven she had created in the wilderness was an intolerable violation.

With a furious cry and without stopping to consider the consequences, Olivia rushed forward shouting, "Go away! Go away!"

The blacks stood still, looking in dismay at this distant squawk of objection. To them she looked like some mad bird, fat, waddling, screeching with arms flapping, prepared to take on the tribe's finest hunters in a defiant but hopeless attack. When it became obvious this being was human, female and pregnant, amusement stilled their defensiveness. Their confusion as to the reason for this apparition was explained by one of the men who had sighted the shipwreck. They spoke quickly, then moved forward as a group and stood waiting to exchange greetings with this irate survivor.

Olivia saw them unite and seeing the weapons

they all carried, their superior strength and sheer numbers, wondered briefly at her headlong rush into the arms of certain death and, with fear taking over from rage, stopped and squeezed her eyes shut waiting for a spear to hit her. She stood, her face in her hands, her last thoughts of the fate of her unborn child.

When she lifted her head again the beach was deserted. Nervously, she walked slowly toward her shelter expecting wild men to leap from the bush brandishing spears. But all was quiet. Olivia found the revolver, then sank to the ground, tears flowing down her cheeks.

Eventually hunger and the pressure in her womb from her baby forced her to rally. She had known this pioneering life was going to be harsh and here she was going to pieces within days. Resolutely, she set about gathering grasses that had dried in the sun and twigs to build a small fire. Then, searching desperately for some means to light it, she rummaged amongst the mess of her possessions but realized it was useless. The tin of matches had been lost. She stamped a foot in frustration and despair. Her attention turned to what supplies she had. As unappetizing as the cold, uncooked food would be she had to keep nourishing herself and her child.

As she pondered these possibilities a blur of movement at the edge of her vision suddenly caught her attention. For a moment she thought it was an animal. There was a brief flash of color, then in a gap between the trees she saw a dark naked man. Olivia couldn't quite believe her eyes. There was no doubting it—he had her straw bonnet bouncing merrily on his buttocks, its red ribbons tied across his belly. She hastily moved to stare back at the beach and saw to her dismay two other natives standing once again by her wicker hamper which had held her damp clothing. One had a petticoat tied around his matted hair and the other was holding up one of her best high-button kid boots in some puzzlement.

"Shoo! Go away!" Olivia advanced in outrage, then dashed back to fetch the revolver. After fumbling with it, she managed to fire a shot in the general direction of the two Aborigines on the beach.

They raced away, clutching her clothing.

With trembling knees, Olivia tried to think calmly what to do next. Still carrying the revolver, she began to gather up the clothes she'd spread to dry. She was stooping awkwardly to pick up undergarments off the sand when from behind her came a shout.

"Hoy there!"

Dropping the clothes, Olivia spun around and leveled the revolver in the direction of the voice. She was surprised to see the tall figure of a white man coming from the direction of the little headland. He wore a woven straw hat and loose white shirt with breeches and boots. She also saw the holstered gun stuck at his side and knew this man was no shipwreck survivor. As he strode toward her she saw, following some distance behind, a smaller man of oriental appearance with straight black hair and a strange small hat.

Her first impression of the white man was that he seemed quite at ease and was strikingly handsome despite the stubble on his face. He was tall and dark with a rosy glow to his generous smiling mouth and tanned cheeks that showed off his sky blue eyes. He kept his curling hair longer than most men favored but he was most recognizable by the large pearl he wore threaded through his left earlobe. It took only seconds to absorb all this and she was instantly alert and fearful as she recalled the captain of the *Lady Charlotte* telling them tales of the unsavory and often dangerous rogues who sailed the waters of northern Australia. He'd spoken of groups of unscrupulous beachcombers trading in illicit liquor, women and whatever they could find or steal to sell to passing boats.

"Who are you? What do you want?" she called to the advancing man.

He stopped and stared at the revolver pointed at him.

"What do *I* want?" he queried in a bemused voice. "Madam, I thought you might be the one in need. Please have no fear." He raised his arms above his head in mock surrender.

Olivia blushed, realizing she was still pointing the revolver at him and lowered it to her side. Her relief at seeing a white man was still tempered by nervousness and she noted he approached her just as cautiously.

"How did you manage to come ashore safely when it seems all others have perished?" Without pausing he answered his own question as he noticed her protruding belly previously screened by the pile of clothes. "Ah I see, in your condition you were given favored status."

"Not so," Olivia swiftly snapped back.

They both stared at one another. She recognized his Irish brogue though it had something of a Yankee twang to it, she thought. But he was well spoken and courteous. They exchanged a brief smile.

Now he could observe her closely, he thought her very pretty with a pert nose, green eyes and full lips.

"Madam, I have to ask if you are all right? I am Captain John Tyndall. I have my boat in the next cove. I came ashore when I saw the wreck on the reef."

Olivia swallowed, thinking of the acquaintances and crew they'd known so briefly and who had met such an untimely end. "Did no one survive?" she asked.

"None, I'm afraid. This coast is littered with unmarked reefs, it is hazardous at the best of times but now is cyclone season. Are you alone?"

Olivia hurriedly answered, "No, my husband is with me. We were put ashore before the storm. We are taking up land further inland."

"So I cannot offer a pretty shipwrecked lady a berth to Broome then," he said with a smile. "But seriously, this is rough country, surely you are not planning on traveling by foot? I should warn your husband the journey will be difficult. Especially in your delicate condition. Where is he?"

"No. It's all right. Thank you just the same," said Olivia quickly. The man made her uncomfortable. "Conrad has gone to Cossack for horses and we will stay there until I give birth and we are able to get to our farm."

The man looked dubious. "That is quite a journey. You are brave to stay out here alone. Have you met the local inhabitants yet?" he asked. She looked no more than a girl trying valiantly to hide her fears, though she certainly seemed to have spunk.

"I saw some natives. Are they dangerous? We were told in Fremantle of the monstrous murder of explorers in their sleep at La Grange some time back."

"There are always two sides to a story, especially in this part of the world. I think you'll find, dear lady, that that event was in retaliation for an unprovoked attack on twenty Aboriginal women, children and old people. I suggest you befriend the local people here. I doubt they'll think you are a danger or a threat."

Olivia's mouth twitched but she remained prim and stood her ground insisting she was capable of fending for herself. She glanced apprehensively at the Asian man standing silently behind the white sailor. Their eyes met briefly and he flashed a smile that disconcerted her. "Thank you for your offer of assistance. Perhaps we might meet up in Broome some day," she said with forced politeness.

He swept his hat from his head, gave a courtly bow and answered. "Indeed we might." Turning on his heel he strode back along the beach toward the shipwreck cove. Olivia assumed they would salvage what they could and sail away.

However, had she followed the two men she would have seen them turn into the scrubland and make their way to where some of the local Aborigines were camped. Here the white man, who spoke enough of their language to be understood, asked that they keep a watch on the woman on the beach. Some other matters were discussed with the tribal elders and the two men returned to their schooner.

Olivia, meanwhile, sat on the ground, limp with mental and physical exhaustion. Leaning back against a tin trunk she thought of course she couldn't have gone with him, but perhaps he could have sailed his smaller boat into Cossack. Maybe she should have asked him to wait for Conrad. Instead she had dismissed him like a lady at a tea party. But at least the unexpected visit had broken her sense of utter isolation. Oh dear, she hoped Conrad would be back by nightfall. Thinking of the evening she suddenly realized she could have asked him for matches. She rose and struggled along the beach to the rocky point but to her dismay there was no sign of any boat.

Nor was there any sign of her husband by the time the dusk drew in. Forlornly Olivia looked at the little pile of dried grass and twigs she'd been unable to light. She ate some dried oats, drank some water and crouched at the water's edge to splash salt water on her face, knowing the salt would be uncomfortable on her skin, but thought it best to save the precious drinking water. She was tired and sat on the damp sand, soaking her feet in the sea water to relieve their swollen soreness.

It was twilight by the time she made her way back to the shelter. For a moment she thought she smelled smoke, but the sky around her was clear. However, as she arrived at the makeshift camp she stopped and blinked to make sure she wasn't imagining the sight before her.

One of the Aboriginal men she'd seen earlier sat cross-legged at the site of her failed campfire. Concentrating on his task, he twirled a thin stick on a piece of wood, stopping to blow on it as a spark flared, then another, then a thin wisp of smoke was visible and the grass smoldered and caught. He gently blew on the embryonic flame, dropped wisps of shredded grass on to it and a fire was started. He ignored Olivia who squatted opposite hardly daring to breathe as he performed this delicate task. Once he had it burning brightly he straightened up and gave Olivia a beatific smile.

"Thank you," she whispered.

His reply, short and guttural, meant nothing to her and was like no language she had ever heard. Gratefully she held out her hands over the flame which represented security as well as a practical aid for light and cooking. Suddenly anxious to build the fire, she heaved herself to her feet and went to where she had stacked some wood.

When she turned back to the fire the man had gone, melting into the softly falling night.

She slept fitfully that night, driven to distraction by the attacks of flying, biting insects. When the dawn finally came, Olivia threw a branch on the fire embers and was relieved to see it flare into life. She felt a renewed spurt of energy and was confident that today Conrad would arrive. In anticipation she stowed and packed the things she had scattered about her shelter and gathered more wood. She longed for fresh food and was concerned at how low the water had sunk in one of the barrels. Perhaps the native who had kindled her fire might lead her to water. She had heard and seen nothing, but somehow knew they were close at hand and watching her.

By late morning she was weary, her limbs ached and she felt very strange, which she put down to lack of proper food. She sipped some of her water and to distract herself decided to walk through the coastal fringe of growth behind the white low sandhills. But after some distance with nothing but low scrubland, sandy red soil, spindly trees between sparse large gums, the heat began to affect her. So when she came upon a small clearing she sat down in the shade. She closed her eyes then gulped in shock as she felt her body become gripped in an iron clasp of pain. She drew up her knees as another spasm rippled and stabbed at her and the terrifying realization hit her that she was going to have her child all alone in this wilderness.

Crying out aloud, she struggled to her feet, her arms cupped beneath the weight of the child which was pushing insistently and agonizingly downward. After staggering a short distance, the pain once more forced her to the ground. Curling up on her side, Olivia rocked and moaned as the contractions rippled through her body. She lost track of time and sense of where she was, as she focused on the point within her body that was causing this anguish. She was vividly aware of her predicament, fearful of its outcome and screamed for her husband. Finally, she lapsed into semiconsciousness.

Through the mists of her mind Olivia became aware of a gentle hand soothing her hot brow, and firm hands straightening her legs. She felt herself being lifted.

"Conrad, I knew you'd come," Olivia sighed and struggled to regain consciousness. Opening her eyes with relief, instead of her husband, she found she was staring into the dark eyes of a black woman. Two other Aboriginal women murmured words that had no meaning and pulled at her clothes but Olivia was too wracked by another contraction to fight them. She soon realized they were there to help her, and she began to work with them. Her voluminous skirt and petticoats were dispensed with and she squatted forward, supported front and back while the third woman directed proceedings. She felt the baby slide from her body as she arched and heaved with a panting cry and the satisfied grunts from the woman in charge comforted her. In a rush it was all over and the child was turned to face the earth, the cord pulled free and cut with a sharp stone flint. Olivia felt a hard push on her belly to expel the after-birth.

They settled her and busied themselves with the baby after lifting it to her with broad smiles, showing her it was a son. Olivia, weak and shaking, could only gasp until they placed a wad of gummy substance in her mouth. She sucked on it as they had shown her and could soon feel her energy returning. Now trusting these women completely she watched as they tended her by rubbing some kind of ash paste on to her torn parts. Then they turned their attention to the infant. A small fire was burning. Olivia had no recollection of it being started or of the hole being dug in which they were now burying the placenta. After placing green leaves on the fire and holding the baby above the smoke they drew a pattern on its pale skin in ash and red paste.

The three women were chanting softly together, words of a familiar and ancient rite as they tended the baby, joining it with mother earth and giving the child its Dreaming place, its place of belonging, the place where its spirit would return when its time in this place had passed. But Olivia understood none of this, seeing only her child, calm and alert in capable hands. When they handed the child to her, Olivia put it to her breast and, for the first time, she smiled.

Later she slept and as night fell the women who had squatted patiently by, helped her and the child return to the shelter. The fire was burning and the smell of food gave Olivia great pangs of hunger. A fish was cooking in the embers and as Olivia settled herself one of the women dragged the fish from the fire with a stick. After letting it cool, she then scraped away the burnt skin, broke off the cooked white flesh and handed it to Olivia who ate greedily. They threw more green leaves on the fire which gave off a pungent smelling smoke and left her and the child to sleep. Olivia lay by the fire with her son, delighting in the wonderment of this small and perfect being she cradled in her arms.

CHAPTER FIVE

The day came wrapped in a wet blanket. Olivia felt as if she was being smothered by the moist air, her limbs were heavy, her skin clammy, insects were annoying her and the fretful baby. She felt lethargic and drained and knew it was not the reaction to giving birth but to the physical conditions about her. As she struggled to settle the baby at her breast, a depression born from feeling abandoned seeped into her like the dampness soaking through her uncomfortable clothing. Had something happened to Conrad? Why hadn't he come back with the dray? The realization of responsibility for this small dependent creature she held in her arms was daunting under ideal conditions, but here was the added weight of loneliness and helplessness. It was almost overwhelming. How was she going to get through the next few hours, let alone face the days and months and years ahead? Olivia weakly tossed a branch onto the fire, knowing she should rouse herself and eat to keep up her strength.

As Olivia sat cradling the baby she heard voices, then saw that the three Aboriginal women had returned, bringing with them a young girl who eyed Olivia with shy curiosity. The women had brought food which they put before her in a little wooden dish. The older woman gently reached for the baby then held him to her breast. Olivia was stunned and felt an urge to reach out and snatch the baby away from the black breast, then relaxed. The gentle smiles and tender handling of her baby reassured her. She no longer felt so lonely or abandoned and gingerly sampled the strange food. The young girl, who looked about ten years old, giggled and made eyes at the baby. The women loosened the cotton shawl and let the naked baby stretch in the warm air. One waved a swatch of green grasses over him, keeping the insects away.

Olivia found the food delicious, a sort of seed cake soaked in wild honey, and a nutty tasting, finger-sized white "cigar" she couldn't identify and from its slug-like appearance she decided not to look at too closely. When she finished she felt better and she gave them all a smile of apprecia-tion and licked her fingers. The women stood and with gestures, unfamiliar words and laughter made it clear to Olivia she should come with them. Olivia was a little reluctant to move, but these seemingly primitive women had been so car-ing and she knew she had to trust them. They unrolled a simple string sling lined with kangaroo fur and hooked it over her head so it hung across her chest. The baby was put in the bag where he snuggled comfortably against his mother. Leading her from the shelter they pointed inland. Suddenly lamenting the loss of her straw bonnet, Olivia tied on her second best hat and, taking the stick the little girl handed her, followed the women into the bush.

It was a slow walk, but the women were patient and in no hurry, sometimes pausing to pick wild berries. Olivia tired quickly and she realized that these people must think it normal for a woman to walk soon after giving birth. It was a great contrast to the customs in her world. One of the women offered to carry the baby, and Olivia gratefully handed over the weighty little baby bag.

How she wished she could communicate with these women as they chattered softly amongst themselves, but she was glad enough for their company and felt safe in their care.

They soon came to a billabong surrounded by pandanus palms and river gum trees and they all settled in the shade. Olivia sat with her back to a tree and watched the women gather food from the water plants and shrubs in the mud beneath a floating carpet of broad-leafed plants. One of the women found a huge water snake that was brought ashore with shrieks of delight and quickly killed. With gestures they indicated to Olivia that it was going to be part of their next meal.

On the way back to her camp they stopped and used their digging sticks to unearth two large eggs buried in the sandy soil, to catch a small goanna and to whack a tree and shake free its seed pods which were collected in a little wooden scoop. The short heavy sticks with a fire-hardened pointed end seemed to Olivia to be of huge importance and no woman moved far without this versatile and practical implement. They left their grinding stones at the main camp but around their waists they wore a braided hair belt into which they tucked small tools, which left their hands free to carry children and to hunt. Olivia was fascinated at their skill in catching small animals.

Late in the day several men came out of the scrub further along the beach. The women signaled to them to come into Olivia's camp. The men hesitated, chuckling and discussing the entreaty before edging forward as a group. Olivia felt as shy with them as they obviously were with her. Their near nakedness embarrassed her but nonetheless she couldn't help admiring their lean and muscular physiques. The three women pointed at the sleeping baby and were obviously talking about the food they had prepared for Olivia. This brought a surge of talk, with the men pointing to the water's edge. For the first time Olivia noticed a long low stone wall of loosely packed stones that ran across the mouth of an inlet between two rocky outcrops. This wall was covered by the sea at full tide and as the water receded through the gaps between the stones, fish were trapped behind the wall, making it an effective trap. It was now low tide and the men and women went to the trap and began scooping up the fish. Mollusks and shellfish were also collected and added to the stock of food.

Back near her camp small fires were lit and allowed to smoke to keep insects away, while a large cooking fire blazed in a ring of stones. When it had died down the fire was scraped to one side and the fish and shellfish were buried in the hot sand and covered over with ash and hot embers to cook. Olivia watched from a distance, marveling at their self-sufficiency and skill. How interested Conrad would be in this, she thought, and with a pang realized it was the first time she'd thought of him for many hours.

She sat by her own small fire in front of her shelter not wishing to intrude, for she had noticed their etiquette involved periods of simply sitting and observing. When the time was deemed appropriate, it was the young girl who shyly approached and gestured for her to join the others.

The men had finished eating by the time the sun began to dip into the sea. Sitting to one side, they regarded Olivia with clinical detachment. She was handed the seafood and ate hungrily. How could she ever repay these people? She just hoped they would stay around until Conrad returned. She had no doubt he would turn up safely. He simply *had* to, she told herself. So she sat with the baby in her lap and watched and listened as the group talked. She suspected they were part of a bigger group who were some distance away as she noticed food was put to one side to be taken with them.

Olivia gave them a grateful smile and indicated the food was good. They nodded with satisfaction. They obviously understood how ill-equipped, mentally as well as physically, she was to survive alone here, and for the first time it fleetingly occurred to Olivia that these people were actually playing host in their own land. Was she, Olivia thought, on land already owned?

Her thoughts were pushed aside when the baby began whimpering. Turning away from the men, she went to put it to her breast, then thought how silly it was to be modest when everybody else was virtually naked. So she ignored her feelings and watched the infant suckle greedily.

At sunset they doused the fire, collected their tools and weapons and the women followed the men into the bush. Only the young girl gave Olivia a backward glance.

Olivia realized the smaller smudge fires of the Aborigines had indeed kept the marauding mosquitoes and sandflies at bay, so she copied them and lit two smaller fires from her campfire, putting the same leaves on them. The pungent smoke was effective and Olivia crawled into her rough brush shelter and curled up to sleep with the baby beside her.

In the morning Olivia found she was following a basic routine just as if she was in a house. She took the baby to the sea and cautiously bathed him in the ocean, returning to the camp to sponge off the salt with fresh water. She felt full of energy, delighted in her placid baby and knew in her heart Conrad was on his way. She tidied her camp, found it too hard to identify and unpack whatever container held baby items, so she ripped a petticoat and made diapers and cotton wraps for him. Then, settling the baby in the Aboriginal sling, she set off along the beach. Olivia found she enjoyed the exercise and was amazed at her ability to be up and about after giving birth, rather than languishing in bed sipping consommé as would have been the expected routine in London.

She found some shells, including a magnificent trochus, wiggled her bare feet in the wet sand as she'd seen the tribal women do, and to her delight collected a half dozen small mussel-like shellfish.

When she returned to her camp several men were at the water's edge setting off on what she assumed was a fishing expedition. One man pushed off in a small dugout wooden canoe while two others balanced precariously on mangrove log rafts. They were carrying nets and spears. One of the men she recognized from the previous evening lifted an arm in acknowledgment and pointed at her shelter. When Olivia reached it she found a curved and smoothed piece of bark with a soft hide lining it and she realized it was meant to be a baby cradle. Delighted with this gift, she lay the baby in it and he rested comfortably, staring trustingly at her. How right the white man she'd encountered on the beach had been in telling her to make friends with these people. She and Conrad had read the writings of early explorers who described the natives as primitive barbarians. While they could be seen as primitive and their lifestyle simplistic compared to the trappings of Olivia's civilized world, sitting here she began to consider that maybe they had evolved a system which best suited their needs.

She and Conrad were about to travel to what they believed was free territory, a lapsed leasehold bought from the government in Perth. They had a dream of clearing the land, building a home, planting crops, raising livestock. The dream did not include the Aborigines or the vagaries of nature in an alien land. It did not acknowledge the chance of failure or the possibility that all trace of their presence could be obliterated as easily as footprints in the sands of the north-west dunes. Yet already the land was perplexing Olivia. It seemed so terribly harsh. The Aborigines, she observed, lived with it, flowing along to where the food, shelter and friends were. They seemed—her thoughts struggled for the right word—comfortable. Yes. That was it, comfortable with the land.

Olivia sighed. It seemed too big an issue about which she knew very little, but she resolved to learn what she could and wished she could speak the local language. Sitting peacefully in the shade by her child, she watched the men paddle along the shore over the patterns of light on the moving surface of the water. She heard the call of strange birds, felt the humid breeze lift a strand of hair, and absorbed the rhythm of the place while she stoically waited for the return of her husband. She felt no need for anything further in her life at this moment. The sense of oneness was calming and she wondered why she'd never experienced it before in her life.

Some distance north, a small white schooner drew into the sandy shallow water of a tiny island close to the mainland where sandy bays and inlets were a rich trepang hunting ground. The island was two kilometers long and half a kilometer wide but the main beach was a hive of activity. A small fleet of *praus* from the Dutch East Indies, a scattering of huts and the smoke of many fires along the beach gave the island a settled air. John Tyndall, master of the sailing schooner *Shamrock,* grinned as he took in the scene and with a practiced efficiency lowered the mainsail, then held the bow into the wind. His Malay crew hand, Ahmed, stood by the anchor chain as the boat drifted toward the shore. When it was calculated to be close enough that they could row ashore in a minute at low tide, Ahmed hit the securing pin with a hammer and the anchor chain rattled over the side with a clatter that set the seagulls on the beach shrieking into the air. Tyndall relaxed at the tiller and once again scanned the shore, recognizing some of the boats. This was the life, he reflected. A tropical paradise, more or less, and a chance to do a little business. The problem however, was that it was indeed a little business and John Tyndall yearned to do big business.

He found life full of surprises, delighted in its unpredictability and had decided there was no such thing as coincidences in this world. It was all a matter of recognizing a passing possibility of a new direction and boldly grabbing it. As soon as you settled on a plan, those so-called coincidences fell into your path. He was told he had the luck of the Irish, he always said it was a matter of "jumping off the cliff, knowing without a shadow of a doubt, you'd fly!"

John Tyndall sometimes marveled at where life had led him with its joys, sadness and adventures. Apprenticed to a Belfast shipwright the sea had always been in his blood. He'd gone to sea on trawlers as a boy. Being a bright lad, he had learned quickly and had graduated to working on windjammers crossing the Atlantic where he earned his Second Mate's certificate. He was never short of female attention but Tyndall, despite his sea roving life, was shy in his flirtations and hesitant about any serious involvement—which had made him a sitting duck for the ambitions of pretty Amy O'Reilly. She worked as a serving girl in a boarding house and what she lacked in formal education she made up for in streetwise survival tactics and a deep ambition to make something of her life. John Tyndall with his good looks, cheerful disposition and blossoming career presented a chance to break away. She contrived to cross his path and, as she planned, he found her charms and beauty irresistible. Before he knew it, at twenty Tyndall found himself with a pregnant wife who urged him to improve and change their circumstances. He snatched the opportunity to sail to Australia to find what opportunities existed.

Upon his arrival in Sydney, he obtained work immediately with a shipwright in Balmain and sent his first substantial savings home to Amy, advising her he was going to sea again, on a whaler, as he could make more money that way.

Amy was not impressed with his description of Sydney or their prospects for the moment and began to rethink her situation. Unbeknownst to Tyndall, she used the money he had sent her to travel to London to look for work and be ready to join Tyndall on his return. When Tyndall's second draft of money arrived at their Belfast home, Amy's drunken father with whom they had lived, had promptly cashed it and spent it on booze. Shortly afterward he received a letter from his daughter lamenting that she had lost the child she had been expecting some time previously and was in a bad state, as conditions in London were tough due to an epidemic. She asked if more money had come from Tyndall. Her father sent her a note denying any money or letters had come and saying that he was upset to hear of her miscarriage.

Not one to miss an opportunity to better her circumstances, Amy teamed up with an elderly

Scottish landowner and traveled north with him. With the loss of the child and a husband on the other side of the world she chose immediate comfort. In the meantime, during the flu epidemic in London, her boarding house was burned down and some people died. The local priest in London wrote to Amy's father with the news of the fire and of Amy's disappearance. He hoped she hadn't been one of those who died in the epidemic. In a drunken state her father relayed the confused news to drinkers in the pub that Amy had died. That night staggering home, he fell into a pond and drowned. When Tyndall's next letter arrived, the village postmaster returned it and wrote to inform him of the sad demise of Amy and her father.

Neither of them had close family so Tyndall had then turned his back on the old world.

Now, at twenty-five, he was a handsome bachelor in transition from adventurer to solid citizen of the north-west of Western Australia, a frontier that attracted the adventurer, but a developing area that appealed to his business instincts. He was respected and well liked among the waterfront people and merchants he serviced along the coast. He could drink his way through the night with a bunch of seafarers down by the wharf, then scrub up and next night be all charm, wit and tact at a dinner party given by one of the middle-class merchants with a daughter or two of marriageable age. The daughters of the rather limited upper class and very wealthy also eyed John Tyndall, but not with serious intentions. They were simply fascinated by his handsome looks, swaggering nature and the stories that were told in whispers about his past, stories more often based on fantasy than fact.

Tyndall felt no pull to cement his boots ashore. He loved the sea and his boat. He loved the freedom. He had dallied with dusky maidens on a score of islands from Tahiti to Thursday Island, but was yet to meet another woman of his own race to confuse his reasoning with any sort of love he had briefly experienced with the now forgotten Amy. He believed that out there, somewhere, was a woman of spirit, beauty and loyalty who was ready to match his spirited run at life. John Tyndall had his dream, too. But in his philosophy, in love, as in war, it was every man (and woman) for himself.

The little temporary settlement on the island beach reminded Tyndall of the odd circumstances in which he found the Hennessy woman on a beach some days ago. He grinned to himself. At least no one was going to pull a gun on him on *this* beach. She had guts, he reflected, but was she really strong enough to survive this rough and remote land? Like so many from the old country, she probably didn't have a clue what lay ahead of her. Her husband was lucky to have such a pretty and plucky mate at his side. He hoped all went well for her and made a mental note to sail past the beach on his return to Cossack to see if there was any sign of the Hennessy camp.

A soft word from Ahmed snapped him out of his reverie and he prepared to go ashore.

This island had been used by the Macassan trepangers for several generations. The economy of many Sulawesi towns relied heavily on trepang, which was sold to the Chinese merchants. The men sailed from Ujung Pandang, blown in their *praus* on the north-west monsoon to the land they called Marege in about ten days. They had their regular routes and bases and some *praus*, manned by up to twenty men, ventured down to the Kimberley waters. They had long ago established trading and social rituals with the local tribes-people and each year returned home when the south-east trade winds began.

Aboriginal women were offered freely to the Macassan captains and many of these liaisons were re-forged each season. Children they fathered were absorbed into the extended Aboriginal families. Occasionally the Aboriginal brides who had been taken away to Sulawesi and the other islands returned to visit.

Already the beach resembled a village. The *praus* and their wooden canoes were beached along the sand, portable bamboo smoke houses had been erected to dry the trepang, and men were busy at the lines of circular stone hearths stretched along the shore where iron cauldrons of the sea slugs were boiling before being dried. Piles of cut and dried mangrove wood, prepared on a previous visit, were heaped by the hearths. Several men sat pounding kaolin clay rock to make caulking paste for the boats. Crude thatched shelters were scattered under shady trees and at a large campfire sat Aboriginal elders from the nearby mainland and the leaders of the Macassans who were offering around their tobacco pipes.

They hailed Tyndall as the dinghy came to rest on the beach. Speaking in Malay and a local pidgin Aboriginal language, he greeted his friends.

After stumbling upon this place two years before, Tyndall had returned annually and learned much from the visitors and local tribespeople. It had also proved a valuable bartering situation. He brought fresh food, rice, flour, sugar, jams, fishing gear, kerosene and small boat gear which he exchanged for dried turtle and shell along with some trepang that he sold to the Chinese in the towns along the coast and in Fremantle on trading trips.

Tyndall realized that the present peaceful coexistence of these two disparate communities and their trade alliance had developed through patient understanding of each others' customs and etiquette. He had heard stories of occasional hostilities resulting from the theft of coveted items, disagreements over women or some breach of custom that warranted reprisal. But for centuries it had been largely a peaceful and mutually beneficial arrangement, ritualized with obligation and traditional behavioral patterns understood and reciprocated.

Once, on a trip inland with a group, Tyndall

had been shown ancient rock paintings of these encounters on the coast which had passed into Dreaming stories and the fabric of their oral history in song and dance.

Tyndall joined the men at the fire and they swapped news. Later would come the exchange of gifts and that evening "good food" would be prepared and possibly some of the Macassans' liquor shared.

They talked, too, of barter and one of the Aboriginal elders asked Tyndall if he had brought a much desired new long-handled axe. Tyndall told the old man that he had indeed brought the axe and, what's more, a special stone for keeping it sharp. There was a nod of gratification from the old man who immediately launched into a long discussion with other Aborigines that Tyndall had trouble following, but it was connected with some future walk-about into the back country. Tyndall waited until he had nearly finished a mug of tea before turning the conversation back to the axe and payment.

To his surprise the Aboriginal elder pointed to Tyndall's pearl earring, gestured with cupped hands and pointed south. From his adequate grasp of the language, Tyndall was quickly able to gather that payment was to be the opportunity to harvest some mother-of-pearl and perhaps find a pearl or two at a spot only known to the tribe. The offer pleased Tyndall as much as it surprised him. The roll of the dice, he thought, might just be going my way.

Tyndall went back to the beach where his dinghy was anchored and without having called for him, Ahmed was suddenly at his side. Without a word they pushed the boat into the moonlit water and Ahmed took the oars. Ahmed had been in the camp of the Bugis men to hear news from the area he once called home. He had not been back since he was rescued by Tyndall two years ago from an uninhabited island in the Timor Sea. A cyclone had sunk the Broome pearling lugger Ahmed was working on and he had been the sole survivor. Ahmed believed Allah had sent Tyndall as his savior and ever since had been his devoted and loyal offsider.

Good as their word, the following day several Aborigines set out with Tyndall and Ahmed in dugout canoes to travel down the coast to the place of the pearls. Ahmed and Tyndall were not as proficient paddling the canoe as the Aborigines were and they struggled to keep up. The bulky and crude dugouts slid down the coast, weaving between reefs and over sand bars until they came to where a swampy river emptied into the sea and mangroves shrouded the shoreline. They pulled into shore and the men settled themselves on the narrow strip of gray sand amidst the sprouting tips of roots and mangrove shoots. They explained the water had to leave and so they waited.

When at last the tide ebbed, the men took long sticks and began prodding and wiggling for shell with their feet.

Soon, amid whoops of laughter, they picked up

fat shells, sealed tight and crusted with a covering of slimy growth and miniature crustaceans. Ahmed and Tyndall prized the shell halves apart to reveal the meat and muscle lying in the iridescent shell. Before long three shells had yielded small gleaming round pearls which Tyndall slipped into his pocket with great satisfaction. They worked through the day, piling the dugouts with unopened shells. Finally, as the tide rose, they pushed out and with the canoes low in the water paddled in the twilight back to the trepang island.

Tyndall was elated. Now he knew where the beds were he could make dry shell pearling a profitable sideline. What's more, the Aborigines had told him there were other pearl beds further south and out to sea.

An idea began to form in Tyndall's mind. Over the past twenty years pearling had become a highly lucrative activity despite periodic slumps in the world market for mother-of-pearl and disasters such as the cyclone that wiped out forty luggers and several hundred men. It was an industry pursued by wild risk takers who were fiercely competitive and secretive about the pearls they found. But if he had access to a rich source, aided by his friends' local knowledge, and a partner with capital he could expand to make this a serious operation and challenge the existing pearling masters.

That night as he sat by the fire with Ahmed he couldn't resist opening more shells while the trepangers went about their work, the fascination of mother-of-pearl and the lure of possible pearl finds had him hooked. He rolled the shining moon-colored globules in his palm and said at last to Ahmed, "Friend, I'm thinking of becoming a pearler. We'll start off dry shelling with the schooner but hopefully we'll soon be able to get a new boat."

Unfazed, Ahmed merely nodded. "We build a number one lugger, tuan."

"We'll work out of Cossack to start with, but no one must know about this place. Soon enough we'll make our way and head for Broome ... I think this is the break that I've been looking for."

"It is fate, the time is right, tuan."

Tyndall grinned at Ahmed's devout Muslim belief that fate ruled their lives and that there was little either of them could do to alter what was preordained. His calm acceptance of the good and the bad that life threw at them sometimes irked Tyndall, but right now he, too, felt the gods were on his side.

CHAPTER SIX

Conrad Hennessy did not think of himself as a brave man. To him bold and brave men tackled feats he could only marvel at from the safety of his hearthside armchair. They were reckless, even foolhardy in their quest to conquer and achieve. Yet in his modest way he knew he had courage of heart and, while not flamboyant, was steadfast and diligent. He had never imagined that he would win a bride as sweet and plucky as Olivia. And now here he was, crashing through wild terrain in a strange and inhospitable country, in charge of two large horses dragging a small wagon through bush where only a wild animal track existed.

Many times he had had to stop and, with the axe, hack a path for the small wagon he had acquired in Cossack after two days of searching and negotiation. His natural caution was cast aside in his desperation to reach Olivia, who would have been expecting him days ago. He tried not to think about the return journey with a pregnant wife and kept urging the horses forward, glad that he had bought bushwise and hardy animals. The journey on foot had been much further and rougher than it appeared on the basic map. From the brief conversations he had had in Cossack, he realized the north-west was very much more untamed than he'd imagined from afar. This might well offer opportunities to adventurers, the risk takers and brave men and women prepared to soldier through the hardships to establish a profitable new life, but he had hoped for a softer land, a little more order and more amenities. He hoped the land he had bought lived up to expectations and the favorable government report that had persuaded him to take this chance.

Deep in thought and trying to control the horses in the rough terrain, he didn't notice the log and boulder which lay across their path. The vague track fell away into a small dip, screened by the undergrowth and thick scrub. One horse stumbled and rolled onto its side bringing down the other horse and wagon.

Conrad was thrown clear and lay momentarily stunned as a frantic horse, pinned by the wagon, tried to get to its feet. Conrad rescued one horse but had to shoot the other. The wagon was damaged but the wheels functioned and after unharnessing the dead horse, he used the other to drag the wagon upright. Feeling shaky and dispirited he traveled on more slowly after checking his compass.

• • •

For Olivia the time passed slowly but she was not lonely or dispirited. The Aboriginal women, usually with their children, came to see her several times a day. They ensured she had food and water and in return seemed more than happy simply to be able to share the delights of the baby whom they fussed over with lots of chatter and laughter.

Olivia was surprised at how fast her strength returned and one morning took the baby with a group of women working the tidal fish trap. She sat on the sand as they hunted the trapped fish, watching the sandpipers dancing on the wet sand and the gannets diving for fish. She found herself pondering the unity of the whole scene—every one, every thing getting food, a natural harmony that was so enchanting and yet she was also conscious that she, a white woman from another world, really wasn't a meaningful part of it. She felt alien, but at the same time was aware of a yearning to belong. Nothing in her past experience had evoked such thoughts, and she mused on them while absently stroking her baby's head.

The next day when the tide was low, Olivia left camp for the fish trap before the Aborigines arrived, leaving the baby asleep in a little canvas shelter. As she approached a large flock of gannets and several pelicans arrived and began noisily feasting on the trapped fish. Waving her hat wildly and shouting at the birds, Olivia began to run toward the trap, and several Aborigines burst out of the scrub and chased after her, laughing and shouting with delight.

At this moment, Conrad crested the rise of a sand dune, and the spectacle of his beloved wife being pursued by natives waving their arms and spears and shouting was unbearably shocking. Surely he hadn't arrived at this last moment to witness his wife's murder! He lifted his rifle and fired.

However, the horse, slithering down the dune on its hindquarters, sent Conrad's shot astray. As he saw "the black devils" bolt for cover, Conrad was amazed to see Olivia turn and run toward him now waving her arms.

He heard her voice echoing faintly across the beach, "No! No, Conrad!"

Leaping from the wagon he ran to her, gathering her in his arms as she sobbed, "They are friends, Conrad—they have helped me."

"My dear, dear Olivia." He held her tightly, overcome with relief. When he stepped back from her, he realized she was wearing only her undergarments, camisole and petticoat, her feet were bare, her hair loose about her shoulders, and then it hit him, the bulge of her belly was gone. He reached out and soundlessly touched her, feeling the loose softness of her flesh, no tightness of skin over a body stretched wildly out of shape.

Olivia smiled tenderly, and took his hand. "It's all right, Conrad, come with me."

Excitedly she led him to her shelter as he mumbled at the nightmare the trip had been, how he'd feared for her safety, trying to grapple with the idea she had given birth. She pulled him down to his knees and, reaching inside the little tent, drew out the bark dish-like cradle in which the baby was sleeping. She lifted the torn petticoat covering the infant.

"We have a son, Conrad," she said gently.

He touched the baby's cheek, loath to disturb him. "But how did you manage, my dear? Alone, here . . . oh it must have been dreadful."

Olivia calmed him. "No, I had good care. The women, the Aboriginal women, they looked after me."

Conrad stared at her aghast, realizing he had fired on these people.

Olivia touched his hand. "You'd better see to the horse, and I'll put the pot on to boil. Don't worry too much about the shot. I'm sure they'll come back. Perhaps we can make amends with them in some way. Oh, I have so much to tell you."

"And I you," he said, suddenly feeling exhausted. "It is a miracle I am here. I really don't know how we are going to forge our way back again. It is truly ugly country to travel through. This coming ashore was not a good idea."

She pressed his hand. "Conrad dear, the *Lady Charlotte* . . . it has been wrecked. All are lost. We did make the right decision."

He shuddered and held her close.

"Don't worry, Conrad," pleaded Olivia. "Just see the bright side—we have a son."

Olivia returned to the beach and collected two fish that had been thrown onto the sand. She called out to the Aborigines. Even though there was no response of any kind, she felt sure they were watching.

Conrad led the horse to a patch of shade, tethered it and contemplated the wagon stuck in the sand. He asked Olivia for some water and looked at the near empty barrel of water. "Maybe they can show us where we can find water. We will need this replenished for the journey."

"Conrad, stop worrying. Come and rest, the fish will be cooked soon. Now tell me. What is the town like?"

Conrad bit his lip. "A ramshackle place I'm afraid. Not what I expected, but we can get all the supplies we need. There are sheep arriving in a week or so on one of the trading vessels. I plan to buy some to start us off. I think we should set out as soon as you feel ready, my dear. I don't think you'll be too comfortable in Cossack, I mean, there are very few women and it's a bit of a rough place."

"I understand. I'll do what you think best, Conrad. You know, I've learned so much from these people. I do hope there are tribespeople close to our farm."

Conrad stared at her in astonishment. He hadn't anticipated sharing his land with the blacks. He didn't want his precious stock stolen or hunted nor the fear of reprisals or attack at any time. "We'll see." He smoothed the baby's head. "He *is* a handsome child, Olivia."

They exchanged their first relaxed smile. "Pick him up Conrad, he won't break."

Later, after their meal, Olivia walked to the sea to
throw the fish bones into the water and to look
for some shellfish. Conrad sat at the camp with
his son in his lap, examining the small fingers
and toes. Suddenly a shadow fell across him.
Looking up in surprise he saw three Aboriginal
women staring at him. They had bemused
expressions at seeing the man cradling the baby.
They crouched before him, squatting down to
touch the baby and point to Conrad's face. When
they started chattering in their own language,
Conrad guessed he was being discussed and
immediately felt uncomfortable and awkward.
He tried to smile at them, and they broke out in
laughter. When Olivia eventually appeared he
was much relieved.

She took the baby and handed him to the
women, who nodded with satisfaction, smiled and
patted his round belly.

Conrad tried not to look at the swaying breasts
of these women or the barely modest grass covering over their private parts. Some of them wore
woven arm bands but they were, on the whole,
totally unadorned and unclothed. But there was
no mistaking the goodwill they exuded. He patted
his son's head, pointed to Olivia and then said
carefully to the women, "Thank you."

They laughed again and Olivia took Conrad's
hand and held it out to the oldest woman who
had delivered the baby and joined their hands

together. She understood the gesture and nodded solemnly. Then, picking up their string baskets and dilly bags, the women headed to the beach to collect the fish from the trap.

Conrad watched them and remarked, "Ingenious idea, that wall. Do you suppose we could get it across to them that we need to find fresh water?"

Olivia picked up the baby which had started to whimper and began to loosen her camisole. "Take the empty barrel to them and show them the water that's left. I'm sure they'll understand. Their camp can't be too far away."

"Yes, I'll do that." Conrad turned his eyes away from Olivia's exposed breast, fetched the water barrel and carried it along the beach to the women.

Olivia closed her eyes as the baby suckled contentedly, then as she changed the baby to the other breast she heard a footfall behind her and turned to see if Conrad had had success with the water and found instead she was staring up at the tall figure of Captain John Tyndall, the man from the schooner.

He coughed discreetly and averted his eyes as she pulled her top about her.

"Oh excuse me," he said a little awkwardly. "I saw the smoke from the fire and realized you were still here, so thought I'd see if you were all right." He looked down at Olivia seated on the ground, her bare toes peeping out from the now ragged hem of her petticoats, the baby at her breast, her hair falling softly about her pretty face.

Bedraggled though she was, it was a heartwarming picture. "I see you are doing very well. Congratulations. How did you cope with having the baby on your own?"

She gave him a hesitant smile. "I had help. The Aboriginal women were wonderful . . . they just came out of nowhere to help me."

He nodded and refrained from mentioning his talk with the elders on his previous visit. "And your husband, what news?"

"He arrived back this afternoon, he is looking for water with the women."

Tyndall looked about the camp and saw the wagon further along the beach. "I'm amazed he made it through. I believe the country is very rugged."

"Yes, he says it's going to be difficult returning with us all. He arrived and started shooting at the Aborigines, which was an unfortunate misunderstanding."

"He didn't wound or kill anyone, did he?" asked Tyndall, looking concerned. "He could find himself with a spear through his leg or worse. They have a payback system."

"Oh, dear me. No, no one was hurt. Do you suppose he is all right?" Olivia peered anxiously toward the beach.

"I'll go see," he said, striding away.

The two men returned together a short time later deep in animated conversation. When they stopped to inspect the wagon, Olivia laid her sleeping baby down and went over to join them.

"Hullo there, my dear," Conrad greeted her.

"What a stroke of luck Captain Tyndall found us. Saw the smoke, he said."

"Did you find water?"

"The women showed me a small spring, very fortunate."

"And we made our peace with the menfolk," added Tyndall.

"He speaks their tongue," said Conrad, impressed.

John Tyndall turned to the wagon. "I doubt that horse and wagon will make the return trip," said the captain dubiously. "I suggest you allow me to carry you back to Cossack. My schooner could take you and your belongings, I believe."

"That's a kind and generous offer," said Conrad, but Olivia looked worried. "Don't you think so, Olivia?"

"I don't like the idea of going back to sea."

"Believe me, Mrs. Hennessy, the seas have gone down and it will be a lot easier and quicker."

"Well, if Conrad agrees. That would be very kind of you."

They were under way late the next morning after Ahmed had brought ashore food from the galley— a fish curry and some rice. That night she slept in a narrow berth in the cabin of the *Shamrock* which was cramped, hot and stuffy. She found herself almost pining for the rough tree and crude canvas shelter by the comforting light of her campfire and insect-repelling smudge fire.

The next day Olivia sat quietly on the deck-house holding her son, who was yet to be named. Conrad stood beside John Tyndall at the helm while Ahmed, on the bowsprit, guided them through the mangrove-lined stretch of Butcher's Inlet. They had brought what they could with them, leaving the rest at the campsite and releasing the horse into the scrub.

Out on the water, the heat sapped her energy almost immediately, hitting her like the blast from a fire. Jarman Island, four miles offshore, served the estuary as a breakwater and most ships sheltered here due to the near fifteen-feet tidal drop and passengers and cargo were rowed ashore. However Tyndall and Ahmed sailed carefully but confidently into the creek and anchored at Deep Hole jetty on the opposite side of the creek to the township, where they could remain afloat.

Stepping ashore in Cossack, she felt too tired and dispirited to find anything positive about the bustling shanty town built on a strip of sand, surrounded by mangrove swamps and rocky hills. Several stone public buildings—the customs house and post office—gave some air of permanence but Olivia was disturbed to see a row of buildings with solid chains strung over the roofs and bolted into the ground around the foundations.

She glanced at Tyndall, who shrugged. "Willy willies—winds can get pretty high in a cyclone."

Settling Conrad and Olivia in a sulky, Tyndall gave them a swift tour of Cossack while Ahmed loaded their belongings on a dray to take to Tyndall's house.

The township crouched between two hills, Nanny-goat on the eastern side and Reader Head, a crag that overlooked the sea. From the south a causeway ran through the mangroves to Roebourne. There was a wooden church and a couple of stores but by far the most active and colorful section was the Chinese quarter, also known as "Jap town" which spread out towards the western boundary near the cemetery. They drove past the Chinese stores, the Indian tailor, a Japanese store, a Chinese bakery, a Turkish bath-house, opium dens and Japanese pleasure houses. Sly grog shops were plentiful and obvious. Some of the houses were little more than humpies, while the Aborigines, he said, had set up their *mia-mias* further out on the edge of town.

Olivia thought that the people of differing races all seemed coarse and disreputable and she only saw two women, a tired-looking older European woman and a painted Japanese girl in garish kimono who swiftly disappeared into a dim house.

That evening after Olivia and Conrad were settled in Tyndall's simple but functional house they talked over their plans for the immediate future.

Conrad wished to go to their land as soon as possible but worried about Olivia's strength. "You should be resting, with someone caring for you and the child. But I am loath to see us stay too long here. They say the wet season is horrendous and I was hoping we would be settled in our place before then."

Olivia still felt a little weary from the birth and the voyage but she had no hesitation in agreeing to move forward. The prospect of staying in the seamy town didn't appeal to her and, as hard as establishing their new home might be, it was preferable. "I think we should set out then, Conrad. You know, seeing how the Aboriginal women live has made me look at things differently. It's hard to explain, but I got a sense that it's better to be part of the country rather than trying to keep it apart from us. And I felt good being up and walking on the beach rather than lying in a dark room. So, I say let us go. I'll try to pull my weight as best I can."

He leaned over and kissed her forehead, feeling a deep love and pride. "You just care for yourself and the baby. One day I promise you'll have a grand home and the beautiful garden you've always wanted."

"Let's start with a roof over our heads first," smiled Olivia. "I wonder what the little cottage on the farm is like."

Neither was prepared for the harsh reality that confronted them. The trek to the land they had bought was slow and difficult. A team of horses pulled their wagon along a sand and dirt track and, by following their rough and inadequate map, they eventually located the area they presumed to be their acreage. Some of the land was as described, and could hopefully carry sheep, but most was rough country. Thankfully, the permanent water-hole and creek were as marked.

The "cottage" was built from slab timber and bark packed with a mud made from old termite colonies, with a hard dirt floor and a verandah front and back. Its galvanized iron roof was covered by a thick thatch of brush for coolness. Wooden shutters on greenhide hinges acted as windows for the two large rooms. A lean-to attached to the back had a fireplace with mud-brick chimney. Several pieces of rough hewn furniture remained and the hand of a woman was unmistakable—a dog rose rambled up one side of this sad looking home and brought a lump to Olivia's throat. She plucked a flower and inhaled its delicate scent, wondering what had become of the family that had started here with such dreams and hopes. She looked about with sagging spirit and wondered if they would fare any better.

"I suppose we can be glad squatters haven't moved in," said Conrad, desperately trying to make some light remark in the face of this shock. "It seems things are not quite as we were told in Fremantle."

"Well, we'd better do something before dark," said Olivia briskly, shifting the baby in her arms while trying to hide the disappointment and twinge of fear eating into her heart. Using her skirt, she attempted to wipe a thick layer of dust from a stool, and sat to feed the baby. Conrad went to the wagon to haul down the first of the supplies but instead rested his head against the load and closed his eyes in pain and frustration as he felt scalding tears burn against his lids.

A few days later, with the help of the two hired hands who arrived with another dray of gear, things were better organized and Olivia had even managed to prepare an evening meal of bully beef and damper and a simple pudding made with dried fruits and sugar. Roses in the center of the rough table gave a festive air and the soft glow from the kerosene lantern disguised the harshness of their surroundings. The baby, now known as James, slept in his cradle close to Olivia's feet.

Conrad put down his mug of sweet black tea and took Olivia's hand. "Olivia dear, I think perhaps we should give thanks to the good Lord for this meal and ask that he bless our home." Remembering the simple prayers of his father, Conrad bowed his head and said, "Thank you, Lord, for this food upon our table, the roof over our head and for your guidance and protection."

Olivia whispered "Amen" and thought of the Reverend Albert Cochrane back in London and wished he could christen the baby. While it was a simple thanksgiving she believed Conrad's dedication to work would see that they achieved their goals.

But as the weeks went by, and Conrad inspected their land more closely, they discovered the terrain was worse than they thought and would prove difficult for sheep or cattle. The waterhole was not big and a place for a well would need to be found. It was apparent the last wet season had not been a good one. The country was hot and dry and the only things that flourished were the flies. Their first sheep were soon due to arrive in Cossack and Conrad planned to ride to town with one of his stockmen to bring them back, as he knew nothing about handling stock and was ill at ease on a horse. He had also hired John Tyndall to bring the rest of their goods and extra supplies out to them by dray when his next shipment arrived from Fremantle.

In the soaring heat of a summer's morning, Olivia worked in their small house. She was tired from lack of sleep, as James had been fretful and cried most of the previous night. Conrad was completing the shed he was building, while the two hired men were across the property, fencing a holding paddock around a dam. At mid-morning she tied Conrad's lunch of pickled meat and damper in a small cloth and prepared to take it to him with a billycan of hot tea. She checked the baby, who was sleeping in a cradle crudely fashioned from a wooden box and set up near their bed. Normally she carried him with her in a sling like she'd seen the Aboriginal women use, as it kept him calm and seemed to stop his fretfulness by being close to her body. But for once he was sleeping well after a long feed instead of short bursts of fussy eating. She decided to leave him where he was and set out to where Conrad was working.

Conrad was having difficulty stretching a length of wire and asked Olivia to help. They worked together, talking little, until the task was finished.

Wiping his brow Conrad looked about him. "A hot wind has sprung up," he observed, then smiled at her, "Come and share my lunch."

"I've eaten, and I've left James sleeping."

"Olivia, do sit with me for a moment." They moved to the shade of a tree and sat with their backs against the tree trunk. "I know it is hard at present, but I feel sure the sheep will do well. We need the wet to boost the feed and I will look into other means of making our way. Maybe cattle at some stage." He talked on with a desperate buoyancy, describing how he saw the eventual layout of their land. She knew he was seeing sheep and cattle grazing and yarded in organized paddocks dotted with sheds and horses, and herself tending flowers she loved so much before a large and gracious homestead.

But for Olivia, tired and depressed, all she saw was the hardship of the reality before them—heat, flies and loneliness. And smoke, and a strange smell . . .

Olivia jumped to her feet. "Conrad, that smoke . . . there's too much for the chimney . . . quickly!"

Scrambling to his feet Conrad raced with Olivia through the trees and over the little crest to where they saw their cottage partially smothered in flames and smoke.

"Oh my God—James!" screamed Olivia, tripping over her long dress as she ran. Conrad, fear clutching at him, sped ahead of her. The kitchen lean-to was already burned out, the roof was alight and as they ran they saw to their horror the fiery roof cave in over the rear section which they used as sleeping quarters. Like some voracious monster, fanned by the hot breath of wind, the flames swallowed their little home. With gasping wrenching cries of agony, Conrad tried to push forward, but the heat, smoke and flying sparks seared his skin and hair and choked his breath. Olivia, not hearing the screams that were torn from her chest, grabbed at him and they fell to the ground, clutching one another as if mortally wounded while their son and their future, died before their eyes.

In the silent bush, partially burned by the fire that had leapt from the house to nearby trees, no bird sang, no small creatures moved. Olivia had lost track of time, and squatted, motionless at the graveside, seeing only the nightmare scenes unroll, rewind, and roll forward once more, and she could do nothing to change the scenario of events that had burned into her soul. She crumbled a handful of the red dirt from the tiny grave, staining the palms of her pale hands, still blistered from her puny grab at the wild thing that had taken her child. She nursed her grief, crouching by the mound of earth marked by a plain wooden cross, her hand still clutching the coarse, dry red dirt.

She heard the slow steps but did not look up. The grief-stricken eyes of Conrad caused her pain and guilt and she had spurned any broken advances he made to comfort her.

There was a slight cough and a gentle male voice, "Mrs. Hennessy . . . words fail me . . ."

She slowly raised her head and gazed into the concerned eyes of Captain John Tyndall. He squatted on his heels beside her, taking off his hat. She made no response and barely acknowledged his presence.

"I brought your supplies and hoped to find you progressing well . . . I didn't expect to discover this . . . this tragedy. I would like to say something to comfort you, but . . . " The wounded expression in her eyes, her crumpled body by her baby's grave, touched him deeply. He remembered her vitality and strength, alone on the beach after she had given birth. He reached out and took her hand and patted it in a gesture of comfort.

She finally spoke in a whisper. "He wasn't christened. We wanted to call him James. He won't go to Heaven . . . he'll be left here . . . all alone . . ." Tears rolled down her cheeks.

Tyndall felt helpless then tightened his grip on her hand. "The Aboriginal women who helped you when you gave birth . . . tell me, did they do a little ceremony?"

She nodded and told him briefly as best she could of the ritual she'd seen. A small light seemed to glow in her eyes and she studied him intently. "What did it mean?" she asked.

"It means your son is safe. He has returned to his spiritual home. That was a birth ceremony, they believe that the spirit returns to its place of birth, its Dreaming place. A place where he will find peace and joy and return to his own spirit world. Your son was christened without a doubt, Mrs. Hennessy . . . Aboriginal style."

She stared at him, her face softening with relief for an instant. She started to look back at the grave but Tyndall took her arm and helped her to her feet. "Let's go back to the camp," he said softly. "I'll help you both back to town and you can stay at my house as long as you like. I will stay on my boat." He anticipated her protest. "No, I assure you it won't be an inconvenience. I'm busy making some changes on board for a new enterprise."

He held her arm supportively in his and they walked in silence back to the tent Conrad had set up near the ruins of the cottage. Conrad was tending to the horses from Tyndall's dray but his shoulders drooped and he moved with little energy. He suddenly looked an old man. Olivia walked to the tent while Tyndall approached Conrad at the wagon. Reaching into a bag under the seat, he pulled out a bottle.

"The sun isn't over the yardarm, Mr. Hennessy," he said, brandishing the bottle, "but I declare it is nevertheless time for you and me to have a little something that braces the spirit."

He picked up two enamel mugs from beside the fire, tossed out the dregs of tea and poured a couple of stiff slugs of rum. The two men walked back to the dray and sat in its shade against a wheel, their legs stretched out in the dirt.

"To the future, Mr. Hennessy," said Tyndall softly, raising his mug in salute.

Conrad looked at him with glazed eyes, fighting back tears. Slowly he raised his mug. "The future," he choked a little over his words. "The past has so far been a bloody disaster . . . ever since we arrived in this godforsaken country." He forced the mug to his lips and swallowed hard.

Tyndall drank, too, then cradled the mug in his hands. "Yes, it can be a cruel land, and for you it has been crueler than anyone would expect. But life must go on. What do you plan to do now?"

"Quit this place," snapped Conrad with bitterness. "I doubt we really have the skill or the will now to make a go of it. Perhaps there is some opportunity in town. I still have some capital left."

Tyndall said nothing for awhile, but sipped thoughtfully at his rum.

"Well now, that's an interesting prospect," he said at last. "You told me about your background when we sailed to Cossack and it seems to me I have a little project that might be just what suits you."

Conrad stared at him. "And what might that be?"

"Pearling, my friend, pearling."

•　　•　　•

Inside the tent Olivia carefully emptied the handful of red dirt she had brought from the grave into a small jar and tightened the lid. Biting her lip, she put it safely in the trunk that held her remaining clothes, shut the lid and went outside.

CHAPTER SEVEN

The three men picked their way through the oily red slick of the tidal mudflat trying to avoid the sharp points of new shoots, ducking between the spread of mangroves until they reached a cleared area where the lugger lay on its side, shrouded in damp hessian sacks like a veiled bride.

Conrad watched Ahmed walk around the boat, lifting a sack, tapping on the hull, peering into its belly.

Tyndall studied the rigging then walked around checking the deck and fittings. Looking thoughtful he turned to Ahmed crawling out of the fo'c'sle hatch. "So what do you think eh, Ahmed? We take her to sea or not?"

"Must sail it, tuan."

"I suppose it's the only way to tell if a boat is seaworthy," offered Conrad, taking off his hat and wiping his brow. He found the heat and humidity of the mangroves oppressive.

"That's the final test. Ahmed can tell if she'll

ride well and be what he calls a 'setia' boat—a loyal one. He has a sixth sense about boats," explained Tyndall. "Like some men with horses. This is an old boat but a good one. She's made from kajibut timber, built inland, put on wheels and carted to the coast. She's given good service."

On the full tide the *Bulan* was refloated and Conrad marveled at the synchronicity between Tyndall and Ahmed. He sat on the deck doing as he was directed and wondering if he would ever feel at home at sea. As they headed through the channel to the open sea with billowing sails he drew a deep breath, relieved to feel the wind and seaspray after the muggy, sluggish atmosphere of the mudflats, and began to understand a little better what Tyndall had told him about the lure of life at sea. He had never imagined that he would be involved in something as . . . he searched for the right word to describe his ambivalent feelings . . . as buccaneering, yes, as buccaneering as pearling. It was a long way from the Bon Marche Emporium owned by Olivia's father in Southwark. He was still cautious about this undertaking, but Tyndall had been persuasive, explaining how lucrative the pearling industry was—though not without risks, for it was dangerous work with no guarantees. However, with his knowledge of new shell grounds, his contacts, sheer bravado and salesmanship, the odds seemed to be in their favor.

While Ahmed and Tyndall put the *Bulan* through its paces, Conrad reflected on the last few weeks since they had arrived in Cossack.

Tyndall had brought the shocked and grieving Hennessys into Cossack, settled them into his small house and then broached the idea of going into partnership in a pearling lugger. When Conrad had protested he knew nothing about this business, Tyndall had countered by asking what he knew of farming and running stock.

It was Olivia who had surprised them both by speaking up. "Conrad, I think you should consider the idea. You have organizational skills, a business head for numbers. I'm sure Captain Tyndall didn't see you at the helm of a lugger. I think we should move in a new direction."

She didn't add that in her heart she had never felt that Conrad was cut out for life on the land, particularly land as harsh as the property from which they had just fled. Had James lived, she would have stayed beside her husband and battled on, trying to make good in the wilderness. But since meeting Captain Tyndall again she began to think Conrad should participate in something that held the promise of quicker profit as well as a total change in their lives. She still hadn't totally assessed what kind of man Tyndall was, for his rather swashbuckling ways disturbed her, even his charm caused her disquiet, but her inclination was to trust him. His relationship with the Aborigines put him in a different category to most of the Europeans she'd met. They generally despised the blacks, dismissing them as worthless and of no account.

•   •   •

They were all sitting in a Malacca cane lounge on the verandah of Tyndall's house in the cool of an early evening, the men drinking a fine label of whisky from Tyndall's bar, Olivia enjoying a lemonade.

"The best time of day in these parts," Tyndall assured them. "Ideal for a relaxed look at the world and to marvel at the opportunities it offers us. Cheers," he said, raising his glass to the Hennessys. "Now about the deal—here's how I see it. I have the plan and a few assets, but not much ready cash. You have some capital and need a project that offers better prospects than chasing scrubbers and starving sheep all over the outback. And I need a good business head running things on shore. Have I missed anything?"

Conrad nodded. "No, that about sums it up."

"Right. We go fifty-fifty in the profits. We'll need most of your capital for the lugger. We aren't deep-sea pearling to start with, so we can use the schooner, and the cyclone season won't be a problem for a while. By the way, we'll have to move to Broome. That's the heart of the pearling industry these days."

Conrad fussed with his glass.

John Tyndall was addressing him, for it was the man who made these decisions. But he was uncomfortable about making such a radical change and also the fact that most of their capital had come from Olivia's inheritance after she sold her late father's business. It had been her idea to come to Australia. She had read about fortunes

141

made by luck and hard work, and she thirsted for something new and challenging in her life. A childhood dream of adventure, to not be like the other women she knew, had seemed just a dream. But with the early demise of her widowed father and with few ties left to England, an opportunity had presented itself and she had finally convinced Conrad they must seize it.

He took a sip of his drink. "It sounds a bit risky, but then that may be because I know absolutely nothing about pearling. It would mean sinking all that we have left into the enterprise." He sounded unsure of himself and unwilling to take the decisive step of commitment.

Tyndall rose. "I'll take a turn around the garden. You must want to talk in private, please do so." He strolled down the wooden steps into a far corner of the sparse garden to a frangipani tree and began picking some blooms.

Before Conrad could speak Olivia whispered firmly, "Do it, Conrad." The decisiveness, the determination in her voice stunned Conrad. He was not used to such a reaction from his young wife. "But we know so little about him, even though he has been extremely good to us. He has been trading the coast for some time but is new to pearling. Though he does seem to be reasonably respected hereabouts."

"Frankly, I don't think we have a choice but my instinct tells me we should join forces with him. As for being respected, anyone who is sober and owns a decent pair of shoes is regarded as respectable in this town. But I must admit, there is something about him that gives me confidence. Don't ask me what it is."

Conrad's uncertainty dissolved in the face of his wife's attitude to the venture, an attitude he felt revealed a recklessness that he had never seen. Trying to sound confident and comforting, he put an arm around her. "Then the answer is yes. We'll throw our lot in with him. I just hope I can contribute as much as he expects in the on-shore operation."

"Of course you will, dear," said Olivia, taking his hand. "But just one thing I want you to mention to him . . . I want to be part of this venture as well."

"What do you mean?" Conrad was genuinely puzzled. "You are an investor, it's your money, too, my dear."

"I mean work . . . I want to work in the business. Help in the office or something." Her voice then crumbled a little, and a vulnerable young woman now replaced the reckless decision-maker of moments ago. "I need something desperately, Conrad. An interest would help me." She paused and went on. "Help me . . . cope."

"Yes, my dear. I'll mention it." He squeezed her hand then rose and went into the garden and talked with Tyndall, both of them lighting their pipes as they leaned on the picket fence beside the dusty road. Soon they shook hands and returned to the verandah.

"It's a deal then," announced Tyndall buoyantly,

leaping up the steps. "Welcome aboard. And for you, Mrs. Hennessy, some flowers to mark the occasion." With a dramatic flourish he offered a small branch smothered in frangipani blooms. "Mind the sap," he added and Olivia laughed.

"Thank you, kind sir," she responded with exaggerated politeness.

After Tyndall had left she sat alone on the verandah with the flowers in her lap while Conrad got dressed for dinner. When he came looking for her she was quietly weeping.

"My dearest, you are having regrets?"

"Not about business. About James. Oh, Conrad," she sobbed. "Our beautiful son. The horror of it. Will we ever recover?"

"Olivia dear, I understand how you feel. This will be a new start for us."

He took her in his arms and held her tightly for a long time.

At sea Conrad was uncomfortable and awkward and hoped his duties wouldn't involve too many seagoing activities. Tyndall had assured him he would be running matters ashore, but that wouldn't be until they had a crew and their first haul.

"But while we are at sea," Tyndall had said, "you can make some business enquiries about the place, Conrad. We need to know who is trustworthy when it comes to prices and shipments, who is the best pearl cleaner and who are the best buyers."

It all sounded foreign to Conrad but he nodded

and said he'd do his best. He still found it hard to adjust to Tyndall's seemingly haphazard and cavalier attitude to life and business.

The lugger raced across the sea as a stiff breeze filled the sails and Tyndall and Ahmed nodded to each other. "I think we've got ourselves a decent boat, Conrad," called Tyndall. "Now we have to negotiate a deal."

"What happened to the fellow who owned this?" asked Conrad, wondering why the owner was no longer in the pearling business.

"Shark took his leg. He's staying ashore nowadays. Has no use for the *Bulan* so we'll make him an offer he can't refuse," grinned Tyndall.

"What does the name mean, Ahmed?" Conrad asked the silent Malay who was tending to some ropes. He found Tyndall's shadow a bit unnerving. The little Malay seemed to be quite languid most of the time, but his dark inscrutable eyes never rested. He missed nothing. He seemed to anticipate every move of his master, and the two of them appeared to communicate so much of the time with subtle gestures and looks. His devotion to Tyndall was clear, but Tyndall's regard for the skills of the Malay was also obvious. They made an effective team but Conrad couldn't help thinking of the little brown man as a servant and bodyguard. The silver *kris* he usually carried in an ornamental wooden sheath in the waistband of his sarong enhanced the bodyguard image.

Looks like a bloody pirate, thought Conrad. Wouldn't like to cross him.

"*Bulan* means moon, tuan," answered Ahmed. "Bad luck to change a boat's name," he added firmly, just in case Conrad had any such thoughts.

The inference irked Conrad and again he felt the unease that came from contact with Asians and Aborigines. Conrad knew he was of superior race and standing, yet he felt vaguely threatened and insecure. Strange, he thought, that Olivia seemed quite at ease with the colored people. He rationalized that her experience with the natives at the birth of their child must have something to do with it.

Tyndall spent some time with the one-legged owner of the lugger to settle on a price. Tyndall and Conrad then signed the papers and handed over the money. They strode enthusiastically up the street to register the change of ownership, and Tyndall slapped Conrad on the back. "We got a bonus as well, he has an old office down by the wharf in Broome, says we can use it. He never goes there. Spends his time in the brothels and the pubs."

Conrad rushed back to break the news to Olivia. "We got it at a bargain price," he gushed. "By God, that Tyndall is a card. Drank the best part of a whole bottle of whisky with the old fellow before getting down to details of the deal. Talked about everything from pearls to the pope."

Olivia laughed. "I think you had a fair share of the whisky as well. So, now we are pearlers. Hard to believe it's real, don't you think?"

Conrad gave her an effusive hug. "It's real, by

jove. At last I'm beginning to feel good about this country."

On arrival in Broome, Olivia and Conrad rented a bungalow in Walcott Street from the Bateman family, who ran a general agency business and usually rented the house to French pearl buyers who came to town for three months of every year. Tyndall rented a smaller cottage close by the seafront on Hamersley Street, owned by a Chinese merchant.

He wasted no time in making the rounds of the hotels, back street drinking dens and boarding houses used by the polyglot collection of men from Asia and the Pacific who worked the pearling fleets. Because the season was almost over, some crews had already been laid off so he had no trouble finding several hands with good credentials. Before signing up the men, Ahmed was able to check the credentials of all of them with their fellow countrymen working on the fleet.

Broome was an extraordinary place and Olivia was enchanted by its boisterous, bustling atmosphere and air of derring-do. Even conservative Conrad admitted that it had a certain colonial charm and projected a sense of excitement.

It was home port for several hundred pearling luggers collecting mother-of-pearl shell used mainly for the buttons in clothing manufacture all over the world. Any pearls found represented a bonus— a little for the crew, a lot for the pearling master. In season and during the lay up months, the town was alive with stories, more often rumors, of pearls found, prices fetched, deals done. Shrewd dealers in pearls came from Paris, London, New York, Singapore, Hong Kong and Shanghai to buy Broome pearls for the world's greatest jewelry houses. While the handling and marketing of shell was a very open business with few secrets, everything about pearls seemed to be surrounded with secrecy and intrigue. Stolen pearls, or snides, were filched by divers and crews and sold to known snide buyers or anyone prepared to resell them at a profit.

The ramshackle town was built overwhelmingly of corrugated iron, and paint was not considered important. The bareness was broken by efforts at gardening in some of the better homes, but by and large the town stood exposed and unadorned, baked by the sun or lashed by monsoonal storms, depending on the season. The commercial area was dominated by Chinese merchants who also acted as financial agents and money-lenders. The residential areas were divided into white and Asian quarters. While the power and authority rested in the minority European community, Broome was wildly individual, a white man's culture veneered over a mix of Asian subcultures.

The most notable building was Cable House, an elegant iron and wooden structure with a splendid billiards room. This grandeur befitted the marvel of contemporary technology housed within—the telegraph cable connecting this remote outpost of the British Empire to London.

Within days of their arrival Conrad had called on the Resident Magistrate C. R. Hooten who, swiftly ascertaining that he was a gentleman with a wife of good background, made a note to add the Hennessys to his invitation list. Social stratas existed within the white community and new arrivals were carefully vetted.

"I'm sure my wife will have your good lady over to meet the other wives as soon as possible. There are few ladies of standing in the community, though there are more than enough of questionable lineage." The broad wink he then gave shocked Conrad, who was a trifle unsure of just what the RM was alluding to, though he had heard about the proliferation of brothels from Tyndall.

Briefly Conrad told him of their sad life since arriving in the state.

"Rotten luck, a bad business all round," commented the RM. "By the way I'd suggest to your good wife that she not mention her, er, contact with the Aborigines. We don't mix with them, of course. Mind you, some are good workers, but only if they've been mission-trained. Most are lazy and take off at inconvenient times. Walkabout, you know. I never quite trust them. Always wonder if I'm going to get a spear hurled at me in the dark of night."

"Why would they do that?"

"Oh, they get some idea they've been slighted and blame any white person for an injury some other white fellow might have caused. There have been some dreadful attacks on white women and children left alone on farms. You're well out of that land deal, I would say." He then began to tell Conrad of his own arrival in Broome. "Badly organized. Damned low tide it was. There I am in all the finery, plumes, medals, the lot, for the official welcome and I have to plough through blooming smelly mud for a good half mile. Sorry sight I was to greet the town!"

Now into his stride with a fresh audience the RM prattled on about the town and conditions. "Always trouble with mixed nationalities. The Koepangers, Malays, Japs, and of course the blacks, all present problems fighting among themselves as much as with other racial groups. And when the pearlers aren't smuggling, drunk, or supposedly killing off their crews, they complain about lack of facilities." Hurriedly he added, "Naturally a gentleman pearler like yourself will be welcome. They're not all rogues, a few master pearlers are decent fellows. Some of them have done very well, too, though they keep it quiet of course." He roared with laughter and Conrad smiled tentatively, wondering which category John Tyndall belonged to.

The formal card inviting Olivia to afternoon tea at the Residence arrived several days later and she received it with mixed feelings. Olivia was keenly looking forward to the pleasure of a social occasion but hoped she wouldn't be called upon to repeat her story, as she still grieved for her lost child, and talking about the accident pained her greatly. Well meaning as people were, beneath the solicitous enquiries she sensed a salacious thirst for details that hurt her further.

Dressing carefully and paying attention to her toilette for the first time since her arrival in the northwest, Olivia stepped down from the verandah in a black taffeta day dress, a hat and gloves, her hair coiled. To her surprise she found Ahmed waiting at the front in a small sulky. He helped her into the seat.

"Tuan sent me. Said you should make a good appearance at the Residence."

"How kind of Tuan Hennessy," she said with warmth.

"Tuan Tyndall," corrected Ahmed as he swung into the driver's seat and picked up the reins. Glancing over his shoulder he warned her with a slight smile, "Not so good with horsies as boats, Memsahib!"

"It's only a short distance, I had planned on walking."

"You soon be a lady pearler wife, no walk," he admonished.

Olivia enjoyed the drive to the long low Residence building, its wide formal verandah screened by palm trees and set in a lawn flourishing on bore water. A young white aide and Malay manservant directed her through the airy building to a shady portico at the rear. Here, the guests were gathered, seated on cane furniture. She was led to Mrs. Hooten who greeted her warmly.

The Malay houseboy in starched white and wearing a small turban handed her a teacup. She was introduced to the ladies and the conversation soon turned to small talk about life in Broome. Advice was offered on all manner of subjects related to running a house—a Chinese or Japanese cook, a Koepanger boy to supervise children and polish the silver, an Aboriginal to look after the garden, a Chinese for the ironing, and an Aboriginal woman to do the washing.

They also delicately probed to find out more about Olivia and Conrad, their family background and their future plans. When Olivia murmured that circumstances had changed their plans, that pearling was quite a new and unexpected undertaking for her husband, Mrs. Hooten was soothing. "Many pastoralists have become pearlers. It's difficult country for grazing stock and only the men with big backing seem to be really successful. In theory everyone should make money, the growth in the wet is so prolific, and there is just so much land for the taking. But yet there are so many failures."

Olivia was stung by the suggestion of failure. It must have shown, for Mrs. Hooten quickly added sympathetically, "Of course you really didn't have a chance to see how you would have made out. It was so tragic." Then she continued enthusiastically,

"But I'm sure that fate has now turned in your favor. Believe me, Mrs. Hennessy, the pearling industry is taking off, so my husband says. A pity it attracts so many riff-raff, don't you think? I mean, at the lower end, the Asians and the like."

Before Olivia could think of anything to say in response, the wife of one of the leading pearling masters took the conversation in another direction. "I know you'll be wanting to join some of our social committees, Mrs. Hennessy, and it will be a delight to have your talents to help those of us who have been here so long that we're rather out of touch with what's happening back home. The social life is looking up thank goodness, now that more wives are coming here. We have balls, races, concerts, and the most wonderful picnic that is becoming a really major annual event."

"Well, I was rather thinking of doing some work," replied Olivia brightly, and there was an immediate freeze in the conversation.

After a moment Mrs. Hooten broke the silence. "Work, Mrs. Hennessy, what sort of work?"

"Pearling . . . or rather something connected with the pearling business. Perhaps in the office."

"Really?" responded the hostess with raised eyebrows, absently fingering the lorgnette hanging around her neck on a chain set with large pearls. "How *interesting*." Then she turned to address the room with a voice that almost rattled the teacups. "Now ladies, I feel that it's cool enough for a little croquet. To the lawn everyone."

Olivia realized she had made a social faux pas

and decided to be more discreet in future about her involvement in the business, although she was more determined than ever to do what she wanted to do. At the same time she recognized that in such a small community acceptance by the wives of the leading families was probably very important for the business. With this in mind, she joined in the exodus to the croquet lawn, making an effort at light-hearted enthusiasm and anticipation that was obviously welcomed by the elite ladies of Broome.

Later, Ahmed was waiting patiently at the gate and he drove her along Dampier Terrace, past crew camps, shell sorting and packing sheds, the jetty where the luggers tied up, a boat builder's yard and sail maker, a saddlery and bootmaking shop, a general store and the Dampier Hotel, popular with the Japanese, Ahmed informed her. He stopped outside a two-storey white wooden building which housed several offices and a pearl cleaner's workshop.

Ahmed pointed proudly to a new sign by the narrow doorway: STAR OF THE SEA PEARL CO.

Olivia was puzzled.

"That's us, mem. Tuan give us a name." With studied formality he helped her down and pointed upstairs.

Lifting the hem of her dress Olivia ascended the rickety stairs to two separate small rooms.

Conrad was sitting at a desk covered with papers and new folders. He sprang up when Olivia entered, stepped around the desk and hugged her. "We're open for business as of today. Not that there's any business . . . just a lot of paperwork. What do you think?" he asked, gesturing toward the spartan furniture and bare walls.

"A suitably modest start, I feel," said Olivia approvingly.

"Modest? You'd better take a look next door," said Conrad with a grin.

They walked into the next office to find Tyndall leaning back in a swivel chair with his feet on a desk empty but for a whisky bottle. The rest of the room was in chaos. There were piles of rope, sails, diving apparatus, bags of sugar, cartons of tea, some nautical charts pinned to the walls along with an Aboriginal pearl shell breastplate on a cord. In a corner was another desk and chair where Ahmed had been carefully packing waterproof canisters with curry powders and other spices that filled the room with exotic smells.

Olivia was stunned.

Tyndall slowly took his feet off the desk and stood up. "Savor the scene, Mrs. Hennessy. The beginning of a commercial empire. You can breathe the sweet smell of success in it all, can't you?" he said with exaggerated earnestness.

"Frankly, all I smell is curry," said Olivia with a grin. "Whatever is all this stuff?"

"A job lot. The fellow who sold us the lugger had a stock of supplies he no longer needed. Buyer's market. Got the lot dirt cheap this morning," explained Tyndall with considerable satisfaction.

"Did it require another bottle of whisky?" asked Olivia, instantly wishing she hadn't made such an impulsive response.

Tyndall was stung and stared at her for a moment, then responded angrily. "As a matter of fact, yes it did."

"Just trying to come to grips with the ways of business in these parts," said Olivia lightly, anxious to defuse a situation she felt was getting a little beyond her. "Who came up with the name of the company? It's nice, but maybe I could have put in a suggestion, too."

Tyndall was appalled. He was just feeling relieved that she had changed the subject from the purchase of the supplies when she swept in under his guard with another punch. Stay calm, he told himself. He hadn't met any woman who so confused him. "It was my idea. Conrad left it up to me . . . I didn't think to ask, just assumed you would not be interested."

"Olivia . . ." interjected Conrad quickly, but Olivia went on as if she hadn't heard him.

"I am very interested, Captain Tyndall. I am a partner in this business, too. I have discussed it with my husband and told him that I would like to be involved in any small way I can. I have very little else to interest me."

Tyndall understood this as a reference to the loss of her child, but at the same time sensed there was more to this young woman than he suspected. There was a hidden strength beneath that youthfulness, and it was striving for expression.

With quiet politeness he said, "Forgive me. It was thoughtless."

Olivia responded in kind. "It's a pretty name. I hope it augurs well."

"How was the tea? Were the ladies pleasant?" asked Conrad, anxious to change the subject as he found Olivia's forthrightness a little embarrassing.

"Yes. It's strange observing formal customs here. I am expected to call on them over the coming weeks. That will give me a chance to get to know them better, but they certainly enjoy the chance to gossip."

"And you must join the Club, Conrad. It will be useful for business as well as for the social activities," suggested Tyndall.

Conrad nodded in agreement. "Yes, the RM already suggested I should join the Freemasons. And I was rather thinking I'd like to join the Cricket Club, more for the sport than the social side of things. I miss swinging a bat."

"Do you belong?" Olivia asked Tyndall.

"Haven't got around to it yet. I'm still considered a bit of a blow-in round these parts. But when I'm more settled, I'll get around to it."

He grinned and Olivia had a feeling he was not really about to join an elite white men's club. Tyndall led a very private and casual life from what Olivia had observed. He didn't seem comfortable ashore and gave the impression it was a temporary arrangement. He was happiest at sea and living on his schooner.

"I'm sailing back down the coast and going to hook up with some of the Aborigines who showed me the shell beds. I'll hire some of them to work the shallow water and dry shell for us. Want to come along?" Tyndall asked Olivia with a lifted eyebrow.

"I have work to do here getting our home set up. But thank you for asking," she answered, ignoring his teasing air. "Next time I will come along," she said archly, with a tilt of her head. As she noticed Ahmed by the door, she softened and turned back to him.

"Thank you for providing Ahmed and the sulky. I feel I made the right impression arriving in style at the Residence."

They exchanged a quick smile and Conrad turned to Tyndall.

"I say, that was decent of you. We'll have to arrange for transport."

"Better sell a haul of shell first. I rather hope that Star of the Sea will start making money soon," remarked Olivia, emphasizing the last word.

"I guess we've got our orders, Conrad," chuckled Tyndall with some relief as Olivia swept from the room. However, underneath he was wondering just how well he was going to get along with his partner's wife.

With Conrad happily settled behind a desk, Tyndall and Ahmed put to sea, both pleased to be away from the office. With their crew they sailed the *Bulan* south to the untouched shell banks in shallow water that Tyndall had been shown by his Aboriginal friends. They readily enlisted several men to dry shell—a form of beachcombing at low tide—for payment of tobacco, flour and sugar. Sharp eyes were needed to spot the flat gray shells embedded in the muddy sand. As the tide moved over them, they drifted away.

It was slow work because for so many hours of the day the mud flats were covered by the ebb and flow of the tides, but steadily the stockpile on the beach began to grow and the two Koepangers hired as crew were kept busy opening and cleaning the shell under the watchful eye of Ahmed. They had good reputations, but Ahmed trusted no one when it came to pearls and he knew that it took only the slightest hand work to conceal a pearl if temptation struck.

When the hold of the lugger, and the space in its engine room, were filled with shell, they lashed to the deck the bags of unopened shell from the final few days' work and headed home.

They sailed into Broome with the tide and as soon as they were alongside the wharf Ahmed was sent to alert Conrad, who hastened down the wharf and clambered on board the cluttered deck to shake Tyndall's hand.

"I say, this looks like a really great haul. The hold full, too?"

"To the very top, Conrad. And good shell at that. Not many pearls, mostly small baroque, but we still have the deck cargo to open. How have things been going with you?"

"Met most of the dealers in mother-of-pearl and talked about arrangements. Nothing settled yet. I must say some of them are very shady characters. Had a telegram from Perth from the representative of a European pearl merchant wanting first option on any pearls we find. How do you think they found out we're in business?"

"The bush telegraph, mate. The pearl business is a cut-throat one and there's big money at stake. Information is worth money, too, and I don't doubt that someone in this town has made himself something out of passing on information on our venture to contacts down south."

The tide was still on the make and Conrad and Tyndall wanted to get as much of the cargo unloaded before the *Bulan* settled on the mud below the deck of the jetty. Soon the crew were stripped to the waist and slinging bags of shell off the lugger while Conrad kept tally and supervised the hired dray hauling it along to their foreshore shell camp.

The next day the Koepangers and Ahmed began work on the unopened shell before they went off to the foreshore camp. They had barely started when Olivia arrived, unannounced and unexpected. The three men stopped work when she pushed open the galvanized iron sliding door and stood silhouetted against the bright sunlight outside. For a moment she could see little in the dark interior, but as her eyes adjusted she took in the frozen tableau in a far corner of the shed—three men, some large metal drums, and a small mountain of bagged shell. The men were sitting on tiny stools surrounded by piles of shell, some unopened. They stared in surprise at the sight of a white woman in their domain.

"Apa kabar," said Olivia brightly, a greeting she had picked up from Ahmed before he had set out on the trip.

"Ah, baik, baik, saja," responded Ahmed with delight. "Please come. Come see your shell."

Olivia was instantly overwhelmed by the smell of stale oyster, then as she reached the group became aware of a fresher, saltier smell of the live oysters being opened. Ahmed offered her his stool and she sat down, looked over the pile before them, then picked up one of the oysters.

"Good shell, mem."

"I'll take your word for it, Ahmed." She turned the shell over in her hand, marveling at its size. Most of the shells were the size of saucers or small dinner plates. She stroked it, feeling the roughness of the uncleaned shell that had nestled undisturbed in the muddy waters, marveling that her life was now so closely linked to such an unlikely object. Whatever would they think in London, she thought and smiled. "Hard to imagine, looking at it now, that inside might be a lovely pearl."

Ahmed took the plump shell and, using a broad flat knife, inserted it deftly into the muscle that held the two halves of the shell tightly together. Rolling his fingers into the rubbery visceral flesh enclosed in the fold of tissue known as the mantle, he pulled out a small, odd-shaped pearl. Being a baroque pearl, it was of little value, he explained but, nevertheless, Olivia was delighted and fascinated by the strange creature revealed to her. She paid rapt attention as Ahmed identified the parts, using both the Malay and English words, which Olivia repeated carefully and committed to memory. The Koepangers began to feel relaxed with the white woman and chuckled at her studied repetition of the Malay words. Ahmed showed her the strong adductor muscles that joined the two half shells and the fringe of fine hairs which strained the water flowing into it, capturing the plankton and oxygen.

She tried her hand at opening a shell, an effort that reduced the crew to laughter as the shell remained stubbornly and tightly shut. This failed attempt caused several cuts to her hands, which she, too, laughed about.

"Nothing serious," she said, wiping them with her handkerchief. "All part of the learning process, but I think I'll leave this part of the operation to you."

Olivia took to visiting the foreshore camp each day, sometimes bringing a tiffin carrier of food from her Chinese cook for the crew. It was an uncommon gesture and news of her deed traveled quickly through two communities. The whites who heard about it raised their eyebrows and pointed to the sun and muttered about "spoiling them." The Asian pearling community accepted the gesture with puzzlement but respect; the new white lady in town was certainly a curiosity.

As part of the daily routine she arranged to pass on to Conrad the tally of the day's work and the little bag of fairly ordinary pearls, mainly baroque, that the shells yielded. The onshore work was completed a week after they arrived back in port. As Olivia left the shed that day, she wished the crew as much success on their next trip. While walking her to the door, Ahmed noticed an unopened oyster amid the debris on the floor and absently picked it up. He thanked her, as he always did, for the food.

"Think nothing of it, Ahmed. It gives me an excuse to stay a little longer in the shed in the hope of being there when you find a really worthwhile pearl."

"Sorry, mem. Maybe next time," he said consolingly. He turned to walk back into the shed, then paused and pulled out his knife to open the oyster. He probed the flesh and knew the moment his fingers touched it that this was no ordinary pearl . . . it was a real gem. He rolled it around in his palm . . . a beautiful mellow gold-toned pearl of at least twenty-four grains, glowing with what seemed to be an inner light.

"Ah, Allah is great," he whispered, then ran to the door and was about to call to Olivia, who was now down the track that led back into town, when he hesitated, pocketed the pearl, and threw the shell in a bag. The Koepangers exchanged glances, but said nothing.

Conrad was elated at the figures in his ledger and the collection of pearls which he kept in a small locked cash box that he took home each night.

"On paper at least we're doing nicely," enthused Conrad as he and Olivia made their way to the Continental Hotel where they often took lunch. "Of course, we have a lot of expenses coming up, crew wages when they are paid off, boat repairs, and so on, but I must say things are looking up."

Over lunch Conrad broached the subject of her visits to the camp. "It's not really necessary, you know. Ahmed can be trusted to bring me the figures and so on."

Olivia very deliberately took a spoonful of soup before replying. "I know he could, Conrad, but as I've said before I'm part of this business and I'm learning quite a lot. The men have taken to telling me a lot of stories about pearling and pearlers. Some of them are funny, some of them very tragic. It's really fascinating, Conrad, and I want to keep doing it."

Conrad felt awkward. Some chaps at the club had made a couple of remarks about her visits to the shell camp which clearly indicated that town gossips were at work. "It's just that, well, some people find it a bit odd, dear."

"I imagine they do, but they will have to get used to it," said Olivia determinedly, then changed the subject. "That Ahmed is an impressive man. I'd trust him with my life, I think."

Conrad took up the theme, glad to avoid any further tension with his wife. "He's certainly devoted to John and works very hard. Funny business though, he doesn't seem to want much for himself. Probably has something to do with being a Muslim. He's always praying. Bit off-putting, I must say. John saved his life, you know. I suppose that's why he is so devoted to him."

During the following week Tyndall and Ahmed made changes to the rigging and storage on the lugger, innovations they devised from experience at sea and actually working the boat for the first time. Before setting out on the next trip Tyndall and Conrad asked Olivia to join them at the Continental for lunch.

"An unexpected pleasure, Captain Tyndall," said Olivia after they had ordered and the waiter had poured glasses of champagne.

"For me as well, it's a special occasion."

"Oh, then that explains the champagne. But what is the excuse for such a midday extravagance?"

Tyndall reached into his pocket and passed a small cloth pouch to Olivia. "The first return on your investment," he said nonchalantly.

She looked at Conrad who was smiling. "Well, open it," he urged her.

Olivia picked up the bag and shook out into the palm of her hand a large pearl set in a gold ring. She gasped.

"Ahmed found it. Said it was in the last shell he opened," explained Conrad. "We all agreed that you should have it."

Olivia looked at them both in gratitude, momentarily lost for words. She slipped the ring on to her right hand, admired it, then looked at them both. "It's so lovely. Thank you both very much. And Ahmed."

CHAPTER EIGHT

Olivia had taken to walking along the seafront at sunset, watching the red ball of the sun slip into the brilliant turquoise waters of Roebuck Bay. The color of the water fascinated her as did the activity around Streeter's Jetty, a straggling long wooden wharf, built by the English pearler of that name, through the mangroves near the path that led to the three native wells east of Dampier Creek when the town was still a bush settlement. It was here that the luggers offloaded their hauls. When the great drop of the tide ran out, the luggers rested on their rounded beams. To Olivia it was as if some hurricane or tidal wave had swept through, tossing the sturdy boats to one side as it passed.

There was always activity around the area as the crews swarmed about the boats either unloading or preparing for sea. Olivia knew she was being watched with suspicion and curiosity by the many races working, shouting and singing as they went about sailmaking, repairing, sorting shell, loading and offloading cargo. But they gradually became used to the beautiful white lady who, unlike the other white women, wandered amongst them watching everything with interest, exchanging shy smiles with them and greeting them in Malay.

One sunset on the full tide she saw the *Bulan* sail back in with Tyndall at the helm. She walked the length of the jetty as they moored. Seeing her, Tyndall raised his skipper's hat, giving her a salute and a thumbs-up sign. "How did you know I was coming in? You just knew I'd made a good haul and thought you'd check up on your investment, eh?"

Olivia laughed. "Pure coincidence, I can assure you, although Ahmed did say this morning that you were due any day now. He's kept tabs on the shed, the sorting and packing and all the other details. Though I think he missed being at sea this trip. How did you do? Is there reason to break out the champagne?"

He hauled on one of the mooring lines to get the boat closer to the jetty, then extended his hand to help her on board. "We did well enough. Conrad will be able to write up another tidy profit in those immaculate records of his."

Not wanting to accept any implied slight on her husband, Olivia leapt to his defense. "Immaculate they should be. That's the only way to run a business. Efficiently."

Tyndall threw up both hands in mock defense. "I'm sorry. No slight intended. You are right of course. It's just that I've never been that keen on bookkeeping. Come have a look in the hold."

The two Koepangers had already unlashed the canvas over the hold and on a word from Tyndall quickly removed the thick planks that made up the hatch. The hold was packed with bagged shell but the smell made Olivia put a hand to her nose.

"We found a good patch of shell but I think we're on to the last of it. One more trip should clean it out."

They moved aft and went below into the cabin.

"My goodness," exclaimed Olivia in surprise, "It's remarkably tidy."

"The only way to run a ship, I reckon." He grinned, then added mockingly, "Efficiently."

Olivia stiffened slightly and turned to find him smiling at her. "Point taken," she said graciously and sat on one of the two bunks. "I rather think I would like to come on the next voyage."

Tyndall was stunned. "Whatever for? It's . . . " He was momentarily lost for the right word. "Well, it's boring . . . uncomfortable . . . not the done thing."

"Not the done thing," she echoed. "My goodness, you sound like Conrad in one of his conservative moods. But I have heard of pearling masters' wives going to sea at times and in any case I don't think it would be boring and I can quite easily cope with discomfort . . . as you well know, Captain Tyndall."

Tyndall changed tack to what he confidently believed was a safe course. "All right, if Conrad agrees, then you can come. Now, let's get ashore and let the crew get on with the unloading. I want to get back to sea in a few days."

Conrad was bemused at Olivia's suggestion that she sail on the next trip of the *Bulan* and was taken aback when he realized she was serious. "Out of the question. Dangerous, uncomfortable and not the done thing. Not the done thing at all."

Olivia had to fight to suppress a smile. She quietly reminded him that it was not that uncommon for wives to take the occasional trip with their pearling husbands. Some had even lived on board for the entire season.

"Ah, but you won't be going with your husband," he observed with a note of triumph.

"Does it matter?" she asked.

"Does it matter? Does it matter?" exclaimed Conrad in a rising voice. "Have you taken leave of your senses, Olivia? People will think you have a touch of the sun."

"Don't be insulting, Conrad," said Olivia angrily.

"I'm sorry. But what will people think?"

"I am sure Captain Tyndall can be trusted, Conrad. And since everyone knows that I'm an active partner in this enterprise I believe it a perfectly reasonable request. It will be a great adventure for me. I'm going, and that's it."

"You get seasick."

"I got sick on the trip from Fremantle because I was pregnant and it was a long trip in rough conditions," Olivia countered, then hesitated before going on with a look of sadness and a voice trembling with emotion. "There's another reason I need to go, Conrad." She collapsed into a cane chair and rested her forehead in the palm of her hand. "We can call into Cossack on the way down. No matter how hard I try to get on with life here in Broome, part of me is buried in Cossack. I really need to go back. I need to visit his grave. Can you understand that, Conrad? He's our son."

Conrad went to her and knelt down, taking her other hand in his. "I understand now, but this is not a decision to be taken lightly." Then he suddenly smiled, confident he had found the solution to the dilemma. "Well, if you feel that strongly, then go. But only if John agrees. After all, he's the captain and what the captain says goes."

"Of course it does," smiled Olivia and she warmly embraced her husband.

Tyndall was sitting on the port gunwale engrossed in splicing a rope when the carpet bag thudded to the deck beside his feet. He looked at it intently for a moment and thought, "My God, she's done it," then slowly turned to look up at a grinning Ahmed standing on the wharf with Olivia a little behind him.

"Well, I'm here," she announced with a note of challenge in her voice.

Tyndall smiled. "Indeed you are. Welcome aboard." He extended a hand and with Ahmed taking her other arm she was lowered onto the deck.

"I really didn't think this madcap scheme was going to come to anything," confessed Tyndall. "But I'm pleased it has," he added warmly.

"I suppose it is madcap, but somehow it doesn't bother me, even if it raises eyebrows in town. Practically everything that has happened to me since I arrived in this country seems slightly unreal to be quite honest."

Her countenance changed slightly and Tyndall saw signs of sadness in her eyes and the firmer set of her mouth. He quickly changed the subject as he took her bag and turned to the cabin hatch. "Well, the weather is looking good. With luck we'll have a smooth passage. Come and I'll help organize the state room for you." He was pleased that the exaggerated description of the cabin made her smile, albeit fleetingly.

At his office window Conrad watched the *Bulan* sail down the mangrove-lined channel into the bay and out to sea. The image of Olivia standing in the stern, looking back, her skirt billowing in the breeze, one hand holding her straw hat, the other giving a brief wave in his direction, burned into his mind. He had a swift, gut-tearing feeling that his wife was sailing out of his life, but dismissed the thought at once. No, he reasoned, Olivia was simply growing . . . changing . . . that was to be expected. But, good Lord, she was becoming unpredictable, and yes, unconventional. But the grief they had suffered, the pain, that must be the explanation. A little madness, perhaps. Quite understandable. But it will pass. Conrad sighed and turned to his desk, much comforted by his rationalization.

The sails filled with a steady breeze, a white-capped foamy wake on either side of the bow as the *Bulan* cut through the aqua water. Olivia stood by the main mast holding on to a halyard and taking deep breaths of the salty air. Once they had cleared the creek and were in the bay, she had slipped below and emerged in her "sailing gear." Dispensing with the impractical long skirt and restricting blouse, she had made herself an outfit of loose black pajama pants teamed with a long white top that hung over the pants. She had copied the outfit from that of her Chinese cook. It was cool, comfortable and practical. On her feet she wore canvas plimsolls.

Tyndall disguised his initial shock. "Very sensible outfit," he commented with raised eyebrows.

Ahmed said nothing and displayed no obvious reaction, but Olivia thought she detected a faint glint of amusement in his dark eyes.

The lugger rode smoothly over the slight swell and heeled to port as the sails were set for the run south-west with the wind almost on the beam. Olivia closed her eyes to focus more keenly on the feel of the wind, the rolling, surging movement of the boat, the soft vibrations of the hull that came from the deck, the quivering of the rigging and the sound of singing in the stays. There was an occasional flap of sail, a slap and splash of water as the bow dipped and cut through the sea. There was a fresh smell to the air and she licked a faint saltiness from her lips.

She found the whole experience exhilarating. A sense of elation, freedom and contentment took hold of her. For the first time since the death of James she felt really relaxed, almost peaceful. She stayed there undisturbed for almost an hour, the crew sensing her need to be alone.

When she finally broke her reverie Olivia looked astern. Ahmed was at the helm, alternatively eyeing sails and compass. Tyndall was splicing rope again and the Koepangers were repairing holes in hessian bags. It all looked so ordered and reassuring, and she smiled warmly when Tyndall lifted his cap in salute. She moved down the deck, carefully reaching for rigging for stability, then without a word sat on the deck beside him, back against the gunwale and, with arms wrapped around her knees, concentrated on the eye splice he was making in the thick rope.

They anchored for the night and, by the light of a lantern and the clear moonlight, Ahmed cooked their meal of rice, fish and vegetables with a spicy sauce over a small portable fuel fire. Sitting on the deck, eating off tin plates, the water lapping against the hull and the stars bright above, Olivia thought it one of the most enjoyable meals she could remember. The sea air had made her drowsy so she retired to the main cabin, opened the portholes and fell instantly into a sound sleep. On deck Ahmed and Tyndall, in swaying hammocks slung under the booms, talked softly in Malay and English.

They had been at sea for two days before Olivia raised the matter of a stopover in Cossack so that she could visit her baby's grave. Tyndall agreed without hesitation.

Olivia walked slowly to the small, lonely cemetery where her son had been formally buried what now seemed an age ago. Their brief stay in Cossack held only sad memories for her and she gave thanks again for the entry of John Tyndall in her life. Broome and pearling had helped her cope with the loss of James. But she needed to say goodbye, to make some gesture to show she hadn't abandoned him.

At the cemetery Tyndall stood back a little as Olivia went to the grave, knelt on the barren sandy soil and laid a small bunch of wildflowers at the foot of the tiny tombstone. She thought of all the things she would never do or share with him. Never to see him grow and discover the world, never be able to show him the love that ached in her. Her arms and heart felt empty and she cried softly. Then she prayed silently, and absently stroked the mound slowly for some time before kissing her fingertips and lightly touching the headstone. As she rose Tyndall took her arm and their eyes met briefly, then she turned and together they walked silently to the road and the hired sulky.

For the rest of the journey Olivia spent a lot of time sitting alone in the shade of the sails looking out to sea or at the passing coastline, but not really seeing. Ahmed took her food and drink from time to time, saying little, and getting no more than a nod and a fleeting expression of gratitude. Tyndall kept his distance, occupying himself with the wheel, and tried to understand the emotional turmoil she must be experiencing.

One morning, after hot black tea and toast with treacle, they got under way and by lunchtime were nosing into the strip of coast where they had established a rough camp. They moored and as Ahmed rowed them ashore welcome calls rang out from the bush land and soon the Aborigines were milling about exchanging greetings and news.

To Olivia's delight, among another group making their way to them, she recognized the women and the men from the people who had helped her when she first came ashore. Tyndall glanced at her, then swiftly and gently explained in their language the fate of Olivia's baby. The women made a clicking sound with their tongues and spoke quickly.

While Ahmed spoke to the men in pidgin, Tyndall said softly to Olivia, "The women say your baby has returned to his Dreaming place and is well."

Olivia crumbled and Tyndall reached to take

her arm and felt her choke on a sob, then stiffen and pull herself erect. "Please tell them I am very grateful for their message." She hesitated, then went on, "Tell them that I'm glad they gave James a Dreaming."

Tyndall struggled with the message but the reassuring nods from the women did much to hearten Olivia. They took her by both hands and led her off to a huge spreading rain-tree and in its shade formed a circle and began a ceremony of wailing, weeping and chanting. Almost in a trance Olivia sat through the ceremony, quietly sobbing, her mind a blank. When they had stopped Olivia felt a strength that came from the companionship of sharing grief. She was more grateful than ever to these strange people.

Back on the beach Olivia found the first of the supplies coming ashore with the help of several of the Aborigines. Tyndall made no reference to the ceremony that had taken place, recognizing that it was "women's sorry business" and that it was better to talk of other things. He informed her that the negotiations for dry shelling were completed and that the men would begin work in two days. The delay was for some ceremony they were organizing.

"Can't put off a ceremony, not for anything," explained Tyndall. "We either do things to their time, or not at all."

"Time seems irrelevant out here, don't you think?" mused Olivia.

"A lot of our world is irrelevant out here," he

replied and went back to helping unload the dinghy.

Olivia sat on the beach and took some deep breaths, quietly watching the activity. She reflected on Tyndall's parting remark, at the same time acknowledging the ease with which she had accepted the Aboriginal expressions of grief, and how incredibly moving the experience had been for her. She realized she had been through a cathartic experience in the ceremony and now felt a remarkable sense of relief and freedom. James was safe. It was no longer so painful to think about him.

When the Aborigines were ready to work they waited till the tide ebbed, then fanned out along the exposed coral and mud sea bed, filling small woven baskets with shell during the few hours that the mud flats were exposed. Some of them waded out further, bobbing beneath the sea as their feet or keen eyes found shells. Several men and two young women set out in the dinghy, diving over the side feet first with knees drawn up under the chin, then once in the water, angling their body to swim downward. Some dived off the lugger into a depth of three or four fathoms, resurfacing with several shells.

Tyndall watched the work with satisfaction. "They're natural divers but they were terribly abused in the old days," he told Olivia. "Twenty, thirty years ago the early pearlers, well, the more unscrupulous ones, used to virtually kidnap the natives and make them work their guts out diving for shell. Women, too. In fact the women were said to be better than the men at underwater work." He paused, then added with a raised eyebrow. "Not that they did all the work underwater."

Olivia was shocked. "How terrible it must have been. Why didn't the authorities stop it?"

"Well, they did. At least they passed a law in the Parliament, but while the arm of the law is long, it has trouble reaching some of these parts. They at least stopped the auctions of Aborigines and islanders. The barracoons were slave sales."

"Do the natives use the modern diving suits on luggers?"

"A few do, but other races are better at it, especially the Japs and Malays. This mob are too inclined to go walk about at the drop of a hat. Money isn't too meaningful to them. Like time," he smiled.

"And the Malays?" asked Olivia,

"Like all the East India men, not too bad, but a bit easy going. Can run amok at times with their bloody ugly knives. Have cut up a few captains over the years. And hung for it."

"Ahmed seems very attached to his knife ... *kris*," she said, correcting herself.

"Ah, don't you worry about him," said Tyndall reassuringly, "Ahmed is different."

A breeze blew up from a new direction and Olivia recoiled as a vile odor washed over her with

a near physical blow. Seeing her grimace, Ahmed
and Tyndall laughed.

"Poogie tub," explained Tyndall. "Come on,
you have to experience it all."

He handed her a clean white handkerchief and
she followed them along the shore holding the
hanky to her nose.

Two wooden casks sat in the hot sun, and one
of the men gave a cask a stir with a stick, raising
putrid fumes. Each tub was filled with small shells
and sea water, which fermented and decayed in
the heat, and as the shellfish rotted away the
pearls dropped to the bottom to be retrieved
later.

"Smelly but effective," said Tyndall. "The big
shells are opened on the lugger and ashore."

Late in the day Olivia, barefoot and grateful
she'd made her pants "half mast" below her
knees, helped drag the shell-filled baskets to the
dinghy which the Koepangers then rowed to the
lugger. She enjoyed the physical labor and despite
the straw bonnet tied on her head, her cheeks
glowed from sun and wind.

Later as they sat around the campfire the
Aborigines sang traditional songs, chanting and
swaying, clicking and tapping the rhythm on
carved music sticks and boomerangs. It was hypnotic and Olivia felt her head drooping with
drowsiness. Tyndall leaned over and whispered to
Ahmed, who quietly rose and led Olivia down to
the dinghy. As they rowed out to the lugger, Olivia
sleepily listened to the rhythmic splash-splash of

the oars. The faint moonlight outlined the fat shape of the *Bulan* and it crossed her mind it looked like a ghostly moon ship. Behind, on the shore, the bright blaze of the campfire flickered over the dark shapes of the figures huddled around it. The haunting music drifted across the water.

"What are they singing about, Ahmed?"

"Their people song. They always sing about their people and this place. They bin here long time, mem."

Olivia slipped into her bunk and fell asleep, feeling very at home in the strange cramped womb of the lugger.

In the morning there was much activity as the *Bulan* prepared to get under way. Olivia realized they were not going ashore again and was disappointed she was not able to farewell her Aboriginal friends. Standing at the rail as they were about to raise the anchor, she saw two dugout canoes paddle toward them. Ahmed and Tyndall went to the starboard side and hailed the approaching canoes.

Joining them, Olivia asked, "What do they want?"

"Just saying good-bye, we won't see them for who knows how long," replied Tyndall, lifting his cap to salute them.

The men in the first canoe called and waved. The other craft held an elder and the two women Olivia regarded as her friends and benefactors. They signaled that they wished to come in close and, bumping gently against the *Bulan*'s beam, threw a small package onto the deck and shouted a message.

Tyndall picked up the parcel wrapped in woven grass cloth. "They say it's a gift for you. For good luck."

"Oh my, I wish I could give them something in return. Tell them that, and thank you," she said in a rush, overcome by the gesture.

Tyndall called down to them and they shouted back in return. He turned to Olivia. "The women would like your hat. Are you willing to part with it?"

"Of course," laughed Olivia.

Tyndall tilted her chin and swiftly undid the ribbon. Lifting the straw bonnet from her hair he threw it down to them. Both women reached for it, but the one who grabbed it promptly tied it over her unruly bush of hair.

Olivia was delighted at the sight of the near naked woman in a straw hat.

Well pleased with themselves they turned and paddled back toward the shore. As the small dugout faded in the distance, the anchor of the *Bulan* rattled over the bow and the mainsail slid up the mast. Olivia stood gazing in the direction of the shore until it became a thin black line on the horizon.

When they were safely at sea Olivia unrolled the parcel. Inside was a bangle with a dark brown and green pattern woven into pale plaited grass. She slipped it on her wrist but it was too large.

"It's an amulet, a symbol of their family line," explained Tyndall. "It's supposed to bring good luck."

"How lovely." Olivia slipped it over her muslin sleeve. "I'll keep it close to me."

The affinity she felt for these women was strengthened. She knew they wished her well and in their own way were helping her, and the knowledge gave her a sense of well-being and security. Their friendship was very special to her and she resolved to see them again.

A stiff breeze sent the heavily loaded lugger barrelling along, but a rising swell made the deck sloppy with wash so Olivia went below. Soon a bank of clouds appeared on the northern horizon and Tyndall tapped the barometer. "It's dropping," he said in Malay, then added quietly, "I don't like the look of this, friend. If it gets lower we'll have to make a run for shelter."

"A long way till a break in the coast, tuan."

"Get me the chart."

The Malay opened the hatch and dropped down the steps beside the bunk on which Olivia was resting. He smiled, found the map and bounced back on deck.

Shortly afterward she felt the boat change course and begin to roll dramatically. She stumbled up the steps. "Whatever is happening?"

"We're heading out to sea." Tyndall gestured to the fast-moving clouds to the north. "There's a bit of a blow coming up. I'm running for shelter at an island I know. Just a precaution," he said calmly, but at that moment a wave of green water came over the port gunwale, swirled deeply across the deck and caused the boat to roll violently.

Olivia screamed.

"Now, don't panic, woman. We're not sinking, but we'll have to ditch some of the deck cargo." He shouted to the crew and they leapt at the lashings, slashed them with their knives and quickly dumped the bags over the side. "Right men, the sails," he shouted as soon as they were finished. "Olivia, on deck," he commanded. "I'm going to put her nose into the wind. Take the helm and hold her there while we take in the sheets."

She clambered out of the hatch, lurched to the stern and stood by Tyndall as he swung the *Bulan* into the wind and the waves until the sails were flapping wildly. She took the wheel, panic rising, but remembered how Tyndall had shown her how to point into the wind when they had dropped anchor at the beach. She held the boat steady for the few minutes the crew needed to expertly reef in the main and mizzen.

Tyndall then dashed back to her, swung the wheel and instantly the smaller sails filled and the lugger surged west, handling noticeably better.

He turned and smiled at her. "Thanks. You look lovely when you're wet."

She was suddenly aware that she was drenched with spray, her hair plastered, clothes clinging to her body. Then, choosing to ignore her appearance and his remark, she asked, "How serious is it?"

"A willy willy on the way, I'd say. We're coming

into the monsoon season so it's not that much of a surprise. It could peter out or blow like the devil. I'm not taking any chances. There's an island a couple of hours away where we can shelter safely. You'd better get below."

He spoke lightly and calmly but Olivia could sense a tenseness. However, his air of being in control of any situation reassured her and she stumbled back across the heaving deck to the cabin.

For several hours she sat on the bunk listening to the crash of the water and the howling wind, and became worried when the night began to set in and they were still at sea. It was a huge relief when Tyndall shouted triumphantly, "Land ho."

The island was not much more than a dark smudge rising and falling behind the waves but the entrance to the sheltering lagoon was clearly marked by the white wash of the pounding surf on the rocks. They went in at speed with the wind astern and immediately found themselves among a fleet of luggers at anchor.

They anchored well clear of the other boats and paid out a lot of line for a secure hold on the bottom. The Koepangers and Ahmed scurried to the fo'c'sle for shelter and Tyndall climbed into the cabin and secured the hatch.

It was stuffy and muggy and Olivia felt uncomfortable patches of perspiration well from her body. "It sounds like it should be cold, not hot," she said, as the wind howled around them.

"It's going to get worse. We'll be down here for

some time I'm afraid," said Tyndall. "Have some water. When the eye comes, it'll be calm for a bit, then comes the other side of the storm and we have to sit that out. But at least you know it's almost over," he added with a grin.

During their seemingly endless wait, Olivia asked Tyndall about his early years in Ireland, but he brushed that aside and regaled her instead with outrageous tales of adventure from his sailing days on whalers.

Olivia sat and listened, her eyes wide, her laugh often disbelieving. "It all sounds like something out of an adventure book. What wild places you've been to, Captain Tyndall. Are you ever going to settle down to a normal life?"

"What's normal?" he asked, but before she could compose a reply Olivia became aware of a lull in the storm.

The silence and stillness of the eye of the storm was eerie, and they sat in silence. Then as if someone had opened a door, the wind returned.

The stuffiness and pitching of the boat made Olivia feel queasy and she began to doubt the wisdom of going on this trip. She lay back and closed her eyes, trying to think of anything but where she was.

Just as she thought she could bear it no longer, it was over. They went on deck for fresh air and to see if there was any damage. All was intact. Ahmed and Tyndall exchanged a satisfied look, both pleased the *Bulan* had come through this test.

They all spent a restless night as insects and

mosquitoes swarmed over the lugger from the nearby mangroves and thick cover of trees.

In the morning Ahmed made a breakfast of sweet rice and dried fruit which they ate on the deck.

"All seems quiet on the other boats. They must have stayed ashore," commented Olivia.

"We'll go see what's going on after we've checked the boat," said Tyndall.

While the men worked the deck, checked the hold and then the rigging, Olivia straightened the little galley, marveling at how Ahmed turned out meals on a small kerosene spirit stove in such a cramped space. She washed herself in a bucket of water and put on her second pajama outfit and bound her hair up on her head where it felt cooler. She took a small jar of rose-scented face cream from her small bag and rubbed it into her face to protect her skin, which was growing darker by the day.

At mid-morning Tyndall and Ahmed lowered the dinghy, waited for Olivia to expertly clamber into it and they rowed ashore. They followed a sandy path through the scrubby bush when suddenly they heard voices, laughter and shouts. Tyndall and Ahmed arrived first at the break in the trees and they stopped in shock at the sight that met their eyes.

Before Olivia could see what was going on in the clearing ahead, Tyndall pulled off his battered skipper's hat and handed it to her. "Put this on, pull it down low. Don't talk to anyone and stay well back," he commanded urgently.

At the tone of his voice she didn't argue and peered past the two men standing in the shadows of the trees, their presence as yet unnoticed.

Olivia's hand flew to her mouth at the scene before her.

In the center of the clearing, a small wooden platform had been erected and standing along it were six miserable naked women, roped together. Varying in age, four were Aborigines, one was of mixed Chinese and Aboriginal blood, while the other, the youngest of them, was an exotic mix of races and stunningly beautiful. Her wide, frightened dark eyes, and lithe tall body made Olivia think of a forest deer.

"What is going on?" she whispered in shock.

"It's a *barracoon* . . . slave market. Didn't think it was still going on."

Olivia was too stunned to answer.

Ahmed nodded his head. "There's the boss, tuan. Same fella make trouble everywhere."

He indicated a man walking up and down amongst the motley group of white men gathered around the platform, eyeing the women like horse traders. Short and heavily built, he had a dark complexion with a bushy black beard and a gold earring in one ear. Atop this, he wore a large woven straw hat made from pandanus fronds. A long whip curled over one shoulder and a gun tucked in a wide leather belt gave him a menacing look.

"Karl Gunther," hissed Tyndall.

"He looks positively vile," Olivia murmured.

The man began prodding the women with the long bamboo whip handle, poking it into buttocks, between their legs and flicking at a breast. His voice boomed out, "Righto men, step forward, you've had a chance to eye the goods, let's see who'll be taking home these lovely ladies tonight!" He gave a coarse laugh and leapt up on to the platform as the men gathered around him to start bidding.

Ahmed spoke urgently to Tyndall in Malay, and they seemed to reach agreement over something.

"Am I too late, or is new blood welcome?" Tyndall strode forward, leaving Ahmed and Olivia hanging back in the shadows of the trees.

Gunther watched the tall man stride toward him, noting the figures of his Malay offsider and young boy in the black and white tunic in the background. "Captain Tyndall, no less. New blood, new money, is always welcome."

Gunther's eyes were cold and hard and there was no welcome in his voice. Olivia realized these men had crossed paths before and there was no love lost between them.

The bidding started, the strongest women going first, payment being handed to Gunther who slashed the rope from the wrist of each woman and handed her over to her new owner.

Olivia cringed. "This is barbaric. Why can't they at least cover their bodies? It's shameful."

"Be quiet, mem, if they find out you here, could be big trouble," warned Ahmed.

Tyndall stood quietly and calmly to one side, his arms folded, watching the proceedings. There were two women left, the beautiful girl of mixed race and a defiant Aboriginal woman who glared at the men, her fists clenched by her sides.

"She looks like trouble. A tough one," commented one of the men loudly.

"Have a bit of fun breaking her in then," shot back Gunther.

The young girl stood meekly, her head hanging down, her long straight black hair falling over her just-developed round breasts.

"Here she is. The cream of the crop, a little black virgin, ripe for the plucking," shouted Gunther. He knew this one would fetch a high price and had even considered keeping her for himself. But he no longer ran a lugger or had use for an untrained woman, in his bed or his business. There were plenty more out there. Even though the practice was outlawed, he kept this as a lucrative sideline. Once the men had finished with the women as divers and sexual chattels, they could be sold as servants or to brothels. Few of the women had the heart or health to run away by then, but for the moment these poor wretches had little knowledge of just how bleak their future would be.

The bidding for the virgin was brisk but Tyndall remained passive. Then as the bidding settled down between two men, Tyndall called out a price—double that of the last bid. He spoke firmly and clearly and even Gunther paused and repeated the price.

"He's *not* going to buy that girl!" Olivia could barely contain herself.

Ahmed put a restraining hand on Olivia's arm. "I ask him to save her, mem. She Macassar girl. She belong to my people."

One of the men made a half-hearted bid to better Tyndall but knew it was a lost cause. Tyndall would not be outbid. Gunther waited, hoping the price might double again, but the other men shook their heads.

"She's yours then, Captain Tyndall," said Gunther ungraciously. "Enjoy her."

While Tyndall paid Gunther, Ahmed pulled Olivia back into the trees, out of sight. Tyndall then led the girl away, loosening the rope on her wrists and throwing it away. Pulling off his shirt he put it over her shoulders. She clutched it to her body, never lifting her eyes from the ground as she followed him. Scowling, Gunther watched them go. He didn't trust Tyndall not to turn him in, despite his being party to the proceedings. Gunther instantly planned a voyage that would keep him away from the north-west for a long time.

Tyndall stayed ashore while Ahmed rowed Olivia and the girl to the lugger. Olivia went aboard first and the girl nimbly followed. Standing on the deck, she lifted her head and stared curiously at Olivia who took off Tyndall's hat and gave her a gentle smile. The girl was still fearful but curiosity at the sight of a white woman got the better of her and she studied Olivia carefully before giving her a half smile.

While Ahmed rowed back for Tyndall, Olivia took the girl's hand to lead her below deck, but at the sight of the small hatch leading into what appeared to be a dark hole, the girl wrenched her arm away, ran across the deck and jumped over the side.

Olivia shrieked as she hit the water, rushed to the gunwale and peered over the side. The girl's head bobbed to the surface. Tyndall immediately plunged into the lagoon and struck out for the girl who was smoothly kicking her way to the other side. When he grabbed her she beat him with her fists, her flailing arms and legs sending them both below the surface. Finally with an arm locked across her chest and pinning her from behind, he slowly side stroked back toward Ahmed, who rowed quickly to help. Together they dragged the spluttering naked girl into the boat. Tyndall swam to retrieve his shirt from the water and Ahmed shouted at the girl in Malay, "We're helping you! We are your friends."

"*Kawan?*" She echoed the word and looked confused.

Back on board the lugger, Olivia looked at the bedraggled girl. "Ahmed, ask her what her name is."

He spoke to her quickly. "Her name is Niah."

"Niah," repeated Tyndall reflectively. "Well, Niah, at least we know you can swim! Might make a diver of you yet!"

"What!" Olivia exploded. "I thought you were going to let her go."

"Well, not here any ways. Gunther would snatch her back in a minute. Besides, I paid a high price for her." He grinned at Olivia's furious face. Turning to the girl, he said, "So Niah, what are we going to do with you?"

He spoke to her in Malay and she answered, giving him a smile that made Olivia look from the girl to Tyndall then to Ahmed. "What did he say, Ahmed?"

Ahmed was grinning and turned away. "Nothing, mem."

Tyndall lifted an eyebrow and explained. "She made me an offer some men might find hard to refuse. Would you be so kind as to give her something to wear?"

Olivia glared at the three of them and stomped below to pull a long white shift from her bag.

With the island now behind them, Olivia sat on the deck and hugged her knees watching Niah, who was sitting comfortably cross-legged in the simple cotton shift, calmly braiding her long dark hair. Olivia noticed she wore a striking flat, carved shell pendant around her neck. Looking close, she reacted with surprise—it had the same pattern on it as the gift the women had given her. Ahmed and the Koepangers busied themselves opening shell and Tyndall stood at the wheel whistling, steering the *Bulan* toward Broome.

CHAPTER NINE

Captain Tyndall's return to Broome with a nubile young black woman did not go unnoticed in the town. Nor indeed, did the fact that Mrs. Hennessy had accompanied him on the voyage.

The two women, followed by Ahmed with the luggage, walked solemnly along the jetty after the *Bulan* moored. Niah was a step behind Olivia, who was now demurely dressed in her formal day clothes. But sharp eyes watching the small procession quickly identified Niah's white "dress" as a woman's petticoat, probably Olivia's.

Tyndall brought up the rear, cheerfully whistling and carrying his battered leather Gladstone bag containing documents, money, pearls and the inevitable bottle of whisky.

As they reached the end of the jetty Conrad came hurrying to greet them. He embraced Olivia and over her shoulder he glanced at Niah, giving Tyndall a quizzical glance and raised eyebrows. Tyndall responded with a grin and a wink.

"My dear, I saw you sail in. It was such a relief to see you home safe and sound. I heard there was a bad blow down the coast." Conrad released her and put his hands on her shoulders. "Did you enjoy yourself?" One glance at her sparkling eyes, flushed cheeks and eager smile answered his question.

"Oh, she has quite a story to tell," commented Tyndall.

"Was it successful?" asked Conrad.

"Indeed it was—despite a small loss along the way," answered Tyndall. "Your wife coped admirably, all things considered. I don't know many women who would have done so well under such trying conditions."

"She didn't get seasick or get in the way?" Conrad asked teasingly.

"No, Conrad, I didn't. I even took the helm once," interjected Olivia sharply.

"You'll hear all about it, but pour yourself a rum first," advised Tyndall. "Nice having you on board, Mrs. Hennessy, you made the trip quite memorable." He strolled off, whistling again. Tyndall was relieved things had gone so well, for it hadn't been an easy trip by any means. However, now her whim had been satisfied, he doubted he'd see Olivia go to sea again.

Niah had been standing quietly to one side and now Conrad gave her a curious glance.

Olivia waved toward the girl. "Oh, Conrad, this is Niah. She's coming home with us." As Conrad's jaw dropped, she took his arm. "I'll explain it all later."

"I get sulky, mem." Ahmed handed her bag to Conrad and hurried away.

Conrad lowered his voice. "Olivia, what is going on? This is all very awkward. I've had a bit of explaining to do down at the club about you going on this trip. They understood about visiting James and so forth, but some of the old hands did say they thought it 'a bit rum, old chap'. How am I going to explain this girl?"

"You don't have to whisper, Conrad, she doesn't understand English. We're going to look after her for a bit and we'll just say she is going to be my maid and help in the house."

"A bit difficult when she doesn't speak English and you don't speak Malay," commented Conrad, throwing her bag into the sulky and helping her climb up.

"Then I'll have to learn Malay, won't I? Oh Conrad, wait till you hear her story!"

Niah was shown to a small room in a separate part of the servant's quarters, much to the dismay of the Chinese cook. He was immediately concerned he might have to train the girl—whom he considered no better than a savage—in domestic duties.

Olivia called the Malay house boy away from his dusting to explain the details of the house and her situation. She then rejoined Conrad on the verandah.

"Now Olivia, sit down and have a cool drink and

tell me all about this . . . adventure, and how come we now have a new, er, resident," said Conrad.

Olivia dropped into the nearest chair and poured out the story.

"Oh Conrad, it was just awful . . . the poor girl . . ."

Once over the dismay of hearing of the women's barracoon and the possible danger Olivia could have encountered, Conrad was rather bemused by the new addition to the household. He saw it as another example of the swashbuckling exploits of his colorful partner, but he was concerned at his wife's involvement and her complicity in concealing details from the police. He was upset with having to go along with the whole business.

"I have grave reservations about all of this," he said finally.

"Well, we really haven't got much choice," said Olivia decisively. "But we say nothing until we talk it over with Captain Tyndall tonight."

Around sunset Tyndall arrived at the house and he and Conrad settled themselves on the verandah with a bottle of rum and freshly squeezed lime juice set on a silver tray.

Olivia, dressed in a cool, flowered muslin dress, her hair softly combed into a twist at the nape of her neck, joined them. The men rose to their feet as she sat on the small wicker chaise. "Would you like to join us for supper, Captain Tyndall?" she asked. "Now that peace has settled on the household."

"There's been a bit of fracas with the girl. She

argues with the house boy. God knows what's going on," said Conrad, looking concerned. "I hope she isn't going to cause difficulties. Is she actually going to stay on with us, or do you have other plans for her?"

"I'll work out something with Ahmed about her future. In the meantime, Mrs. Hennessy has assured me she will look after her. It will be an ideal opportunity to learn Malay."

"I'm planning to do so," said Olivia, taking up his challenge. "You and Ahmed won't have any secrets from me in the future," she added.

Tyndall raised his glass to her. "Then a toast to you. And thanks for your company on our voyage. May I add, you are looking very fetching this evening."

Olivia smiled in acknowledgment. She could tell he'd already put several rums under his belt, and that the compliment was a reference to the very different attire she'd been wearing on the *Bulan*.

"Oh, thanks for the invitation to dinner, by the way, but I've got to meet some chaps for a drink or two," said Tyndall.

"Socializing tonight, eh?" interjected Conrad, feeling a little uncomfortable with the bantering conversation.

"I've been doing a bit of that at the Conti already," he said easily. "My, we are the talk of the town."

Conrad looked concerned. "Oh dear. I hope the RM hasn't heard about Olivia's little adventure."

"People will always talk. I ignore them and just live my life," said Tyndall.

"That's all well and good, but when one aspires to a certain standing in the community, one has to consider one's actions to a certain degree. It's not possible to simply do as one wants to, no matter what." Seeing the expressions of Tyndall and Olivia, Conrad realized he was sounding pompous.

"Is that what you want, Conrad? To aspire to a certain standing in the community?" asked Olivia gently. "I'm sorry if my actions have embarrassed you."

Tyndall glanced at the contrite Olivia, but suddenly knew from the light in the depths of her green eyes she wasn't the least bit sorry for taking the trip on the *Bulan*.

"Don't worry about it, Conrad. Your wife's reputation is intact. Now, we must discuss business for a moment or two. We have to start deep sea pearling and that will mean further investment."

"What sort of investment?" asked Conrad cautiously, knowing that funds were low.

"We have to equip the lugger with a new pump and gear and make more room to accommodate a crew. The schooner will act as mother ship. And we have to find a diver and tender."

"That's all your department," said Conrad. Enthused by the idea, he added, "The more I learn about the pearling business, the more I like it."

"He's got the bug now," said Olivia, pleased that Conrad's normal reserve and caution were swept aside by the heady business of pearling, with its lure of finding valuable pearls.

Like so many men before him, the mystique of pearls was affecting Conrad. He had begun to read what he could find on the industry and had talked to as many people as possible about all aspects of pearling. The loose rounds, baroque and blister pearls attached to the shell were considered a bonus, but enough were found in the deeper waters off Broome to make it a lucrative sideline to pearl shell. Not all the pearls collected were officially reported to the Customs authorities for duty and record keeping. It was a great temptation, especially when good pearls were found, not to declare them and sell them on the snide market or send them to buyers in Singapore, Hong Kong or Melbourne.

Conrad was glad to be able to report his own small success. "Actually, while you were away, I made a good friend of the town's best pearl cleaner, so we can hand over the first batch of pearls to him. His name is Tobias Metta."

Tobias Metta was from Ceylon via Singapore. Conrad had taken to frequently visiting Toby's nondescript office where his work bench was spread with the most basic of tools—a magnifying lens, a goldsmith's file stuck in the end of a champagne cork, a knife with several blades honed to their ultimate sharpness, file board and clamp, emery paper, ruby powder, a soft cloth and a pair of scales.

His round face, that looked as if it had just

been oiled and polished, always broke into a welcoming smile. Fortunes came or fell away from his fingers as he delicately operated on flaws that marred a pearl's beauty and value. The art lay in his hands—surprisingly squat stub-fingered hands—but the agility, lightness and swiftness of touch was like watching two creatures perform a dance, so delicately they twisted and spun the pearl beneath the blade or file. Like a doctor, the pearl cleaner was believed to have healing hands. Though luck, skill and judgment were just as important. Despite the pressure of his work, Tobias Metta still managed to chuckle and talk all the time while he worked.

"It's the risk the owner takes, Mr. Hennessy, to sell immediately at a small profit or gamble that beneath the surface is a perfect beauty. If it isn't there, I cannot produce it. I am not a magician," smiled Toby. "But I can make more beautiful a pearl whose true qualities have not been shown to the world," he added with some pride.

Conrad was amazed at how lackluster pearls became shining iridescent gems, sometimes in only minutes. Misshapen pearls sometimes yielded valuable gems, but just as often turned out to be worthless.

"How exciting! I would love to watch him at work," exclaimed Olivia. "Would he mind? I absolutely must go with you when we collect our pearls and tackle the buyer."

"Toby is quite unperturbed about visitors being around as he works. He's amazingly deft, and very fast. It's hard to believe he is working with something valuable and that one slip could destroy it," marveled Conrad. "I'll introduce you tomorrow, my dear."

Tyndall put his glass down and thanked them both for the sun downer. "By the way, before I go, I'll speak to Niah. I'll attempt to settle her down and explain what the situation is. May I see her now?"

"I only wish I could communicate with her, help her. She doesn't seem to be adjusting to our household at all well," sighed Olivia.

As the two men walked to the rear of the house, Conrad asked, "How wild is she, John?"

"All women can be wild at times," said Tyndall lightly, but then continued more earnestly, "She's from the Indies, Conrad. Quite a different culture from the blacks."

Niah was sitting cross-legged in the center of the camp stretcher in the simple whitewashed room. She glared at Tyndall when she saw him, then let forth a stream of urgent questions.

"*Lambat.* Slowly," said Tyndall, speaking softly and choosing his words carefully. The girl listened and then Tyndall called for Yusef, the house boy, who was sitting at the servants' communal eating table outside the laundry and cook house.

"Yusef, you must watch her, and be her friend. Mem Hennessy will have clothes made for her because it might take a while before we can send her back home."

Niah jumped up and clutched at Tyndall, crying

and talking in a jumble of her native language which he had trouble following. He calmed Niah and turned to Yusef. "She doesn't want to go back home? What was all that about a bad man?"

Yusef translated. "Tuan, she say she is given to old man, a bad man, for husband. She no want to go to him."

"What about her family? Will they take her back, is there anywhere else she can go?"

Niah shook her head vehemently in response to this and nervously clutched at the shell pendant around her neck.

"She stolen by bad white man and put on boat with others. No can go back, tuan," said the boy, giving Niah a sympathetic look.

"Hmm," muttered Tyndall. "It seems we can't send her back."

At this Conrad looked shocked and shook his head. "Well, we can't just keep her or indeed, let her loose in the streets."

Niah reached out and clutched Tyndall's shirt, talking urgently.

He unhooked Niah's hands. "She says she belongs to me now because I saved her."

"Oh," said Conrad, now quite confused by the fast-changing situation.

Olivia overheard this last exchange as she approached, wondering what all the noise was about. "Well, you certainly can't keep her, Captain Tyndall. We'll have to talk to the church people. Maybe she should go to a convent. I'm sure there must be a mission that will take her."

Tyndall bit his lip and didn't answer. Turning to the girl, he spoke soothingly, before asking Olivia to get the cook to make her some food. "I think she feels a bit better now she's sounded off at all of us."

Olivia glanced back at the girl who still looked haunted, but there was a small gleam in her big brown eyes. She recognized the glint of victory when she saw it.

The next day a very hung over Tyndall announced he had found a diver for the next season. "A Jap. Good record with the fleet. But my God he can drink whisky!"

Olivia raised an eyebrow. "Will you be coming with us to the pearl cleaner?"

Tyndall screwed up his face and slumped low in his office chair, lifting his feet up on the desk. "I couldn't handle Toby Metta this morning. Never stops talking. All too much. As for the pearl buyer, well my advice is, be tough."

"Don't worry about it, John, we'll look after everything," said Conrad with some confidence.

Just as she was enchanted with the rundown shell shed on the waterfront when she first went there, Olivia was excited by the atmosphere of the workshop of the Asian pearl cleaner. He greeted her effusively, fussily dusting off a bent wood chair, and rubbing his hands together with enthusiasm.

"It is very good of you to come to my humble little place, Mrs. Hennessy. It is rarely graced by the presence of a lady." He bobbed and smiled and clasped his hands. "You are most welcome any time."

His singsong accent and excessive politeness amused Olivia, but she warmed to him immediately. "I hope that together we will make some wonderful pearls, Mr. Metta."

"Oh indeed, indeed, Mrs. Hennessy. We most certainly will. But already you have some very excellent pearls." He reached into a drawer and from a labeled black velvet bag emptied a small cluster of pearls from blue tissue paper into the palm of his hand, then spread them on the bag on the desk. "There," he said triumphantly.

Four pearls of intense gold and rosy luster shone like beacons on a moonless night. Olivia gasped lightly. "Oh, they're beautiful. Conrad, isn't it exciting."

"Only a few skins had to be removed," explained Toby. "Very simple little task, just like peeling an onion. A most lucky start. They will bring a good price even though they are not that big." From another bag he emptied two dozen smaller pearls. "Your petty cash," he laughed. "I lost four. They were flawed to the heart. So sorry."

They paid his fee and accepted an invitation to Sunday tiffin. His reputation was such among the pearling masters of Broome that there was no racial discrimination when it came to accepting invitations to Toby and Mabel's tiffin. Not only was the food good, but very little happened in Broome concerning pearls that Toby did not know about, and occasionally he discreetly let slip some useful information.

With the pearls rolled into a small chamois bag and tucked into Olivia's handbag, the Hennessys continued on to the Continental Hotel to meet with Monsieur Jules Barat, the pearl buyer.

After exchanging introductions and greetings, Monsieur Barat carefully closed the door behind them.

The pearl buyer was a short man, quite young despite his courtly manner, with a large hooked nose, pointed goatee and gold-rimmed spectacles that magnified his bulbous brown eyes. He was immaculately dressed from Faubourg St. Germain and the combination of his élan and distinctive Gallic style made him glaringly out of place in Broome.

They sat around a small wicker table and he opened a flat wooden case. Its lid was lined with green baize. Beside this he set up a small set of gold scales, a jeweler's eyeglass, and a small note pad.

He spoke with a smooth and seductive French accent. He bowed slightly to Olivia. "Would Madame excuse me if I remove my jacket?"

"Please." She gestured to him to go ahead, and he slipped his jacket on the back of his chair. Conrad, dressed in tropical linen and not haute couture, stayed as he was.

Olivia took the pearls from the little bag and placed them on the green baize. It was a modest collection and Olivia spoke up a little defensively.

"As you are aware, this has been our first season. We expect to increase our output significantly with each season."

"Of course. Quality, not just quantity, is what we strive for in the jewelry business," he responded with a slight bobbing of his head.

Monsieur Barat went through what was obviously his personal ritual—the adjusting of the metal expanding bands that held up his shirt sleeves, the flexing of fingers, the wiping of his glasses, which he put to one side, the screwing into place of the eyeglass. Only then did he pick up and study each pearl. After careful scrutiny, he weighed each and made a note on his pad. Another thoughtful look at each pearl, holding them at a distance, and finally a calculation on the pad. He tore off the sheet, turned it around and slid it across to Conrad. After a brief perusal, Conrad silently handed the paper to Olivia. He looked pleased—it seemed a fair price, quite in line with the estimate Toby had made for them. But Olivia pursed her lips.

"Monsieur Barat, surely this is not your final offer?" she challenged him.

Conrad and the pearl buyer blinked at her.

"Mrs. Hennessy, I am a professional dealer, not a horse trader."

"I understand, of course. But . . ."

"Olivia . . ." began Conrad, appalled at her questioning of the offer.

The falcon eyes of the pearl buyer from Paris didn't flicker as he stared at Olivia without expression. "I have considerable expenses. If you would prefer to travel to Rue Lafayette or Hatton Garden yourself . . . " He gave a shrug. "Besides, you are first-time clients, we have not established a trading relationship as such where I can offer you *un prix special* . . ."

"It seems to me this is the time to do so then," said Olivia sweetly. "A special price now will assure we continue to do business with you, for we will know you are a fair and reasonable man. It would save us the trouble of negotiating with other buyers."

Conrad decided to maintain his silence. Olivia had scored a point. He was at once surprised at and proud of his wife's boldness.

The pearl buyer unfolded his glasses, slowly put them back on and reached for the scrap of paper. He drew a line through the bottom figure, wrote a new figure and handed the paper back to Olivia. "Does that establish a relationship between us, Mrs. Hennessy?" he asked with a thaw in his formal demeanor.

She gave him a brilliant smile. "Indeed it does. Star of the Sea Pearls looks forward to seeing you next season, Monsieur Barat. Isn't that so, Conrad?"

"Er, yes, quite so . . ." he glanced at the note pad sheet Olivia handed to him.

The pearl buyer stood and put on his jacket. "Please allow me to celebrate our business dealing with an aperitif in the Lugger Bar." He held out his arm for Olivia to take as Conrad opened the door for them and they all stepped into the garden.

Niah appeared to have settled down. Olivia had had an Indian tailor run up several simple outfits for her, as Niah was reluctant to wear European clothing and preferred sarongs. Olivia had to agree privately she thought this a far more practical outfit and wondered if she might ever dare wear one, away from public gaze. In the back of her mind was the possibility she might take another trip on the *Bulan* and she imagined how perfect such attire would be on a boat. She wished Conrad enjoyed the sea more so that they could take some trips together.

While the sea might not have held any lure for Conrad, shell and their possible haul of pearls certainly did. He began spending more time in the packing shed when the shell openers and cleaners were at work.

"So, we've got you away from the figures at last," said Tyndall, who was watching the men drag the crates of shell to one side ready for shipment.

"I'd like to be writing up more pearl sales as well as shell," remarked Conrad with enthusiasm. "I must say it was quite an experience dealing with Monsieur Barat. There really is something special about pearls, isn't there. Everything about them has a different excitement—the find, the peeling, the selling. When do we start deep diving?"

Tyndall laughed. "Bejesus, Conrad, you've really taken to this business, but you'll have to be patient during the wet. It'll be a few months before we get back to sea. There's plenty to keep us occupied. Got to finalize the crews, and there are the changes to the lugger."

"The new diving suit we ordered from Perth should be on the next steamer," added Conrad.

"I thought I might take a turn on the bottom," announced Tyndall casually. "Can't be that difficult to get the hang of."

"Do you think that's wise, John? Damned risky business. One hears such terrible stories . . . And what about the chap we got the boat from. He's not good for anything now." Conrad was genuinely concerned at the prospect.

"Don't worry about it. I'll have Ahmed on top keeping an eye on me, and I'll get plenty of advice from our diver. Which reminds me, we'd better sign him up."

Olivia was excited at the prospect of them being "proper pearlers," as she put it. She wanted to know every detail of the changes to the lugger and the new gear which they were accumulating in Tyndall's office. She even suggested that she join in negotiations with the Japanese diver.

"Now that's one area of business you're not sharing," admonished Tyndall, shaking a finger at her. "We wouldn't get anyone to work for us if a woman got involved in the act."

Olivia glared at him in reply.

"It's a cultural thing, no insult intended," he

explained, then hurriedly changed the subject. "Hey, have you seen the diving gear? Just had the helmet overhauled." He led her to a corner of the room where the baggy diving suit was hung, metal boots and helmet piled on the floor beside it.

"Those boots look terribly big," said Olivia.

"Here, try them on," enthused Tyndall, pulling them out while Olivia slipped off her shoes.

She put a foot in each of them, then burst out laughing. "They're ridiculous. I can't move they're so heavy."

Tyndall bounced back to the pile and lifted the copper and brass helmet. "Might as well do the full thing, try the hat," he laughed, carefully placing it over Olivia's head, resting it on her shoulders, then stepped back.

Olivia's muffled giggle gave way to a sudden cry for help, but it was too late. Her legs buckled as she tried to lift her feet, and she toppled over. Tyndall dashed forward and caught her in his arms, but he was off-balance and they both fell to the floor, overcome with helpless laughter.

"Good Lord, Olivia, whatever are you doing?" gasped Conrad as he took in the scene having just come up the stairs. "What's going on?" he snapped.

"Just testing the gear, Conrad. Testing the gear." On his knees Tyndall helped lift the helmet off Olivia's head.

Olivia lay flat on the floor, her feet still stuck in the diving boots, and looked up at Conrad, first seriously, then burst out laughing again at the absurdity of the situation.

"Really! This is very embarrassing. You're behaving like a child," Conrad reprimanded her and then stomped off to his office.

Tyndall helped Olivia to her feet, and they exchanged mock grimaces behind Conrad's back.

Several months later the Star of the Sea Pearl Company was back in business with the *Bulan* refitted for deep-sea helmet diving with accommodation, new hand pump and tender's equipment in place, crew hired and the *Shamrock* fitted out as a mother ship to deliver supplies and collect shell hauls.

Prior to setting out to sea, Tyndall joined the Hennessys for dinner. Niah helped wait at the table, she and Olivia showing off their respective limited knowledge of English and Malay. Niah knew this was a farewell for Tyndall before he and Ahmed went away to sea again.

Tyndall and Conrad celebrated the forthcoming enterprise heartily with far too many drinks. When Olivia bid Tyndall good-bye and good luck she knew he was going to head to the bars in Chinatown.

She wagged a finger at him. "You behave yourself and don't miss the tide in the morning!"

"Ahmed will get us to sea, don't you worry. What are you going to do while I'm away?" he slurred. "You'll find it very dull without me around. You'll have to go and play ladies again."

"We'll manage perfectly well without you,"

she answered, trying not to sound upset at his drunken state. "You just bring back lots of good shell and pearls."

"Don't you wish you were coming, too?" He lurched a little as he peered intently at her face, but her expression was hidden in the shadowy night.

"Good night, Captain Tyndall," she said firmly from the verandah. "And bon voyage."

Conrad was already snoring lightly in his chair and Olivia sighed as she watched Tyndall, staggering slightly, disappear into the night. It would be an adventure to go out to the pearling grounds where the banks of shell were hidden fathoms deep. Maybe . . . one day.

The next morning as Conrad walked carefully about the house complaining of feeling out of sorts, a worried Ahmed arrived on a borrowed bicycle. "Mem, mem, tuan no on schooner."

"I knew it," she said, slamming her hand on the door post in exasperation. "He went to Chinatown after he left here late last night. Conrad, you'd better help Ahmed look for him."

"He could be anywhere," agonized Conrad, holding his head.

"I know his places," said Ahmed. "Crew all ready, must not miss tide."

"Tell me where to look for him while I get the sulky ready," sighed Conrad.

After they left, Olivia had a sudden thought.

She hurried from the house and down to the office. Conrad's room was locked, but hearing a thud next door, Olivia cautiously opened the door.

There was Tyndall, sprawled sound asleep on a cane lounge, one foot having dropped to the floor. He was still in his clothes from the evening before, stubble showed on his chin and he was breathing heavily, lips slightly parted. There was an empty whisky bottle on the floor.

"Tyndall!" Olivia shouted and banged the door loudly behind her.

It took a few seconds for him to open his eyes and focus on the figure standing over him.

"Have you been here all night?" demanded Olivia.

"Nope." He sat up, rubbed his eyes and his rough cheeks and chin and stared at her before asking, "What time is it?"

"Time to sail. Ahmed is looking for you. The crews are on board. You'd better get going."

"We'll get there. Full steam ahead." He climbed slowly to his feet, pulled on his skipper's hat and gave her a cheeky salute.

"John Tyndall, you are incorrigible."

"What would I do without a partner to keep me on the straight and narrow?" mused Tyndall as he stumbled past her to the stairs.

Still feeling somewhat appalled and annoyed, Olivia returned to the house where she was confronted by a distressed Yusef.

"Mem! Niah gone. No here. Run away."

"What!" Olivia rushed to the servants' quarters to find Niah's room empty of her few possessions.

It wasn't till that afternoon, when the *Shamrock* was well out to sea, following the *Bulan* and several other luggers, that the Japanese diver came on deck looking quite flustered.

"Stowaway," he said, pointing to the main cabin.

Tyndall stepped through the hatch to find Niah sitting calmly on his bunk. She looked up at him and flashed a happy smile.

CHAPTER TEN

A message was sent to Olivia and Conrad informing them of Niah's whereabouts via a lugger returning with a sick diver. Aware that Tyndall was less than pleased at her presence, she initially kept very much to herself. A bunk was rigged for her behind a canvas curtain in the small compartment for'ad of the main cabin, an area that contained water tanks and the sail locker in which Niah had concealed herself until the schooner was well out to sea.

As the days at sea and on the pearling grounds passed routinely, Niah became more and more involved in helping around the boat, establishing a polite but discreet working relationship with the crews on both the *Shamrock* and the *Bulan*. The cook on the *Shamrock* treated her like a servant, sending her to the galley for more rice, or mugs of sweet black chicory coffee during meals. She talked mainly to Ahmed, their homeland links providing the foundation of a more relaxed relationship. Together they made several trips in the

216

dinghy between the two vessels, occasions Niah used to question him about the unusual white man who had saved her from slavery and who was now at pains to ignore her.

Ahmed answered her questions discreetly. Out of loyalty to Tyndall he avoided responding to those he thought were too personal. He found it enjoyable having her on board for she was no trouble, had an easy sense of humor and was incredibly beautiful, a matter that he found more than a little disturbing. It was also a matter that made him ponder on his master's attitude to the girl. The forced distancing from her would be hard to maintain much longer, and then . . . ah, everything is in the hands of the Almighty One, mused Ahmed.

Some evenings, particularly on Sundays if the weather was calm, many of the luggers and schooners working the grounds would anchor within easy distance of each other, and crews and skippers would exchange visits, enjoying shared meals, drinks and gambling with dice and cards. Tyndall was busy building up friendships with as many skippers as possible, particularly those working independently or belonging to the smaller fleets. He saw the chance for profit next season by acting as a mother ship to other luggers, packing and carrying shell as well as selling food, fuel and grog.

Tyndall had a firm rule for Niah when other crews came on board the *Shamrock* for social evenings—she must keep to herself in the main cabin. He instructed that she venture on deck only after the last of the visitors had left.

One evening she was sitting with her back against the main mast, her chin on hunched-up knees, looking across the moonlit water. As she listened to the soft slap of water on the hull and the lazy rattle of the rigging, she could see that nearly all the boats had doused their lanterns, except the schooner *Ambrosia* run by "Wild" Bill Leven. A waving lantern held over the side vaguely illuminated a tiny rowing boat into which a man was trying to clamber. There was a shout, a thump and a curse and then laughter from two men as the little craft rocked violently. After shouted slurred farewells, the boat zigzagged toward the *Shamrock*.

She sat still until the dinghy bumped alongside the rope ladder amidships and she saw Tyndall fumbling with the rope to secure the craft. Without a word she went to the side, leaned down and took the mooring line, holding it firm while Tyndall climbed clumsily aboard, missing his footing several times. He stumbled to the main cabin without a word, as if he hadn't seen her.

After she had secured the dinghy astern she padded silently after him. In the dark cabin Tyndall was sprawled across his bunk, one leg and one arm hanging over the side.

Niah bent down and pulled off his plimsolls and socks, and as he opened a weary eye, she tugged at his shirt and, with some assistance from Tyndall, dragged it off. He watched her without saying a word as she leaned over him and unbuckled his belt, methodically undid the row of buttons and, taking the bottom of each trouser leg, slid off his pants. Tyndall tossed his undergarments to the floor and lay there naked, without moving or speaking.

Standing by the bed Niah looked down at him for a moment and gave a small satisfied smile, then undid the knot of her sarong and let it fall to the floor. A faint change of expression swept fleetingly across Tyndall's face at the sight of the nubile golden body softly lit by moonlight through the portholes. Niah then laid her body gently on his and his outstretched arms tightened around her.

The *Shamrock* strained at its mooring, the wooden planks groaned gently and rigging quivered as it lolled in the arms of the sea and Niah sighed sensually in the strong arms of Tyndall.

In the morning Ahmed quietly boarded, got a steaming mug of black tea from the galley and went to the main cabin to wake the tardy skipper. In the hatchway he paused, seeing Niah sleeping snugly curled into Tyndall's side.

Before he could retreat Tyndall opened his eyes, yawned and gave a small smile. "Leave the tea thank you, Ahmed. I'll be up and about shortly."

Ahmed nodded, his face impassive, and went up on deck and busied himself with bags of shell.

It was some time before Tyndall appeared, looking pleased with himself and surprisingly refreshed. He made no reference to Niah and, after calling for *makan* from the cook, heartily announced, "Today is the day I go below."

Ahmed looked up in surprise. "Is this wise, tuan, when you have had such a . . ." Ahmed paused delicately, ". . . such a night? Liquor in the blood is not good when diving."

"Slept that off," replied Tyndall cheerfully. "No, my mind is made up. Tell Yoshi, today he can rest on deck for awhile and I'll go over the side. Only one way to find out what it's all about. Can't have these divers pulling the wool over our eyes and having us believe their fancy stories if I haven't seen it for myself."

Ahmed knew better than to protest. He nodded and rowed over to the *Bulan* to alert the crew that the skipper wanted to dive.

Tomoko Yoshikuri, the Japanese diver, was not happy at what he regarded as a mere little adventure by the captain, for they would lose at least half a day's work, and he was being paid a bonus percentage of the shell take. On the pearling grounds when the skipper was not aboard, the diver had control of the boat and when the diver was below, his tender guided the boat's movements, dictated by the diver below. Yoshi could disagree with Tyndall's wish to attempt a first dive, but Tyndall was owner and pearling master and his sea skills were respected. Before signing on, Yoshi and Takahashi Ono, his tender, had made their own enquiries. Some Malay crews were considered lazy but Ahmed had a solid reputation and his fierce loyalty to Tyndall was considered a credit by the two Japanese, and the word was about that the master ran a tight, efficient ship.

Yoshi went and sat in the shade and waited. Tyndall would only try this once, he reasoned.

He was contemplative as the tender and Ahmed set out the gear for Tyndall's dive. A placid man, Yoshi's calmness came from an acceptance of knowing his path in life. The old samurai who had opened a small school in his village after the overthrow of the shoguns had taught Yoshi that success came from hard work and knowledge, and also from attending to one's fellow man by being loyal, trustworthy and kind. As a schoolboy he had dreamed of the world beyond his village. Japan was changing, turning from feudalism to embrace ideas and ways of the Western world, with merchants replacing warriors as the men of high esteem.

Yoshi's village in Taiji on the coast of Wakayama Prefecture on Honshu was as different as the distance that separated it from the Kimberley coast. It was five years now since he had last wandered among the dark forests of elm and ash, fir and pines that grew in a solid green wall almost to the edge of the rugged steep cliffs over a sea-swept rocky shoreline. As the land was impossible to farm, the villagers made a precarious existence as fishermen and whalers. Yoshi still recalled the dreadful day when, as a young boy, he watched the abler men of the village row out to capture a whale calf, only to have their boats smashed by the enraged mother who, hearing the cries of her calf, charged and smashed the boats, killing all the men.

Many young men left the village to find work elsewhere and some found their way to north Australia on small boats working the waters for seafood delicacies and pearl shell. Their natural ability as divers, their innate understanding of the sea, and their strength of will and body, earned them a big reputation and thus began a traditional link between an island of Japan and a remote part of the great Australian continent. Soon master pearlers right across the north were bidding for their services.

Throughout his teens, Yoshi heard tales from returning divers and yearned to join them in what seemed to be a great and rewarding adventure. So when agents of the Thursday Island pearlers came recruiting one summer, Yoshi signed up and was indentured. He learned his trade with the Torres Strait fleet, then contracted with a pearler moving west to the newer and richer grounds of Western Australia. He missed the coral and palm-fringed islands of the Torres Strait, but accepted the rough and barren Broome landscape with equanimity. The rewards were good. There was money to spare to send back to his brothers and sisters, to secure some property in the village. Whenever he was ashore he went to the small temple built by the tight-knit Japanese community in Broome and burned incense and offered prayers for his mother who had died during his first year abroad.

Yoshi had yet to make a trip back home to his village, but such absences were not uncommon among Japanese divers. When he did go back it would be with the money to afford a wife whom he would bring to Broome.

Yoshi was now in his late twenties, a senior diver with many years good work left in him, provided he was careful. And there were few divers on the coast as wary of the hazards as Yoshi. He had one rule . . . never take unnecessary risks. There were too many examples about Broome of divers who had—men crippled and wizened with bodies crushed and warped by the pressure of the sea, causing the dreaded paralysis, which, if it didn't kill them, damaged them for life.

Yoshi thought Tyndall was taking an unnecessary risk. He had no need to go down. It was a decision that he had not expected from his new boss, and it worried him. He thinks it a bit of a game, reflected Yoshi as he sipped at a small blue china mug of warm tea. Taki his tender had brought it to him with a raised eyebrow and a nod toward Tyndall who was wrapping himself in layers of flannel while Ahmed fussed with the diving suit. Niah, in a sarong, sat on the aft gunwale, smiling at Tyndall's comic antics as he pulled on layers of clothes to combat the cold below.

"Yo, ho, ho, Yoshi," shouted Tyndall in good humor. "I'm ready to don the suit of the finest and bravest diver in the nor-west. How do I look?"

Everyone on deck, including the Malays, looked at Tyndall with inscrutable faces. Tyndall knew he looked ridiculous—a tall pole of a man wrapped in multicolored layers of long johns, strips of flannel sheets, several undershirts and pairs of long socks, none of them matching. But nobody smiled, except Niah, who broke into a giggle which she smothered with a hand, earning a wicked wink from Tyndall.

Ahmed and Taki helped Tyndall into the bulky canvas and rubber diving suit and then laced up the heavy lead-weighted boots, and pulled on the gloves. Yoshi kept a professional eye on every detail, without moving from his squatting position on the roof of the cabin. Only when the team prepared to put on the helmet did Yoshi move and take his place beside Tyndall. Yoshi watched carefully as the corselet of brass and copper was guided over Tyndall's head and screwed to the reinforced neck of the suit. A coir rope was tied around his waist within easy hand reach to signal Taki from below and for Taki to signal him.

Yoshi spoke at last. "Breathe slowly. Never panic. Concentrate on the job. No time to look around pretty place. Look where you put feet all time. Remember, one pull, more air, two pulls, slack off line, three pulls help quick smart. Three pulls from topside, you come up quick time." They rehearsed the routine several times, Tyndall feeling increasingly uncomfortable and sweaty in the suit.

Ahmed grinned. "No work today, boss. You just look around at pretty places." He knew it would annoy Yoshi, but the Japanese diver showed no reaction.

"No, Ahmed, it's not a holiday. I've got to come up with something, or I'll be the laughing stock of the whole coast." He took a couple of steps toward the ladder, then paused. "Hey, shouldn't we have a ceremony or something?"

All divers were superstitious and most carried lucky charms, prayed before diving or conducted some small personal ritual before sinking through the fathoms to the sea bed. They made countless dives, but knew each one could present some terrible accident that could claim their life. Yoshi carried a miniature red torii, the simple two uprights crossed at the top by two horizontals which was a powerful symbol of Shintoism. The first tales he had heard of pearl diving were accounts highly colored about devils that lurked beneath the sea. There were so many beliefs and customs. One must always bow before silver fish in a bowl. Two fish fighting meant sharks were around. It was not good of the master to joke about such things before a dive.

Niah leapt off the rail and ran to Tyndall, taking off her carved pearl shell pendant as she moved. Niah dropped it over his head, pushing it inside the suit. He glanced at the carving, and smiled into her eyes. It was a good omen, he told himself, though he was not sure why. The spontaneity of the gesture pleased him.

The copper helmet was lifted and placed over his head and locked into place on the metal collar. The glass panels in the helmet had been rinsed with sea water to prevent them steaming up with his breath, and these too were locked shut.

Lifting his hand in salute, Tyndall stepped backward and flopped into the water. He put a hand to the valve on his helmet and there was a hiss of air deflating the suit and he sank beneath the surface into a watery world of changing light and color. He hit the bottom gently, quickly readjusted the air valve to get the right pressure, enough to keep the water pressure off his body, and yet not high enough to send him shooting to the surface. He was more conscious of his body than the world around him. He could feel pins and needles of pain spiking through his head and joints as his body rebelled against this unnatural state. He could hear the unexpectedly loud hissing of his breathing, the click-clack of the air pump on the deck transmitted down the hose, and the rush of bubbles each time he exhaled. Once he was comfortable, he sent a signal up the line and the tender began playing out line so he could start exploring his underwater world.

Slowly Tyndall began trudging along the sea bed, his lead boots kicking up clouds of sand. Initially the transparent walls of water around him were disorienting. He looked down at the sea floor. It was grubby-hued sand littered with rocks, weed and small outcrops of corallite—the decaying skeletons of coral formations. He was glad there wasn't the "grass" that divers talked of—the lush, bright green weed that sometimes obscured the bottom and hid treacherous holes, shell and dangerous marine life.

As he became accustomed to the floor he started to pick out the shell, generally bunched together, grayish-brown, some covered with weed and coralline. Looking more closely, Tyndall could see the giveaway small ridge line in the sand where concealed shells had "breathed." He bent down and began picking up shells and placing them in the woven baskets strung on the extra line.

Above the surface Taki followed Tyndall's groping movements as the line played through his fingers. Ahmed kept the *Bulan* head reaching, ensuring it was close up to the wind, moving stern-first with the tide, its direction guided by the rudder and a small jib to stop her drifting away with the current too quickly and dragging Tyndall with her.

Niah moved to the side, looking down to where the air-hose and lifeline disappeared into the tranquil sea. She glanced at Ahmed and found him watching her intently. If the crew had not been present she suspected he would have spoken to her about joining Tyndall in his bed. She saw a warning in his dark eyes and knew immediately that should she ever do anything to hurt or upset Tyndall, she would have to answer to Ahmed. But she did not cower under his intense gaze. Instead she felt a rising knowledge of the power she had over Tyndall. She reciprocated Ahmed's challenging stare and then suddenly, laughing, she ripped the sarong from her body, and dressed in only a brief strip of cloth that wrapped around her buttocks, she pulled herself up onto the gunwale, and dived smoothly into the sea.

Tyndall was four to five fathoms below and he caught his breath at the shadow and movement at the edge of his peripheral vision, fearing a shark. But as he turned his head he saw, like a sea siren or mermaid, the near-naked shape of Niah, as she glided toward him, kicking her legs, her hair streaming behind her. He could see the laughter in her eyes and he reached out a clumsy gloved hand toward her bare breasts. She blew him a kiss and grasping the shell bag slid it up the manila rope line as she kicked toward the surface.

Two of the crew eagerly helped her back on board, lifting the half-filled bag onto the deck as they eyed the glistening figure of Niah.

"Is that all he has? Send the basket back down," said Ahmed, ignoring Niah.

Yoshi made no comment, remembering the first time he went into the world below and how sometimes, now, he regarded it as his real world. No one knew he sang and hummed as he worked, the pleasing sound reverberating in the metal helmet as he sang the folk songs of his childhood which his mother had taught him. It was a world that was familiar, and while he was ever alert to danger, he felt at peace in the sea, and despite the often intense cold, he enjoyed the work. The wildness of the other divers during lay up, the intrigues, the fights, the brothels and gambling, the fierce loyalty of the other Japanese "club" members, did not interest him. He had the reputation of being a loner and it was one of the reasons Tyndall and Ahmed chose him.

Now dressed and ignored by the crew as they went about their jobs, Niah hung over the side again watching Tyndall's air bubbles lazily pop to the surface in a steady stream.

For Tyndall it was all fascinating and he felt he'd been down for hours. His body and head ached and he had lost track of time. If it hadn't been for his boots planted firmly on the sea bed and a glimmer of light slanting through the water above, he would have easily felt disoriented and imagined himself drifting into a silvery aqua oblivion. He concentrated and focused on tiny objects and watched a small marine creature inch its way across a coral-encrusted rock.

It was Niah whose attention was diverted from the stream of bubbles breaking the surface to a distant movement on the water. It was fleeting, and for a while there was nothing more to be seen and she was about to look away when it came again, a brief spurt of water. She called out, "Whale!"

All heads shot up and they stared in the direction of her pointing arm. The seconds, a minute, ticked by in silence. Yoshi was standing, shading his eyes, Taki held Tyndall's line, poised to give three rapid tugs, the shell openers sat with motionless knives as they too scanned the sea. The two men on the pump were the only ones moving. Ahmed looked back at Niah with a raised eyebrow.

She was about to shrug and protest that she was sure she had seen the blow, when, so loud, so fast, so surprising they were all stunned, a massive whale breeched beside the lugger, slapping its giant flukes against the hull.

Niah screamed and the *Bulan* shivered with the impact of the brush from an old bull longer than the lugger. The crew sprang into action, Taki sending an urgent message to Tyndall they were bringing him up as Ahmed and the crew began to set the sails.

"Quick, bring back tuan, quick," cried Niah, tugging at Taki's arm as he methodically wrenched in the lifeline. Ahmed shouted at her in Malay to move back and she stood by wringing her hands. Once again the whale surfaced, regarding them with a small imperious eye and showing a hide encrusted with barnacles.

There was near panic on board as the whale scraped along the starboard side as the boat heeled well to port. The tender fell to the deck and momentarily lost control of the lifeline and air hose which were over the port side of the boat.

Tyndall, who had been unceremoniously jerked toward the surface, now dropped back to the sea bed, wondering what the hell was going on. Then, before he could make sense of the situation he was again jerked upward. He felt the pressure swell inside his head, and he gasped long sucking breaths of air, wondering what had happened. Then all movement stopped and he was left dangling like a puppet on a string. He tilted his head to stare upward.

As if looking through the wrong end of a telescope, the scene above him seemed unreal and he felt his heart squeezed with fear. The silhouette of the *Bulan* was dwarfed by a great black lolling shape just below the hull. Tyndall was astern the lugger and as his vision adjusted he saw the flukes of the great tail were directly between him and the lugger. He watched in helpless horror. The whale moved upward so its back was against the *Bulan.* Tyndall waited, terrified the whale would flip over the lugger.

On the deck everyone was again flung off balance as the *Bulan* rolled and shook while the whale started scratching the barnacles off its crusty hide.

The lugger began to move forward now that sails were going up but they couldn't get fully under way until the master was safely on board, and that was impossible now that the whale was between the boat and the diver. Taki took a turn around a bollard with the hose and lifeline. Yoshi and Ahmed conferred quickly and Ahmed shouted to Niah and the crew to get anything metal—wok, tools, anything—and to start making as much metallic noise as possible in the hope of scaring the whale away. Niah ran to the main cabin and grabbed Tyndall's rifle, checked it was loaded, then dashed back on deck.

"*Tidak,*" shouted Ahmed in alarm when he saw her. A wounded and enraged whale could destroy the boat in seconds. At that moment the boat heaved again, throwing Niah off balance. She dropped the rifle which went off, the bullet whizzing into the sea. The sharp crack of the bullet seemed to have an effect, for as suddenly as it appeared, the whale disappeared from sight. For a few seconds everyone stood there in a frozen tableau, incredulous at their luck. Then, with Niah screaming for them to hurry, and Ahmed shouting instructions, Tyndall was hauled toward the lugger.

Then, into the small gap of water between Tyndall and the hull roared the train-like bulk of the whale. It crashed against the side of the boat as it charged past and dived, its white speckled triangular flukes catching Tyndall's lines and ripping them like strands of hair.

Tyndall's body spun wildly and painfully in the surging wake as the whale tore the lifeline and air hose. He felt the helmet was going to be wrenched off his shoulders and his hands instinctively flew up and miraculously caught hold of the light line used for hauling baskets of shell to the surface. He felt himself choking as the air in his suit was pressured out of the broken hose. He had to use both hands to hold on to the rope for he would sink like a stone if he let go. Panic was almost instantly replaced by terror as he struggled without effect to haul himself up the line to the surface.

As soon as Taki gave the alarm Niah was over the side, struggling to disentangle her sarong. Yoshi and Taki flashed past her, strong strokes taking them to Tyndall within seconds. With one on either side of him and Tyndall hauling on the rope they suddenly broke the surface, and with Niah grabbing the remnant of air hose and holding it above water, were hauled to the ladder by the cheering and shouting crew.

Tyndall was nearly unconscious and too heavy for the rescuers to lift on board. They held him by the ladder while the chest weights were removed and the helmet unscrewed. The rush of fresh air revived Tyndall and he managed to stagger the few steps up the ladder before he was dragged over the side. He collapsed on the deck, bleeding from nose and ears, his skin gray-white. Niah crawled over the side and rushed to cradle his head in her lap as the men began to take him out of the boots and suit. Niah pulled off his gloves and rubbed his hands and, as Tyndall coughed and the color began to return to his cheeks, she kissed the shell pendant still around his neck.

Ahmed got the *Bulan* under sail, noting that several other luggers, having seen the whale attack, were also under way.

Tyndall had recovered by the next day and insisted they stay to finish the patch of shell. Yoshi agreed, but for the first time since he had begun diving, he was fearful as he went over the side, remembering the death of his father's fleet by a whale.

However, the rest of the trip was uneventful, and Tyndall found great joy in the arms and the happy laugh of Niah, who made no secret of her devotion and attachment to him.

One evening she sat cross-legged on the bunk, his head in her lap, massaging his scalp. She asked him, as all women were wont to do he thought, about the other women in his life. She wanted to know about Mem Hennessy and he tried to explain they were friends, business friends.

"Why you have no wife?" she asked, using a new word she'd learned.

Tyndall closed his eyes in pleasure as her strong fingers ran through his hair, soothing his head. "Um, I did once. In a far away place. Very cold. You wouldn't like it." He hadn't thought of Belfast in years. It was his past, of no relevance now.

"Where wife go?"

"Heaven I suppose. Spirit place. She died. Big sickness." He didn't want to talk any more and moved her hands down to rub the back of his neck.

"Mem Hennessy wife, too," said Niah after a while, causing Tyndall to look up at her, slightly puzzled.

"Yeah. That's right. She's a wife." He was prepared to let it rest at that.

Niah was silent for a while, quietly massaging.

"You like Mem Hennessy?"

Tyndall stiffened and grabbed her hands, looking up at her. "Good Lord, girl, what are you getting at? Like her? Well, she's a nice young woman. Why do you ask?"

"Mem Hennessy no like me. No like you get me."

"Rubbish."

"You see," said Niah sadly. "She send Niah away."

"Nonsense," said Tyndall and he pulled her

down and she lay on top of him, light as a sea breeze, her hair and skin smelling of salt. She licked his ear and nuzzled her face in his neck, clinging to him like a lovable puppy. Tyndall realized however that she saw Olivia as a threat, someone who might send her away. It began to dawn on Tyndall that this romantic interlude was coming to an end and that soon they would be returning to Broome and the prying eyes of a small community. Suddenly the thought of giving up this pretty and affectionate girl was an appalling idea. As he felt his passion rise under Niah's expert hands he decided to worry about what to do with her later.

The same thoughts had been on Ahmed's mind and one evening while he and Tyndall rowed back to the *Shamrock* he delicately raised the question of Niah's future.

Tyndall was vague. It troubled him that he'd become so attached to her. He hadn't realized how empty his life had been. How he had envied Olivia and Conrad their shared life and companionship. "Don't know. S'pose she could make herself useful round the place. She doesn't want to go back home, nowhere to go really."

"Being useful could cause plenty talk, tuan," said Ahmed gently.

"Hmmm," said Tyndall in half agreement.

"No good for business. No good for Mem and Tuan Hennessy. All people have their place in Broome. You break rules," sighed Ahmed.

Tyndall gave a weak smile. "I know what you

mean. But she's a nice little thing. Bright, you know. Easier to get along with than most of the women in Broome, I'll wager."

Nearing the *Shamrock,* he could make out the silhouette of Niah on the deck outlined against the starry sky. He was acutely aware of a pleasant and sudden surge of excitement that was just as suddenly neutralized by Olivia Hennessy striding into his consciousness. Yes, that was going to be difficult, he acknowledged to himself. Explaining away the relationship to Mrs. Hennessy. The old hands of Broome would accept it readily enough so long as both of them were fairly discreet in public. After all, everyone knew what went on in Sheba Lane some afternoons in the lay up season and after dark, but no one talked about it publicly. Ah, to hell with it. But try as he might, the prospect of facing Olivia Hennessy worried him. He suddenly realized that she was more than just a business partner. He didn't want to let her down, not just because they were in business together, but because she was Olivia. It was but momentarily disconcerting. The sight of Niah smiling down at him in the moonlight, her long hair ruffled by the light breeze, and the sensual memories of her body filled his mind with only one thought.

CHAPTER ELEVEN

The arrival of a steamer was always a highlight and families turned out to greet any arrival as it came to the jetty on the high tide. It was a social occasion, the white community paraded in best clothes, ladies in large hats and lacy parasols held the hems of their dresses out of the red dust and were escorted by husbands wearing smart tropical suits. Children leapt about, enthusiastically dashing along the wharf. Chinese and Malay amahs, Koepanger house boys or Japanese house staff watched over the young children or pushed babies in high-wheeled English prams.

The Resident Magistrate, with a party of special guests, were among the few invited by the captain to be entertained on board. Passengers took the opportunity when the tide was out and the steamer sat on the exposed mud, to indulge in the novelty of walking about and examining the underneath of the hull. They also chose to stroll about Broome, wrinkling noses at the smelly shell sheds and tantalizing cooking odors from the Chinese eating houses serving long soup, chop suey and fried rice. They might pass an Aboriginal road gang in chains, they might be approached to buy a pearl by a figure shadowed in a doorway or lane. On the edge of town they might glimpse Mohammed and Moosha Khan leading their strings of laden camels to supply the pastoralists and Kimberley goldfields.

It was a busy time for the crew of the steamer, who had their own business to conduct—snides bought, smuggled goods exchanged and packets passed on to be posted from a foreign port. The European pearl buyers swept ashore like royalty to be greeted by the master pearlers, while Japanese divers, a royal class of their own, sauntered through Chinatown. Notorious Sheba Lane was always busy, the gaming houses and brothels benefiting from the influx of visitors and cash.

About twenty luggers and several schooners sailed in on the same tide, jostling for room at the wharf or going straight up creeks to the foreshore camps.

They created a noisy, hectic and colorful scene as families were reunited and the crews busied themselves with unloading. There was a confusion of wheelbarrows, drays, rail wagons, bags of shell, bags of mail, luggage of the steamer passengers and cargo from the south.

Almost every idler in town had also turned out for the diversion the scene afforded. Through the throng strode Yoshi carrying his helmet like a badge of high office.

By the time Olivia and Conrad arrived on the wharf most of the cargo had been unloaded from the *Bulan*. On the *Shamrock*, Tyndall was starting to cast off to sail to the foreshore camp while the tide was high.

"There they are," cried Olivia, taking Conrad's hand and pulling him forward with excitement. "Captain Tyndall," she called.

Tyndall looked up from the mooring line he was easing off, threw a quick wave then secured the line with a couple of half hitches. "Good to see you," he shouted and went to the side to help Olivia on board. "G'day, Conrad. Hope you've been as productive as our trip has been," he quipped.

Olivia gave him no chance to reply. "Oh, it's great to see you all back, but you came in so early and you've worked so fast. Goodness, you must think we're dreadful partners!"

Tyndall grinned. "No. No. Understand the late arrival perfectly. The beauty sleep could not be disturbed by anything as gross as business at sunrise."

Olivia gave him a playful thump and Conrad forced a chuckle.

"Good trip, John?" he asked.

"Almost beyond belief in one respect. Had a run in with a whale," said Tyndall rather enigmatically. "But more about that later, perhaps over dinner tonight at the Conti. However, from a business point of view, Conrad, you'll be using more black than red ink as you tally up this lot."

Conrad smiled. "Great news, John. And I've got some good news too about expanding the business . . . diversifying."

"Where's Niah?" asked Olivia suddenly, with an edge in her voice.

"Ashore. Went home as soon as we berthed. No need for her to hang around here," explained Tyndall casually.

Olivia was aghast. "You let her go? You just let her walk off, just like that? After all the drama she's caused. Whatever for?"

Tyndall was a little uncomfortable at the outburst. "Easy now, she's a free person you know."

"How do we know she'll go home?" exploded Olivia. "Why did she run away anyhow?"

Tyndall pushed his cap back before replying a little awkwardly, "Well it seems she sorta felt she belonged to me. Stowed away in the sail locker. She wasn't a problem really, as it turned out." He tried to keep a straight face but a silly grin sneaked through and blew out into a big smile that told them everything. "She'll go home all right. To my place."

"Good Lord, man," gasped Conrad.

Olivia was speechless. Her eyes met Tyndall's. His sparkled with embarrassed humor. Hers burned with anger and dismay. She turned on her heels and scrambled ashore, Conrad following, shouting over his shoulder, "See you tonight. Conti at sunset. You certainly know how to make a day interesting."

Conrad went to the office, while Olivia, still

furious and a little confused about the situation, snapped open her umbrella for protection from the heat and strode rather than walked to Tyndall's house. Without knocking she marched into the house calling loudly as she went, "Niah, Niah."

She stopped at the door of the sitting room, taken aback by the sight of Niah asleep on the cane lounge with one of Tyndall's nautical caps over her face. Olivia shook her vigorously. "Wake up, Niah, wake up," she snapped.

The hat slid off. Her eyes opened sleepily. "Hello, mem." She languidly sat up while Olivia sat down stiffly in a chair.

"Well, Niah, what happened?" she demanded. "Why did you run away, and what is going on with Captain Tyndall?"

Niah hung her head. Olivia went on. "We're very angry with you, Niah. You caused us a lot of worry. If you were unhappy, why didn't you come and talk to us?"

Niah lifted her head and, pulling back her shoulders, a little in a gesture of resolution, looked at Olivia. "Captain Tyndall, me, make love. I live here now."

Olivia gripped the arms of the cane lounge and flushed with shock and anger.

"Sorry you and tuan worry, mem. I think mebbe you send me away."

There was a silence as Olivia tried to gather her thoughts. "It's impossible, Niah. Whatever went on at sea . . . no more." She waved her hand with a dramatic message of censure. "You cannot stay here."

The girl bent down and picked up the skipper's hat, fidgeted with it then smiled. "John say love Niah."

Olivia closed her eyes for a moment, stunned by the words and furious at Tyndall for seducing the girl. Then she stood up and spoke sharply. "Right. I'm going to sort this out with Tyndall. This simply cannot continue, Niah."

Instead of seeking him out Olivia went home and sat on the verandah until her anger had subsided and her head had cleared a little. Try as she might, she couldn't ignore the mix of emotions and thoughts swirling in her mind.

By the time Conrad arrived home and the day was cooling, so was Olivia. She raised the matter with her husband as they readied for dinner at the Continental. "It isn't going to be easy to stay civil with Tyndall over dinner, Conrad. He really has gone too far. Obviously he seduced the girl and she's smart enough to take advantage of the situation."

Conrad was sympathetic. "You're probably right, dear, but it's not going to be easy to sort out if he's really keen on her, and that seems to be the case. You know a lot of this sort of thing goes on up here."

"But you must agree, Conrad, it doesn't look good at all. From a business point of view."

Conrad was considering what his lodge members would think, not to mention the Hootens and the rest of the social snobs if it appeared he and Olivia were condoning the relationship.

"It's a tricky one, I agree. I suppose she could be hired as a maid and live with the servants."

Olivia thought this over and could see no other solution. "It could work provided Captain Tyndall doesn't parade her around town. You'll have to speak to him, Conrad."

Conrad sighed and decided on a dressing drink while they got ready. A stiff one. He didn't feel adequately prepared to deal with such sensitive issues that had never before come into his sphere of existence. He also knew he had no hope of changing Tyndall's mind once it was made up. And Olivia seemed unusually overwrought about the whole matter.

"All we can do is hope that we can make him see reason and respect our wishes and feelings," Conrad offered. He sighed again and called for the house boy to get him a gin and tonic.

The verandah of the hotel was crowded with pearlers and their wives along with Broome's varied social milieu. Toby Metta, resplendent in a formal dark suit, moved among the pearling masters in their high-collared white uniforms with shining buttons and spotless white shoes. A whispered message here and there assured him there'd be plenty of pearls coming his way. Mabel, his wife, wrapped in a bright, gold-trimmed sari, waved at Olivia.

Conrad steered Olivia toward the last available cane table and chairs and signaled to a waiter. "G and T and a lemonade." After settling Olivia, Conrad then sat beside her, reaching for the spicy, dried nuts and fruit in a small silver bowl on the table. "I must say, Olivia, you do look fetching. Quite put the crowd to shame."

"Thank you, Conrad. You look splendid, too."

Conrad had, to Olivia's initial surprise, ordered several sets of whites and wore the uniform of a pearling master with aplomb. He had thrown himself into life at the Cricket Club and while she had no idea what went on at the Freemasons weekly lodge gatherings, Conrad found it all very rewarding and "useful".

"Dear me, have you noticed the pearls some of the women are wearing. Bit of a parade to outdo each other, isn't it," smiled Olivia.

"Bit silly to give the profits to the wives instead of selling them, I would have thought," said Conrad pragmatically.

Olivia felt the pearl ring on her finger but didn't answer.

"Going to be a good evening, there's a magician of some sort performing at sunset in the garden I'm told."

"How exciting. Oh, there's Tyndall." Olivia trembled slightly, anger flooding through her as he nonchalantly approached. Half screened by the hanging baskets of ferns, Olivia watched Tyndall make his way across the lawn. He, too, wore his whites, but in typical fashion he seemed to add his own dash of style. While some of the more ostentatious men favored gold buttons—even real gold sovereigns when they'd had an especially big season—most men wore the silver buttons. Tyndall's uniform had mother-of-pearl buttons and from his ear lobe hung the magnificent pearl from a gold hoop. His collar was open, a gesture of studied informality. Olivia had been quite astonished when she'd first seen him on the beach near Cossack, but now she found this flamboyance rather appealing. He looked like he had just swung off the deck of a lugger, his hair curled around his ears and hadn't been flattened in place by a solar toupee like most other men. In contrast, Conrad was immaculately turned out, but looked as if he had just been taken, freshly ironed, from a cupboard.

Tyndall paused to greet a family, the daughters twittering and dimpling at him.

Conrad grinned as they watched. "He's a devil of a man with the ladies. I imagine he could have any woman in Broome, or anywhere for that matter. Yet, he doesn't take any of them seriously . . . and has chosen someone quite unsuitable."

"If word gets out about Niah, there'll be a few young ladies around town with their noses out of joint. Perhaps he should start to think about settling down and that would solve the problem," said Olivia.

"Why?" asked Conrad. "So he won't bring gossip about unsavory exploits down on the head of the Star of the Sea Pearl Company?" He lifted an eyebrow. "I haven't seen any young women with the same charms of Niah that would appeal to Tyndall," he hastily added.

Olivia didn't answer for Tyndall had seen them and was making his way along the verandah. He shook hands with Conrad and bowed to Olivia. Ordering another round of drinks he sank into a chair, stretching his long legs in front of him.

"So," he said.

"So?" repeated Olivia quizzically.

"All is calm on the high seas, I believe."

"What was this whale business?" asked Conrad, anxious to avoid the matter of Niah.

"Ah, bit of a close thing actually."

Tyndall recounted the episode in graphic detail. Conrad sipped his drink, not sure if Tyndall was exaggerating but he knew his story could be easily corroborated. Olivia was fascinated by the tale, but also aware of her churning emotions as she realized how close he had come to being killed.

Conrad shook his head. "I don't suppose you'll do that again."

"Dive? I'm sure I will," grinned Tyndall.

"You like living dangerously, obviously," said Olivia. And he gave her a penetrating look, wondering if she was referring to Niah.

There was an awkward pause and Conrad plunged in. "Now, about Niah. I do believe we have to discuss this."

"Do we have to do it here and now?" Tyndall affected to look slightly bored.

Gently Conrad covered the points he and Olivia had discussed. "I mean, old chap, we are partners and what each of us does affects the other and the company."

"Well, I certainly wouldn't want to cause you both any distress or embarrassment . . ."

"You should have thought of that earlier then," cut in Olivia.

Tyndall's eyes blazed as he turned to her. "Haven't you ever let your emotions get the better of you? Look, Niah is going to be around for the foreseeable future. I've set her up in my house."

The boldness and the bluntness of the announcement left Olivia speechless. Tyndall had no intention of even making an effort at some face-saving pretense.

"Look, I could pretend she was a servant or a cook, but no one in this town would be fooled by that." He looked challengingly at her, then went on. "I'm not going to be a hypocrite. Do you want me to invent some grand lie?"

Conrad stepped in before Olivia had composed her tumbling thoughts and emotions. "Look, John, let's not allow things to get out of hand. I understand your point of view, but you must realize that Olivia and I don't find it easy to accept, particularly so suddenly. If that's the way you intend to play it, then we will have to come to terms with that."

Olivia fussed with her glass, took a sip to give her a little more time to take control of her anger. "If that's how it's to be, then I will go along with it. However, I have to say that while I am very sympathetic toward Niah, I cannot accept her in my house as a guest."

Tyndall nodded in agreement. "Understood and accepted. I am sorry that it has caused some pain but let's hope time will heal today's wounds." He finished off his drink then leaned forward in a clear signal that the matter was closed and he was moving to a new item on the evening's agenda. "Now, some business matters."

Olivia looked out into the twilight gardens, withdrawing from the conversation as the men talked business. A sadness crept over her as she felt the beginning of a rift in her relationship with Tyndall. She blamed him entirely for the seduction of Niah and for spoiling a friendship which she now admitted had become very special to her.

After dinner the magician performed in the main dining room and was well received by the relaxed crowd. He juggled, ate fire and did sleight-of-hand tricks which had the crowd gasping. For his finale he drew out a pack of large tarot cards and picked on members of the audience to tell their fortunes. It was highly amusing and, in most cases, very accurate, though for some a bit close to the bone. The crowd applauded, gasped and tittered, unaware the visitor had done his homework round the shops, sheds and pubs gathering details of the lives of some of the town's personalities. For his last victim he pounced on Tyndall, who with mock reluctance allowed himself to be led to the small table and chair in the center of the room.

The performer dealt the cards then turned them face up, studied them for a moment and pronounced, "Luck and fortune are soon to come your way." This sent a murmur round the room and a few good-natured ripostes about what pearls he may have found last trip. But the magician's next remark brought the house down. "You are very lucky in love. I see four women in your life . . ." When the laughter had subsided the seer added softly, "Their love will come at a high price, but be assured their love will be special." The cards were shuffled quickly into the pack and Tyndall had the fleeting impression that the magician had been about to tell him something else and changed his mind.

Against a background of considerable laughter, cheering and ribald comments Tyndall sat down with the Hennessys and Olivia raised her eyebrows. "Four ladies in your life?"

"Well, I hope he's right about the riches," said Conrad quickly. He took Olivia's hand and helped her to her feet. "It's late, we'll be going now. I'll see you tomorrow at the camp."

Tyndall yawned. "I don't think so, old friend, I'm taking the day off. Staying home." He gave them a broad wink and a grin which Olivia ignored, bidding him a cool good night.

•　　•　　•

The following morning after Conrad had left for the foreshore camp, Olivia set out for Tyndall's house. She had spent a restless night and needed to talk to Tyndall and vent her feelings.

Tyndall's house sat on pillars, its peaked, sloping roof giving the rooms high ceilings. Split cane blinds were tied around the verandah that encircled the house. Drooping poinciana and frangipani trees scattered tangerine and cream blossoms on the dry grass by the front path. Olivia stood for a moment by the row of trees outside the fence, then closed the gate with a purposeful click and marched to the front door. She called out at the open door and eventually a plump Chinese man shuffled out, wiping his hands on a cloth and peering at her myopically. She asked to see the master and he turned and disappeared without a word.

She could hear Tyndall grilling the cook about just who was at the door and in exasperation he came down the hall demanding, "Who's there?"

"It's me, Captain Tyndall, I want to talk to you."

Tyndall arrived at the door looking surprised. He wore cotton trousers and only his undershirt. A towel was slung over one shoulder and his hair was damp. Apologizing for his appearance, he led her along the verandah to a comfortable chair and excused himself. He called for cold lemon drinks and returned a few minutes later buttoning his shirt.

"I suppose I know why you're here. So?"

"What is the situation, Captain Tyndall, and how are you going to resolve it?"

"Resolve what? I thought we had it all settled."

"Just what is the situation between you and Niah, exactly?"

"It's pretty straightforward, I guess. We're lovers. She's moving in here. I'll find something to keep her busy, she's a bright thing, learns fast."

"I'll bet," Olivia snapped. "Really, it's disgraceful. How could you? It's not fair to the girl, nor to Conrad and me. There is no future in this, I thought you were better than . . ." she struggled with the words, ". . . than those other womanizers who have secret native mistresses."

"Is that what's bothering you? Her color? You had no trouble accepting Aborigines as friends when they helped you."

"It's not just that. She's so young! She sees you as a means of staying here and being cared for." Olivia was getting angry at Tyndall's questioning and complacency.

An edge crept into Tyndall's voice. "What's wrong with that? In other cultures Niah would be married by now. I thought you were a bit more progressive in your thinking than this. You sound like the ladies at the Residence teas."

Olivia hesitated for a moment. She had developed an acceptance of the Aborigines which was considered unconventional. She had prided herself on these views and on being a bit of a rebel in local society. So why should she mind so much that Tyndall was also flaunting the rules of white society?

Before she could answer Tyndall went on with

rising anger, "Don't be a hypocrite, Olivia! You think it's all very well to hold those views so long as they don't impinge on your nice little home life. You're just jealous of a girl who is brown, has no education and is culturally different. I thought *you* were better than that!"

"Leave me out of this! It involves all of us! Especially the girl! She's a simple girl and you seduced her—not just physically but by offering her security and false promises. She doesn't understand and just what is to become of her?"

"Do you really care, Olivia? Or is it just appearances you care about?" he shouted.

"Of course I care! And I care about you, John! Moving her in with you is madness." Olivia, too, was shouting.

"You're jealous, Olivia. Pure and simple as that. Leave us be and let the future take care of itself. And you might look at your own feelings while you're about it and stop judging others by standards you only *think* you uphold."

"You might also question your own motives, John Tyndall," she retorted, getting to her feet and brushing past the bewildered Chinese cook who was holding a tray with a jug and glasses on it.

Olivia was hurt and angry and, as she hurried down the crushed shell path, Tyndall's voice, sounding slightly amused, called after her, "Well at least we're on first name terms at last!"

Olivia slammed the gate and, with her head high, stomped furiously along the street toward home. As she walked, her anger cooled, and the sun beating through the white linen parasol began to weary her. She tried to go over the entire conversation again but she couldn't get past the idea of Tyndall accusing her of being jealous. Why should she be jealous? She was a married woman, Tyndall could sleep with whomever he liked. Would she have been so upset if the girl in his bed was an attractive white girl? She realized she had to confront her prejudices. Was she annoyed because Tyndall had chosen a girl the rest of their friends and associates would regard as inferior and of little consequence? Or would she have been jealous of any girl Tyndall chose?

That evening Conrad was occupied with the periodicals and newspapers that had arrived from England, months after their publication. Olivia sat on the darkened verandah listening to the night noises in the garden, the warm breeze carrying the heady scent of frangipani flowers and the faint smell of the mangrove flats exposed by the tide, an odor of Broome that was now a familiar part of her surroundings. She regretted the flare up with Tyndall, but was glad she'd spoken up about something that had wrenched her feelings about so strangely. She decided to let things be and hope that Tyndall would handle matters discreetly or come to his senses. She would maintain a cordial relationship for the sake of the business, but there was no denying that her friendship with Tyndall was strained by Niah's presence. She would go on with dignity for she had nothing to be ashamed about.

And in her head she heard Tyndall's steady voice, "And neither have I."

At the same time Tyndall sat in the shadows on his verandah sipping a nightcap, deep in thought. Niah padded quietly to him and sat by his feet, leaning her head against his knee. Absently he smoothed her hair. The day had been a draining one. He was saddened at the conflict between himself and Olivia. Only now that their friendship was threatened did he realize how much he valued it as distinct from the business partnership. He found himself wanting her approval, a feeling he had difficulty accommodating. Nonetheless he couldn't help contrasting her frosty eyes and formal manner with the windswept vision of her on the *Bulan* in those mad pajamas, learning to laugh again. Niah's hands began to softly stroke his thighs and he became conscious of how she filled a hole in his life, and his thoughts of Olivia soon faded.

Slowly and subtly, the relationship between Olivia and Tyndall changed over the next three years. The business partnership strengthened as mutual regard for their abilities was recognized and while the bond of friendship was still there, their former closeness had faded. Once or twice they would exchange a swift smile as something caused them both to react simultaneously. But when they made meaningful eye contact, a veil would drop swiftly over Olivia's eyes and she'd turn away.

Tyndall learned where the invisible barriers were and never overstepped them. He minded his manners and rarely teased her as he'd done before.

In turn, Olivia was less judgmental and kept her criticisms to herself when she wished she could air them frankly and argue with him as she would have done before. She also missed his bantering, an art Conrad had never mastered. But they continued their use of first names, a surprising legacy of their argument over Niah.

Conrad was pleased at the stability of the relationship between them all, unaware of the undercurrent of restraint between Tyndall and Olivia. The birth of their son Hamish two years earlier had been a time of great joy and created a diversion in their lives. Conrad had been somewhat surprised at Olivia's continuing interest and involvement with Star of the Sea, despite the claims on her time and attention by the baby. However, he realized that Olivia was deeply committed to their pearling enterprise and, as they had staff to help out, he saw no reason why Olivia shouldn't continue to be active in the company.

Olivia took her small son Hamish by the hand and led him along the track to the old jetty. The toddler jumped up and down excitedly as he saw the luggers lined up, all making ready to sail on the tide. Dropping Olivia's hand, he scampered along the wooden jetty on chubby legs making for the *Bulan*. Spotting Ahmed, he waved and called, "A'med, Hamish come, me come!"

The Malay grinned in delight. He and the child had established a special bond, and he reached up and swung him down onto the deck.

Olivia smiled as she watched the two of them. Ahmed was a patient teacher with the child, slowly tying and untying knots, letting him turn the wheels of the pump, and teaching him Malay words and phrases.

"All set, Ahmed?" she asked in Malay.

"Yes, mem. All ready to go," he replied, pleased with her easy use of his language.

"How's the new lugger?"

"*Bagus*. Yoshi is taking the new lugger, the *Annabella*, I'll stay on *Bulan*, tuan will bring *Shamrock* for the mother ship. Reckon this one will be a good trip. I feel lucky."

"I hope so, Ahmed. Good luck." She lapsed back into English. "Hand that monkey back so we can say goodbye to Yoshi."

Ahmed picked up Hamish, who flung his arms about the Malay's neck and squeezed tight, then was lifted onto the jetty. Olivia walked a little further along to where the *Annabella* was tied up. Yoshi, his tender Taki and the second mate were standing on the jetty, Yoshi holding his precious copper helmet. He reacted in mock alarm as Hamish pounced, demanding he wear the helmet.

"Too big, too heavy, little man," admonished the diver. "When big fella you wear the helmet."

Olivia chatted briefly with the crew and wished them well. This was the first time a lugger was going out without either Ahmed or Tyndall on board to oversee operations. Yoshi had proved himself to be trustworthy and honest and while many divers secreted a pearl or two away from the owners to sell as a snide, Tyndall and the Hennessys had agreed to let Yoshi master a lugger this trip. Yoshi bowed respectfully to Olivia, who acknowledged the courtesy with a bob of her head and wished him well. Finally she and Hamish approached the *Shamrock* and called out to Tyndall, who appeared on the deck.

"Ho!" squealed Hamish as he saw him.

"Ho yourself, Hamish." Tyndall sprang onto the wharf and picked him up.

The boy carefully touched the pearl at his ear. "Pretty."

"We'll bring back lots more pretties I hope, eh Olivia?"

"Ahmed says he feels lucky. Are you staying out on the grounds the whole time? Be difficult for Niah, won't it?"

Niah was due to give birth in a few months. Tyndall had broken the news to them casually, but with great pride and genuine delight.

"I'll go south again and take supplies and water out to the fleet as needed."

"If you see my Aboriginal friends, tell them we are well."

"I will."

They paused for a moment having run out of niceties and exchanged a glance.

Niah appeared on deck and waved to Hamish.

"Good luck, Niah. Look after yourself," said Olivia. While Niah had not been invited into the Hennessys' house as an equal, they had established a friendship of sorts. Niah had made herself useful at the foreshore camp while Olivia had taught her many things and in return Niah had helped her become fluent in Malay.

Olivia glanced at Niah who was wearing a long loose shift like those worn by the women of the South Seas. But there was no hiding the bulge of the child she carried with grace and ease.

"I hope that baby doesn't come early," said Olivia with genuine concern.

"I be fine, mem."

"We'll manage if it does," said Tyndall. "You did," he added softly, then regretted the remark in case it brought back past hurts. But since the birth of Hamish, Olivia had come to terms with the loss of her first son. It crossed her mind now that it would be nice to be sailing south on the *Shamrock* with Hamish. One day she'd take him to where his brother had been born and tell him the story.

As Olivia turned to leave, she added, "Conrad sends his best wishes. Good luck."

Tyndall watched Olivia and her son walk back

along the wharf with feelings he didn't understand. When he turned back to Niah she gave him a soft smile. "I give you a son too, Tyndall. You see."

"Not till we're back safe in Broome, I hope!" he laughed.

A few weeks later, while at sea, Niah and Tyndall lay in the night coolness on the deck of the *Shamrock*. The moon was full and hung plump and mellow, shining across the water. But instead of the unbroken path of light, the annual phenomenon known as the "steps of the moon" was taking place. This occurred when some unseen atmospheric disturbance broke the silvery gold light into a ladder of steps leading across the sea and wound up to the moon itself.

"We go walk about up there," said Niah, pointing to the moon.

"You'd never get up there. Too fat," laughed Tyndall, rubbing her belly. She snuggled into him and he put his arm around her. Feeling the shell pendant between her breasts, he idly asked, "Tell me about this."

"It's my people sign. Very old. First girl gets to wear."

"Not the men, huh? And what does it mean?"

"My mother mother come from here. Marry to Macassar man. Leave Australia, go far away."

Tyndall was stunned by her casual revelation of her grandmother's Aboriginal ancestry. "Niah, do you know which Aboriginal tribe this came from?" he asked, touching the shell pendant.

She shook her head and looked wistful and Tyndall realized she was missing her family, especially with the birth so close. "They must have been coastal people." He said no more and they lay there looking at the steps of the moon shimmering on the water. Tyndall felt very contented, this simple girl made him happy, and the arrival of the child would make it complete. Such musings came as a surprise to him for he was disconcerted to realize that he too now wished for the security of companionship like Conrad and Olivia. Now it seemed to him having a child meant he would leave some footprint upon this place. Maybe it was one of the reasons why he'd lived so recklessly—he had no one but himself to think about. He leaned down and kissed her cheek and Niah smiled up at him.

Seeing his pearl earring catch the moonlight, she touched it. "What this one mean?"

"I won it in a card game and I thought it so beautiful I decided to find lots more."

"This one tear of the moon," said Niah softly as she touched the pearl that perfectly matched the color of the moon above. "My mother say these ones—pearls—when the goddess of the moon weeps, tears fall into sea and make pearls."

"That's beautiful, Niah . . . tears of the moon. I like that."

Niah stretched sleepily. "Baby and me go to sleep now."

• • •

The *Shamrock* moored in the cove near where the ill-fated *Lady Charlotte* had been shipwrecked and where Tyndall had first met Olivia. Today the weather and sea were kind, so Niah and Tyndall waded ashore from the dinghy to picnic for a few hours.

He took her across the dunes and along the sandy scrub track to the low line of trees and a small spring-fed creek. They'd brought food and Tyndall settled himself in the shade with his journal. Leaving him to his jottings, Niah set off to explore the area.

Within a short time she noticed tracks and when she eventually came across a mound of discarded oyster shells and shellfish, she knew this was a regular camping site. Like Olivia before her, Niah sat down in the shade near the midden and felt a great peace and sense of security steal over her. She closed her eyes and rested, almost falling asleep, but was awakened by a group of Aboriginal women calling out to her.

Niah had not expected to understand them but, astonishingly, some words and phrases were familiar, greetings taught to her by her Aboriginal grandmother. She repeated them with curiosity and immense excitement. Her mind was whirling as memories and questions flooded her thoughts. The women gathered around and asked about Tyndall, having recognized his schooner. Niah smiled and pointed down the track then, with a widening grin, she pointed to her swollen belly and said, "Tyndall baby."

This brought gales of delighted laughter and as they were about to move away to find him the oldest woman gesticulated and began talking rapidly and seriously. The other women gathered about her. Niah was unable to follow the conversation, but then the old woman pointed at her shell pendant and began asking questions.

Niah trembled as it dawned on her she had a connection with these people. But she couldn't understand their language or few words of English so, with signs, she indicated they all walk downstream to meet Tyndall.

After the formalities of greeting, Niah quickly told Tyndall of their interest in her pendant and her recognition of some of their language. They sat in a big circle under the trees and with his knowledge of the language they slowly established the story of the woman who went to live on the other side of the monsoon winds. An old woman sat down and, with a stick, began to draw in the sandy dirt. She drew the pattern depicted on the pendant, explaining the strokes meant trips across the sea, the big circle meant the moon and the small circles were . . . and here they stumbled on the unknown word until the old woman, with a big grin, pointed at the pearl hanging from Tyndall's ear.

The women clapped their hands then led Niah and Tyndall further down the track and back onto the beach. Here they showed Niah the remains of stone fireplaces built by the Macassans for boiling the trepang.

Niah sat awkwardly on the sand and ran her hands over the old stones, trying to conjure the scene of generations before. Tyndall watched her, realizing how meaningful this was for her. Her childlike excitement had been replaced by a deeper sense of awareness that she had discovered a new link with her family's past.

"I know story of my family. Now I know my family. Now I have story to tell baby."

"It's incredible. Quite amazing really. But then life is full of such surprises," he said. The longing and the joy in her face touched him deeply. "Now you have a Dreaming."

Word was sent back to the rest of the Aboriginal group and by the evening they had all gathered on the beach with Niah and Tyndall around a big campfire. There was much discussion among the elders and it was agreed that a celebration was in order. A corroboree would take place the following night.

It was a homecoming corroboree, the women explained to Niah, holding her hands, and Niah felt tears of joy running down her cheeks. She had found part of her family.

The fires were burning brightly as twilight faded to a soft night. The members of the community not performing sat with Tyndall and Niah in a half circle talking, laughing and playing with children.

Then suddenly, without introduction, to the beat of music sticks and chanting, some men came out of the darkness and began the dance. Some of the ceremonial white clay designs painted on their bodies were the same as the pattern on her pendant. Their dance depicted seafarers from Macassar guiding their *praus* across the sea. Others, playing their own ancestors, welcomed them ashore. Then, in superb pantomime, they mimed the diving for shell, and the cooking of the trepang. The stirring of the pots which gave off a foul odor drew a laugh from the audience. Then a woman was singled out and taken away by the visitors in their boat. There were accompanying wails of sadness as she bid good-bye to her family. But then she returned with a baby and there was much celebration until it was time to go again. The long song of the elders told of the unity of family, of how the spirits of the sea and the great ocean birds carried their messages from land to land and kept them all as one. Tyndall grasped the message, even though he didn't understand all the words, that physical separation could never break the ties that link a family through generations. He saw the tears glistening on Niah's cheeks as the dance ended. She, too, understood this concept of unity and belonging and he was glad for her.

After six weeks at sea the *Shamrock* slid quietly into Broome ahead of the fleet. Niah was close to term and Tyndall had decided to come back to port.

Two nights later, in the early hours of the

morning, Olivia was awakened by Ahmed banging on the front door.

"Mem, Niah baby come. No can find midwife. Tuan says come quick."

Olivia dressed quickly, asked Conrad to look after Hamish, and then drove in the sulky with Ahmed back to Tyndall's bungalow. As Ahmed left her to continue his search for the midwife Olivia told him, "There's an Aboriginal woman down by Kennedy's camp. I've heard she helps at births, see if you can find her."

A concerned Tyndall paced around the bedroom with a glass of rum while Niah moaned on the bed.

"John, you're not being any help. Please go and wait on the verandah," said Olivia firmly.

"Whatever you say," he agreed, glad to escape.

Niah began walking awkwardly about the room, finding it more comfortable. When Olivia tried to get her back onto the bed she refused and then insisted on squatting, rocking to and fro.

Then the midwife, Minnie, arrived, explaining simply, "Ahmed get me."

Olivia nodded, grateful for the strength and calmness of the Aboriginal woman.

Minnie bent over Niah and murmured a few words. Niah reached up to take her hand, responding in the same language, and smiled briefly.

A few minutes later the baby began to push its way into the world. Niah insisted on squatting and the Aboriginal woman nodded in agreement.

"Well, if she wants to have it this way, we can't

argue now," said Olivia. Minnie moved behind Niah and held her against her ample chest. Panting with exertion, the crouching Niah pushed and delivered her baby into Olivia's steady hands.

Olivia cut the cord and lifted up the baby, while Minnie pressed out the placenta and helped Niah back onto the bed. Olivia then cleaned the baby, wrapped it in a cotton shawl and bent down to show Niah. She nodded with satisfaction, smiled and leaned back on the pillow, closing her eyes to rest after the effort.

Cradling the baby in her arms, Olivia went to the verandah where Tyndall was pacing in the shadows.

"John, it's all over. Everything is fine."

He turned to Olivia, who was standing in the lit doorway holding the baby.

"Boy or girl?" he asked in a whisper as he moved quickly toward her.

"You have a beautiful daughter." Olivia placed the tiny bundle in Tyndall's arms, pulling down the shawl so he could better see the child.

"Oh, Olivia," he breathed. "She's a gem."

Olivia felt her throat constrict. "Go to Niah, John."

Tyndall, eyes still glued to the infant he held, walked indoors without another word. Olivia watched him disappear into the house, quietly gathered up her bag and light shawl and slipped through the darkened garden and out the gate, her footsteps muffled on the dusty road.

CHAPTER TWELVE

"Tyndall is a changed man," announced Conrad with a mixture of amusement and mild astonishment. "He's besotted with that baby. Whoever would have guessed?"

Olivia watched Tyndall cradle the baby in his arms, talk to her, and make delighted nonsense noises. She was surprised to feel a twinge of envy. But there were other feelings too, feelings she could not identify let alone explain. She felt a strong attachment to the exquisite little girl she'd helped bring into the world. And since the baby's birth, Tyndall's unabashed joy, his conversation sprinkled with anecdotes of her day-to-day progress and serious queries over baby-rearing matters—despite Niah and the amah's capabilities—had given Tyndall and Olivia a common ground that had drawn them closer together again. Olivia's acceptance of Niah and her assistance at the birth had helped heal the rift between them. Olivia couldn't help comparing the paternal roles of Conrad and Tyndall. Conrad was a devoted but conservative father, who held the philosophy that a baby was the responsibility of the mother and his role as guiding hand came later in life. Olivia noticed Conrad shake his head with a bemused expression as he watched Tyndall sitting cross-legged on the floor with the baby in his lap singing bawdy sea shanties. He tapped his head indicating to Ahmed that the tuan was going "soft." But Ahmed was just as delighted with the child and chuckled at her small gestures and also got down on the floor to play with the baby. After Niah had fed the baby in the early evening, Tyndall frequently took the baby to Conrad and Olivia's. She would sleep contentedly in his lap while the adults shared a sundowner.

Little Hamish stood beside Tyndall watching the new baby with great fascination, sometimes reaching out to touch the small fist and grinning in delight when little fingers curled around his own. He beamed at his mother and stood without moving, afraid of disturbing the baby, but Tyndall scooped the boy up and made room beside him in the chair so he could be close to the beautiful olive-skinned baby girl. Tyndall's show of affection further endeared him to Olivia.

At the Freemasons, Conrad had become very conscious of the raised eyebrows in reaction to Tyndall's domestic arrangements.

Major Ralph White, ex-British Army, old India hand and pastoralist who "dabbled" in pearling, had taken a shine to Conrad. "You picked an odd bod there to throw your lot in with," he declared, his waxed moustache unmoving as he waggled his head in mock dismay. "Decent enough chap, I suppose. Understand he helped out you and your good wife during difficult times, but I must say, Conrad, this baby business is not good form."

"Rather unusual to parade about with it, I agree. But then, Tyndall has always been a non-conformist I suspect," sighed Conrad.

"He's not the first and won't be the last to keep a woman on the side, white or black velvet, but it's rather throwing it in the face of everyone. Especially you and your wife. Very difficult. The women don't like it. Rattles them when one of their own kind lets the side down."

He spoke kindly but Conrad knew there'd probably been a lot of discussion about it and the major had been nominated to talk to him.

Conrad felt a faint flush around his collar at the major's words but replied with some spirit. "Tyndall is my partner and I respect him for his honesty and professionalism, but it *is* his personal business and, frankly, all the talking in the world is not going to change that man. He tends to live by his own rules. However, I will of course point out to him—once again—the inappropriateness of his behavior." Conrad hoped he sounded more positive than he felt, for he knew Tyndall would do just what he liked. He'd have another word with him and maybe Olivia could ask him to be more discreet.

The major changed the subject and talked about his latest cattle venture which was proving very lucrative. "Might even consider going into wool, old boy. Mind you, it's not a piece of cake. Blacks spear animals, damned weather is harsh, staff unreliable, but overall I seem to have a few runs on the board. Speaking of which," he slapped his thigh, "when are we going to arrange another cricket match? You're an excellent bat, splendid addition to the team."

They called for another round and chewed over the highlights of the last club game, when Conrad had enjoyed a moment of glory after hitting several boundaries to give his side victory.

Excesses of weather dictated life in the north-west and this lay up season was proving particularly trying. The humidity drenched the body and numbed the mind, tempers were short-fused and explosive, minor matters became major issues. Small conflicts at sea became magnified into huge injustices in the simmering boredom of life ashore.

Among the Asian community, in particular, there was a lot of tension. Ahmed conveyed this to Tyndall who warned the Hennessys and Niah to steer clear of the Sheba Lane area.

Sheba Lane, also known as Chinatown, Jap town, or the colored quarter, was a collection of narrow alleyways that webbed from the original sand dunes where the enterprising Kamematsu

Shiba had erected the first boarding house for the Japanese. Shanty dwellings, food shops, sheds housing brothels and gambling dens crowded haphazardly together, creating a village of its own within the town.

The alleyways offered escape routes into or away from the various sections of the town, and a man could disappear into shadowy doorways, rickety upper floors, or back rooms at the flash of a knife.

Sheba Lane also accommodated other races and on the whole everyone rubbed along together with the general understanding that it was "them" against the white bosses, the police, the law, and the belligerent members of the Yakuza, linked to powerful secret society leaders back in Japan.

The monsoon was late and for guests at the Resident's garden party, there seemed no promise of relief from the oppressive heat and humidity. Storm clouds gathered, then slipped across the placid waters of the bay and got lost in the desert. The relatively new Australian flag hung limply on its flagpole alongside the Western Australian flag and the Union Jack. The RM liked the way the flags conveyed authority and elevated his position beyond its real status.

Olivia closed her fan and, excusing herself from the group of ladies on the terrace, walked across the lawn to where Conrad was sitting with the RM and Mrs. Hooten, and Major White and Mrs. White.

Of all the wives, Olivia found Amelia White the easiest to deal with because she made no demands on anyone. She drifted, in a haze of gin and lavender, smiling benignly at the world through slightly unfocused pale blue eyes. She was the antithesis of her blustering, loud, hearty, domineering husband and was thankful that while he was around she didn't have to make much of an effort.

Olivia was glad the major had become a friend to Conrad. His cocksure attitude irritated her, but his fatherly advice seemed to mean a great deal to Conrad, who felt the friendship gave him extra standing in the small world in which they moved.

Talk turned, as it had with every group at the party, to the great fight that had erupted that morning between a group of Japanese and some Koepangers. No one was clear as to the cause. There was some perceived insult, shouted words, then the Japanese had chased the Koepangers along the foreshore.

Later in the day each side had gathered support and there had been several clashes resulting in some nasty injuries. Two police officers had intervened and for the last two hours all had been quiet.

Mrs. Hooten gathered the guests around the outdoor buffet table where a large birthday cake was set up for the Resident's birthday. After toasts and several speeches, the Resident blew out the candles and, taking his ceremonial sword, was about to cut the cake, when there was a mighty outburst at the gates of the Residence. The stunned partygoers turned as one to confront a shouting horde of Japanese brandishing sticks, knives and stones.

"What the devil is going on?" demanded the Resident as the women cried out in alarm and retreated toward the house.

"Close the gates," called Major White and two men rushed to the wrought iron gates across the drive.

The demonstrators continued to rattle the fence and shout and someone quickly translated, "The Koepangers have killed a Jap!"

"Good Lord, now we're in for some trouble," said Conrad with concern as Olivia stood close to him, nervously watching the angry men demanding justice.

"Order them away, Ralph," demanded Mrs. Hooten, still holding the cake plates. "They'll ruin the party."

A stone lobbed over the fence and another heated cry went up.

"Get the women indoors, Hennessy" shouted the RM. "Major, run for the police. We'd better get to the bottom of this in a hurry. Could turn very nasty." He turned to an aide. "Get the men organized on the verandah, Jones."

Soon a worried policeman arrived carrying a shotgun. "Sir, seems the Japanese hounded the Koepangers and they were going in all directions and one of the Jap divers ran the wrong way straight into the gang of Koepangers. Beat him to death. The Japs are demanding you round up the Koepangers and have them surrender the culprits."

"Thanks, constable. First thing is to disperse this mob."

"They're not going to listen to reason, sir. They're very stirred up."

"Righto then." Mr. Hooten issued instructions and action was swiftly organized. Within minutes, assisted by the major, he had all of the men assembled behind him. "Right men . . . *Charge!*" The RM raised the ceremonial cake-cutting sword and dashed forward. Behind him came a ragged line of Broome's elite, armed with umbrellas, walking sticks, garden rakes and brooms.

They raced across the lawn and the Japanese were momentarily frozen as the birthday guests reached the fence and banged their brooms and brollies against the railings, the occasional implement poking through to prod a startled protester.

The Japanese suddenly turned and headed toward the Japanese Club and Sheba Lane.

The men returned in triumph, calling for drinks. "It's going to be a difficult night," predicted the RM.

Fighting broke out through the night, with bands of Japanese storming houses, shops, dens and foreshore camps to hunt down Koepangers. They'd given up looking for the guilty—now all Koepangers were in danger. They hid, and many ran into the pindan, hoping no Japanese would venture into the bush at night and that things would be under control by morning.

The extent of the trouble was considered too great for the police and men deemed to be responsible citizens were sworn in as special constables, Conrad and Major White among them.

The next day, as the fights continued, the RM, flanked by Sergeant O'Leary and the special constables, read the Riot Act in front of the Buccaneer Arms Hotel. He announced to a small crowd of citizens that a curfew was being imposed and that arrests would be made if anyone broke the curfew or engaged in unlawful assembly. If the races involved did not cool down swiftly, Japanese and Koepanger rabble-rousers would be held in segregated detention in pearl sheds.

"Throw 'em in together, that'll fix the problem," suggested someone in the crowd.

But despite the RM's pronouncement, no home or building was safe. Stones were hurled at verandahs and there were more reports of sheds, shops and offices being broken into.

With dusk settling over the town and brawls still breaking out, Conrad strapped on his revolver to patrol the streets along with other special constables.

Olivia looked concerned. "Please, be careful Conrad."

"Of course. But we have to show the flag or else they'll think they can take over the town any time they want. These chaps are only after each other, I'll be perfectly all right," he answered more confidently than he really felt. "Tell Minnie to keep indoors and tell Hamish I'll read him a story if he's still awake when I get back."

Olivia gave him a warm embrace and, calling Minnie, who was now their housekeeper, she latched the house as Conrad strode down the street.

First he called on Tyndall who told him he was going to sleep in the Star of the Sea offices.

"I thought I'd check on Toby Metta while I'm patrolling," said Conrad. "I imagine he's staying on the premises, too, seeing as he has pearls there."

"Good idea, Conrad. He's got our five best pearls there to work on. Take care."

"Right. You too, John."

From the shadows beside the house, Ahmed watched Conrad set out on patrol.

The town seemed relatively quiet. The curfew was keeping people indoors although, as Conrad passed one of the lanes leading into Chinatown, he could hear shouts and thumpings on doors. The strange smells that hung around the lanes, mostly a combination of sickly sweet incense and spices, caused Conrad to wrinkle his nose. A shadowy figure slid along the lane and dashed into a doorway next to the Star Hotel. The door opened just wide enough to let the man through and

Conrad glimpsed the bright colors of a kimono in the lamplight before the door was swiftly shut.

Disgusting, he thought, the way the Jap women are used. God knows what they were promised to get them here.

Conrad was ignorant of geisha houses and of the fact that most of the women chose to come here to pursue their profession in the hope of accumulating wealth to take home. They were an essential part of Broome's Japanese community and the money that came from some of the courtesans secretly funded many successful business enterprises. But there were others—poor illiterate daughters of farmers and laborers—who were procured for brothels.

Conrad reached the pearl cleaner's shop without incident. The door was bolted, the shutters pulled across the window, but he could see a faint light within. He rattled on the door. "Toby, it's me, Conrad. You all right in there?"

There was no response for a moment, then Conrad heard something heavy being dragged from behind the door.

"Conrad, my friend," came the hoarse whisper of Tobias Metta.

"Just checking on you, we thought you'd be staying here."

The door opened and Toby's plump arm dragged Conrad inside, slamming it quickly behind him. "You are a brave man to walk the streets alone. Brave and maybe foolish. But it is good to see you. A cup of tea?"

Conrad looked around, noting the revolver lying on Toby's work bench. "Not taking any chances, I see. Yes, a cuppa would be nice."

"I have many valuable pearls here, including yours, of course. I feel it is my responsibility to look after them. I heard some Chinese are selling gelignite. Never miss a business opportunity."

"Gelignite. Good lord, what for?"

"It would put a hole in that for a start," said Toby, pointing to his lead safe in the corner.

They drank their tea in the dim room lit by a small oil lamp. The idea of a break-in worried Conrad.

"So, have you had a chance to work on our pearls?" he asked, lowering his voice unnecessarily.

Toby kissed his fingertips. "Several are superb. They're finished, came up magnificently. Let me show you." Before Conrad could protest, he was unlocking the safe. The pearl cleaner took out a small black velvet bag and slammed the safe door shut again. "Here, Conrad, under the light." He adjusted the lamp on the desk, shook the pearls in the palm of his chubby hand and held them closer to the light. The fat round pearls glowed and Conrad beamed.

"They certainly are magnificent," he enthused, "Olivia will get us a good price for these from Monsieur Barat. I can't wait to show them to her. Could I take them now?"

"Is that wise?" said Toby, tipping them back into the little cloth bag.

"I'm armed and no one would think I'd be

carrying pearls. It will distract and please Olivia, I'm sure. She has been quite put out by all this turmoil. Settling down a bit now the RM has got tough."

"Well, if you insist." Toby handed the pearls to Conrad who slipped them in his pocket.

"You'll be all right on your own?" asked Conrad.

"I have a stout stick here as well as the gun. I feel safe, the troublemakers are after the blood of the Koepangers. It will blow over. Mabel thought it wise I camp here for the night."

"I'll head straight back then, Toby. Done my bit to show the flag in the streets."

"Go safely, good friend. And good night." With this he ushered Conrad out, bolting the door and ramming the heavy oak chair against it once more.

Conrad stepped briskly along the wooden footpath, his footsteps ringing in the quiet night. He stepped down on to the dusty road of Dampier Terrace, his footsteps now muffled. For a moment he thought he heard footsteps behind him, and stopped, but all was quiet. A block further on he crossed the street and skirted a lane way. Banks of clouds had rolled in and obscured the moon. Distant flashes of lightning streaked across them, followed by rumbles of thunder.

Conrad was about to turn the corner and head toward home, when a shadow moved between two buildings. Pausing, with his hand on his pistol, Conrad saw nothing and moved on. He had only taken a few steps when he was grabbed from behind and pressed into the doorway of the Chinese laundry. An arm was around his throat stopping him from calling out, and as his hands reached up to drag away the constricting arm, he felt a sharp sensation burn in his chest and in the second before everything went dark he read, quite clearly, the sign across the street—KIMBERLEY EMPORIUM, ALL NEEDS MET.

His assailant let the body drop to the ground and was quickly searching the pockets when he heard shouts and pounding feet close by. The Koepanger urgently stuffed the pistol in his belt, the little velvet bag into his pocket and was about to run when the *kris* slit his throat. Ahmed sheathed his *kris,* retrieved the pearls and was still crouching over the body when about a dozen Japanese came around the corner shouting and waving sticks. Ahmed pulled Conrad's pistol from the body of the Koepanger and, still crouching, fired two quick shots over the heads of the Japanese. They stopped in their tracks. Ahmed leapt over the two bodies and dived down a lane way as Major White and a group of armed special constables came charging down the street.

The Japanese fled and, within seconds, Major White was beside the bodies. He ignored the Asian and rolled over the European.

"Good Lord, it's Conrad Hennessy," he gasped.

•   •   •

Despite the curfew, the news of Conrad's murder spread swiftly. Tyndall was quickly on the scene. Stunned by confirmation of the death of his friend and partner, he went to Toby Metta, who told him of Conrad's visit. The pearl cleaner wrung his hands, tears running unchecked down his plump dark face.

"I told him, warned him, he was foolish to be out in the streets, especially carrying pearls. But he wanted to do his duty. He was such a good man . . . a good man."

Tyndall touched Toby's arm, unable to speak, nodded in support and understanding, and left to return to the scene of the murder.

Conrad's body was carried away and the major, the RM and the police chief turned to Tyndall. The four white men stood in the shadowy street while police and a small crowd, ignoring the curfew, stood in the background softly discussing the gruesome details.

The Resident Magistrate took Tyndall by the arm. "Captain Tyndall, I know it is difficult, but frankly we think it best you break the news to Mrs. Hennessy. Naturally if you would rather—"

"No!" said Tyndall instantly. "I'll tell her. No one else."

"Mrs. Hooten and the ladies will call later in the morning."

Tyndall shook his head. "I'll let you know when I think it appropriate for all of that. Leave matters to me . . . for the moment." Tyndall was firm and protective but there was something else in his manner that stilled the others from rushing in with offers of assistance and advice. "Please ask the doctor to send sedatives to the house."

Refusing the offer of transport, Tyndall walked slowly through the darkened streets toward the Hennessys' bungalow, trying to frame the words to tell Olivia she was a widow.

When he reached their garden gate, he opened it as quietly as possible. Approaching the house he saw a figure rise from the verandah to confront him.

"Olivia?"

"No, is Minnie, boss. I bin waiting."

Tyndall tried to make out the expression on the woman's face. "You know don't you?"

"Yes. I go get her."

He stood in the darkness, staring up at the scudding clouds and the sheets of lightning illuminating the great expanse of sky.

Olivia appeared, a wrapper clutched around her shoulders. She spoke quietly. "How bad is it, John? Where is he?"

"It's bad, Olivia."

"I want to know, John. What has happened to Conrad?" Her voice rose.

"He's dead, Olivia. Killed on the street. It was quick. I doubt he knew anything . . . Oh, Olivia . . ." He stretched out a hand toward her.

A choking wail was stifled as she clutched the verandah post, hiding her face in her arms. Tyndall reached her as she lost her grip and slid to the floor. Gathering her in his arms, he sat on the verandah step holding the sobbing, shaking woman, wishing he could somehow lessen the pain that wracked her slim body.

He finally picked her up in his arms and took her through the house to the spare bedroom, where he laid her on the bed. As Minnie hovered around them, Tyndall directed her to bring a brandy. Sitting patiently by the bed as Olivia sipped the brandy, he answered her questions honestly, not softening any details. When Minnie brought in the doctor's medication she swallowed it as directed.

Then Olivia lay back in the bed and whispered, "I have to make Hamish understand."

"Tomorrow, Olivia." He took her hand and smoothed her hair back from her forehead.

The pills gradually took effect and she drifted into a nightmarish sleep, though her grip on his hand never lessened. Several times she cried out in her sleep. After one of these cries of anguish Tyndall slid onto the bed beside her and gathered her in his arms, rocking and soothing her as he murmured words of comfort, but she barely registered his presence in her drugged state of shock.

The threatened storm finally hit, crashing and raging over the house, the beating rain on the tin roof drowning Olivia's fitful breathing and sad cries.

By morning, the storm had passed. Olivia was now sleeping calmly and a weary Tyndall slipped from the room, giving Minnie instructions to watch over her.

The town was stirring, but everything seemed different in the light of the night's events. When Tyndall reached his home he was met by a tearful Niah, cradling their baby, whom they'd called Maya.

He held her for a moment then drew back and touched the cheek of the sleeping child. "I've been with Olivia. She's in shock." He ran his fingers through his hair. "Have you seen Ahmed?"

Niah shook her head. "Tuan and Mem Metta come and tell me what happened. I see no one."

Tyndall stood quietly for a few moments, thinking, then poured himself a strong whisky. "Run a bath for me please, Niah."

"You very tired. Need sleep."

"Later. A few things to be done yet."

They exchanged brief smiles and Niah went to the bathroom. Tyndall headed for the verandah, where he sat looking, but not seeing, as he pondered the complexities of his world, a world that had changed dramatically overnight.

He was dressing after his bath when Niah came into the bedroom.

"Minnie come with message, John."

"I'll see her in a moment. See that she's comfortable, Niah."

"No stay. Leave message. Ahmed down near foreshore camp with Minnie's mob."

Tyndall dressed in work clothes and walked nonchalantly to his deserted foreshore camp. He pottered for a few minutes then checked to see if anyone was around before walking quickly by the fringe of mangroves and into the bush. From the upstairs verandah of the shed's crew room he had seen a wisp of smoke from a campfire.

He found the camp in a few minutes, a temporary and shabby collection of humpies made from sheets of rusted roofing iron, sacks and old canvas. The ground was still wet from the night's deluge and the humpies dripped on huddled families. He exchanged greetings in their language and joined a couple of old men sitting on logs arranged under a banyan tree. He offered them cigarettes and they smiled in gratitude and lit up.

After a few minutes Ahmed walked into the camp accompanied by an Aboriginal man with a spear. He squatted down with the group at the banyan tree and silently took a cigarette offered by Tyndall. His face was drawn and sad.

After a few puffs on the cigarette he spoke in Malay. "Sorry, tuan. I let him get too far ahead of me. I was too slow. Was hard to see what was happening in bad light."

Tyndall reached out and put his hand on his offsider's shoulder. "I'm sure you did your best, Ahmed. It was very thoughtful of you to make the effort to follow Conrad. Glad you got the bastard anyway. Problem is, it amounts to murder. Did anyone see you?"

"No. Don't think so. Not close anyway."

Tyndall drew thoughtfully on his cigarette. "Have you told anyone what happened?"

"No. But this mob know things, you know these fellas. Just know things."

"Yeah. But they're not going to talk . . . not to anyone in the law." Tyndall stamped his cigarette butt into the mud and put his arm around Ahmed's shoulder. "I'm going back to the shed. In a few minutes you come along. Just act normal. Say nothing about the affair. Just tell anyone who asks that you spent the night with the mob here. Right?"

Ahmed nodded.

Tyndall had a few words with the men under the tree, shook hands and left.

They spent an hour at the shed and the boats, making out to be checking security, then both went into town. The news of the double murder had taken the heat out of the conflict and the warring factions had gone to ground. Shops were opening again and the hotel bars were packed with men exchanging news and gossip. Tyndall knew he would be expected to turn up at the bars favored by the pearling masters. He also wanted to hear their version of events.

There was little mention of the dead Koepanger, and even less about who killed him. All the talk was about Conrad and all of the men wanted to reinforce their expressions of sympathy with a drink.

It was late in the day when Tyndall staggered to the office quite drunk and fell asleep.

• • •

Sergeant O'Leary knew what he needed . . . a few shots of brandy. It had been a nasty twenty-four hours. Three killings, one a white man and that was bad. A lot of injuries, mainly to Asians and that really wasn't a concern, some minor property damage, and a lot of scared whites. Thank God someone killed the bugger who did in Hennessy. Asian, according to the Japs. Probably a Malay. Not that it helped much even if they were right. Town was full of them. And they'll all have an iron-clad alibi.

O'Leary was an Irish adventurer who had found his way to Australia via a stint with the police force in colonial India, serving the white raj. He had been a city policeman in Fremantle and Perth before taking a post with the mounted police in the north-west. He'd gone north largely out of curiosity and a love of adventure, but found the outback was addictive. He often talked about leaving, but never got around to doing it. Holidays in the south had always left him yearning to get back to the town he now called home. After ten years and a couple of promotions he was respected by whites as a tough but wise administrator of the law. He was feared more than respected by the Asians and Aborigines.

Paperwork was not his strong point. Sean O'Leary worked hard at applying the law in ways that reduced paperwork and court appearances. His boot and fists helped enormously to this end.

And it was the paperwork associated with the recent events that bothered him. It could not be eliminated, but it could be limited.

Tyndall awoke to find Sergeant O'Leary at his desk, feet up and drinking whiskey.

"I was going to give you five more minutes, enough for another drink, then I was going to wake you from your beauty sleep. Fact is, John, I needed a few quiet moments to reflect on this and that. It's been a hard day again."

Tyndall dragged himself to a chair. "Do you mind?" he asked, reaching for the bottle.

"Not at all, mate. It's your whisky after all."

"Is it?" said Tyndall vaguely. He poured a half glass and raised it to the policeman, who raised his glass in salute. They both drank.

"On duty or off duty?" asked Tyndall casually.

"Off duty, despite the uniform."

The two men were much alike, though O'Leary was old enough to be Tyndall's father. They came from the same country, and it was this link to the Emerald Isle that had brought them together as occasional drinking partners at hotels, in the office after work, or sometimes in each other's home. O'Leary used Tyndall to keep in touch with what was happening in the pearling scene. Tyndall knew that, but it didn't bother him. He knew how to be discreet.

"How did Mrs. Hennessy take it?" O'Leary inquired.

"Poorly. As you'd expect. It will take some time for her to get over it."

"Aye, it will t'be sure. A terrible thing is the murder of a white man. But at least we're spared the agony of the killer's trial. He got what he deserved."

"I'll drink to that."

They both raised their glasses, then O'Leary leaned forward and poured them both another drink.

"Rather odd, don't you think, that Koepanger having his throat cut at the scene. Suggests that someone was following him . . . or Hennessy."

Tyndall stiffened slightly, and tried to cover his reaction by taking a long swig of his drink. But O'Leary had noticed the reaction. "Maybe. Hadn't thought much about it."

"The Japs tell me that it was an Asian. Probably a Malay." The policeman sipped at his glass. "Ahmed around?"

Tyndall was now on his guard. He answered neutrally. "Yep. Turned up for work this morning. Checked the shed and boats, then I sent him off."

"Toby Metta tells me that he gave Hennessy some pearls before the murder. They weren't on the body. Now what do you make of that?"

"Sounds like robbery. Damned big loss," said Tyndall, trying to sound genuinely upset.

"Of course. And you were going to mention this business of the pearls to me, were you not?"

"Of course. Another drink?"

The glasses were filled in silence.

O'Leary carefully examined the contents of his raised glass, then looked across the rim at Tyndall before drinking. "It could cause me an immense amount of paperwork if those pearls turned up in certain quarters. To say nothing of the immense waste of government funds on trials and all that."

Their eyes met. "I don't think there's any chance of those pearls causing a problem for you," said Tyndall quietly.

The sergeant finished his drink with a long gulp and smiled. "That's good, John. In a way we might say justice has been done then."

"Without paperwork."

"Aye lad. Without paperwork."

The following day Ahmed appeared at Tyndall's office where he was sorting through Conrad's papers and files. Tyndall looked up and Ahmed reached over and placed the bag of pearls on his desk. The men exchanged a glance but said nothing. Ahmed turned and left the office and Tyndall put the pearls in the safe.

The funeral of Conrad Hennessy was a miserable affair. Rain fell in a relentless, solid sheet. The red clay sides of the hole into which Conrad's coffin was lowered, slipped and collapsed in a slimy mass, covering the sodden flowers on top of the casket.

Olivia held on to Hamish's hand and the bewildered little boy kept casting anxious glances toward Tyndall, Minnie, Ahmed and Yoshi, still unsure of why his daddy wasn't there. Niah stayed at home with Maya and waited for Tyndall, knowing he would be with Olivia. But for once her jealousy of Olivia was tempered by sympathy.

In the evening, when Tyndall had seen Minnie settle the sedated Olivia into bed, he went to the Lugger Bar, drinking until he could barely stand.

He staggered into the cool night air that momentarily cleared his head, but all he could think of was Olivia's tragic face. Of all people it seemed unjust that a decent man like Conrad should meet such a brutal and unnecessary end. The business would survive but the hole in Olivia and Hamish's life was dramatic.

Lurching across the road, he entered the shadowy park opposite the Continental with no idea of where he was going. But within a minute Ahmed was at his side.

"Tuan, I have sulky. You go home now. No Sheba Lane."

"I don't know where I'm going, Ahmed. It's all bloody dreadful."

"Yes, tuan." Ahmed took his arm and guided him back across the road as Tyndall continued, "Poor Olivia. We're going to have to look after her and the boy. Oh my dear Olivia . . ." He muttered and shook his head as Ahmed helped him into the sulky where he soon slumped across the seat and fell asleep.

At dawn Olivia awoke as the effect of the medication wore off, her head heavy, her tongue thick, throat dry. Without disturbing Minnie, she dressed a sleepy Hamish and, taking his hand, walked through the silent muddy town where the humidity hung like a wet steamy blanket. She walked slowly, sometimes carrying Hamish as his legs tired, until she reached the small bluff where Conrad was buried. There she stood by the red mud of the freshly covered grave. It overlooked the sea that stretched so far from this sun-drenched sienna soil by a turquoise bay to his homeland of white cliffs and soft mist. What a long journey their life had been, yet how short had been their time together.

Memories of London crept into her mind; of dusk seeping into her father's shop on a winter afternoon and of Conrad bent over account books. Their simple marriage ceremony, where her widowed father confidently and proudly placed her in Conrad's care. So soon after came her father's death and, at her urging, their bold decision to make a new life in Australia for them and the child she was carrying. Conrad had always told her, "As one door closes, another opens . . ."

She thought of little James, buried down the coast and wondered if he should be here beside his father. Their brief struggle on the land emerged in her memories, and then the fortu-itous partnership with Tyndall which had changed their lives.

"Where's Daddy?" asked Hamish suddenly.

"He's in Heaven, darling. But this little place is where we come to talk to him. He has gone away, but to a wonderful place."

Tears rushed from Hamish's eyes. "Why Daddy go away?"

"Oh, my darling boy. He didn't want to go away and leave us . . ." Olivia knelt down and hugged him fiercely. "Sometimes God asks the angels to take special people up to Heaven. He knows you and I will be strong and good and we have Captain Tyndall and Minnie and Ahmed and everybody to look after us and one day we'll all be together again . . ."

Hamish still cried. "I want my daddy . . ."

Olivia tightened her arms about him and tears came to her eyes as she whispered, "So do I, darling . . ." In a moment or two she pulled away, wiped her son's tears and her own.

Seeing his mother's sadness, Hamish grasped her hand and together they walked sadly back home.

Two shell openers making an early start observed her brief pilgrimage and one remarked, "She'll be on the next boat back to the old country. Sell out to Captain Tyndall, no doubt."

"She's no ordinary woman that one, matey. You heard how she mucks in down at the shed, takes food to the shell openers from time to time. Never heard of that sorta thing before. Still this town's no place for a widow like 'er with a kid."

•   •   •

For the next two weeks Olivia stayed mostly in her bedroom. The wooden cyclone shutters obscured the outside world, air flowed through the funnel-shaped wind scoop on the roof. In the dim stillness of the room she fought to come to terms with the tragedy that had shattered her life. Visitors were turned away. Only Minnie had right of entry, padding quietly in with food which Olivia barely picked at. Hamish was led in at regular intervals to sit with his mother. He didn't really understand what had happened to his father or their ordered life.

For the boy the best part of these difficult days was at sunset when the familiar tall and swaggering Tyndall came through the gate carrying little Maya. Tyndall sat on the verandah and sent Minnie to ask Olivia to join him. She repeatedly ignored his request, so he sat and drank a rum, as he had so often with Conrad, and watched Hamish play with the baby girl he had come to adore.

Finally, one evening, Tyndall finished his sundowner, put down the glass with some force and, telling Minnie to watch the children, strode through the house and tapped on Olivia's bedroom door.

"It's time, Olivia. Time to come out."

There was silence but he knew she was listening. He banged on the door. "Time, Olivia."

"Please leave me alone, John."

"No, I won't. It's time you came out and got on with your life. For Hamish's sake. And Conrad's. I miss him, too, Olivia."

There was a muffled noise.

"Damn it, woman. I'm not talking through this door. I'm coming in."

"No! Please go away." Her voice was hoarse and tired.

Tyndall wrenched the door open and stood in the doorway, blinking in the near darkness. "God, woman, what is this?" He went to the windows where the shutters showed slits of dusk light.

"Please, leave me be," pleaded Olivia in a weak but tense voice that was teetering on the edge of hysteria.

"Throw something if you want." The shutters banged open and a rush of last yellow light, perfumed by the tropical shrubs, surged into the musty room. With it came the giggles of Hamish and Maya. He turned to face Olivia.

She sat hunched in a chair, her hair falling lank and dull down her back. Her face was drawn and pale and she hugged a cotton wrapper across herself.

Tyndall pretended not to notice her appearance and spoke to her with firmness. "Olivia, I expect you to be down at the camp and office tomorrow morning. There's a mountain of paperwork and you will have to take over Conrad's administrative duties. It's all beyond me. Damn cyclone of paper seems to have hit the place. We need to plan the coming season. I was thinking of sailing north."

The outburst achieved its intended effect, particularly the radical suggestion of sailing north. His luggers always went south.

"Why north?" Olivia demanded.

Tyndall sighed inwardly with relief. While she would continue to mourn, he knew he'd sparked a reaction and soon enough she'd be out of this cocoon of grief. However, his demeanor didn't alter. "I've heard rumors of new grounds. I might go check it out." He turned to leave and said casually over his shoulder, "Perhaps you and Hamish might like to come along. Anyway, I'll see you tomorrow."

He left the room, quietly closing the door, then leaned against it and expelled a long breath. Olivia had looked wretched and his heart ached for her.

Olivia stared at the closed door, a sudden flood of anger welling in her. *Typical Tyndall,* she thought with some anger. *Didn't ask if she wanted to go to work, just tells her.* She paced the room a little, went to the window and looked out at the technicolor sunset, then decided to have a bath.

Soaking in the water her annoyance dissolved in a rush of affection for Tyndall's rough kindness. She knew he was right, there was Hamish and the business to think about. Conrad was gone, the life they'd had together was gone. It was no use wallowing in self-pity and sadness. She had to go forward, alone.

CHAPTER THIRTEEN

Olivia began to come to terms with her loss. While she came out of her room and faced the world again, her grief turned inward and became a private pain. Life went on and she went through the motions. But day by day it became a little easier.

Olivia found the morning walk to the foreshore camp a calming experience. The day was yet to heat up and there was something reassuring about seeing the luggers at anchor for refit and repair during lay up. The extraordinary color of the sea never failed to amaze her, and the activity of the foreshore camps was enchanting.

Chinese and Manilamen emptied their fish traps and hurried to the town with baskets of fresh fish hanging from a long bamboo pole across their shoulders. Crews were fussing about the luggers, storing everything that could be moved in tin sheds around the camps. Filipino carpenters were busy with makeshift slips nursing some of the luggers, while Malay sail makers bent over the sheets of canvas, cutting and stitching.

The men working at Star of the Sea's camp were delighted to see her. They all came forward, some with a little embarrassment because of the cultural and social gap, to take her hand and offer words of sympathy and support. Olivia was greatly touched by the reception and responded with a smile and little more than a single word of thanks. It was too moving, almost too emotional to handle and she felt a little weak at the knees, but forced herself to carry on with an inspection of the shed and a boat on the slips, and to wave to Tyndall on the deck of a lugger moored in the bay.

Her equilibrium was shaken back in town when she climbed the stairs and stood outside Conrad's office. She took a deep breath and stepped inside. Documents were spread in a disorderly fashion over his desk, and the top drawer of the oak filing cabinet was open, files scattered on files, testimony to Tyndall's attempt to keep the paperwork moving.

Her attention to the files was total and another hour passed before she knew it. She was disturbed by soft footsteps in the passageway and looked up as Ahmed stopped in the doorway.

"*Selamat pagi,* mem."

"Good morning, Ahmed. Do come in."

Ahmed walked to the desk and ignored her gesture to sit. His eyes burned with pain and sorrow as they looked at each other in silence.

"Mem . . ." said Ahmed, then paused unable to go on.

She nodded her head slightly in support then

realized that he was really unable to put into words what he wanted to say.

Then he simply touched his *kris,* looked into her eyes, and whispered, "Sorry, mem. Too late."

Olivia smothered a small gasp with her hand, but recovered quickly. "Thank you, Ahmed. Say no more." He gave a small bow and left the room. Olivia covered her eyes with both hands and wept quietly.

Later in the morning, Tyndall turned up, pulled out a chair and propped his feet up on the now tidy desk. "John, please."

"I'm glad to see you here," he said simply.

"Thank you. The men were very kind down at the camp."

"They think a great deal of you. They respected Conrad, but they have a special feeling for you. You knew that, of course."

"I really hadn't thought about it. I was greatly touched by their support this morning." She stood and took a file to the cabinet, hoping the activity would somehow bolster her emotional strength. The morning had been more draining than she had anticipated.

As she busied herself at the filing cabinet Tyndall broke the silence. "I've taken an option on a new lugger."

Olivia spun around. "A new lugger! But we haven't had a chance to talk about the future yet. That's rather a rash thing to do, isn't it?"

"Rash, but wise. It's a good deal and life and business must go on, Olivia. We've got to keep things on an even keel. Sit down and I'll fill you in on the details."

Olivia sat and immediately began taking notes as she realized that his idea of keeping the business on an even keel meant sailing at full speed with the wind astern.

"I've made Yoshi the skipper and hired one of his relatives as number one diver on the *Annabella*. Yoshi will dive as well as be skipper."

"That's a good idea. He's proved to be a good worker and loyal."

"So far. Some of the other captains think I'm crazy. Can't trust the Japs, they say. They'll steal the good pearls and sell them as snides. Say they think it's a prerogative that goes with the job."

"Do you and Ahmed trust Yoshi?"

"Totally."

"Then you have my support." Olivia paused to put down the pencil and sit back. "Now, about my future. I intend to stay in Broome and, if you agree, to become a more active partner. I'll take over Conrad's work. And I want to push on with Conrad's plans for diversifying the business on the providore side. There's money to be made in re-supplying the luggers at sea."

Tyndall smiled. "I rather hoped you would. It will be tough on your own, but I'll give you all the support I can. You know that, Olivia," he added warmly.

"Thanks, John, and thanks for being so firm

with me. It wasn't easy to listen to, but it was what I needed to get going."

Several days later Tyndall sent for Olivia and Hamish and asked them to meet him at Streeter's Jetty. To her surprise she found the crews of their luggers along with Ahmed, Yoshi and Taki gathered about the jetty. They welcomed her warmly and Hamish made straight for Ahmed, who picked him up and squeezed him in delight.

"Well, what's this all about, John?" asked Olivia.

"The new lugger. We thought Hamish might like to christen it. We've rigged up a bottle of champagne. He just has to let the rope go."

"What a lovely idea," said Olivia as she made her way through the group to the edge of the wharf. It was then that she clearly saw the stern of the freshly painted lugger.

In black lettering on the white hull was the lugger's name—*Conrad*.

Tears filled her eyes as she looked at Tyndall.

"We hope you approve," he said softly. "Maybe after Hamish has done the honors you'd like to bring him for a run across the bay."

She had difficulty speaking. "We'd like that very much."

Hamish squealed in delight as the lugger heeled over, the water slapping the lee gunwale, sometimes gushing down the deck while Ahmed held him at the wheel of the forty-foot lugger. Olivia looked over every inch of her, from the air compressor for the divers, to the hold where the shell was stowed, to the two water tanks which each held two hundred gallons. Forward of the hold was the small fo'c'sle where the Koepanger crew slept. The crew was evenly divided between Japanese and Koepanger, a system that had proved safe and sensible. In the past many one-race crews had ganged up against the master to mutiny or steal pearls. Often masters had been "lost overboard in a storm" when carrying crews of one nationality. The *Conrad* was ketch-rigged and toward the stern there was a cabin where two bunks were on a level with the deck. The vessel smelled of new canvas, fresh paint and pitch.

Olivia nodded her approval. "She sails well, looks good. I think Conrad would be pleased." It was the first time she had uttered his name without choking up. She gave Tyndall a grateful smile.

He smiled back and patted Hamish's fair head.

From the shore, Niah watched the new lugger skim across the bay. She was annoyed at being left behind—since Conrad's death, Tyndall had divided his life as if he had two families. She understood Mem Hennessy was part of his world of luggers and pearl shell, but now Tyndall was taking an interest in the boy, giving him more attention than Maya. His obsessive devotion to his baby girl had been diverted, as had his interest in Niah. He was preoccupied with work, the new boat, with Mem Hennessy and the crews. Only at night when he was sober and attentive to her, did Niah feel her power and place in his life restored.

Niah walked back toward Tyndall's bungalow. She looked down the length of the sandy street to where the ribbon of road led to the pindan and the coastal country of her people.

Changing direction, she went to the Hennessys' and found Minnie in the laundry sorting clothes for ironing. Niah sat on the steps, Maya sitting next to her.

Minnie glanced at Niah, stopped what she was doing and eased herself onto the step below her. She smiled at Maya and spoke a phrase in their language, then lifted Niah's hand and held it. She patted it gently, the gesture heavy with meaning to the forlorn young woman.

Three years passed, and the relationship between Olivia and Tyndall tightened—their bond through the business giving them mutual ground and interests to share.

Tyndall's respect for Olivia's business acumen, her judgment, and negotiating skills grew to the point where he admitted to her one day she was "just as good as a man." Olivia accepted the comment as a compliment but it irritated her. While she was one of only several white women who were involved in the business and professional world of Broome, she saw no reason why women shouldn't take their place alongside men if they had the inclination and ability.

Tyndall sometimes accompanied Olivia during the pearl sale negotiations with Monsieur Barat, but sat back and let her handle the delicate interplay and exchanges before agreeing on a price. Then Tyndall would step in and take over the social exchange. The friendship that had developed with the French pearl merchant was one that both Olivia and Tyndall valued.

Olivia had come to understand Tyndall's nature much better as she observed him through his working day—dealing with, on one hand, a bureaucratic, petty customs officer, barely controlling his impatience with the man's arrogance and obsession with unnecessary details, then displaying gentle humor and appreciation of craftsmanship in his dealings with a Malay sail maker.

She didn't approve of, but tolerated, his occasional drinking bouts, accepting that in Broome the male-to-male way of doing business often involved a bottle.

They had become an effective business team but she had also come to treasure his emotional support and friendship. Tyndall continued his habit of dropping by for a sunset drink on Olivia's verandah as he'd done when Conrad was alive. Now it was Olivia and Tyndall who discussed business, made plans, and exchanged bits of news about people and events in the town. Occasionally some news from abroad and the southern cities provided fresh subjects for conversation but for most of the time the world beyond the magical waters of Roebuck Bay was barely acknowledged.

Niah and Ahmed seemed more laterally attached to Tyndall while Olivia had gradually become the core of his functioning life. Olivia came to rely a lot more on Minnie, who ran the house and watched over Hamish along with his amah, Rosminah, a young Malay.

Minnie had a daughter and a husband, Alf, an Aboriginal Asian. Alf was never sure which half was more dominant so he drifted between both worlds. He worked as a diver till a bad case of paralysis partially crippled him and forced him to stay ashore, where he worked in the bakery run by his Chinese relatives. He delivered bread by horse and cart early each morning and spent the rest of the day sitting in the shade with cousin Wally down at Kennedy's camp on the knoll above Dampier Creek. Minnie's daughter, Mollie, was cared for by relatives and occasionally spent time helping her mother at Olivia's. Niah and Maya often visited when Olivia was at work and along with Rosminah and Hamish, it was a jolly group that gathered in the back garden of the Hennessy bungalow.

But increasingly Niah felt resentful of Tyndall's close association with Olivia. He dismissed her complaints about time spent with Olivia pleading "business" and "responsibility." Niah felt insecure about her position in the household and about the fact that Tyndall was separating her more and more from Maya. He took the little girl everywhere with him and talked to her at length as if she were an adult. Yet he shared little with Niah.

They weren't a threesome anymore. Niah's role as unofficial mistress of the household was diminished and she felt no more than Maya's nursemaid and Tyndall's bedmate.

The times Niah saw Olivia and Tyndall together at the shed, in the office, about the luggers, she instantly recognized the rapport and friendship between them. She also tuned into an undercurrent, a chemistry that bound them, and which neither recognized or seemed aware of. They could share things she could never share, the only hold she had on Tyndall was at night in his bed. And Maya, of course. For as long as she had Maya she had Tyndall.

Niah didn't voice her complaints—she had few to share her feelings with—but it was obvious to Minnie what was fermenting inside the young woman.

For many weeks Niah held her peace, then one evening she left the bungalow while Tyndall and Maya were at Olivia's. She had arranged to meet Minnie at sundown by the foreshore camp.

She knew Tyndall and Olivia would be sharing their evening sundowners so had slipped out before preparing dinner. The older woman cast a sympathetic glance at Niah. "You got troubles, eh?"

"Yeah, Auntie. I bin feeling sick inside for a long time now." In the way of Aboriginal communities, Minnie had become "auntie" of Niah soon after their Aboriginal links had been recognized. Minnie was from the same clan, but through marriage had become a town dweller. Niah tried to explain her dissatisfaction with life despite having a caring benefactor.

Minnie listened, particularly noting Niah's concern about Tyndall's obsession with the child. She began idly to draw in the sand with her finger the pattern of the pendant Niah wore.

"Why you draw that one, Auntie?"

"That one woman's business sign, Niah. B'long our mob. Ceremony for girls is comin' soon and you 'n' Maya orta go, be in ceremony, eh?"

Niah smiled at Minnie, her eyes bright. "How will I get there?"

"Wally is down at Kennedy camp. He take you when he go back. Long walk but."

"That will be good. When will he go?"

"Dunno. When he ready. You pack few things."

Niah walked in the twilight back to the bungalow feeling contented and purposeful.

She greeted Tyndall a short time later with a happy smile and took Maya to give her dinner, telling her how they were soon going walkabout and trying to explain what it meant in reply to the girl's eager questions.

As the wet season came to an end Tyndall again raised the idea of looking for fresh pearl banks and giving the new lugger a run. He suggested Olivia come along with Hamish. At first, she hesitated, as the young boy had never been to sea. She told Tyndall she would discuss it with Hamish.

"Captain Tyndall has asked us to go on a trip up the coast for a few days, how would you feel about that?"

"On the boat? Staying on it all the time?"

"Yes. You might get seasick. Or bored."

"No, no. It'll be fun. Oh yes, do let's go." His enthusiasm was infectious. "I promise to be good," he added for extra emphasis.

"We'll make it a short trip and you have to do everything Ahmed and Tyndall tell you, absolutely. Understood?"

Tyndall explained the situation to Niah. "Too cramped for you and Maya to come. And I want this to be a special event for Hamish. He misses his father and I'd like him to learn to know and love the sea. Just be a short trip." He lifted Maya and spun her around in the air, making her giggle. She reached out and grabbed at his earring which always intrigued her. He hugged her to him. "You be a good girl while I'm at sea."

"Me come to sea."

"Maybe next trip." He kissed her hair and brushed his fingertips over Niah's cheek.

The *Conrad* slid away from the jetty and Hamish waved to Niah and Maya till his arm was tired.

Niah had helped with the preparations for the trip but said little. Olivia tried to make her feel less rejected. "Niah, I know you would like to come, but I just think it would be too hard on board with both children. Not just for space but for safety reasons. It's for Hamish really." She looked into Niah's large eyes and saw a depth of feeling that shook her slightly. A flash of envy, a quizzical questioning, but slowly she smiled with an openness and warmth that Olivia had never seen before. She returned the smile feeling comfortable that Niah understood. But what Niah saw and understood was something Olivia had yet to recognize.

After the *Conrad* was out of sight Niah decided to take a ride on the little train that ran from the wharf to Chinatown, and held Maya's hand as the old gray horse pulled the open rail car along the street. She got off close to the foreshore camps.

A dusty track wound above the mangroves to a small hillock where there was a makeshift camp.

An older man rose to his feet and lifted an arm in greeting. "Hey girl. Me is Wally. Minnie said ya'd be along." He grinned at Niah and rested his hand on Maya's head. "We gonna take girlie meet family, eh?"

Wally had brewed a billy and handed Niah a mug of hot tea and proceeded to tear off chunks of a freshly made damper. "Corned beef orright?" he asked. Niah and Maya nodded and he sliced slabs of the pink meat and put it on the damper and handed it to them.

"How far do we walk?" asked Niah.

He shrugged. "Long walk. We go tomorra, orright?"

"All right," said Niah, and she felt confident and purposeful for the first time in ages.

They walked slowly back to the bungalow and Niah packed the small dilly bag she planned to take with her.

The following morning, at first light, she said good-bye to Minnie, who enfolded her in a strong hug, kissed Maya and reassured Niah this was the right thing to do.

Niah nodded. "My heart tells me, too. This Dreaming, important for Maya."

"Important for you, too, Niah. You need proper family now."

Wally was waiting for them. "G'day. Gimme bag." He took the dilly bag from her and they strode out.

A little later, when the sun had risen properly, Wally paused at a point on the track and signaled for Niah to wait. He went to a hollow log nearby and retrieved a spear, woomera and a large hunting knife.

The small party walked through the morning, rested in the shade during the hot midday and resumed walking in the stillness of afternoon and the coolness of twilight. Wally sometimes carried Maya, or she trotted ahead of them in little energetic bursts. They camped and caught food as they traveled, Niah learning much about the bounty of a land that appeared so barren. She slept peacefully beneath the stars, usually by fires in sandy creekbeds, with her daughter cuddled close.

The *Conrad* bobbed and rolled as the lugger tacked for a starboard run. The spray blew into Hamish's face and he shouted with laughter and licked the salt from his lips. He was holding tight to the tiller under Ahmed's strong hand. Olivia and Tyndall exchanged a warm grin at the boy's delight. Unlike his father, Hamish had taken to sailing with gusto. The weather had blessed them. At night they sat on the deck, the sea calm, and taught the boy how to spot the constellations and steer by the stars. Tyndall's knowledge of ships and sailing blended with Ahmed's mystical approach to the sea, the wind and the stars, and fascinated Olivia as the men talked to the boy.

Later, swinging in his hammock rigged in the small cabin Ahmed and Yoshi shared, Hamish listened in awe as they talked of the wonders beneath the sea, its strange creatures, great dangers and their many diving adventures.

After several camps, Wally announced one morning, "This country bilong us mob." He grinned at Niah, "Feet can feel 'im. You smell 'im. You listen good, hear 'im songs bilong you." He paused and looked at the ground as if sensing some distant vibration. "Mob comin' t'meet us," he said with satisfaction.

When the *Conrad* returned to Broome, Tyndall left Ahmed in charge of mooring the lugger and escorted Hamish and Olivia to their bungalow.

They were all pleased with how the boat had performed, and plans were afoot to dive further up the coast as it had looked promising. The trip had also successfully distracted Hamish from the loss of his father. Olivia doubted if his infatuation with becoming a pearling master would last, but she was grateful to Tyndall for taking them with him. She too had found the solitude and peace at sea healing and restful.

Tyndall waved good-bye at their gate and hurried home to Niah. He was a little surprised to find the house empty, even of staff. He bathed and changed, reflecting on what a happy time it had been for young Hamish who, once he had his sea legs and learned the shipboard rules, had really taken to life at sea. They'd taught him to fish and given him small chores like winding ropes into neat circles and polishing the compass brass. Tyndall looked forward to the day when Maya was old enough to do the same.

He heard some movement in the staff quarters and called the amah. "Rosminah, where has Niah gone?" he asked.

"Walkabout, tuan."

"Round town? When is she coming back?"

"Gone big walkabout. Said she goin' to see her people. Take Maya her country."

Tyndall was stunned for a moment. "What do you mean walkabout?"

When the full impact sank in, Tyndall sat with his hands hanging between his knees. He now saw how he had neglected Niah and even Maya and had been too absorbed in the business. He didn't blame her for seeking family contact. But he missed them and hoped they would soon be back, for this was their home.

Olivia found him, hung over and morose, at the camp the next day. She made him strong tea. "Perhaps Niah was jealous at us taking Hamish away. She's been a bit reserved lately. And now she's found her tribal family it's only natural she'd want to take Maya to them, for a visit," said Olivia, trying to explain the situation rationally.

"She's *my* daughter, too. She really doesn't belong out there."

"How can you be sure, John?" said Olivia, hating to see the misery in his eyes and feeling a little bit guilty that perhaps it was because of her that the situation had developed in this way. "You can only wait."

Tyndall gazed at Olivia sadly. "You're right, of course. And there's not a damned thing I can do about it. But wait."

Olivia poured his tea and hoped Niah would be sensible and not stay away too long. She'd heard of some Aborigines going walkabout for six months or more. "At least we know she's in safe hands."

Tyndall didn't answer.

In the weeks that followed, Niah discovered her extended family, the rituals, the sacred sites, the stories and sense of kinship. The tribe embraced Maya and in a simple but moving ceremony performed by the women, the young girl was welcomed into the extended family of the clan and given a shell pendant. The small curved shell had the same carved pattern as her mother's. No matter where she went in life Maya had a link with previous generations and a place of belonging.

The old women adored the beautiful girl and entertained her, singing and showing her endless patterns made from twine twisted between fingers. It was a time for both mother and daughter to learn their language and culture.

Niah relaxed and felt comfortable leaving Maya with the old women while she went hunting and gathering food with the other women and young girls. There was much to learn.

One day after they reached the coast Niah felt a need to be on her own. She found herself thinking a lot about Tyndall and Broome. While the others collected oysters and shellfish, Niah clambered over rocks to a deserted inlet. She wandered idly for a short time kicking at the sand, then sat and stared out to sea. Somewhere across the ocean was the island where she'd grown up and where her other family lived. She remembered how her grandmother had sat and told her the story of the land across the sea. It had been a long time ago and Niah's mother told her stories of how her grandmother had sailed back over the sea to visit, returning with gifts and stories of the great welcoming ceremony for her. Niah, by inadvertently returning to the home of her grandmother, felt she had completed the circle.

Deep in thought she didn't hear the footfall behind her. An arm grabbed her around the throat and her arms were swiftly pinned behind her back.

"Got you!" The grinning face of Karl Gunther leered close to hers. "What a pleasant surprise, my pretty. What are you doing up here?"

"I, I, I come with Tyndall," she stammered frantically.

"Oh yeah? And where's 'is boat. I'm moored around the cove, there ain't any other boats 'ere." He dragged her to her feet.

Niah tried to scream but he clamped his hand across her mouth. "Now, now. Don't make a noise. Or I'll hurt you real bad. You're comin' with me."

He dragged her, kicking and struggling, along the sand. She bit and scratched until he gave her a solid backhander and she went limp. Slinging her over his shoulder, he hurried along the beach.

• • •

Niah came to in the dim cabin of a boat. She could tell by the sound and movement that they were getting under way and she struggled to rise, but found she was tied by her ankles, the rope looping up to tie her hands behind her back. She attempted to cry out but a rag had been tied across her mouth. Her frantic heavings sent her crashing to the deck where she lay bruised and sore. A black cloud of fright and despair descended on her.

Once the boat was under way, Gunther appeared and yanked her upright. "So, you fell. Dear me." His voice dripped facetiously. He flung her back on the bunk. "Stop fightin', woman. There's no point. Be nice 'n' things may go easier for you."

She lay there, her eyes burning with anger as she watched him fuss around the cabin. He then threw her one last look and a leering grin. Niah thought longingly of her child—at least she was safe, but her urge to get off this boat and get back to Maya overwhelmed all other feelings.

Hours passed. She felt faint with hunger and thirst. Gunther returned and yanked the cloth from her mouth, loosened her hands and gave her water which she gulped greedily. She sat and glared at him.

"Don't give me the evil eye. You wanna get on in this life, you be nice to me." He flicked a finger under her chin and Niah resisted the impulse to poke a finger at his eye. He tied one of her hands to the ankle rope.

The cook delivered a plate of rice with a few strips of dried fish on it and turned away. Niah spoke swiftly in Malay but he didn't reply. She ate with one hand and waited.

Gunther came to her, drunk, later that night, forcing her back on the thin coir mattress of the bunk. He pulled out a knife, casually slit her sarong and flung it away. Grinning in the lantern light he drew the knife around her nipples and slowly ran it down her chest and belly to her pubic hair where he held it as their eyes locked. Niah remained motionless.

"That's the girl. No point in fighting me now," he slurred. He reached down and slit the rope binding her ankles, kicked her legs apart and held the knife threateningly above her. Niah didn't move. Gunther dragged off his trousers and flung himself on top of her, fumbling and groping, his rum-soaked breath almost smothering her.

Niah kicked out with her legs, pulling up her knee and thrusting it in his groin, making a grab for the knife with her free hand. Her movements were swift and strong and they both rolled to the floor, Gunther gasping in pain. They fumbled for the knife, Gunther having dropped it in the fall. Both their hands fell on it and he swung it, slicing downward toward her neck. Niah twisted and felt it hit her shoulder, cutting deeply. She swung her free elbow, smashing it into Gunther's teeth then, grasping the knife, she turned it back on him. He yelled in pain and rolled away from her and in that second she staggered to her feet and raced up to the deck.

A lantern swung from the rigging and the crew, sitting and eating their meal, glanced up in astonishment. No one moved or spoke as the bleeding, wild-eyed, naked girl stood before them trailing rope looped around her feet and wrists. In that split second Niah knew she could expect no help from these men. Hearing Gunther cursing and crashing his way up on deck, she turned and dived over the side of the lugger.

She sank through the dark water, holding her breath, kicking her legs free of the rope, then swam until she was forced to the surface to take a breath. Treading water, her heart pounding, gasping for air, Niah looked around. The moon was obscured by clouds, so it took her a few seconds to adjust to the dark night. Then she made out the shape of Gunther's lugger, its lights glowing faintly, the distance between them growing as she watched. She turned around and saw the coastline, thankfully not an impossible swim away. But fear clutched at her as she struck out, knowing sharks infested the waters. She doubted whether Gunther would look for her, knowing as she did that he was wounded and it would be an impossible task with no moonlight to guide him.

Her childhood spent in the waters about her island home stood her in good stead. Although she swam strongly, she still needed to rest often.

But thankfully she could feel the current drawing her toward the shore.

She had no idea how long she spent in the sea, but eventually could hear the surf and suddenly there was a rush of water and her legs were raked by sharp needles as she was washed on to a coral reef. She tucked her legs up and with a few strong strokes got herself over the reef to calm water.

She could see a white strip of beach and soon her feet hit the bottom and she tripped, crawled out to the sand and lost consciousness from fatigue and loss of blood.

Dawn found the naked girl still unconscious, her limbs covered with congealed blood from many cuts. Blood trickled from the knife wound in her shoulder. As the morning began to heat Niah became conscious and raised herself to her knees. She was weak but knew she must move to find shelter. Staggering into the sand dunes and scrubland, she found a small water hole and threw herself down to drink. She then peeled a large piece of paper bark off a tree and using it to shade herself she set out to follow the creek upstream following a well-worn track.

Just as she thought she could drag herself no further, Niah saw several small shacks and behind them a large white tower. At the same time a black girl and boy came along the path, squealed in shock at seeing her, turned and ran.

Niah called to them, then sank to the ground and passed out.

Niah opened her eyes and found she was on a small bed in a white cell-like room. A black cross hung on one wall and sunlight and a soft breeze came through a window, framed by open wood shutters. Turning her head, she saw a white man sitting beside the bed, smiling kindly at her. He was wearing a long dark robe. A mug was offered to her and the man helped her sip the cool broth. It gave her some strength and she looked down and saw that she was dressed in a white shift or shirt of some kind. Realizing that her shoulder was bandaged, she tried to lift her arm on that side of her body but found it would not respond. Suddenly she felt hot and then began shivering. Fear gripped her, but the man spoke gently to her, his accent different from the white men she knew in Broome.

"I am Brother Frederick. This is Beagle Bay, don't be frightened. You are very sick. Rest now. Later you try to eat, yes?"

Niah fell back and closed her eyes.

For three days she battled the fever and infection from the deadly coral that had poisoned her. She had lost a lot of blood and Brother Frederick spent a long time praying for this native girl who was so desperately ill. Niah was too weak to speak except once to utter one word in reply to his asking her name—"Niah," she whispered.

As the days passed, Niah's hold on life slipped further and further from her grasp.

Finally Brother Frederick lifted Niah from the bed and carried her across the sandy ground to the whitewashed mud-brick church. Inside it was cool and dim. He went to the altar, put Niah on a mat, lit candles, knelt beside her then raised his arms in supplication.

"Dear Lord, bless this heathen, take her into thine almighty kingdom and shower her with love and thy blessings. Let her life not be in vain!"

Niah opened her eyes and saw the candle-lit altar shining with inlaid mother-of-pearl. A brief smile touched her dry lips and feebly she lifted an arm toward the priest. Brother Frederick looked at her and followed her eyes to the mother-of-pearl shell pendant and knew she had found some recognition or made some connection with the pearl shells on the altar. Then her head fell back and she died quietly in his arms.

Brother Frederick buried her in the small graveyard near the church.

On her grave he added a simple headstone into which he had set the shell pendant with clay and lime paste. The strange pattern puzzled the Brother, but he sensed it was symbolic and meaningful.

Brother Frederick made a note of the event in his journal and never mentioned it again. Life and death were like leaves falling from a tree to him.

A long way down the coast, the tribal women saw Gunther's boat with its black hull and dark red sails move away. In the sand they read the signs of a struggle and found Niah's digging stick. The snatching of Aborigines was not unknown but the women were deeply distressed. They sent word along the coast to watch for the strange boat and rescue Niah.

The women took Maya with them, she was part of their family and they all cared for the little girl, sharing food and love with her as they traveled across the land, all hoping for the day Niah might return to them.

CHAPTER FOURTEEN

With the absence of Niah and Maya, Tyndall swung from depression, to anger, to rum-soaked pity. He took to heavy drinking bouts to try and obliterate the emptiness in his life and his inability to wrench back his daughter from the remote desert country. He cursed Niah for her defection but blamed himself.

Olivia was patient and tried to be understanding. But then, recalling the firm stance Tyndall had taken with her during her own crisis, she confronted him.

He was slumped back in his chair, unshaven, the inevitable bottle on his desk beside a jumble of papers, his skipper's hat and a toy lugger which Maya had always played with. He glared at Olivia when she walked in.

"You have your do-gooders face on," he said bitterly.

"Now, John, this isn't doing you any good. You can't drown your sorrows, you're only harming yourself."

"How original. Stop preaching."

"Look, I don't care what you do in private, but falling around drunk in Sheba Lane bars and your sloppy attitude is threatening the company. The crews are starting to play up and Yoshi and Ahmed have had to break up several fights with our men. A quarter of the fleet have already left and we're still messing around at the foreshore camp."

"How do you know what I get up to?"

"It's a small place, or had you forgotten? What you do is all over town in a minute. People are laughing at you, John. Don't let them think you've gone to pieces because your mistress has run out on you."

His eyes narrowed. "Is that what they're saying?"

Olivia nodded.

"So tell them to get knotted." He pushed the toy lugger off the desk with a sweep of his arm, reached for the bottle and swung around in his chair, his back to Olivia.

"You are being very boorish, John. And downright rude," she snapped.

He ignored her, and took another drink from the bottle.

Olivia leaned across the desk, grabbed his shoulder and forcefully spun him around in the swivel chair to face her. Flushed with anger she shouted, "John Tyndall, you're . . . a . . . an ill-mannered oaf." She turned and stomped out of the office, leaving a stunned and silent Tyndall clutching his bottle and feeling more than a little embarrassed.

Olivia sighed with frustration and went down to the shell shed and looked for Ahmed. He and

Yoshi had taken it upon themselves to start loading the *Conrad* and the *Shamrock*.

"You tell tuan we got to go?" he asked.

"I did. Don't know that it had much effect. He's drinking. And he's mad."

"No can wait for Niah come back. We gotta get up the coast quick smart. Mebbe we shanghai skipper and leave."

Olivia gave a faint smile. It was the best suggestion to date.

Ahmed studied her for a moment, then asked, "You think Niah come back with Maya?"

"Yes, Ahmed, I do! It's only natural she went. She wanted to see her people, and the captain hadn't been paying her a lot of attention."

Ahmed saw the fleeting guilty expression in Olivia's eyes. "Tuan got many troubles and too much business. Niah want everything to be round Niah. She bored. She be back at end of season and everything be number one again."

"I hope you're right, Ahmed. Is there any news of Captain Evans?"

"No, mem. No worries. He at sea, working. Soon need supplies from tuan."

Without saying so, both Olivia and Ahmed were glad their new white skipper was unaware of Tyndall's state.

Thomas Evans was born and educated in Liverpool, but put to sea as a lad before the mast on the Sinclare Line. Eventually he worked his way up in ships trading to India and Australia. The lure of gold and dreams of a fortune attracted him to the Marble Bar goldfields. He made no fortune and missed the call of the sea, so returned to Broome and skippered luggers. A quiet and sober man, he was a mason of Roebuck Lodge No. 56 and had known and respected Conrad Hennessy.

Consequently, Tyndall and Olivia had been delighted when Evans accepted their offer to skipper the *Annabella*.

Now if only Tyndall would come to his senses and focus on the business at hand, thought Olivia. She could understand him missing Maya and his frustration at not being able to reach them. She decided he needed a diversion and to heal the wounds of their recent falling out she sent him an elegant handwritten invitation to dinner.

He confronted her at the foreshore camp, producing the invitation card from his pocket.

"What's this, Olivia? What's the occasion?"

"Dinner, John. Please come, let's say it's a bon voyage and to wish Star of the Sea a good season."

"I hate stuffy dinner parties. All that wah-wah chit chat. Can't stand 'em."

"I'd really like you to be there. Please."

"I might disgrace myself. Insult someone's wife, tell off a stuffed shirt, drink too much."

"You can be fiendishly charming and beautifully mannered on occasion. Don't be late," she said brightly, ignoring his gruff grunt as she left him, her fingers secretly crossed.

He arrived a little late, deliberately, but was decked out in his formal whites to please the hostess. At the gate it occurred to him that it seemed uncommonly quiet for a dinner party venue. There were no sulkies belonging to other guests and he wondered if he had got the time or date wrong. He fumbled in his pockets for the invitation card but realized he had left it at home. So he climbed the steps and was greeted by Minnie with a large smile.

"You on deck duty tonight, eh, Minnie?"

"Just little time. Help cook, then go home."

Tyndall walked into the dining room and stopped in astonishment.

The table was set for two. Candles and flowers in the center flanked by the best china and crystal. Olivia, dressed in a flattering gown of soft material in pale pink, her hair prettily coiled to one side of her head, came to him with a mischievous smile.

For a moment Tyndall was at a loss for words. "Where are the other guests?"

"Seems it's just the two of us," she smiled. "Sit down, John. I wanted my respected business partner—and friend—for company. He's been missing lately."

"You tricked me. I don't like that." His tone was affable.

"You wouldn't have come otherwise and we need to talk."

"We talk all the time." He lifted the bottle of champagne and poured two glasses.

"No, we don't. Lately we've been arguing, disagreeing, and if we do communicate sensibly it's for business. I thought it time we started off on a better foot. Rebuild our relationship."

"What's that mean? I don't like beating round the bush." He handed her a glass.

She twisted the crystal stem in her fingers and spoke softly without looking at him. "We've both suffered a loss and while yours is only temporary, I think we need to offer each other a bit of emotional support." She looked up at him. "I get lonely and there isn't anyone I can really talk to about how I feel. I miss Conrad's company. I know I am always the subject of speculation in town and while the ladies are well meaning I always feel I have to be on my best behavior. I can't be myself."

"Like running around in Chinese pajamas," he grinned.

They both laughed and clinked glasses. "That was a wonderful trip," sighed Olivia. "I think I must have the sea in my blood, too."

It suddenly occurred to Tyndall that the *first* time they went to sea together helped her come to terms with the loss of baby James. Maybe another sea trip would help with the grief she hid so well most of the time.

"How about coming out for a couple of weeks on the *Shamrock*? We'll get the rest of the fleet out, take a run up the coast and do some diving, resupply the fleet. The company might do me good, too."

Relief swept over Olivia. "I think that's a wonderful idea. Yes, I'd like that. Rosminah could help Minnie look after Hamish."

"He'll be cranky at missing out."

"Too big a trip. Besides, he's in school."

The house boy served the food and Olivia passed on what she'd read in the recently arrived London newspapers. Talk then moved on to the possibility of expanding the company.

As the dessert plates were taken away, Minnie appeared to say good night, looking concerned.

"What's up, Minnie?"

"Bin lookin' at the signs. Big wind comin."

"Can't be a cyclone, too late in the season," said Tyndall.

"Signs say big blow," said Minnie stubbornly and wished them good night.

Olivia lifted her eyebrows. 'You don't normally reject 'the signs'. What do you think?"

Tyndall rose and looked at Olivia's barometer hanging on the wall beside a brass ship's clock. He tapped it and looked thoughtful. "It's dropping. But not enough to panic." He walked to the verandah, picking up his skipper's hat. "Thanks for a lovely dinner. And for . . . being a friend. Don't worry. Star of the Sea is back on course." He put his hat on at a jaunty angle and stepped into the night, casting an anxious glance at the sky.

By morning the first clouds were scudding in on rising winds, the seas were building up, the barometer still falling. Olivia gave Minnie a rueful smile and headed to the office. She noticed some of the shopkeepers were shuttering their premises and people were taking precautions, stocking up on water and provisions, lashing down what they could. There was an oppressive heaviness in the air.

She pulled out essential working files and documents to put in the safe only to find Tyndall had the keys. While she was kneeling beside the safe pondering the problem a high wind screeched in, rattling the wooden shutters and blowing an empty drum into the side of the building. It jolted her into action. She bundled the papers together and ran to the foreshore camp. All along the shore of the bay was frenzied activity as men climbed over boats securing gear and putting out additional anchors. On the coast the ocean rolled in a slowly heaving mass as if building up to regurgitate the very depths of the sea bed.

Olivia paused for a moment, listening. Above the noise along the foreshore she heard a distant moan which sent a shudder through her.

At sea the fleet which had tried to run for shelter was becalmed in intense heat as if put in an oven and the air sucked out. It was so hot the pitch oozed from between planks, and metal burned skin.

On the *Annabella,* Captain Evans looked at the wildly dropping barometer and ordered the sails down, hatches battened and everything possible tied down or securely stowed. The two dinghies were hauled in and secured and storm anchors readied.

Early the next morning the cyclone hit the fleet near Broome, making a sudden and dramatic entrance with screaming winds, lashing rain and boiling seas. Some skippers attempted to run under storm sails. Captain Evans and several others decided to use sea anchors and try to ride it out. He knew their chances of survival were slim.

The first casualty was an old schooner loaded with shell that lost its masts and rigging and was thrown by huge waves into a lugger. Both quickly disappeared beneath the waves leaving crew floundering in the sea. There was nothing Evans could do to help them. Despite the sea anchor astern, his boat was hurtling along under bare masts, the rigging rattling and shrieking in the wind. Evans had a lifeline around his waist tied to a bollard and worked the tiller desperately to prevent some of the waves breaking over the stern, threatening to sweep him overboard, and soon stripping the deck.

The dinghies went first, their lashings torn

from the deck by waves. The pump went next, then the fo'c'sle hatch, causing the panic-stricken Koepangers to tumble onto the deck as water surged down. They rallied to shouted commands from Evans and quickly lashed canvas over the gaping hatch. While they were scampering to shelter in the main cabin aft another wave rolled over the stern, bringing down the main mast. When the water cleared off the deck there was no sign of the two Koepangers. Evans looked astern into the boiling sea but could see no one. He kicked at the door of the cabin and shouted for the divers who came on deck at once, sized up the situation, grabbed lifelines, and immediately began slashing and cutting at the rigging and mainmast to get it overboard as fast as possible. They knew that survival depended on how fast they worked and whether luck was on their side this day.

While the storm struck first at sea, it soon reached the coast south of Broome, slashing a path through the mangroves, hurling sheltering boats high onto the shore. It was the wild lashing of the cyclone's tail that hit the town, but nonetheless wreaked great havoc. The swiftness of the attack had stunned Olivia, who had barely reached the buildings at the foreshore camp before the wind threatened to carry her off. Tyndall dragged her into one of the shell sheds as the upper storey of the flimsy building ripped away, the galvanized iron sheets hurtling through the air, slashing into and wrapping themselves around trees stripped bare of leaves by the howling winds.

They could barely hear each other speak and Olivia clutched at Tyndall, shouting in his ear, "What about Hamish?"

"Don't worry, Minnie knows what to do. She'll look after him." He tightened his arm around Olivia as the doors to the shed and the roof were suddenly torn away.

"Let's get out of here, it's going to be flattened. The iron could slice us to pieces," yelled Tyndall. Half-running, half-dragging Olivia, he staggered toward the beach. A lugger belonging to another pearler had been tossed high on the beach and lay on its side, its masts jammed in the sand, the bottom of the hull beam to the wind. They raced to it and climbed into a hatch for shelter.

They were protected from the wind and whipping rain. Occasional waves crashed against the hull, but the boat, driven hard into the sand and mud by its initial impact, stayed in place.

Huddled together, Tyndall wrapped his arms around Olivia. Her thoughts were with her son, praying he was safe and not crazed with fear and worry. Over and over Tyndall kept reassuring her that Minnie would keep Hamish safe.

It was as dark as night, and the noise of the storm so great that Olivia felt the entire world was being broken apart.

Then came a lull, the eye, and they looked at each other.

"Too risky to make it to town. We have to see it out here," said Tyndall.

All too soon, the eye of the cyclone had passed and the terror began all over again. Olivia lost track of time, reduced to an emotional numbness, unable to think or feel, aware only of the warmth and strength of Tyndall's body. Tyndall was thinking of the little luggers at sea. Few would survive. Thanks to his lassitude, Ahmed, Yoshi and Taki were still ashore and he prayed they were safe. He could only trust and pray that the crew on the *Annabella* would be lucky.

By nightfall the winds gradually eased and then stopped. The sounds of the town picking itself up and awakening from the nightmare began to echo through the devastation. In the darkness, Tyndall and Olivia held hands as they picked their way through rubble and mud to Olivia's house, oblivious to what was around them. But in her street they became aware of voices calling and the crunch of wood and tin being moved by residents assessing the damage. The evening sky was still overcast but in the dimness Olivia could see her front fence was gone, the tree in the front garden uprooted and, to her horror, one end of the house had slid from its pole foundations and half the roof was gone. She realized at once which part of the house had caved in.

"It's the bedrooms. Oh, dear God, no . . ." She

clawed her way into the house, tripping and stumbling, calling, "Hamish, Hamish, I'm here. . . ."

Tyndall scrambled past her, calling for Minnie in the darkened house. He wheeled about and shouted at Olivia to be quiet and listen.

Then they heard it. "Mummy . . ." followed by Minnie's strong voice, "In main bedroom."

As Tyndall and Olivia groped their way into the room now exposed to sky, a light suddenly flared. It flickered from the floor and there, from under the big, solid wood four-poster bed, two faces peeped out, illuminated by the candle in Minnie's hand. Tyndall took the candle and helped Minnie out while Olivia scooped up Hamish.

"Big bed no can move. Good place, eh?" grinned Minnie, then seeing what had crashed into the house in the night she murmured, "Cripes, no wonder lotsa noise." She reached into her apron pocket and handed another candle and the matches to Tyndall. "All I had time to grab."

Minnie found cake and made a pot of tea and they settled down in the undamaged section of the house to sleep till dawn.

At first light, Tyndall crept outside. He wondered how Minnie's husband had fared in their small cottage near Kennedy's Knoll.

The impact of the cyclone, even though the town missed the full force of it, was shocking. He headed straight for the bay and saw that a dozen luggers making for Roebuck Bay had reached Entrance Point before being wrecked on the rocks or driven into the tangle of mangroves.

The waters of the bay were stained with flood-waters and along the coastline for miles was a high tide mark of flotsam. A jumble of sea rubbish, broken mangroves, wrecked dinghies and shattered boats were tangled with stores and dead birds. Seamen's personal effects and bodies of men were thrown together in a litter of wreckage and death.

Tales of heroism, survival and tragedy would later emerge: the elderly white captain supported in the sea by his Malay crew until they were luckily swept into shore; shipwrecked men who had the clothes whipped from their bodies and suffered near blindness and excruciating pain as their naked bodies were sandblasted by the wind-driven sand; a shell opener decapitated by a flying sheet of iron; and so many other lives lost by drowning.

As Tyndall trudged through the town it looked as if a small war had been fought in the streets. Shanty houses had been torn apart and blown miles into the pindan, foundations remaining as the only evidence of their previous existence. Some commercial buildings in town were flattened and most were damaged. Sheba Lane took a battering but while many lost their roofs and rickety balconies, most of the buildings stayed upright, somehow clinging together for support.

At the Aboriginal camps, there was little to salvage but all had survived by sheltering in thick scrub between the inland sand dunes. Seeing Tyndall, Alf appeared holding the hand of Minnie's daughter, Mollie. Tyndall passed on the news his missus was all right.

"Tell 'er not to come home for a bit. I'm still pickin' up 'er stuff outta trees," he said with a shrug.

Finally Tyndall had to face the inevitable and he turned along the sea front to the offices of Star of the Sea. The building was partially damaged, but intact. Ahmed was asleep on the office floor, his head resting on a rolled-up sail.

Tyndall woke him and together they set out to assess the situation at the foreshore camp. The shed was a total write-off, but it wouldn't take much to rebuild the simple unlined corrugated iron shed and upstairs crew room. The *Bulan* was aground well above the high-water mark but the hull was sound.

"Going to take a lot of bullocks to drag her back to the water," observed Tyndall. "Reckon that and repairs to the rigging will take a couple of weeks at least."

They rowed out to the *Conrad,* one of the few vessels to stay securely anchored during the big blow. She sat low in the water, the main hold flooded. "A pump job and some rigging. Got off lightly there, Ahmed."

"Good name, Captain. Lucky ship," commented Ahmed with a smile.

"You may be right, Ahmed. A lucky ship." Then they rowed over to the *Shamrock.* She had dragged her anchors and was heeling over slightly, sitting on the bottom at half tide, but the two men were soon able to haul it out into deeper water and reposition the anchors. There was storm water in all compartments, but little damage.

"Another lucky ship, Ahmed. The luck of the Irish is powerful, too," he grinned, aware of just how much import his friend put on superstition.

In all, thirty luggers were lost at sea but the *Annabella* limped back to Broome under a jury-rig, having lost both masts.

Evans was praised for his skill though he modestly claimed a lot of it was luck. "As the divers say, when your day is come, you go."

Weeks were lost while repairs were made and gradually the remnants of the fleet headed out to sea. Yoshi took the *Conrad* and once the masts and pump were replaced, Evans took the *Annabella* back to sea. Only the *Bulan* wasn't ready. Tyndall said he'd bring the *Shamrock* out to supply them and pick up shell in a couple of weeks.

Tyndall had said little to anyone about Niah and Maya, but now he broached the subject with Olivia and confessed he longed to know what had happened to them.

They sat in the shadowy twilight of Olivia's verandah and she reached over and took his hand, hearing the tremor in his voice and realizing the depth of his feelings.

"Maybe we should spread the word a bit more," she suggested. "Can't the police or the black trackers help?"

Tyndall shrugged. "I've already mentioned it on the quiet to my mate the sergeant. Out of their territory. Lumped as 'blackfella business'."

Later Olivia decided to talk with Minnie.

"Captain Tyndall is still upset over Niah and Maya. How would you go about trying to find out where they are?"

"Why? If Niah ready come back, she come back. But I can send word again. Wally find out."

"Wally? Who's Wally? What do you mean *again*?" Olivia demanded. As she studied Minnie's set and closed face, Olivia began to feel cold shivers run through her. Minnie, jolly, honest, open Minnie was holding something back.

"Wally one of the mob. Same as me. Sorta cousin."

"What does he know about Niah?"

When Minnie didn't answer straight away, Olivia was insistent. "Minnie, you must tell me. It's important. If you know anything about Niah and Maya, you *must* tell me."

"Niah take Maya find her Dreaming, learn 'bout her family. Them be all right."

"Minnie! You *know* where they are, why they went?"

"Me and Alf are townies now. Don't keep in touch regular with my people. I dunno what happen. Niah unhappy. She ask me what t'do. I tell her take Maya find her people. Niah belong same people. We all same people. Same family. Wally take 'em. Mebbe if Wally come back he know sumthin.'"

The jerky answers pieced the story together for Olivia, who was still somewhat shocked by this revelation. "Please Minnie. We must find out. It's not fair on Captain Tyndall. He loves little Maya, she's his daughter. And I suppose in his way, he loves Niah, too."

Minnie gave her a shrewd look. "I see what I can find out."

Olivia was about to leave when she turned back to Minnie. "What do you mean, you all the same people. Who are you talking about?"

Minnie lifted a hand in a vague gesture. "My people belong same country you make friends when you come on beach 'n' have your first baby. Wally belong same people. He live in town some time. Some time go bush."

Olivia stared at Minnie. "You mean the women I first met down the coast from Cossack are *your* people?"

"Yeah. But I got taken by police 'n' sent to a mission school." She gave a defiant lift to her head. "Learn white ways, work for white people. I marry Alf, he mix-up blood, too. But I find my people again. We got different lives now. Keep in with 'em, they always family."

"I don't know what to say. Who knows this?"

"Ahmed know. He fetch me when Niah baby

come 'cause he know we same people. He know my people help you. They watch out for us."

Olivia sat down, trying to absorb this avalanche of important information and wondering if she would ever understand the Aboriginal way of thinking, their different attitude to life, different values.

Eventually she said slowly, "Minnie, could you send some sort of message via Wally, when he turns up again, to please find out where Niah and Maya are. If they are all right and when or if they are coming back? Do you think he can find out?"

"Mebbe. We try. Don' worry, mem."

Olivia decided not to say anything to Tyndall until they had some answers.

It took two weeks. By whatever method messages were relayed over the vast distance of the bush, the story filtered back of Niah being kidnapped by Gunther and possibly killed. Looking distressed, Minnie relayed the news to Olivia.

"But what of Maya? Where is she, she's so young, what's happened to her?" Olivia dreaded having to pass on this news to Tyndall.

"Oh, Maya safe. She with her family, all the aunties and uncles look after her. She learn their ways, wait see if her mummy come back."

Olivia was frustrated and angry. "What if Niah doesn't come back, and it seems unlikely. Maya should be here, with her father."

"Maya with her people," said Minnie stubbornly.

"Do you know where she is?"

Minnie shook her head. "They on walkabout. Come back some time. Better Maya stay with her people. Tyndall no can look after little girl proper. No can teach her business."

"But she could have the advantages of going to a school here, learning our ways, too. She is half white, Minnie."

Minnie shrugged. "Maya come back to Broome one day."

Olivia saw it was pointless arguing with Minnie. She knew what Tyndall would say, that if Maya stayed away, she'd forget this life and her father.

Tyndall said little after Olivia quietly told him the details in his office. She noticed Maya's toy lugger was back on his desk. He stood and looked out over Streeter's Jetty and the activity of rebuilding and repairing the cyclone damage. She had expected him to rant and rave and lose his temper. His silent pain was actually harder to bear. "Leave me be please, Olivia. And thank you . . . for finding out what . . . happened."

They didn't speak of the matter again. He didn't appear for their sundowners for a couple of nights and she suspected he was comforting himself with a bottle of whisky. When he did turn up, it was all business.

Ten days later he surprised her by asking, "You still game for a trip up the coast?"

She nodded. "I'd like some peace and quiet. The town is still a shambles."

"I'd like some peace, too. Been through a bit of heart searching. I suppose I've come to terms with things. Nothing much I can do for the moment anyway."

"We've both suffered a loss, maybe this trip is a good idea," said Olivia softly.

Arrangements were made and Tyndall pointed out it was not a recreational trip but a serious pearling expedition. He intended to dive on the new beds they'd explored previously. So far as he was aware none of the Broome luggers had worked this area. The *Shamrock* had been converted for diving and fitted with pumps. Ahmed would act as tender. If the diving proved lucrative they would divert their other luggers to the new grounds.

Tyndall grinned broadly when Olivia first emerged on deck in what he called her Chinese sailing pajamas.

"Not a word," admonished Olivia lightly, wagging a finger at him.

He took both hands off the tiller and held them up in mock surrender. "I'm too much of a gentleman, you know that. I'm surprised it even crossed your mind that I might utter an ungentlemanly remark. You look positively divine."

"Huh!" But she couldn't hold back a grin.

And that was the mood that prevailed as they fell into a comfortable routine at sea, a good humored interaction as Olivia, tanned and toughened, threw

herself into crew tasks, handling the sails, taking
the tiller and even, briefly, working the pump.

The weather was peaceful, the water clear and
calm. But the diving was disappointing. Time and
again Tyndall appeared in a whoosh of bubbles
and once on the rope ladder, before his helmet
was off, he'd give the thumbs down. There was
shell but it was small, the nacre thin and luster
dull.

"These duds won't produce pearls," he
declared in disgust.

Olivia could see he was getting cranky with the
enterprise and so one morning suggested they go
ashore and explore. They took a water container,
rowed ashore, pulled the dinghy up on the beach
and set off.

Following the water course through the sand
dunes they were thrilled to discover it widened
into a deep creek. They waded through the warm
knee-deep water as the undergrowth on either
side of the creek was thick and hard to penetrate.
About a mile inland the creek broadened and,
through the bush, cliffs suddenly appeared.
Clambering round a bend they stopped and
caught their breath. The creek widened into a
large freshwater pool. It was fed from a waterfall
that fell from the high red cliff escarpments surrounding it.

"How beautiful!"

Tyndall waded to the small strip of crystalline
red sand and dropped his shoes, hat and water
container and pulled off his shirt.

"Turn your back, I'm swimming." He pulled off his trousers and plunged in. "Come on, Olivia. It's glorious." He faced the other way while she stripped down to her underwear and slid into the water.

Refreshed and relaxed, they sat in the shade looking at the sparkling pool.

"Bit of paradise isn't it?" said Tyndall, smiling at the damp-haired Olivia. "Glad you came?"

"Very."

They stared at each other for a moment longer, then Tyndall leaned over and gently kissed her. "You look sweet," he said softly.

Olivia felt she was in another world. All that had gone before them slipped away and she and Tyndall were in some time warp, some dreamscape where only these moments counted. She had no thoughts of past connections with people, places or events. There was just this beautiful place, this tranquillity, and this special man beside her. She reached for him as he did her.

Briefly, as Tyndall's hands caressed Olivia's smooth skin the thought flashed into his mind, that this act would lead them into deep and complicated waters. But he dismissed the future and the past and lived in this glorious moment of losing himself in Olivia's arms and body.

Their bodies melded together with ease and felt as one. Their breathing, their mounting passion, the physical pleasure they gave each other was in tandem. Olivia felt no weight from Tyndall's body pressing against and within her.

They moved together, their bodies in a dance of love that carried them along in wild sweeps of energy then into valleys of gentle tenderness, exploring, feeling and absorbing each other. They smiled into each other's eyes as they thrust and lingered, teasing and pleasuring. Tyndall's lips brushed against hers as she wound her fingers in his thick hair and they whispered of the wondrous sensations they were experiencing. There was a frankness, an intimacy and a sharing of the heart, soul and body neither had experienced before.

After lovemaking that left them both breathless and stunned at the wonderment of such fulfillment, they swam in the pool again—this time joyously naked, romping and splashing like children. Finally, they dressed and headed back to the schooner. As Tyndall rowed he gazed at Olivia's sparkling eyes and happy smile. "Your face gives everything away," he chided.

"You look fetchingly rumpled yourself."

They laughed, exchanging an intimate glance, both silently pledging to try to appear circumspect in front of the crew.

Ahmed wasn't fooled for a moment. He glanced from one to the other, noting Olivia's flushed face, her persistent closeness to Tyndall, whose studied nonchalance was contradicted by swift and burning glances toward Olivia.

That evening after Olivia retired to her bunk, Tyndall sat in the main cabin poring over a map by lantern light. Ahmed stuck his head in the doorway. "We movin' somewhere new?" he asked, seeing the map. Ahmed was anxious to get back to serious pearling.

"Yep. Some time back I met an old codger in a bar. Had a wooden leg. Told me the best place he'd ever seen was the Buccaneer Archipelago." Tyndall adjusted a protractor over the map.

"He lose his leg up that place then?" inquired Ahmed.

Tyndall ignored the question, remarking, "Easy sailing. What's a couple of days. Could be interesting. Yes, I think we should go." He looked at Ahmed and couldn't stop the slightly embarrassed smile that spread across his face. "Might never have the opportunity again. Good for Mem Hennessy, after the storm . . . and everything. Me, too." For the first time that day, thoughts of Maya and Niah rushed to his mind and a shadow passed over his face.

Ahmed nodded, his expression unchanged. "*Bagus.* I tell boys we go . . . where we go, tuan?"

"Camden Peninsula, set a course nor-north-east," instructed Tyndall, folding the map.

The schooner rolled in seas off Cape Leveque and the threat of bad weather forced them to pull into one of the creeks that fed into the sea. The mangrove trees were thick and protective, sheltering the creek and spreading into the ocean for several miles. Rarely disturbed, the roots grew upward and entwined fifteen feet above the ground, forming an impassable canopy. Deciding to explore, Tyndall and Olivia picked their way through the maze of broader lower roots, using them like stepping stones. Occasionally they disturbed climbing fish basking on the tree branches and the long catfish-like creatures plopped into the marshy water or flipped across the surface.

When they eventually returned to the boat, they found Ahmed and the crew had caught several fat mud crabs and mangrove pigeons.

From then on they had perfect sailing conditions up the coast. It was plain sailing for two days, passing through Buccaneer Archipelago and Yampi Sound. They skirted a large island reef and moved closer to land and finally sailed past Camden Peninsula to Augustus Island.

"I feel like we're the first people ever to come here," said Olivia, shading her eyes to scan the lush and seemingly deserted island.

They anchored in a sheltered cove where rose-colored sandstone cliffs soared three hundred feet to a plateau upon which several large baobab trees stood sentry on the skyline. Lush tropical growth fringed the base of the cliffs. They could hear the screech of birds and distant sound of waterfalls that glinted on the pink cliffs. Before them was a crescent-shaped white-sand beach, with tall trees casting shadows which led to crystal green water. At one end of the island the deeper green indicated the ocean floor dropped off to a greater depth.

Tyndall nudged Olivia. "There's a perfect place to dive."

"It's so beautiful," sighed Olivia. "It's got a strange mood, don't you think? It's really inviting, but there's also something mysterious about it. Or am I imagining things?"

"Well, let's go ashore and find out," said Tyndall buoyantly.

They went ashore in two dinghies—Ahmed, the tender and the second mate, who had brought a rifle along, followed by Tyndall and Olivia. After pulling the dinghies high onto the sand they all went in different directions to explore.

"One shot, we shoot food, two shots quick quick, need help," said Ahmed.

"What about us? What if we need help?"

"Give a cooee. Don't worry, I have my pistol," grinned Tyndall.

Olivia produced a knife in a leather sheath from her pocket. "I can look after myself," she added, taking up an aggressive stance which had the crew chuckling.

They plunged into the thick undergrowth discovering strange plants and exotic flowers. It was green and cool and so unlike the heat and barrenness of Broome. Tyndall saw a tree snake looped and draped like a vine hanging from a branch, but decided against pointing it out to Olivia.

They found a rough track that wound up to the plateau. As they climbed, they rested frequently to admire the view across the glassy waters to the model-sized schooner and islands beyond. In an overhang they spotted caves and, almost at the plateau, they came upon a ridge where a narrow ledge led to several caves.

"Feel game enough to explore?" asked Tyndall.

The ledge along the cliff face was wide enough to walk along, but there was a sheer drop to the jungle floor a long way below.

Olivia nodded and followed him, her heart thumping. She swallowed hard and looked only at where she was putting her feet.

They entered the center cave, which was the biggest, and found themselves in an antechamber with smaller passages leading off it. Tyndall reached for Olivia's hand and they ducked down a short passage to an inner cave. It was quite dark but no sooner had their eyes adjusted to the gloom than Olivia let out a screech and jumped back. Before them lay whole skeletons and assorted human bones. Skulls glared at them from sightless holes and teeth were bared in snarls.

"Ugh. How awful. What is this place?" she whispered.

"Aboriginal burial cave. Hey, look at this." He moved forward.

"Don't disturb them. It might be bad luck."

"I won't. I just want to have a closer look." He pointed to one set of bones. "This fellow brought his favorite things with him."

Olivia saw a large mother-of-pearl breastplate lying amongst the bones. "Do you think it came from round here?"

"Could be."

"Let's leave. This place frightens me."

They retraced their steps and made the final ascent to the plateau. Far below was the speck of one of the dinghies rowing to the schooner.

"Maybe they're going to sail away and leave us," said Olivia in jest.

"Well, if we're going to be marooned we might as well make the most of it." He grinned and took her in his arms and kissed her. They made love on the grass, by the baobab tree, at the top of a magical island, and felt they could touch the clouds. Olivia, naked in the daylight, surrendered herself to the caress of the breeze, the warmth of the sun and the whisper of Tyndall's lips.

The next day Tyndall made the first dive off the point of the island. He rose within an hour and a basket of pearl shell spilled onto the deck. His enthusiasm bubbled over. "It's magnificent down there. Olivia, you must see this. You said you wanted to try a dive. This is perfect. It's only twelve fathoms and so beautiful. You'll love it."

His eagerness swept away her momentary apprehension. She had always wanted to see the world beneath the sea. Tyndall and Ahmed schooled her closely and she'd watched enough dives to be familiar with the procedure. Tyndall would be able to dive with her as they'd set up two hand pumps on the *Shamrock*.

The weight of the suit scared her and as she sank through the water, she felt she would never rise to the surface again. Then she felt lightheaded, as if she could float away and realized quickly she had to adjust her pressure gauge.

By the time she felt comfortable, Tyndall was in front of her, giving her hand signals and she looked about her. Nothing had prepared her for the wonderment of this eerily silent blue and green world. Tiny multi-hued fish darted at the glass panel in her helmet, peering in at her and darting away as one in a colored cloud. The underwater garden waved and swayed to sea music she could only imagine. Coral, which exploded in brilliant bursts, housed all manner of microscopic life and fish. Tyndall pointed beneath a coral ledge and for a moment she couldn't make out anything. Then two eyes came into focus and she saw the fleshy lips of a huge groper with a mouth that looked big enough to swallow a diver's boot. Everywhere she turned was something of incredible beauty or fascination. At first she was aware of Tyndall watching her carefully, but as she moved slowly through this absorbing underwater world she forgot about him and lost track of time.

Finally Tyndall indicated she should follow him, and he led her along the bottom to where a strip of sand ran between two coral outcrops. He pointed to a ledge and when she shook her head, uncomprehending, he bent over and picked up a large pearl shell. Olivia suddenly saw the others, so simply camouflaged yet now so obvious. They collected half a dozen and then Olivia pointed to the coral and made a querying gesture. Tyndall peered at where she pointed, then reached his gloved hand in and felt for what appeared to be a pearl shell nestled in the coral. It was well concealed and hard to dislodge, he struggled and was about to give up when Olivia pushed her hand beside his and together they pulled it free. Tyndall turned the shell over in his hands. It was very large, plump and heavily encrusted. He put it in the bag and pointed to the surface. They tugged on their lines, signaling to the tenders to bring them up.

It wasn't till after they'd eaten and sailed well clear of the beach to anchor for the night that Tyndall and Ahmed opened the shells. One yielded a perfect round, but very tiny pearl. Nonetheless Olivia was elated. Tyndall then opened what he announced to the crew was "Olivia's shell."

It was stubborn, the muscles tightly holding it shut. Tyndall worked the knife until it slipped through and the shell fell open. Without even removing the meat they could see the glow of a fat round pearl.

Olivia, crouching beside Tyndall, leaned forward. "There's more than one," she breathed and the crew gathered around, moving the lantern closer.

Tyndall carefully scraped away the meat.

A collective gasp went up as they saw on one shell, seven fat, spherical pearls. Each on its own would fetch a goodly price but what caused the crew to murmur in amazement was the formation. The seven pearls lay joined in the shape of a star.

Olivia and Tyndall stared at one another in disbelief.

"My God, it's fantastic." Tyndall's hand shook slightly as he studied the shell in his palm, tilting it to and fro to catch the light of the lantern from different angles.

"It's worth a fortune," Olivia whispered in awe and behind her the crew broke into a gabble of exchanges in Japanese and Malay. Ahmed gave thanks to Allah in a silent prayer.

"The great gem buyers of the world will be fighting like hell to get their hands on this," crowed Tyndall.

"We'll have to call it the 'Star of the Sea,' of course. Odd, isn't it, that the shape of the pearls matches the name of our company," said Olivia, her voice still reflecting the awe in which they all held the freakish pearl find. "Spooky in a way."

"Everything that led us to finding it is a bit odd in a way, when you think about it." Their eyes met for the first time since the shell was opened. "It's going to change our lives, Olivia."

She nodded in silent agreement, then they both looked down at the shell again, transfixed by its beauty.

CHAPTER FIFTEEN

Maya still missed her mother. The women had told her that Niah had gone to live with her ancestors among the stars but she watched over her and was always with her even though Maya couldn't see her.

"Sometimes when the wind come and blow your hair and brush your face, that your mummy touching you. When you eat good and find clean water for drink, that your mummy looking out for you," they told her.

Maya struggled to grasp this abstract concept— she missed the lilting voice, the embrace and sweet smell of her own mother.

She missed her father, too. His laughter and teasing and the great stretches of time they spent together "out in the world." While her mother had been part of this outback world, her father belonged to another world. She remembered the noise and smell of the shell sheds; sitting on the deck of a beached lugger while the men worked; playing on the floor of Tyndall's office with her own toy lugger; seeing the streets of Broome from her father's shoulders; holding onto his curling hair with one hand, the other resting over his ear with the pearl.

While these memories were vivid initially, they were soon relegated to the nether regions of her mind while she focused on the daily events of life around her. Being part of a family group was a revelation for her, as was having playmates and so many aunties and uncles and grandmothers. She walked obediently beside the girl designated her big sister, played with the other children when they rested at a water hole, and at night, sleepily climbed into the nearest ample lap as the women grouped themselves around the campfire after eating.

As the weeks passed, the thought of losing Maya gnawed at Tyndall and he tried again to send word via his Aboriginal friends to find where they might be. He'd learned that the people he and Olivia had befriended down the coast had moved on.

Monsieur Barat wasn't due for a few more weeks and Olivia and Tyndall had kept tight-lipped about their pearl find, though there were rumors circulating. Olivia was well aware that collectors and serious buyers wouldn't buy a pearl that had been "shown" or shopped about.

"We'll just have to keep quiet. At least the gossip isn't about us." He gave her a playful grin.

"Do you think they will? Talk about us? Surely not. No one knows anything."

Tyndall laughed at her worried look. "You ashamed of me or something?"

"It's not that. I am still officially in mourning and you aren't unattached." Olivia finally voiced the thought that had disturbed her most about their relationship. "What will you do if Niah comes back?"

"I'm not sure that she will." He looked distressed. "It's not Niah I want back, but Maya. Niah is delightful, but she can't give me what you can, Olivia. I can talk to you, we share a common background and that counts for such a lot. You make me feel a whole person. I treasure that." He spoke hesitantly and almost shyly.

"Where are we going, John?" she asked softly.

"We need time, Olivia. We need to go slowly down this path we're following and avoid the glare of gossip and interfering outsiders. I'm afraid we're going to have to be devious."

"I understand. I'm not ready to rush into anything, John. And I have Hamish's feelings to consider."

So the new turn in their relationship remained their secret. The closeness with which they had worked and supported each other over these trying months was maintained and no one in the community noticed any change.

But they stole opportunities to be together and, in a flash of inspiration, Tyndall suggested they go away to Perth together. "I cabled

Monsieur Barat to see if we can meet him there. It is the logical thing to do—to see him there and arrange the sale of the pearls. We've tried to keep it quiet but enough people know to understand why we'd make a business trip south." Tyndall suddenly became quite demonstrative, waving his arm in the air. "Oh Olivia, just think, we can stay in a nice big hotel in Perth, visit good restaurants, do things together and stay anonymous." For a few moments he was just like an excited schoolboy.

For Olivia, the thought of a romantic interlude with Tyndall was bewitching. "Let's do it!" she agreed with equal excitement.

They decided to wait till the end of the season to take the trip. Everything was arranged—Minnie would care for Hamish, Captain Evans would supervise the refit of the luggers, and Ahmed the sorting and packing of the shell.

Once on board the steamer to Fremantle, they put their precious parcel of pearls in the captain's safe and, despite having separate cabins, enjoyed shipboard life.

Upon arrival in Fremantle, they took a riverboat up the Swan River to Perth and booked into a discreet hotel as Mr. and Mrs. Johnston. Their days and nights together were every bit as wonderful as they'd hoped and imagined.

Monsieur Barat came to their hotel and greeted them warmly.

His sensitive antenna picked up that there was something between the two of them, but his discretion prevented him from showing any reaction. Instead he addressed the business at hand. "If you have come to me, rather than wait for me to come to you, I must assume you have something special to show me?"

Olivia carefully unrolled the velvet wrapping to reveal the shell with the seven pearls on it. Monsieur Barat was speechless, an involuntary short gasp the only sound in the room.

"Is this special enough?" asked Tyndall quietly, with a slight smile.

Monsieur Barat did not take his eyes off the pearls but nodded in agreement. "It's a miracle. Where was this found?"

"Somewhere special indeed," answered Olivia softly. "But even if we were to return there, I doubt we'd find anything like it again."

The Frenchman picked up the shell with both hands, lifting it with reverence, as if it was a sacred object. "One could live several lifetimes before seeing something like this. I am honored you have shown it to me."

"You're our friend and we trust you," responded Olivia and Monsieur Barat acknowledged her with a slight bow.

He examined the pearls on the shell more closely. "I am glad you didn't try to remove the pearls. They could have come apart and they are worth more, initially, in their original state. A buyer can decide what is to be done with them later."

Tyndall and Olivia exchanged a relieved

glance. "Tobias Metta advised us to leave them intact. He is sworn to secrecy about them," said Olivia.

"He is a wise man. Collectors are strange people and some prize more highly pearls that have not been publicly advertised. The sale must be handled very discreetly."

"Indeed," said Olivia, inviting him to continue.

"I would travel to London and sell it privately in Hatton Garden. There are agents there for buyers with the sort of money this treasure will bring. But, of course, that is up to you to decide." He placed the shell back in its velvet wrapping.

Olivia and the French pearl buyer haggled briefly over the commission and the finer details of the transaction as they always did and Tyndall sat back and listened with faint amusement. It was a delicate dance, an exercise they both enjoyed with the toing and froing, pauses for consideration and suggestion, rather like a game of chess.

Monsieur Barat later joined them for dinner and when they bid him goodbye he warned them it might take a little time to find the right buyer "with the right amount of money."

Over the next season, losses from the cyclone were more than recouped.

"These are boom times," declared Tyndall as record yields of shell were sold.

The Broome fleet now numbered in the hundreds and adventurers and entrepreneurs from many countries came to seek their fortunes on the pearling grounds. Some put their life savings into a boat or talked an investor into backing them, but most failed from inexperience, greed, or bad luck.

The Star of the Sea Pearl Company now had twelve luggers.

"We can't expand and keep a close watch on any more than we have now," said Olivia. "It's getting harder to find honest men to work for us, we need white shell openers on every boat to watch every shell that's opened. I still think we're losing pearls, even with the pearl boxes."

These were an ingenious invention carried on all luggers where pearls were dropped down a funnel into the box, which was then padlocked so that only the holder of the key could retrieve the pearls. As soon as Olivia saw this device she put one on every boat.

"You're a tough businesswoman, Olivia," teased Tyndall, leaning down and kissing the tip of her ear.

She blushed and whispered, "Be careful, someone might come into the office."

Tyndall picked up one of their pearl boxes and rattled it. "What lugger did this come off, sounds promising."

"Captain Evans brought it in from the *Annabella*. But he says the tally isn't as good as from the banks they worked last year."

"Hmm. Might be time we went back to some of the old beds," said Tyndall thoughtfully. "The pickings should be ripe again."

"Let's keep it to ourselves. No point in having half the fleet shelling in *our* waters," grinned Olivia.

"I wish there was some way of replenishing the pearl shell ourselves," mused Tyndall. "If we could get the spat to grow in controlled conditions and harvest the shell ourselves, we'd make a fortune. And guarantee they'd produce a decent pearl for good measure," he added.

"Is that possible?"

"I've heard rumors of some experiments and I'd like to think that anything is always possible."

"Always the optimist, aren't you? Well, figure out where we're going to send the boats next season."

"This season isn't over yet. Perhaps we should take two of the luggers and do a little exploring."

Tyndall and Olivia took the *Shamrock,* with Ahmed on the *Bulan.* The fewer who knew where they were going, the better.

They sailed north to King Sound. The waters were so turbulent that it didn't surprise Olivia when Tyndall told her few boats ventured into this area off the entrance to the Sound.

They had brought Yoshi to dive with Ahmed on the *Bulan* and Taki to act as tender for Tyndall on the *Shamrock.*

Tyndall's first drift over the sea bed produced nothing and he signaled the boat to move on. An hour later in deeper water and descending to thirty fathoms, Tyndall still had no luck. Finally, he signaled to them to bring him up. This was a long, slow process as he had to be staged, resting at intervals on his ascent, hanging on to his lifeline, impatiently waiting, in order to prevent bubbles of nitrogen entering tissues of the body and causing excruciating pain known as "the bends."

After they had raised him out of the water, he collapsed on the deck. When his helmet and boots were removed, he moaned, "What a damned waste of time. Absolutely nothing."

"What's wiped out the shell?"

"Not what, Olivia, but who. Poachers it seems."

"Do you suppose Ahmed and Yoshi are having any better luck?"

"Let's go see."

They sailed close to the *Bulan* and called across to Ahmed who shook his head and gave a thumbs-down.

In the morning the two boats set off and headed out toward Adele Island to try their luck in completely new grounds.

Late the following day the crewman on watch called their attention to a smudge on the horizon. They changed course to port and sailed toward the small island. From a distance it appeared rocky and barren, but on the seaward side they found an inlet and a narrow strip of beach.

"Look at the palms, it's quite tropical, and there's smoke inland a bit," said Olivia, handing the eyeglass to Tyndall.

He accepted the glass and, scanning the island, remarked with curiosity, "According to the map the island is 'uninhabited'."

The boats slipped in and moored off the beach as the day faded. Ahmed and Yoshi rowed alongside and Tyndall climbed into the dinghy.

They pulled the dinghy onto the shore and made their way into the trees following a well-worn track. Ahmed nudged Tyndall and tapped his nose. Tyndall could smell cooking, too, and soon they could see firelight and hear the noise of a small community.

Long thatched bungalows stood next to stone and wood buildings. Next to several fireplaces, there was an open communal eating area sheltered by a roof supported on poles. Several Aboriginal women were tending food at the fireplaces. One of the bungalows had wooden doors and Tyndall saw the metal bolt on it was padlocked. Some Aborigines were sharpening tools and cleaning several large tortoise shells.

An elderly Aborigine straightened up and stared at them as the little party walked into the clearing. He responded to Tyndall's greeting with "G'day boss."

The women melted into the background as the men gathered around, curious and friendly.

Tyndall and Ahmed were trying to find out what the unexpected settlement was all about when the crowd parted and a solid middle-aged man dressed in tattered cut-off trousers and cotton undershirt came forward. Despite his bare feet and casual attire he presented a figure of authority. He beamed and announced, "Father Anders. Welcome to our mission." His booming voice had a thick Dutch accent.

"Mission? This is a mission?" Tyndall tried not to look disbelieving. "Way out here?"

"It is a leper mission. The people you see here are relatives and, er, helpers to those afflicted," explained Anders. "*They* are in a special area," he added as Ahmed and Tyndall glanced around.

"I see. Do you have help, and what about supplies? The wood and water trains don't come out here, I imagine," commented Tyndall, referring to the boats that supplied the fleets.

"We look after ourselves," replied the Dutchman enigmatically. "We have our own boats, there's a safe harbor round the point. I assume you came via the beach."

Tyndall nodded. "We'll moor for the night and if we could avail ourselves of some fresh water, maybe a coconut or two . . . we'd be grateful."

Father Anders smiled and gestured with both hands. "Whatever we have, the Lord wishes us to share."

"We'll be back in the morning then." Tyndall shook the Dutchman's hand and they headed back to the beach.

"What do you think, Ahmed? I don't think our Dutch friend is a priest or do-gooder at all. Didn't trust him for a minute."

"Why they lock up bungalows? What they got in them?"

"I think we should look at their little harbor."

The three of them set off, scrambling through the fringe of tropical growth and over a small headland. In the rising moonlight they could see the opening to a calm inlet. Several luggers and a ketch were moored. Dinghies and canoes were pulled up on the beach and the boats looked deserted.

"Me go and check 'em out, eh, tuan?" offered Ahmed.

Tyndall hesitated, he and Yoshi would arouse suspicion. Another Malay might not. He nodded.

Ahmed chose a small dinghy and rowed silently to the boats, studying them closely. Then to their surprise, he tied a rope to the ketch and climbed on board. They saw him crouch on the deck and lift a hatch cover.

As silently as he'd left he was quickly back on the shore and they stood back amongst the trees.

"The hold is filled with shells, tortoise and pearl shell," Ahmed reported.

"I can guess where they've been getting the shell," muttered Tyndall.

"This poacher's place. No mission. What we do, tuan?"

"Leave quietly and report them later. The boats are clearly from the Indies. Dutch-owned, I'd say. And the natives no doubt have been blackbirded—slave labor."

But as they moved through the trees, Yoshi, who was bringing up the rear, gave a small shout. The others turned around quickly to find one of the Malays they'd seen at the mission tugging at Yoshi's arm.

The man spoke quickly. "Please, help me get away from this place. I want to leave, go back to my wife and children. They bring me here and I can't escape."

Ahmed asked rapid questions and the man told them he was hired to work as crew on one of the Dutch boats, but had been brought here with other Koepangers and Aborigines against their will and could not leave. He told them the Dutch priest was actually a ship's captain who had established this base for poaching. It was known that many of the Malay islands were used as piracy bases for gun running, spoils of poaching and blackbirding.

Tyndall and Ahmed conferred quickly, and agreed to take the man with them. With some urgency, they hurried to the darkened beach.

When they reached the sand, they found a reception committee waiting for them. Tyndall let out a cry of rage when he saw who was in charge of the small group—Karl Gunther.

Tyndall sprang at him, catching him by surprise, attempting to throttle the squat and powerfully built man. The men around them fell on the two men, wrenching them apart and the two groups, now all brandishing knives and pistols, held back their two leaders.

"Where is she?" shouted Tyndall. "What have you done with her?"

Gunther, dazed for a moment, didn't register what Tyndall had asked him.

"How did you find us here? Who told you to come here?"

"No one! This is a happy accident, Gunther! Now, where is Niah?"

Comprehension dawned on the hawk-like features of the swarthy German. "She's gone. I did nothing. She dived from my boat. Kaput. Sharks get her."

Tyndall went limp, suspecting that Gunther was telling the truth. "And why would she leap overboard . . . to get away from you." His anger resurged and he made another lunge but was held back by Yoshi and Ahmed on either side. Ahmed held Tyndall's arm with one hand and his *kris* with the other.

Gunther took a step forward. "You can't leave here. We'd better visit Anders."

"Don't be mad, Gunther. No matter what you do to us, our crew will sail straight to the authorities. Better you let us go."

"Why should I do that—" Before he could finish the sentence, a pistol cracked and a bullet sprayed sand beside his feet, causing him to leap backward. The shot came from the trees and two more rang out in quick succession, sending up tufts of sand between the two men. Gunther and his three men turned and fled into the trees, dragging the Malay with them.

Taki and Olivia emerged from the trees and ran across the sand. Olivia was carrying the pistol.

"John, are you all right?" she called in a frightened voice.

They fell into each other's arms. "Yes, no harm done, but it looked nasty for a minute. Good Lord, you could have shot any of us," he exclaimed.

"I aimed low," she said, grinning. "Well, say thanks."

Tyndall laughed, hugged her quickly and led everyone back to the dinghies on the beach.

"Whatever made you come ashore, and with a pistol?" he asked as he rowed back to the two boats.

"You seemed to be gone so long, and it was getting dark, and something told me to do it." She shrugged her shoulders. "Don't ask me what or why. Just one of those things. We had no sooner reached the trees when Gunther and his mob turned up, so we waited and watched."

The last of the fading breeze got them safely out to sea and, in the distance, they could see the flame torches on the beach, and heard the reverberation of a shot, probably fired in frustration.

As they drifted into the night, Tyndall told Olivia of the encounter with Gunther and of Niah's fate.

Olivia took his hand as he choked up. "I'm so sorry for you, John. It's a terrible thing. Can the police do anything? We'll have to tell them."

"No, there's no point, there's no evidence that will stand up and there'll certainly be no evidence here within a few days, you can be sure of that."

• • •

Minnie was quiet and said little when Olivia relayed the news of Niah's death at sea.

"I worry about little Maya, out there. She hasn't led that sort of life. Will she be all right?" Olivia asked.

"She learn quick. They look after her."

"Will they bring her back, Minnie? Tyndall *is* her father after all."

"She know her story when she bigger. Maya decide that."

"It doesn't seem fair. But at least she is with family. I imagine the poor little thing is missing her mother though."

"Niah my family, too."

Seeing Minnie's sad face, Olivia spoke gently, "Don't blame yourself, Minnie. You did what you thought best for them both." Then it dawned on her that Maya must be remotely related to Minnie too. The complex family connections of Aborigines were confusing, but maybe it meant that there would be some hope that Maya would be returned to Tyndall one day.

Eventually a steamer arrived with mail that included a letter from Monsieur Barat. It elaborated on a cryptic cable which had arrived months earlier, indicating that a satisfactory sale had been achieved.

The "Star of the Sea" pearl cluster had been sold for a record price to an Indian prince. The flamboyant prince, well known in London society, had no objection to publicity and the purchase had been written up in the London newspapers. Accompanying photographs showed the lavishly dressed prince, music hall chanteuse and actress on either arm; the pearls still on the shell which the prince was sending to Tiffany's to be made into a brooch; and, supplied by Monsieur Barat, a photograph of Captain John Tyndall, "the dashing pearling master of Broome, Australia" who made the fabulous find.

Having discussed what to do with this sudden wealth, Olivia and Tyndall chose to plough the bulk of the money into the business, but Olivia decided to put some aside to buy a house in Fremantle as an investment. Tyndall announced he was going to build a new house on a hill overlooking the sea, not far from the foreshore camp.

Some weeks later when he unrolled the blueprint on Olivia's verandah, she was flabbergasted.

"It's a bit of a palace, isn't it, John. I mean, it's so large and the garden rambles everywhere, though I love the terraces. It will have a great view to the bay from the front verandah."

"You can watch for the fleet coming in," he said shyly.

"From your house?" She gave him a puzzled look.

"Well, yes, Olivia, I was rather thinking it would be your house, too."

Her heart did a flip-flop and she caught her breath, then gave a teasing smile. "Are you asking me to formalize our relationship?"

"Formalize our relationship?" he repeated in astonishment, missing the humor in her voice. "I'm asking you to marry me." His tone made it more of an explanation than a question. "I've always loved you, Olivia. Since the moment I first saw you on the beach. I never thought there would be a chance for me, and I was content to be close to you. I loved working beside you and thought you were an extraordinary woman. But these past months, since we have come together . . . I can't bear having to hide my feelings and not being able to be with you, all the time, has made me realize . . ."

Olivia started to tremble. She had never admitted to herself that there had been some fateful pull between them since they'd first met. She had fought her feelings, fought against the sheer physical attraction of the man, determined not to be conquered by him. For as she'd always known, once she let herself go, and fell into his arms, she would be bound to him for ever. She'd never known such sexual passion, such a deep sense of knowing they belonged together.

Since they'd become lovers she had dared not think past every moment they'd shared.

"Olivia . . . say something." He reached for her hand and felt her trembling.

She put her fingers to his lips. "It's all right. Everything is all right. I love you, too. Yes, John Tyndall, I will marry you."

He swept her into his arms and kissed her fervently, his mouth lingering on hers.

Later, holding hands, they broke the news to Minnie.

Minnie beamed and nodded sagely. "Thought so."

Olivia told Hamish when they were alone together after dinner that night. He was immediately delighted and relieved. Since his father's death he had felt insecure and worried about the future. The burden of responsibility for his mother quickly slipped from his young shoulders.

Tyndall was against a formal announcement and they simply told friends and acquaintances about their plans as they saw them. However word spread quickly around the community. The news did not surprise anyone. Most people considered it a logical and convenient arrangement. But few realized the depth of passion and emotion between them. For both what had gone before was special and not to be demeaned or dismissed; but this connection between them, this physical and emotional bonding became their life blood. They gave each other's life new meaning and fulfillment. They were almost afraid to show the world how joyous they felt.

Plans for the house were eventually finalized and building began. Tyndall and Olivia would start and end each day by walking hand in hand about the site, visualizing the rooms and what would be in them.

The wedding date was set for several months ahead—a simple affair in the small wooden church to be followed by a reception in the garden of the Continental Hotel. They'd tried to keep it simple but the town had taken the event to its heart and everyone wanted to be involved, help or just attend.

"It's probably going to be the most egalitarian and mixed party they've seen here for a bit," laughed Tyndall. "The RM and Mrs. Hooten rubbing shoulders with our crews and everyone we do business with!"

Indeed, it rankled a little with some of Broome's white society when Tyndall and Olivia made known their plans to include all races and classes of their friends. Ahmed was to be best man, Hamish would proceed his mother down the aisle and Mabel Metta would be matron of honor. Minnie was given her own invitation and had bought bright new hats for herself and her daughter Mollie especially for the occasion.

The day before the wedding, the steamer from Fremantle arrived on the afternoon tide. Tyndall and Olivia planned to sail on it after the wedding reception for a honeymoon in Perth.

There was the usual flurry of activity and socializing when the steamer docked. But one of the passengers elicited more interest than most. She was an attractive woman, although some ladies might be inclined to regard her as a little bit "loud" in manner and dress. A white linen ensemble showed off her curvaceous figure and trim ankles, and under close scrutiny her hair appeared unnaturally fair, her lips artificially red.

She stood on the wharf, her blue eyes sweeping over likely candidates to assist her. Holding her hat and a parasol, she had a cabin boy fetch a porter. An enterprising Indian boy, a relative of the Mettas, was first to hoist her bags.

"There are still trunks to come, I do hope there is some conveyance at hand."

"Oh yes, mem, many sulkies and carriage to take you to hotel. No trouble at all."

"Oh, I'm not going to a hotel. I'm going to my husband's house."

"Very good, mem." He hastened ahead and put the first of her bags in a sulky and helped her settle herself.

She snapped open her parasol. "I'm very hot. Could you get the rest of my luggage later?"

The boy hesitated and the driver shrugged. "Very good, mem. Where you stay?"

"With Captain John Tyndall. The pearling master. I am his wife—Mrs. Amy Tyndall."

The porter and the driver stared at her.

"Captain Tyndall? He know you comin'?" asked the Indian driver.

She gave a pretty smile. "No. It's a surprise. I've come all the way from London."

The Indian porter shrank back through the crowd as the sulky pulled away. Instead of retrieving the trunks labeled "Mrs. Amy Tyndall," he raced along Dampier Terrace directly to the offices of Star of the Sea and rushed up the stairs.

CHAPTER SIXTEEN

Tyndall had difficulty grasping what the perspiring porter was telling him. It was too fantastic to believe.

The porter struggled to get the words out. "White lady, yellow hair, fancy clothes, say she wife of Captain Tyndall and tell my brother take her to your house. He tell me I tell Captain Tyndall, quick smart. I got her trunk there; in sulky." He wrung his hands feeling wretched, fervently wishing he wasn't the bearer of this unwelcome news.

Tyndall flipped a coin at the man and thanked him. Then he leaned back in his chair and closed his eyes.

He saw himself as the hesitant young man who had been spellbound by the flirtatious blue eyes, laughing mouth and lusty body of Amy. His father had warned him to stay away from "a girl like that," but she contrived to be in his path wherever he went. The seduction had been swift, and he an eager accomplice. How naive he'd been. She wept and fretted and wailed when she found out she was pregnant. So, once he was over the shock, he had shouldered his responsibility and married the prettiest girl in the village.

The memories of the sagging narrow bed, the smoky grimy cottage, the coughing of her inebriated father, the nagging and whining and paddy temper of what he recognized was a spoiled and lazy girl, drove him swiftly to Belfast and then to London seeking work. He wanted to make the marriage work and hoped that once they were on their own, things would be better. He recalled the freedom of being at sea and the feeling of guilt at leaving his young wife. He had never intended to shirk his duty to Amy. It was simply easier to earn good money at sea. The eventual news of the loss of the child and Amy's apparent demise had saddened him but also given him a welcome sense of relief, of freedom from guilt.

Her bursting back into his life set his mind spinning and emotions churning. Tyndall felt a burning anger. Why should she come back into his life now, just as he was about to find the joy he'd always sought with Olivia?

He sat bolt upright. My Lord. He'd have to be first to tell Olivia. What a nightmare! He realized he must still be legally wed to Amy, unless she'd had the marriage dissolved, citing his disappearance so many years before. But his heart sank again at the knowledge that she was here and claiming to be his wife. Well, this had to be stopped and sorted out swiftly. He sprang to his feet, snatched his hat and rushed from the office.

Rosminah and the Chinese cook hurried to meet him as he came up the path, noting the sea trunk on the verandah.

"Lady come, tuan, she no go away. Come inside, sit down, want tea and lemonade. She say she Mem Tyndall. She no listen to me when I tell her go away," cried Ah Sing, the cook.

"Don't worry about it, Ah Sing. I'm fixing things up. Where is she?"

The cook, in a lather of sweat, his round face shining, answered. "She in sitting room."

Rosminah padded behind Tyndall as he strode down the hall. "Mem tell me unpack and wash her things. What I do, tuan?"

"Do nothing, Rosminah. I'll speak to her." Tyndall drew a breath and walked into the formal room that he rarely used in the center of the house. He stopped and stared at Amy sitting in a cane chair, neither spoke as the years vanished and they sized each other up. They would have recognized each other in an instant. She'd kept her figure though the voluptuous curves seemed laced in place.

She was holding a tea cup which she carefully put to one side. Holding out a soft hand, she said triumphantly, "Hello there, Johnny Tyndall." There was obvious amusement in her expression and she looked more than happy as she took in the striking and handsome man before her. "You look well. I chose you for your looks and you haven't disappointed me."

Tyndall stayed where he was. "Why are you

here, Amy? This is bloody madness. I still can't believe you've just walked into my life as though nothing had happened. You should have written and told me. Not just landed on the doorstep."

"That's not much of a welcome. It's been a long trip to find you."

"And it's going to be a long trip back. You can't stay here."

"Now, you can't mean that. I'm your wife. You're just in shock," she said placatingly. "I know how you feel, Johnny. It was a shock for me, too, when I read about you in the London *Telegraph.* After all these years, suffering over what had become of you, how you'd run off and left me. Your little wife. What did I ever do to deserve that, Johnny?" Tears welled in her blue eyes and her voice dripped with self-pity.

"I thought you were dead for God's sake," shouted Tyndall. "You couldn't wait like a dutiful wife. No, you had to go to the bright lights of London then just take off and let your father and me believe you'd died. What the hell have you been doing?"

"I don't believe you are entitled to shout at me," she snapped in a steely voice. "It wasn't easy for me, you know. I lost the baby, there was a flu epidemic and I went to Scotland while waiting for you to come back. But you never did, did you?"

"There was no point in going back. The priest wrote to me that your father had died and that they had heard you'd died in London. What was I to do? And how did you get to Scotland?"

She lowered her eyes. "I had a kindly benefactor. I would have been lost without Lord Campbell . . . and his dear family," she hastily added.

"I see," said Tyndall, seeing too clearly how Amy had survived. "So why are you here now? If it's money you want, you could have written."

"Would you have answered such a letter?" she asked, giving him a challenging stare.

"There are some honest men left in this world, it might surprise you, Amy."

"I don't want money. Oh, indeed no."

"So what do you want?"

"*You*, my dear husband. I feel God and fate have reunited us after a dreadful misunderstanding. I am here to take my rightful place by your side." A cloying smile curled about her lips.

"That's what you're going to tell everyone, is it?" He imagined she had rehearsed her lines carefully.

"It's the truth, isn't it?"

"No, Amy, it's goddamned not! I've had a lot of time to think about things over the years and you know what . . . I came to the conclusion you tricked me. And I'll tell you something else, Amy. You're too late. I'm about to marry the woman I truly love."

"How can that be?" she asked calmly with mock sweetness, spreading her arms in a querying gesture. "You're married to me."

"Not for long. We're getting a divorce. No way can you walk back into my life. You smell money. You're only here because of the pearls."

Amy's face was hard, her mouth set in a firm line. "I will never give you a divorce. I will fight you every inch of the way. I have come prepared with documents, marriage certificate and letters. I can claim you deserted me and get . . . restitution." She resumed her artificially sweet pose. "Is it such a poor proposition, Johnny? For me to be your wife? Many men would envy you. There is nothing for me back there. I intend to stay here. With you."

"But I don't want you!" Tyndall shouted in frustration. Through his anger came the dawning realization that this woman was dangerous, conniving and unpleasant.

"Think it over. This is a shock. You'll get used to the idea. By the way, you'd better inform your lady friend of your true situation," she added with some smugness.

"You can't stay here," said Tyndall stubbornly, feeling the ground giving way beneath his feet.

"What are you going to do? Send me to a hotel? Throw out your wife? I would be very distressed at that. Whatever would people think?"

Tyndall conceded momentary defeat. The pretty but manipulative girl who'd led him to the altar had become a shrewd, calculating and experienced woman used to getting what she wanted from life.

He slammed out of the house. Oh God, how was he going to tell Olivia? It would be hard, but he had no doubt Olivia's depth of understanding and love for him would help them to cope with the trauma. He'd get rid of Amy no matter how much it cost.

It took a few moments for Olivia to absorb the full import of what Tyndall told her. She asked him slowly to repeat the basic details.

He stumbled through a brief explanation and floundered to a halt as Olivia sank back into her office chair and stared at him across the desk. She'd come to work as usual to tidy up loose ends before their wedding and honeymoon.

Tears of hurt rage spilled down her cheeks. "How could you not tell me you were *married*? Had been married, whatever . . ."

"I thought she was dead. I haven't thought about her in years! I was a lad, she just disappeared . . ."

"And you didn't try to find out what happened to her? You were her *husband* . . ."

"I was barely twenty years old. I was on the other side of the world. The priest wrote and told me . . . for God's sake, Olivia, try and understand . . ."

"I *am* trying to understand. Understand how the man I love, the man I believed my soul mate, the man I saw spending the rest of my life with, joyously with, has lied to and deceived me."

"Never, Olivia . . . Never intentionally . . ."

"What else have you not told me, John? How can I ever trust you again?"

"Olivia, we'll sort this out. I know it's unfortunate, her timing is bad, I agree . . ."

"*Unfortunate!* I would say her timing was perfect. What if we were married? You'd be in gaol for bigamy . . ."

"We're still getting married, Olivia. This might delay matters but I will fix it. Damn her, she's just after money . . ."

"I don't think so, John . . ."

"Don't think what? That she's after money?"

"That we should get married."

"Olivia . . . you can't be serious! We can't throw away our happiness because of this wretched . . . intrusion."

Olivia turned away from his anguished face. "It's not just her being here . . . it's the fact that you didn't tell me . . ."

"*I didn't know!*"

"But you should have told me, we talked about your past. This is very hurtful. Of course I can't stay in the town." Olivia stood up, suddenly decisive. "I'll make plans to move. Fremantle. Hamish will go to school in Perth and I'll find something to occupy myself."

"Are you crazy, Olivia? Don't be so rash. And what about Star of the Sea? It's half your company. You can't walk away from it."

"I'll be a long-distance partner. If you'd rather buy me out . . ."

"Olivia, stop this, please . . ."

"John, I think it best if you leave me be. You aren't going to change my mind. You've hurt me deeply, I have to come to terms with this. It is all very . . . difficult. And just how are you going to handle this publicly? What about my reputation? This will give everyone something to talk about."

"Olivia, if that's what's worrying you, I'll make sure everybody understands the situation."

"It doesn't change matters though, does it?"

"I'll get a divorce, and then we can go back to where we were."

"No, we can never do that. And has she agreed to a divorce? Why has she come all this way, if not to be with you?"

Tyndall had no answer and he mumbled unhappily, "She only just arrived. I wanted to make sure you heard about it all from me first."

"Oh, they're already talking about us are they? John, please leave."

Tyndall moved toward her, his arms outstretched but Olivia shrank back. "No!" She turned away from him, her face and body stiff and tightly held.

Looking wounded and dazed, Tyndall walked slowly from the office. Olivia heard him go, her heart breaking, swamped by the knowledge she might never again touch the man she loved.

The glaring light seared into Tyndall's eyes. He pulled his hat down to shade his face and found his vision was blurred by hot tears. He still thought Olivia's reaction unreasonable. Why should he have mentioned what was, to him, a brief incident in his past that he felt was of little significance? All he wanted now was to spend the rest of his life with Olivia.

A seething resentment of Amy drove him back to his bungalow. How dare she just settle in under his roof? She was a total stranger. He couldn't remember any treasured moments they'd shared. He had been lured by first-time sex with a girl who knew more than he did. It never occurred to him at the time to wonder at her experience, but he simply lost himself in his own fulfillment and release with a willing and eager partner. After their hasty wedding, a mere formality, he recalled several blazing rows, tearful tantrums and a determination that he try to make a better life for them. What a load it had been on his bewildered twenty-year-old shoulders.

He slammed back into his house, bellowing for Rosminah. "Where is mem?"

"Mem Amy resting, tuan. She make me unpack clothes, I no can say no, tuan," she said miserably.

"Then start packing them again. She's not staying here."

He banged on the door of the guest room and flung open the door when Amy coolly called, "Come in," as if she had been in residence for months.

She was sitting at the dresser, brushing her long blond hair, a satin wrapper about her white shoulders. She gave him a coy look. "You shouldn't barge into a lady's boudoir, Johnny. But then, you are my husband."

"I've ordered Rosminah to repack your things. You're not staying here."

"*I'm your wife.* The whole town must know it by now."

"A bit of paper back in Ireland might say so, but that is all about to change. I want a divorce as soon as possible."

"On what grounds? I don't want a divorce and you're going to look pretty foolish, not to say a blackguard, for treating me this way." She turned back to the mirror and glanced at his reflection. "And what did your ex-fiancée have to say?"

Tyndall simply glared at her. "Amy, I want you out of this house. I will pay your expenses."

"I know you will, Johnny. But nonetheless, I'm staying here. This is my home too, now." She gave a tight smile but there was a malicious dare in her eyes that sent a shiver through Tyndall.

"Very well, I shall move into the Continental."

"That seems an unfortunate waste of our money, Johnny. I shall be here a very long time. Why cause more gossip than necessary?"

He was silent for a moment. She had a point, but if he allowed her to stay, it was tacit acknowledgment of her rights as his wife. He had to think through his tactics. He turned and stormed out of the house, heading for the foreshore camp.

Amy wasted no time in dressing. She had already learned as much as she could from the nervous Rosminah, and her enquiries on the steamer had given her sketchy details of the Star of the Sea Pearl Company. When she was ready, she selected a parasol and sent Rosminah to fetch transport.

• • •

Olivia's mind was racing from one plan to the next, mentally sorting through the tasks ahead of her. By concentrating on the immediate details of readjusting her entire life, she tried to stop thinking of the ultimate outcome of a new life without Tyndall.

The tap at the door caused her heart to stop. She didn't want to talk to anyone. She dropped the last of the files and ledgers into a box and sighed, "Come in."

She swung around and stared in shock.

Both women frankly and silently assessed each other.

To Olivia, Amy looked out of place, overdressed, in her frilled white high-necked pintucked blouse, cinched waist and cream silk skirt swept up to one side in a ruched swathe. Lace-edged gloves matched the parasol and to set it off she wore a pert hat peaked at the back with a small feather and a glittery pin.

To Amy, Olivia looked unstylish and uninteresting. Olivia's simple lilac dress, sashed at the waist without the benefit of laced corset, hair looped at the nape of her neck with a black velvet bow and no accessories, indicated to Amy a woman who didn't care about keeping up appearances or wasn't in touch with the mode of the day. However, she conceded a grudging admiration for Olivia's natural beauty. Amy had to enhance her natural assets, Olivia did not.

"Hello, I'm Mrs. John Tyndall. You must be Olivia Hennessy."

Olivia stiffened at the stressed "Mrs." "Yes, I am Olivia Hennessy. Just what can I do for you?" She wasn't about to repeat Amy's name.

Amy rested her parasol against the wall and began to pull a glove from her hand. She was perfectly relaxed. "I thought I should get to know my husband's business. Could you explain matters to me? Seeing as I'm now part of it all." She gave a bright smile.

"I beg your pardon?"

"I'm Captain Tyndall's wife. Whatever he has is also mine. I'd like to see some of the pearls."

Olivia flushed and tried to hold her temper. "We don't keep pearls just lying around. Nor are they just picked up by the handful from the bottom of the ocean," she snapped.

"Really? This *is* a pearl business, isn't it?"

"It's a *pearl shell* business. I'm sorry, I don't have time to discuss this. There are plenty of other people who can explain it to you in simple terms. And, incidentally, I am fifty percent owner in the business. A *working* owner, I might add."

"Then I suppose that makes us partners, too." The smile hadn't left Amy's face.

Olivia dropped all pretense of civility. "There is no way you will be involved in this business while I'm a partner."

"I'll see about that. But I do hope we can get along. Because I'm planning on staying here.

With my husband." She picked up her parasol. "Good day to you, Mrs. Hennessy."

Olivia watched her sweep from the room. Then, quickly striding across the room, she slammed the door behind Amy with a crash. As her fury dissipated, she sank back into her chair feeling utterly defeated. She had now summed up Amy, which was no doubt the intention of the visit. She saw there was no way Amy was going to give up Tyndall or her position. Amy was avaricious and attracted to perceived wealth as much as to the man. Their relationship might well have been fleeting and orchestrated by Amy as Tyndall described, but it was obvious she had found a comfortable new status in life and would not give it up without a fight. And Olivia recognized that in a fight she was no match for Amy. Nor was Tyndall.

Olivia sent word for Ahmed to come and see her and she tensely explained her plans.

Ahmed had already heard about Amy from Tyndall and Toby's cousin, the porter. He wrung his hands in distress and shook his head. "Oh, mem, this very bad news. She no good lady. Tuan say he send her away. Soon be all right. You stay, mem. We need you." He gave Olivia a half smile. "We like you, mem. You and tuan get married, later."

"Ahmed, there is a small fair-haired obstacle in the way of that happening. And for me, once the trust between two people is broken, things can't be the same. I simply can't stay here while all this is going on. I have some pride, too, you know. And I tell you, Ahmed, that woman is trouble. Dangerous trouble."

He nodded understandingly. "I no like you go away. But maybe for little time, is best. How can Ahmed help?"

"I need two boys to help pack and move my things to the ship. I'll arrange for the house to be locked up. Minnie will keep an eye on things and I'll try to get Yusef settled as a house boy elsewhere."

"He and Rosminah bin plannin' to get married. Maybe he can work at Tuan Tyndall house."

"Yes, I'm sure he'll have his hands full with madam-in-residence. I can't believe she has moved into his house. Well, actually I can now, having met her."

At the foreshore camp Ahmed passed on the news that Amy had already confronted Olivia, who was definitely planning on leaving on the steamer in two days' time.

Tyndall kicked the nearest chair. "That damned woman. How dare she upset Olivia. Did you try and talk her out of going, Ahmed? Tell her we need her here for the business? I need her, too, but she won't listen to me at the moment, I'm afraid."

"Mem say this lady trouble. But you upset mem,

too, tuan. She say trust gone." When Tyndall stayed silent, he shook his head sadly. "This a bad business, tuan. Very bad."

"Ahmed, I swear to you, I'm going to fix this mess. God knows how. It may take time, but I will get Olivia to marry me come hell or high water."

At sunset when Tyndall quit pottering about the luggers he had no clearer idea of how to remove Amy nor how to persuade Olivia to give up her wild idea of moving to Fremantle.

He trudged into the silent house with some trepidation, wondering where Amy was, and called the house boy to fetch him a drink. He had thought of going to the Lugger Bar but couldn't face the questions he knew would come his way. By now the entire town was agog with the news. Amy had made frequent stops on her morning tour of the town to make herself known to shop-keepers.

The house was ominously quiet and he called for Rosminah, but the Chinese cook appeared instead. "No here, tuan. Gone with mem. Help her carry up her t'ings."

"Mem has gone?" Tyndall's heart leapt. "Where has she gone?"

"New house, tuan. Mem ask why such little t'ings here in rich man's house. Rosminah tell her you move to new house after wedding."

"*What!* She's gone to our new house?"

The cook nodded, edging backward at the sight of Tyndall's outrage.

Tyndall charged from the house. This was too

much. She was trespassing in the home that he and Olivia had designed together and planned to move into after their wedding.

He ran without pause to the bluff and stood outside the house panting. Olivia's trunks had been moved outside onto the verandah. Windows were open, Amy's sea chest was by the door, open and half-emptied.

Nearly choking for air with rage and exhaustion Tyndall surged forward, bellowing for Rosminah. The girl ran out of the door, clutching one of Amy's hats and a pair of her shoes.

"Rosminah, drop those," he ordered, gasping. "Get home at once."

"Tuan, she say I must help her." Tears started to tumble down her cheeks.

Tyndall snatched Amy's clothes from her and said quietly, "Rosminah, you are to have nothing to do with the mem. You do only what I, tuan, say. Understand? Now go home and stay there."

"Really, Johnny, such a fuss. You're frightening the girl. There's no harm in her helping me, surely. How else am I going to get settled?" Amy appeared at the door, calm and sweetly reasonable.

Tyndall threw the hat and shoes at her feet and shouted, "You are *not* moving in here!"

"But I'm already in, dear. I thought you wanted me out of the other house. This seems a very satisfactory arrangement."

"Like hell it is. I want you back on that steamer and out of Broome. Go to Fremantle and we'll negotiate from there."

She gave a tinkly laugh like a patient mother with a recalcitrant child. "But there's nothing to negotiate. As I'm your wife, my place is here and I don't for one moment expect you to see me starving on the streets of Broome. What would people say?" She settled herself in a chair on the verandah. "Now, Johnny. Don't be difficult about this. I spoke to Mrs. Hennessy today. I must say, she was rather ungracious, but she tells me she is moving to Fremantle, so that solves that matter doesn't it?"

Tyndall was speechless.

"By the way she told me she was a partner in your pearl business. I imagine you'll need me in her place now, seeing how things have changed rather."

Tyndall stared at Amy, seeing her steel inside for the first time. He was aghast at how fast things were moving. And moving out of his control. His mind raced, desperately searching for some way to take command of the situation.

"Very well, Amy," he said, finally. "Stay here— *for the time being*. I will stay in the old house. As soon as I have sorted out the divorce *and* the settlement, you will be on your way."

"Johnny, dear. When are you going to get it through that handsome head of yours that I am not going to give you a divorce. I am not going anywhere. You'll get used to the idea." She gave a coquettish smirk. "You'll find I'm not so undesirable as time goes on. I'm very good company. Or had you forgotten?"

"Yes, I *had* forgotten . . . all about you. And I have no desire to attempt to rekindle any sort of relationship. It's over, Amy. Dead and gone."

"We'll see, we'll see," she answered affably, walking back to the door. Unruffled, she turned to him, all trace of the mock goodwill gone. "Don't forget, I said I had documents. And copies are lodged in Perth. You'll find changing the *status quo* frightfully difficult. By the way, if you are going to be selfish about your staff, I'll have to hire more servants. Naturally all my expenses are being charged to you." She swept inside and Rosminah sidled out, giving Tyndall a sympathetic look.

For Olivia, the next two days passed in a blur. The nights were a black hole she swam through in some mindless nightmare, waiting for the dawn, when the same reality faced her. She struggled to explain the dramatic change in their lives to Hamish.

The boy looked at her, puzzled, frightened. "Why has this lady come here? Why didn't Uncle John send her away? He was going to marry you, and we were going to live together."

"These things sometimes happen in life . . . things don't work out the way you wanted. And sometimes grown-ups fall out of love and things . . . change."

"I don't think I want to be a grown-up."

"Oh darling, I promise you things will be all

right. You're going to have a lovely exciting time at a wonderful school in Perth, and I'll be close by in our house in Fremantle. On weekends we can do all sorts of interesting things."

"What about Uncle John and Ahmed and Yoshi and everyone?"

Olivia swallowed. "You can come back . . . school holidays . . . we'll still have our house here." She couldn't bear the thought of coming back, not while she was on the verge of fleeing. But she couldn't let Hamish think everything he knew and loved was being cast aside. "Your father and I always planned to send you away to boarding school. This way, I'll be close." Seeing his hurt, Olivia hugged him to her. "Oh Hamish, just believe me and don't worry. You must trust me, darling."

Toby and Mabel Metta were a constant support and help. They had agreed to transport Olivia and Hamish down to the steamer at the last possible moment to avoid her having to face too many people.

"Olivia, I beg you to think this through. Are you sure you simply aren't running away? Give John time to sort matters out," pleaded Tobias.

"He hasn't stopped loving you, nor you him," said Mabel supportively.

Olivia looked up from her packing. "Yes, I have thought this through. And, yes, I am running away. I cannot bear to be here and be reminded of the dreadful situation that has developed and how I was so deceived all this time."

"It was not malicious. We men tend not to look backward, his past is his past. There are many people in this town who have a past they never talk about. You know yourself, sadly, that life goes on."

"He should have told me. I might have been better prepared," said Olivia stubbornly.

"We have been over this many times. If we can't change your mind, dear Olivia, then let us help you as best we can."

"Thank you, Mabel. Here are letters to people like the Hootens, briefly explaining my change of plans, if you'd send them for me."

"I'm sure no explanations are needed, Olivia."

"That's just the point, Tobias. I do want to explain. This is my decision. I want to keep some shred of integrity."

"What about the business side of things? You can't stay away too long, Olivia." The pearl peeler still regarded her rushed move to Fremantle as an overreaction.

"I'll think things through in more detail when I'm settled." She gave a rueful smile.

"I always knew you were a strong woman, Olivia. You do what you think best." Mabel embraced her. "We'll be here keeping an eye on things and you only have to ask if you need anything."

"Thank you. Thank you both." Olivia embraced them.

This was their tearful and private farewell.

•   •   •

At sunset the Mettas drove Olivia and Hamish to the wharf and helped them onto the steamer. Most of their bags had been sent ahead and Olivia did not want to stand about before they sailed on the tide. After another brief farewell and an enveloping hug for Hamish, the Mettas made their way back along the wharf, Mabel dabbing her eyes with a handkerchief.

Hamish was instantly absorbed in exploring every detail of the cabin and didn't notice his mother's set mouth and pained expression as she lifted the name tag—CAPTAIN AND MRS. TYNDALL—from their stateroom door. What was to have been the honeymoon suite had a bottle of champagne waiting with a welcoming note from the steamer's captain. Olivia threw the note away and sank down onto the bed.

Hamish was standing on his bunk, busily peering out the porthole, and didn't see the tears sliding down his mother's face.

The foreshore camp crew worked as normal packing up at the end of the day, all aware of the steamer's imminent departure.

Ahmed had watched the activity from the office window, knowing Tyndall was at the foreshore camp with a bottle of whiskey. How strange were the ways of Allah, he thought. While he suffered with his master he nonetheless believed there was a higher reason for this alarming and sudden disruption in their lives.

Tobias Metta arrived at the shed at the foreshore camp, loosening his collar and tie.

Tyndall looked up but couldn't raise a greeting.

"Well, she's on board. She's going through with this sad scheme. Mabel and I tried our best to talk her out of it. She's a strong-willed woman, John. And one in a lot of pain. This has hurt her dreadfully."

"I don't understand women," mumbled Tyndall with despair in his voice. "I hurt, too."

"Mabel tried to make me see that men and women react differently about things."

"They certainly do. Why couldn't she have stuck by me, Toby?"

"Her feelings and pride are hurt. We have to let her ride things out a bit. Yes, we must let the storm pass, then maybe we will see the way ahead."

Tyndall topped up his glass and pushed the bottle toward the pearl peeler.

Tobias poured himself a stiff drink. He wasn't a drinker, but right now he needed a bracing snifter. He took a sip. "Mabel wonders why you're not down there. At the steamer."

"What the hell for? To make more of a fool of myself? That'd give 'em all something else to talk about. Anyway, she sent word none of us were to go near the wharf. I didn't want to upset her."

"Mabel thinks you should be down there dragging her off the damned steamer. She says you're both in love with each other and both being stubborn and silly." It hurt and embarrassed him to say this and he took another sip of whisky to cover his anguish.

Tyndall looked at his friend, then suddenly slammed down his glass, grabbed his skipper's hat and ran from the shed.

Tyndall reached the wharf as the day disappeared into the deep shade of a lavender night. Only a few people remained at the end of the wharf, waving occasionally as the departing steamer glided across the bay, its lights twinkling on the calm aqua waters.

From the porthole Olivia could make out the dark sweep of bay and mangroves that sheltered foreshore camps. Her eyes filled with tears. For one wild moment, as the mooring lines were being cast off, she wished he had rushed to her, but he had not.

In the shadows of the wharf, John Tyndall also wept.

CHAPTER SEVENTEEN

Two years passed and still the situation had not improved. Amy stuck to her guns and refused to budge. Tyndall's battle to divorce her was bogged down.

Meanwhile, Olivia had been steadfast in her resolve not to have contact with Tyndall, other than on a purely business level. She checked the accounts now kept by a relative of Toby Metta employed by Tyndall, and dealt with Monsieur Barat directly in Perth. Pearls and ledgers were delivered to her by registered mail and once, at the end of the last season, Ahmed had traveled to Fremantle to deliver the pearls to her.

While it was not the perfect arrangement, and she missed the excitement of seeing the pearls come to life under Toby's deft hands, it worked satisfactorily enough. She was glad to see Ahmed and catch up on all the news of friends and life in Broome. She did not ask about Amy but from the snippets of information offered by Ahmed, she gathered Tyndall's situation remained unchanged.

The very personal questions she wanted to ask, Ahmed couldn't have answered anyway.

She didn't know whether to believe the small remarks dropped by Tyndall in with the business correspondence. Things like, "My situation remains difficult and unresolved, but I will not give up."

Amy had initially cut a swathe through the town. The Hootens had given a small afternoon tea for her where Amy had elaborated on the tale of how she and her husband had "lost" each other and what a joy it was that the find of the "Star of the Sea" pearls had reunited them. Most took her gushing affection with a pinch of salt but said nothing. Rumors had been doing the rounds about the volatile relationship between Tyndall and Amy.

However, she managed to flirt and charm her way through the Residence tea.

"What a little dazzler, eh?" commented the RM. "I wouldn't be losing her if she were mine."

"Strange story, turning up on the eve of the wedding. Felt sorry for poor Olivia," said Major White.

"I imagine it was a planned marriage of convenience, business convenience that is. No doubt Mrs. Hennessy will find herself a new husband in Perth soon enough."

The women had also felt for Olivia. The embarrassment of it all.

"No way I'd stay here and be the discard on the shelf," was the general reaction.

"Tyndall is certainly a good catch. Handsome devil. But I bet that wife of his gives him the rounds of the kitchen."

"Is it true they live in separate houses?"

"I'm sure there are visiting hours," snickered another wife. "I hope he's keeping an eye on her. I wouldn't trust that woman round my husband."

"You mean you wouldn't trust your husband," came the quick retort.

None of them knew of the great love that had burned so fiercely between Tyndall and Olivia, nor realized the pain they had both suffered these past two years.

It had taken Olivia many months to adjust to life in Fremantle and to the loss of Tyndall—for she regarded his betrayal as the death of their relationship. Hamish had settled in quickly, enjoying King's College, and had made good friends.

Now that her days weren't filled with activities related to the pearling enterprise, which she missed dreadfully, Olivia had looked for something to occupy her time and energy.

Through friends of Monsieur Barat's she had been invited to work on a hospital charity. There she had met a Doctor Gilbert Shaw who was setting up a special girls' home under the auspices of a community-based foundation. A rich widow had donated a small house in the port city of

Fremantle. Olivia had volunteered to work on the fundraising committee but soon became more interested and more involved. Doctor Shaw noted this and one day asked her to work with him in setting up an institution for homeless girls and young women "in trouble . . . You know, pregnant and unmarried."

Doctor Shaw was older than Olivia by fifteen years. He was an attractive man, slimly built with silver temples, a soft voice, caring manner and kindly gray eyes. His was a popular practice as women found him one of the few doctors with whom they could comfortably discuss personal problems. His invalid wife had died three years before. There had been no children. Since her death he had become a leading figure in campaigns for helping the destitute and needy.

After a tour of the seedier areas around the docks of Fremantle, Olivia saw the need for a girls' shelter. Young girls of mixed blood—Aboriginal and Asian—were cast into the streets after running away from harsh employers and unscrupulous men who abused, mistreated and took advantage of them. Scavenging and prostituting themselves were preferable to the near slavery they endured.

She accepted a position to work directly with Doctor Shaw in setting up the girls' home in Cantonment Street. It had a small staff including a young nurse and Olivia tried to make the refuge feel more like a friendly interim home than a charitable institution. She had visited other public institutions—an orphanage, a home for wayward girls—and found them cold and intimidating.

Olivia and Gilbert Shaw walked through the freshly painted house, which Olivia had decorated simply but in soft colors, unlike the other drab institutions.

They settled themselves in the cheerful dining area and Olivia made them tea, knowing just how he liked it. Gilbert gave her a smile across the table and thought how comfortable Olivia was to be with. "This place certainly has a more friendly atmosphere. You've done a splendid job, Olivia."

"I had a lot of help. But those other places do seem deliberately inhospitable. A scared or sick girl isn't going to go there by choice unless she is utterly desperate."

"This home is not a charity that will give these girls a soft ride," said Doctor Shaw gently. "We can't feed, house, clothe and care for them indefinitely. It's not an open house."

"I understand the financial constraints," said Olivia, "and I agree this home shouldn't be looked on as a free boarding house, but the girls need to be redirected, advised and helped back into the world."

"Then that is your role, Olivia—to help the staff achieve that. If you are prepared to take on the challenge."

"I should welcome it."

Gilbert reached across the table and pressed her hand. "I'm glad. You've brightened up my life, too. You're a delightful lady, Olivia. I'm sure we'll achieve a lot together."

There was no innuendo or hint that the remark was overly personal. Olivia admired his gracious manners and charming warmth and had noted how he treated all women with courtesy and respect.

Gilbert Shaw might not have shown any deeper clue to his feelings and made sure he didn't treat Olivia any differently, but he was conscious that she stirred feelings in him that he had thought long buried. He found himself looking forward to their meetings and kept finding excuses to spend time at the refuge.

Olivia felt needed and useful, and the stimulation of the work took her mind away from Tyndall and Broome. The remuneration was small but she was financially stable. She lived in a house in Phillimore Street in Fremantle's better residential section which she'd bought with some of her share of the sale of the "Star of the Sea" pearls, which also paid for Hamish's school fees. She tried not to think about what her life might be like if they'd never found the fabulous pearl constellation. She drew her percentage from the Star of the Sea Pearl Company and, despite her offering to reduce her share as she was less involved, Tyndall had refused to change their fifty-fifty arrangement.

For Tyndall, these days were empty of feeling, units of time in an emotional darkness that seemed to stretch to infinity. He dreamed that one day he would emerge into bright light and find Amy gone and Olivia smilingly in her place. He had no idea how to achieve this, the fight having gone out of him, so he trudged through the hours clinging to some forlorn hope that fate would intervene.

The opening ceremony for the girls' home was simple, although Olivia had been acting rather mysteriously about the whole event. She had arranged for several local dignitaries to attend a small tea where the simple plaque by the front door was to be unveiled by the Mayor.

Nervously she took Gilbert Shaw aside and made a private little speech. "Doctor Shaw ... Gilbert ... seeing as you left most of the decisions up to me, I took the liberty of making one without consulting you." He raised a bemused eyebrow as she went on, "We had to call our girls' home something and in the time I've worked here and talked to all kinds of people in Fremantle I have been so impressed by the respect and esteem you command. You're a fine man, Gilbert, so we decided to name this place Shaw House ... is that all right?" She smiled with an expression of concern that he mightn't actually approve.

"All right? Olivia, I'm overwhelmed. And very touched. I didn't get into this to create some sort of monument to myself, but the fact you say others approve of my work is most gratifying. It's truly a lovely gesture." He leaned forward and kissed her on the cheek. "No one has ever done something so thoughtful for me before. Thank you," he added softly.

This time, as he looked into her eyes, she saw a glow and depth of feeling she had never seen before and knew suddenly it was meant for her alone.

Amy was feeling frustrated and a little bored. Tyndall hadn't melted one fraction and was as determined as ever to end their marriage. It piqued Amy that her feminine wiles had no effect on him. She had tried to charm, flirt and seduce him to no effect. Worse than the rejection was the ridicule he threw at her. He had also managed to reduce her spending by refusing to honor charge payments she had made in town and so she could no longer tick things up to Captain Tyndall. Streeter and Male's Emporium politely refused such requests, asking for the captain to come in person to confirm the charges. Amy's charm had worn thin and Tyndall had worked hard to convince storekeepers not to indulge or cater to Amy's spending.

She had gone through three sets of servants. Rosminah, now married to Olivia's house boy, Yusef, stayed at Tyndall's house. Minnie and Alf lived at Olivia's house as caretakers and Minnie took on part-time work for the wife of a wealthy Chinese merchant. Minnie had made one trip south to Fremantle—her first trip on a steamer and to a city—to take her daughter, Mollie, to work for Olivia.

Amy's demands, temper tantrums and unreasonable requests soon became known throughout the domestic servants' network. The social invitations dried up, though the white community and the pearling masters' wives remained civil. Despite Amy's volatile nature, she was, after all, one of them.

Amy's boredom evaporated one day when she was taking a meal alone at The White Lotus, a clean and small establishment run by a jolly Chinese couple, Junie and Henry Wang. The pearling masters and their wives often ate there, as did the top divers. It was a reputable, friendly and noisy establishment and only at night did the sound of gambling marathons filter in from the back and upstairs gaming rooms, where serious money, gold sovereigns, even pearls were won and lost.

Even though it was unusual for a white lady to dine alone, Amy was unperturbed. While waiting for her order Amy was reading the catalogue off the last steamer which showed the latest London fashions—now already a year out of date. She decided she would have a new dress made, even though there were so few occasions in Broome for dressing up. A new dress, she decided, would cheer her up.

She cut into small pillows of dough and nibbled the filling of pork and thick sweet sauce. After an unsuccessful battle with chopsticks, she had switched back to a spoon and fork.

The waiter placed another small woven steam-damp basket in front of her which held two crisp triangles filled with spiced, shredded vegetables. She finished her meal with small squares of sweet bean curd. Draining the last of the pot of China tea, Amy felt amply satisfied and glanced around the room. It was not yet lunchtime, so the tearoom was empty save for a Japanese couple, an elderly Chinese man drinking soup from a bowl and a white man engrossed in a newspaper.

Her gaze rested on the white man, who suddenly put down his paper and regarded her with a frank, amused and appraising look. He folded his newspaper and inclined his head in her direction. It was a courtly gesture but seemed incongruous coming from such an unusual man. He was of swarthy complexion and his dark tangled hair had an oily shine to it, as did his moustache. Two dark bushy eyebrows which almost met in the middle and dark, intense eyes gave him the look of a wild pirate. He was dressed in a coat cut in the European style and a silk scarf was knotted and tucked into a white shirt. He lifted a hand and Amy saw the flash of a large gold and diamond ring.

She gave a brief smile and immediately became engrossed in the catalogue again.

He passed close by her table as he left, trailing a pungent smell of cigars.

Amy thought no more about the man until an hour later when she was in a small shop with rolls of fabric spread like colorful silken rivers before her. She lifted several lengths and held them up to her body.

The Japanese lady behind the counter made complimentary noises like a chattering bird. "Velly plitty, velly good kimono silk, this one. Make plitty dress."

"Indeed it would," boomed a voice behind her.

Amy spun around.

"Good day to you again, madam," added the man from the tearoom, raising his hat with an exaggerated gesture.

He was shorter than she had thought, but of muscular build and she had no doubt he could hold his own in a fight. She noticed the thin white line of a scar running along one cheek. Nonetheless, his amused arrogance and looks attracted rather than repelled her.

The lady bobbed and nodded and jabbered in Japanese and waved toward the back of the store.

The man turned away, saying over his shoulder, "I should take the red if I were you," and he disappeared behind a beaded curtain.

"Who was that man?" asked Amy in a low voice.

"Velly rich man, I think. Does lot of business . . . you know . . ." She rubbed her fingers together and put a finger to her lips.

"And his name?"

The girl hesitated, thinking hard. "Him my boss friend, him Mister Karl. Mister Karl Gunther."

Amy purchased the red silk and left the shop.

• • •

Over the next two weeks, Karl Gunther crossed Amy's path on several occasions. She began to wonder if it was just mere coincidence. They finally connected at the Continental Hotel, where Amy was due to have lunch with Mabel Metta. Amy had issued the invitation saying she wanted some advice from "a family friend." She realized the Mettas were friends of Olivia's as much as Tyndall's but Amy needed information and she hoped by saying she was concerned about Tyndall that Mabel would agree to meet her.

Mabel duly arrived at the hotel on the day arranged. Settling the folds of her sari about her round body, she said politely, "How can I help you, Amy?"

"It's Johnny, he has become very . . . difficult. He drinks more than is good for him . . ."

"He's always hit the bottle when he's down."

"Well, he has been muttering about business being bad. They haven't found any pearls . . ."

"That's not so!" Mabel bit her tongue and let Amy continue.

Amy dropped her head and lowered her voice. "Sometimes I fear for my safety. I know he resents me . . . but he is my husband, what am I to do? I don't wish to leave him. I just want to make him happy. And he spurns me so . . ."

"Oh my dear . . ." Mabel looked at the brimming blue eyes now gazing forlornly at her. Had she misjudged Amy? "I really don't know what advice to offer. I know it's hard to accept, but time, you know, is a great healer."

"I am prepared to wait. I just wondered if he had other problems he wasn't sharing with me . . . troubles with the business perhaps. But you say Mr. Metta says they are doing well?"

"Oh yes, you have no worries on that score."

"That's a relief then. I'd wondered, what with still having to pay Mrs. Hennessy such a large portion of the profits . . . never mind, I'll have to try and cheer him up as best as I can then."

Mabel's sympathy immediately evaporated. "Mrs. Hennessy is a part-owner and has always reinvested much of her earnings back into the company, as I understand it," she said tersely. "Not that I wish to gossip about the private affairs of good friends." She rose. "I'm sorry I can't stay for lunch. I have to see to the children."

Mabel departed, furious at being manipulated by Amy. She hoped she hadn't said too much, for Tobias had told her Star of the Sea had reaped some excellent pearls this season. And she knew Tyndall tried to keep such matters to himself.

Amy went ahead and ordered lunch, aware she had ruffled Mabel, but satisfied at extracting the information she wanted.

It was then that Karl Gunther happened by and paused at her table on the verandah.

"Dining alone, Mrs. Tyndall?"

She looked at him, saw the challenging smile lurking at his mouth, and tossed her head. "I was thinking you might like to join me—Mr. Gunther."

"Seeing as how we seem to already know each other, in a fashion . . . I'd be delighted." He slid into the seat opposite and settled himself like an old tom cat before a bowl of cream.

They were as different as two people could be, yet, between the melting blonde woman with wide china-blue eyes and the dark-eyed rough diamond, there smoldered a recognition that within them both ran a streak of self-interest and self-preservation. Both were ruthless, both were ambitious, both were fearless risk takers, if needs be. For him, a pretty woman was always a challenge to be conquered. For her, the dandy had never appealed. Aggressive, rough lovers had been ultimately more fulfilling than the wealthy, aged fops like Lord Campbell.

Danger appealed to Amy and as the lunch progressed she began to see she might have found a match in Gunther. Beneath the banter, the exaggerated and glossed half-truths of edited life stories, each was wondering how they could use the other. For despite the sexual undercurrent that zapped between them on one level, each began to think the other could be a means to an end.

Tobias Metta, expecting his wife to be dining with Amy as planned, stepped out onto the verandah, but seeing Amy in animated conversation with Karl Gunther, he made a hasty and worried exit.

• • •

When Tyndall heard of this sighting, he at first found it hard to believe that the man who had been the nemesis of the women in his life had struck yet again. For a moment he was almost glad the two had made contact, it seemed somehow logical Amy would find something appealing in the blackguard. And maybe he had recognized the same streak in Amy. Each on their own was a potential threat, together they could be a deadly team.

Tyndall stormed to the house and shouted at Amy for belittling, embarrassing and shaming him in public.

"Why, Johnny, surely you're not jealous," she grinned.

Olivia's words came back to him. "Listen Amy, while you are here in Broome, what you do reflects on me and the company. Furthermore, that man is not what you may think, he's responsible for some vile acts."

"Really? Like what?" She raised her eyebrows in feigned amused interest.

Tyndall ignored her question. "I forbid you to see him again—for your sake, Amy." He turned away.

"Is there a more suitable gentleman you could recommend I have a discreet dalliance with then?" The smile still twitched at her mouth and for a moment he couldn't tell if she was serious or not.

"Why don't you just leave, Amy? There's no future for us. You're wasting your time. Find yourself a proper husband."

"I have one. Although he doesn't treat me like a wife. You do have marital rights you know." She dropped her eyes and Tyndall glared at her. How did she manage to sound so demure and yet look so provocative?

One night, drunk, lonely and longing for Olivia's arms he had felt overwhelmed by sheer sexual urge and had walked to the house. He had stood, looking up at the lattice-screened dovecote built at the top of the house for such hot humid nights. Knowing Amy was asleep up there, he'd been tempted to go to her, but desire had turned to bitter anger and he'd resorted to Sheba Lane. There, as thoughts of Olivia flooded through him, he had wilted, sadness and hopelessness replacing the fierce fires of passion and he trudged dispiritedly back to his own empty bed.

Looking now at Amy, it was as if she knew about this and that one day she knew he might succumb to her. But she merely replied, "I have nowhere else to go, Johnny. I'll wait."

Tyndall left, defeated. There was no more to say.

But Amy was far from triumphant. The brazen facade with which she challenged him fell away and she retreated to the bedroom. Falling amongst her pillows, she glanced out at the bay below. The tide was out. Green mangroves and gray skeletons of dead mangrove trees rose from the mud flats. She suddenly felt as if a moat lay between her and the rest of the world. She felt trapped, bored and lonely. Why did she stay? She had been unable to seduce Tyndall and he still controlled the finances. If she could get her hands on the money, which had been her original intention, she could escape. Her dream of teaming up with her handsome husband and leading a life of luxury and excitement in Australia had not come to pass. She had always seen Tyndall as a ticket to a better life, yet in her eyes he had failed her. In the past, she had grasped many opportunities in a life dictated by lust and greed, but they had proved only temporary indulgences.

As she tossed restlessly on the bed, she realized that her options for happiness in Broome were very limited indeed.

Tyndall was fed up. His anger, frustration and the constant worry about what Amy was up to—for she created agitated waves about her as she sailed through her days—were getting him down. As always, his solution was to go to sea.

He left Ahmed ashore, taking the *Shamrock* with a minimum of crew out to the pearling grounds to victual his luggers and try the grounds further north once more. It was agreed that Ahmed would rendezvous with him in four weeks' time.

The trip proved a blessed relief for Tyndall. The companionship of the crew, the routine of the days at sea, the peace that always came to him as he looked across blue water and cloud-tinged sky. The steady rhythmic movement of the boat, the rattle of the rigging and the sighing flap of a wind-filled sail—all these things calmed his aching mind.

After two weeks Tyndall decided to leave the rest of the fleet and do a little searching up toward the Lapecede Islands.

It was easy sailing for the first two days, then the weather closed in. Rain and high winds lashed the *Shamrock,* but it ploughed gamely on as Tyndall checked the chart and gave instructions to the first mate.

Late that night Tyndall checked course, spoke to the crew, then went below to snatch a few hours' sleep. "Wake me if the wind rises or the swell gets worse, we could run into a cockeye bob."

"Aye aye, Cap'n. No worries." The thin and dark-skinned Koepanger gave a confident grin.

He never did get a chance to wake Tyndall. The *Shamrock* was picked up by a freak wave in the storm, breached and was flung beam on into a reef with a sickening crunch. The impact threw the two men on deck off balance and the next wave washed them overboard. Waves lashed over the schooner which lay on its side, the sharp edges of the reef slicing through the wood. A stockily built Manilaman crawled out of the hatch. At that instant, one of the dinghies broke loose and crashed into him, knocking him unconscious and pushing him into the sea. The dinghy then splintered and was swept away. All men were lost from sight in seconds, leaving Tyndall alone on the shattered schooner. He crawled along the deck, now tilted at forty-five degrees, and groped for the rope still securing the second dinghy. In the darkness, gray waves and stinging rain beat at him as he fumbled with the knots. At last the dinghy gave way. He flung himself into it as the *Shamrock* began to roll. It started to break up as it was sucked down by a wall of water. In its wake, the dinghy was almost immediately swamped.

Tyndall lay in the half-submerged little boat, watching the black shape of his beloved schooner disintegrate with a wail of splintering wood and disappear from sight. He wept and screamed his fury at the sea and the storm.

Amy knew she was secretly looking for him. She set out each day about the town visiting the dress-maker, stopping at The White Lotus, browsing through Streeter and Male, walking along Dampier Terrace, and taking afternoon tea at the Continental.

She had just decided he'd slipped out of port when on her way home she decided to stroll along Streeter's Jetty. She saw him standing on the deck of a black ketch with red sails, berating a cowering Malay. His shirtsleeves were rolled up his muscular arms and thick black hair protruded at the base of his throat. He saw her but didn't acknowledge her presence other than to give the man a clip over the ears and send him scuttling away.

Amy put her parasol on the other shoulder, turned and walked back along the jetty, slowly. Swinging onto the jetty, he strolled along behind her until they reached the street. He moved up beside her.

"Good afternoon, Mrs. Tyndall," he greeted her.

"Good afternoon, Mr. Gunther."

"Going anywhere in particular?"

"Just out strolling. I've had a busy day."

"While the cat's away, eh?"

She gave him an arch look. "Whatever do you mean?"

He gave a brief laugh. "You're all on your own, why not join me for dinner?"

It was a casual invitation but as they glanced at each other Amy knew they were at a juncture. It was up to her to decide which road to take.

"That wouldn't appear seemly, what with my husband away," she replied.

"Depends who knows. Maybe it's a business meeting. I conduct my private dealings in private. At the Cable Palace."

"What or where is that?"

"A very large, very private home over on Cable Beach. You'd find the owners interesting people, I'm sure."

"I didn't think there was anyone interesting in Broome. It sounds intriguing."

"I'll send one of my men to collect you. Say seven?"

"Will I be safe do you think?" She gave a coquettish toss of her head.

"I think you are a woman who can look after herself. I like that. Bring one of your staff if you feel so inclined." He nodded curtly and wheeled away from her in the opposite direction.

Amy watched him go, feeling slightly faint, with nerves or anticipation, she couldn't decide. He really was an ugly man, barrel-built, squat and muscular, oily skin and hair, his body covered in the same thick dark hair. The black eyes had no warmth, the voice was harsh with traces of his guttural accent, yet he radiated an animal-like magnetism that drew her to him like a spider in a web. Amy chuckled to herself at the picture of Karl Gunther as a hairy black spider in the middle of a web, thinking he was all powerful. "Hah, Mr. Gunther, have you ever heard of black widow spiders? The females devour the males!" she said to herself.

Feeling assured of her invincibility, Amy set off for home deciding which particularly alluring dress she'd wear for her secret rendezvous.

The Aboriginal women arrived at the coast before the men. Maya always loved this season when they camped by the huge shell middens where generations had feasted on shellfish. The ceremonies held here were different to those performed in the desert. For Maya this was a special place. When they arrived she always walked down to the water's edge and stood with her feet in the ocean, feeling the watery link stretching between this shore and some faraway land of her ancestors across the sea. It was an unconscious symbolic touching of her mother and made her feel happy.

The memories of her mother had faded from the forefront of her mind these past two years, but impressions and senses and feelings of her were pressed into Maya's essential being ... on her skin, in her heart and in that special part of her soul.

She walked out of the water and sat on the sand, watching the very little children play close by while the women began setting up camp and searching for food. Maya examined her feet, now protected by a thick tough pad. So much walking. The clan had traveled over vast distances, following the seasons and traditional food gathering patterns that hadn't changed for centuries. They camped while food and water were plentiful, moving on to the next site of robust growth, where the cycle was repeated.

Maya had developed a walking sense as she'd grown. Previously she'd playfully pattered along with the women until she felt weary and then sat on the ground until someone scooped her up and carried her. Now she was older, walking was a life experience. The elders showed her things, the women pointed out animal tracks and edible plants. Other times in her head Maya imagined she was a bird or an emu or even a big fish and she swayed and danced along as she walked, imitating the animal's movements. Sometimes strange images and memories came to her and she let them drift through and out of her mind without curiosity or fear.

The women watched her with pride. She had grown into a beautiful girl, her svelte frame strong and healthy, and her skin, fairer than the rest of them, had tanned to a deep gold. Her long dark hair fell straight down her back with streaks of auburn gold glinting through it.

Maya loved and accepted this tribal family life, but sometimes she felt different to the others. She let a handful of sand dribble through her fingers. Opening her hand she closely studied the remaining grains clinging to her fingertips. Each one was different. Not quite the same size or shape. She blew on them gently and they fell back on to the beach to be indistinguishable from all the other grains of sand. Maya tilted her head. This meant something she thought, but couldn't decide what. She jumped up and ran to play with the little ones who were digging a hole with large shells.

Soon after camp was made on a creek behind the dunes, a group of women and children, including Maya, set out to get "white fella tucker." It had become their custom over the years to visit the nearby mission where the friendly Brother gave them sugar and flour. There was a ritual attached to these visits. They had to sit and listen to him talk about "God" before getting the rations. In their eyes he was an unusual and likable man, quite different from most of the pearlers, stock men and policemen who crossed their paths. Brother Frederick had learned the rudiments of their language, enough to make his stories about "God" understood. He helped heal their ailments and gave the elders advice, when they sought it, on dealing with the law of the white man, which they found violent and confusing.

The women and children trailed into the sprawling mission, shouting greetings to resident Aborigines, some of whom were relatives who spoke the white man's language, even sang songs in the language and went to a sacred place, the big white building where the Brother talked to "God."

There was a lot of talk and laughter as the visitors and mission blacks settled in the shade of spreading mango trees to exchange gossip. Soon Brother Frederick appeared in the doorway of the white church. Waving both arms in exuberant welcome, he strode briskly across the sward of grass shouting more greetings in their language and reaching out for the hands of a swarm of children who ran to him, giggling and jostling.

He sat among them in the shade and methodically acknowledged each woman in the group, needing little help in remembering names and family connections. When he came to Maya, he paused and thought for a few seconds. "Now who have we here?" he asked. After Maya was introduced to him, he asked for her mother and looked around the group. They explained that "aunties" now looked after Maya, her mother had been taken across the sea. Brother Frederick interpreted this as meaning the mother was dead. He studied the smiling girl, concluding her father had been a white man, but he did not pursue the matter, knowing in all probability he would not get an adequate answer.

The courtesies of greeting over, he then began telling them a story from the scriptures, parts of which were embellished and explained by relatives. Then he led them in a song about his God, enthusiastically backed up by resident Christian converts. The bush people understood nothing of this hymn but joined in rhythmic clapping and burst into a chorus of appreciative noises and laughter when it ended. They knew these expressions of joy pleased the white man enormously.

While the rations were handed out and the talk under the trees continued, the children ran off to explore and play.

From the moment she walked into the mission, Maya had been fascinated by the big white building with the little tower and bell. It brought back images of another time, another place, images that were vague but which she knew were related to her past. She slipped away from the other children and made her way to the open door and peeped inside. It was dimly lit and cool. Cautiously, she stepped inside, and as her eyes adjusted she saw that much of the interior was decorated with mother-of-pearl shell. The sight of it made her gasp with astonishment and excitement.

"So pretty," she said aloud, in English.

"Yes, very pretty," echoed a soft voice in the shadows to her left.

Maya jumped with surprise and turned to run.

"Please, don't be frightened. Stay. Have a good look," urged Brother Frederick with warmth, holding out his hand to her.

Maya paused, then tentatively took the out-stretched hand.

Together, they walked slowly around the church, Maya sometimes running her fingers over the shells, the priest occasionally asking a question, sometimes pointing out a religious feature of the decorations. He suppressed his surprise at her knowledge of English, even though she often had to think hard before finding the right words. But there was no doubt in his mind that God had delivered this child to him for salvation.

Some days later a small party of Aborigines from the mission came down to the bush camp. The women in the group sought out women in Maya's family and there were long discussions, all conducted away from the men. It was "women's business", and it concerned Maya. The next day the women trooped back to the mission for more talk, then a meeting with the priest.

Weeks passed, idyllic days for Maya, who romped in the sand and the sea with the other children, fished and gathered mussels and crabs. At night she would fall asleep around campfires against a background of singing and dancing.

Soon it was time for the clan to move on. One

morning Maya had to go with some of her aunties to the mission. She was disappointed that no other children came along but she planned to try and get some of the hard sweet lollies from the man in robes to take back to her friends.

When they had settled under the trees at the mission with relatives and friends, the women explained to Maya that she was not going back to the camp. They told her she was going to stay at the mission for awhile. The white man was going to look after her, give her special food and clothes and teach her important things.

Maya was stunned. Her lip trembled, then she began to cry softly.

As the women gathered up the sacks of flour and sugar, they waved to Maya, who was now standing forlornly outside the church, her hand held by Brother Frederick. Maya half-lifted her free hand in response and fought back more tears as her family disappeared down the track.

The man squeezed her hand and she looked up at him. He smiled and reached into his cassock and pulled out a brightly wrapped sweet. "Here, Maya, have a lollie. I know you like them," he added brightly.

She took the rock-hard gift and slowly unwrapped it. Popping the multicolored ball in her mouth, she savored the sweetness for awhile before pushing it to one side, making her cheek bulge.

Brother Frederick smiled again and took her hand. "Come. Let's go and get you some decent clothes from the store."

CHAPTER EIGHTEEN

Tyndall stirred and lifted his head as light rain washed over his red raw skin. His mouth came unstuck, his swollen tongue feeling relief as the water ran over his parched and split lips. He'd lost track of time but had a vague memory of night seas pounding the damaged dinghy. As the rainwater trickled down his face, he slowly became aware he was lying on his back, his legs across the smashed seat of the little boat. Chest-deep water sloshed in the splintered hull. He tried to lift himself out of it but had no strength. Sinking back into the watery bed, he closed his eyes once more.

A shudder and a crunch dragged him back to reality. The dinghy was scraping over an ironstone reef and the next wave rammed it into a crevice, splitting the hull apart. He was swept out of the boat, and over the reef and into deep water. The dowsing shocked him into full consciousness and he began to swim. His blurred vision made out the shape of two low islands in the distance. He realized he was in the channel between them. Under normal circumstances it would have been an easy swim for him, but his clothes weighed him down and his limbs felt like lead weights. The days adrift in the dinghy had drained him and, just as he thought he couldn't lift an arm or kick a leg a moment longer, he was nudged by a great shape that glided beside him. Tyndall lunged out. Flinging his arms across the barnacle-encrusted shell of an old green turtle, he held on. It was swimming just below the surface and Tyndall was just able to keep his head above water as the turtle stroked its way toward the larger of the two islands.

The shoreline was reef and rocks, but the turtle swam through a narrow split between them and Tyndall felt its undershell scrape the bottom as the turtle launched itself up the beach. He rolled off and lay there for a moment before dragging himself up. Dozens of turtles were making their way to a thin stretch of sand, where, come sunset, they would begin busying themselves digging holes in which to lay their many eggs. Unable to hold himself up any longer, Tyndall collapsed on the shore.

In the coolness of evening he awoke and crawled to one of the sand-covered nests. Digging with his hands, he pulled out an egg and bit into it. Reviving a little, he slowly and painfully made his way to some shelter and curled up and slept, planning on looking for more food and water at first light.

●   ●   ●

Amy decided to wear the dress made from the red kimono silk that Gunther had admired. The bodice, edged in black lace, sat at the very edge of her shoulders, the low *décolletage* showing the swell of her ample white breasts. The silk clung to her figure, stopping in a scalloped hem above her ankles. She slipped her dusty-pink stockinged feet into black shoes with rhinestone buckles, and carried black gloves, a fan and sheer black chiffon wrap to cover her exposed skin from insect bites as she traveled to the Cable Palace.

By Broome standards the house could have passed for a palace. It was large, set up on high pillars with a broad flight of steps leading to the colonnaded verandah with sets of French doors along its length. But if one looked closely, it was a flimsy construction, with peeling paint and a temporary air. Soft lights glittered through expensive curtains—a rarity in a town where homes relied on shutters and lattice for privacy. The house was very secluded, set behind a high brush fence and heavily screened by palms, frangipani, banana trees and rampant climbing bougainvillea. Amy thought it strange that such an apparently imposing place was located in such an isolated area.

Gunther was waiting on the verandah and came to help her from the sulky.

Amy's initial misgivings were quickly dispelled when she realized everyone there had something of a colorful past or were vague about their present activities. A slick, superficial explanation of their reason for being in Broome only added to the mystery. There was a Viennese pearl buyer who said he also bought gold and precious stones for "private clients", a Japanese businessman who was accompanied by a very young, very pretty kimono-clad Japanese girl who spoke no English but giggled and remained attentively close by his side. There were several other businessmen and a slightly built Malay man who wore a lot of jewelery. The few European women present were plainly dressed when compared to Amy, who shone at center stage like a music hall queen. While by no means classy or distinctive themselves, the women eyed Amy with some distaste. The men favored her openly with appreciative stares.

"Who owns this place?" Amy asked Gunther in a low voice after they had been served several drinks.

"He calls himself a trader. Antoine Dollinger, known as Captain Dolly. He buys and sells . . . anything. A very useful man to know." Gunther winked.

"You know him well?"

"Well enough. I've had various business dealings with him. I'm hoping to close a transaction that will make me a large sum of money." The smile hadn't left Gunther's face.

"And I don't suppose you're going to give me any clues about this . . . big deal?"

"Curiosity killed the cat. Why are you so interested? Ladies are just supposed to look pretty and not ask questions about men's business."

"Some of us can be pretty *and* clever," she teased.

He studied her for a moment. "Yes, but you're rare birds."

"I might be thinking about business opportunities, too. I'm looking forward to chatting to Captain Dolly."

"You talk to me if you have any clever ideas. I'll look after your interests."

"Will you indeed? Business or personal?"

"That is up to you, my dear. I'm full of surprises. You could do worse than throw your lot in with me. It's a hard, cold world out there, only the strong—and the clever—survive."

"I know that, believe me. But I've managed quite well. Up till now. As I said, I'm seeking opportunities. I don't plan to hang about Broome forever."

"And Captain Tyndall? What do you plan to do with him?"

"He looks after himself."

"Perhaps that's the problem, eh? You need an interest of your own."

"I was thinking of a money-making interest." She lifted his hand from her waist. Amy still hadn't decided if Gunther was as clever as he tried to appear. She'd seen his type before, always about to make the big killing, always talking but still waiting for the fortune due to come their way. Yet for some reason, her antenna was registering positive, telling her this man was about to strike his mother lode. She still wondered why he fascinated her so. Despite his ugliness, he exuded a power that was sexually attractive.

Gunther expounded his business philosophy a little further. "You want to make money, you have to take risks. Bend the rules. Live dangerously. Might not suit your way of doing things."

"I wouldn't say that." They exchanged a frank look that spoke volumes more than the conversational jousting.

"Maybe what you're looking for might come along sooner than you think. When it does, you have to up anchor and sail where the wind takes you."

"That's how I've lived my life," said Amy softly.

Gunther instantly recognized he'd met one of his own. One of those who took in order to win and didn't mind the consequences.

The evening passed too quickly for Amy. She felt heady from the wines and port and from the snatches of conversation between Gunther and the other men she'd come to realize were all connected in a loose network devoted to illegal but profitable dealings. She decided that she wanted to be part of it in some way, for she saw the paths of this company led to exotic places, wealth lavishly spent on indulgent pastimes and lifestyle, with a dash of danger and excitement thrown in.

On the way home, Gunther and Amy discussed the party in detail, Amy questioning him about what he knew of some of the other guests and of their host, the rough diamond, Captain Dolly. It appeared to be a social exchange after an intriguing evening, but beneath the surface there was an undercurrent of indefinable electricity that zapped between Amy and Gunther. It excited Amy, she loved the sport of the male and female chase.

They pulled up and Gunther walked her to the verandah steps.

"This has been a very special evening. Thank you, Karl."

"I hope there are going to be more opportunities to enjoy your company. I have plans that might interest you. Seeing as I now understand better what you might be interested in, where you are going, so to speak. You are an independent woman. I like that. We should discuss things further."

"No more merely social occasions?"

"That, too, of course. It's up to you and how you handle your . . . personal situation."

"Well, if you're leaving matters up to me. . . ." Amy leaned forward and kissed Gunther on the mouth.

He kissed her back, roughly drawing her body to his and running his hands around her buttocks. Briefly he pulled back from her. "There's a rule—never mix work and pleasure," he murmured.

"What a shame," whispered Amy. "Which side of the fence does that leave me? On the business or the pleasure side?"

"I should add, that was a rule I broke long ago." He kissed her grinning mouth once more and she thrust her breasts against him, leaving an invitation hanging in the air.

They drew apart, Gunther giving her a friendly squeeze.

"I'll see you again, I'll send a message," he offered.

"I look forward to it." And she did. Suddenly life was a lot more interesting. Amy's hips gave a saucy twitch as she climbed the verandah steps and disappeared indoors.

As Gunther departed, a figure stepped out of the shadows then turned into the house.

Ahmed sailed to the rendezvous point in the *Bulan* and, within a day, learned Tyndall had sailed north and no one had sighted the *Shamrock* since, though none of the fleet had ventured off the pearling grounds. While it was feasible he could have found a good patch of shell, for him to miss their rendezvous was unusual. Ahmed waited one more day, then left a message with the nearest lugger that he was sailing north to look for Tyndall. After conferring with the first mate they set out on the course always taken by their skipper.

Ahmed was worried, it wasn't like Tyndall. Even if he wasn't himself, being depressed over the situation with Amy and Olivia, he was always on top of things at sea. A gnawing sensation in Ahmed's gut told him Tyndall was in trouble.

If Tyndall had sailed up as far as the Buccaneer

Archipelago they could miss each other between the many islands that rose straight from the sea. But Ahmed held his course and patiently waited for some sign.

When it came, his heart sank. The crew dragged on board a splintered piece of wood with a sodden lifebuoy tangled around it. SHAMROCK was written in red letters on the lifebuoy.

Slowly they backtracked, searching the sea in a pattern. The crew kept careful watch, for they knew they were sailing through badly charted waters.

They came across some more wreckage but found no signs of life. They continued in the same search pattern until forced to anchor for the night.

Tyndall was sick of turtle eggs and had managed to catch a bird and eat what he could raw. He had also found some rain-water in the hollows of rocks. But he was not prepared to wait and hope for an unlikely rescue. Estimating the coast to be about twenty miles away, he decided it was too far to swim in his condition, but with the currents and wind in his favor, not too far to paddle. He still had his knife strapped to his belt so he cut some supple young branches and bound them together with vine for a makeshift raft. Clinging to this, he stroked his way back across the channel to the reef exposed by the low tide.

The abandoned dinghy was a shell, a mere buttercup, but it was better than his raft. Using a broken plank, he managed to lever the dinghy free. With the next surge of water over the reef he pushed off. Crouching in the fractured dinghy and using the plank as a paddle, he struck out for the distant line of land.

Ahmed's searching was proving fruitless. In the bright light of the fourth day, he sat staring at the map looking at the pinpoints of atolls and islands wondering if Tyndall was alive on any of them.

It was a Koepanger in a bosun's chair hoisted to the masthead who caught the first glimpse of something in the water and called for a change of course. More wreckage, they thought, until, drawing closer, they saw the body of a man collapsed in the tattered dinghy. He had secured himself to the broken seat by his shirt and the exposed skin of his back was blistered raw. They had no idea if he was dead or alive.

Ahmed stood to one side, praying desperately as they dragged Tyndall on board.

They rolled him over and found he was still breathing. Water was dribbled into his mouth and the dried sea salt rinsed from his face. He coughed and spluttered, his eyes rolled back in his head, then slowly refocused. Through sunburnt lips he tried to speak but only an incoherent babble of sounds escaped from his swollen mouth. They treated him as best they could and Ahmed set a course for Broome.

• • •

Amy met Karl Gunther on two more occasions. To some who saw them together, they seemed an unlikely couple—the coarse adventurer with an unsavory reputation, and the stylish, if overdone, beauty who was used to men of some substance fawning over her. But it was apparent to Gunther and Amy that they had much in common.

They saw themselves as gamblers prepared to take risks, provided the stakes were high enough. They used people. That was just part of the philosophy of grasping opportunities as they presented themselves, feeling no remorse or guilt if the other party suffered. Each acknowledged that they put themselves before all else and saw this as a virtue.

Gunther had never met a woman like this before. Women were chattels, useful for tending all his needs, available anywhere, any time he wanted them. But he soon realized Amy was as used to calling the shots as he. She had a strong will and he suspected that despite her pretty trappings, she would just as readily tough it out under rough conditions if it meant getting what she wanted. She was impatient and was looking for quick and easy money. He couldn't see her sitting it out in Broome much longer. But plotting to peel Tyndall's wealth off him was obviously proving harder than she anticipated. Amy would use her body just as readily as her head to get what she wanted. She had played rough in her time he had no doubts, but she'd met her match in Tyndall.

"That Hennessy woman has some hold over

him," she told Gunther over a late afternoon tea at The White Lotus.

"What are you going to do about it?"

"I thought I held the trump card, being his legal wife, but it's not doing me much good when all his assets are tied up in the business."

"What about the pearl harvest? I heard he's had more than a fair season."

Amy gave him a rueful smile. "That's more the sort of asset I was hoping to get my hands on."

"Ah, you see yourself strutting around this small town—or elsewhere—wearing strands of fabulous pearls."

"No, not at all. I see them as a means to an end."

"You have an idea or plan in mind?" He raised an eyebrow.

"Not yet. But I'm open to suggestions."

"If you could get this asset, would you consider a business proposition?"

"From you?"

"Does it make a difference?" He grinned.

"On the contrary, I think it would have definite advantages." Her bantering mood hardened. "However, I have to, er, acquire the capital, shall we say."

"That's your problem."

"Well, give me some helpful advice. When are pearls sold? Where are they kept?"

"Star of the Sea use Metta for their cleaning. I'd say once he's done with them, they sit in the office safe till they're shipped south for sale."

"That gives me a little challenge then, doesn't it?" She smiled at him.

Amy did her homework, visiting Tyndall's office on her rounds about town. A sleepy Koepanger sat by the stairs but leapt to his feet at Amy's arrival. "Nobody here, mem. All outside . . . at sea."

"Everybody?"

"No, some work at foreshore camp. Me help, mem?"

"Give me the key. I know what I want."

The boy shook his head fearfully. "Ahmed say me no give key to nobody."

"Quite right. But that doesn't mean me, Mem Tyndall. I have business to attend to. Now give me the key, I'll just be one minute." She held out her hand and glared at him.

"You give back one minute?"

"Of course. Wait there." Amy hurried up the stairs.

She unlocked the door to Tyndall's office, glancing around at the scattered gear, ropes, whisky bottles and rug thrown over an old chaise lounge. She swiftly riffled through the piles of papers on his desk but, finding nothing of interest, turned her attention to the safe. It would be difficult but the right skilled person could possibly pick the lock. She opened the desk drawers on either side, flipped through their contents, and took out a folder detailing pearl sales. She then pulled the center drawer. It held a flat bottle half-filled with rum and a set of keys.

"Mem? You there, mem?"

"Yes, I'm coming down." Amy hurriedly slammed the door closed, locking it with the set of keys she'd taken from the desk. Smiling, she slipped the keys in her pocket and went downstairs.

"I have locked the office. There is no need for you to go up there."

"*Terimah kasi,* mem." He put the key in his pocket and settled on the chair again.

The next message she received from Karl Gunther was an invitation for dinner. It was dark when she set out in the sulky he had sent for her. At the jetty, the driver helped her down and, without a word being exchanged, she followed him along the wharf past several dark boats to where Gunther's red and black schooner was moored, a lantern burning on the mast. He appeared on the deck and helped her on board.

"Wait down below, we're going out into the bay. Tide is dropping, don't want to get stranded on the mud. Always like to be able to make a quick getaway."

"Me, too. So what am I supposed to do? Swim?"

"I guess you're at my mercy."

They anchored and the sole crew member made himself scarce.

Gunther poured himself a rum. "Only got

rum." He poured a shot into a second glass and pushed a bottle of sweet lemonade to her. "Put some of that in it."

"It's not my favorite drink exactly," said Amy. "But I guess the French champagne will come after I strike gold, eh? So tell me what it's all about."

"Pirates, my dear, pirates."

Amy paled. "We're not going down that path, Karl," she snapped. "Ye gods, man, you could look like a pirate readily enough, but count me out of joining in your swashbuckling fantasy." She paused, thought for a moment, then cocked her head to one side and queried cautiously, "Or is it just the rum talking?"

Gunther threw back his head and roared with laughter. "Ah, you're a cargo of fun, Amy. No, we're not going to become pirates, we're simply going to do business with them." He reached over and topped up her glass with rum.

"I was not aware that piracy is still a business," replied Amy, both puzzled and amused at the suggestion. "Do you mean skull and crossed bones on flags and all that sort of thing?"

"In a way, yes. You see, my pet, in the Sulu Sea to our north, piracy is a way of life for some of the natives. Small boat stuff, but quite a pretty penny in it. Problem is they're being out-gunned by an increasing number of patrol boats from colonial governments. And that is where we come in. Guns, Amy."

"Sounds dangerous," she said guardedly.

"Not really," he responded with a dismissive wave of a hand and leaned back against a bulkhead with his drink. "The trick is to have better guns than you're trading."

"Is there good money in it?"

"Not money . . . gold. Much easier to dispose of and there's no need to deal with banks that might ask questions. Besides, the Sulu Sea mob are rather keen on hoarding gold, so there's no waiting around for payment. They're willing to pay big money for the latest weapons, particularly some of the new American rifles."

"And where do we find a cargo of American rifles? At Streeter's?"

Gunther roared again and slapped his thigh, almost choking on his drink. "Oh, you're a card, a right good one you are, Amy. At Streeter's . . ." He laughed loudly again.

"Well, I'm waiting," said Amy with a grin, rather pleased that her little joke had gone over so well.

"Nah. We'll give Streeter's a miss. We'll pick 'em up in Darwin. Friend of mine there has a load coming up from Sydney. What the larrikins down there call 'salvage'. Sort of got lost in a warehouse one night some months ago. Of course, the shipment won't be through the usual channels. We'll take delivery at a place not overrun by customs and the like. Then we sail up to a friendly island chief I know and spread the word that we're open for business and make 300 percent profit."

Amy's head whirled. Gun running was not an

option she had imagined in her fantasies. Still, 300 percent profit had a lovely sound to it.

"About the security you mentioned, the better guns?" She pushed her glass over to him.

He poured them both the rum, sloshed lemonade into her glass then looked across the table and grinned. "The Sydney boys have that in hand. They have also acquired an army Lewis machine gun. It's as good as having a score of riflemen on board. An expensive item, I'm afraid, but an essential investment." He gave her a while to take this in, then asked, "Well, are you in?"

Their eyes met and locked in an unblinking transmission of messages. Messages that said we both know who we are, what we want and what we can give each other and we both know the answer is yes.

Amy decided to lay her cards on the table. "I have no ready cash of my own, but as Tyndall's wife I am entitled to a share of the business. The pearls in the safe will be my share. It's fair. Tyndall gets his freedom in return."

"A divorce?"

"If he wants to do the hard work. I'm not going to bother." She flicked a hand dismissively. "And after this little enterprise, what then?" she asked.

"You'll have money, you can do what you want."

"I would be looking for further opportunities in return for my investment," said Amy. "I have to think of my future."

He gave her an appraising look. "If we get on, we could consider another business project or two."

"Just business?" Amy leaned forward and ran her tongue over her lips. Raising an eyebrow, she whispered provocatively, "Maybe we should see how well we get on."

Gunther glanced down at her breasts and reached for her hand. He pulled her to her feet. "The bunk's in there. Let's see how compatible we are then," he said, giving her a gentle shove.

Amy fell back through a curtain onto the bunk, giggling, and watched him strip off his clothes. She felt slightly lightheaded from the strong liquor. She knew it would have to come to this at some stage in any relationship with Gunther and besides, she enjoyed sex. Tyndall's rejection of her had made her feel frustrated and undesirable. She desperately craved the attentions of a man.

Gunther wasted no time in delicate foreplay. Amy had been prepared for rough copulation and expected Gunther to roll away when satisfied. What came as a shock—a wildly erotic and stimulating one—was the untold pleasure he aroused in her. He gave a lusty laugh as she cried in ecstasy.

Later as she lay back satiated and sore but immensely satisfied, he revealed his secret. Taking her hand, he rubbed it along the shaft of his penis till she felt a strange hard bump on the underside.

"What's that? Is that what made it feel so good?" she asked.

"Ah, a woman who doesn't mind admitting she likes sex," grinned Gunther. "It's a pearl. The best baroque, placed in just the right place under the skin to please the ladies. Learned it from a Jap diver. They pierce the skin and stick in the penis pearl. Skin grows back over it and you drive the women crazy."

Amy had to agree with him as she realized with delight that a partnership with Gunther was going to be profitable in more ways than one.

Early the following morning, before dawn, as the sulky traveled through the quiet streets back to the house on the cliff, Amy reflected on the events of the night. As always seemed to happen to her, an opportunity came along just when she was feeling trapped and bored. Whether she created the diversion or it was coincidence or both, she never bothered to consider. Moving forward hopefully to a more advantageous situation was uppermost in her mind at these times.

She didn't totally trust Gunther, but she knew he could lead her into a world of richer pickings than Broome could offer. A shady world, possibly a dangerous one, and if it came to a choice, Gunther would save himself before Amy. But then she would do the same. If a better opportunity presented itself, Amy would take it. They were using each other as long as it suited them both. She did pause for a moment to wonder about this unlikely alliance and the fascination the rogue skipper held for her. Putting this to one side, she began to think over the details of Gunther's plan. It sounded good. And very profitable.

• • •

Amy sent word to Gunther to meet her at The White Lotus. Over jasmine tea she was all business.

"If we agree on matters, how soon before we could leave here?"

"I'm flexible. You seem anxious. We might have to wait in Darwin till the shipment arrives."

"Be safer than waiting here. Once I have, er, retrieved my investment I think it best if I were not around. I wish to leave before Tyndall returns and discovers the loss."

"You've figured out how to extricate the pearls?"

She gave him a flirtatious smile. "I have the keys to the office, but not to the safe. I need a professional hand to get in there."

"You're asking me? What makes you think I know how to crack a safe?" There was an amused glint in his eye.

"If you don't, you'll know someone, I imagine."

"It will cost you." He continued to smile.

Immediately Amy knew Gunther had the nimble fingers and tools that could pick a lock. He looked too confident and relaxed about her request. "I imagine the cost could be negotiable?"

"Indeed." He became serious. "I'll need a day or so. How about Wednesday night?"

Dressed in a dark dress, Amy walked down to the waterfront just before midnight and went quietly into the Star of the Sea building, tiptoeing up the flight of stairs even though the building was empty. She unlocked the door to Tyndall's office and sat behind his desk and waited.

After a while she walked to the window and looked across the moonlit bay. It was an absolutely beautiful evening, the full tide flooding the mangroves and slapping against the old jetty. She became entranced, almost hypnotized by the scene. It was all so peaceful, so beautiful. But suddenly, she felt uncomfortable because the emotions evoked by the view were so at odds with the purpose of her midnight visit to the office. How strange, she thought, that I have come to the other side of the world and in such a short time find myself about to rob a safe and sail off to do deals with pirates. It was not the prospect of the deeds that disturbed her but rather the mystery of the process that led to her easy acceptance of them. How did it happen? What forces had come into play that had led her from a village in Ireland to this place at this time? It was a rare moment of introspection for the streetwise and sharp-minded Amy who held there was no profit in analyses of life's mysteries. She did not consider that when some people make a choice, they are capable of great good, or great evil. Amy didn't bother to reflect on choices in life. Amy looked out for Amy.

A hand suddenly clamped on her hair, tipping her head back and causing her to gasp. Gunther leaned down and bit her ear. "You didn't hear me, did you?"

"No." Her heart was beating rapidly and, looking

at him, she suddenly wondered if he'd open the safe, take the pearls and be gone from her life. But such doubts were fleeting, disappearing totally in the flood of excitement that surged through her body as he pulled her to him and kissed her roughly. He then went to work on the safe.

He looked at it for some time, using a candle shaded by the palm of his hand to illuminate the lock.

"An easy one," he finally announced in a whisper. "They put a lot of money into the steel, not enough into the lock." He chuckled and unwrapped a small canvas roll to reveal a collection of slim metal tools.

She watched him work on the lock with several pieces of wire and then thin, shaped steel. He cursed frequently, and, at one stage, stopped work and searched the office for a drink, eventually finding the half-empty bottle in a drawer of Tyndall's desk. He sat it beside him and resumed work, sweating and cursing with the strain of concentration and frustration. Amy sat in silence, barely able to breathe so great was the tension.

After two hours, during which Gunther had finished the bottle and startled Amy by kicking the safe several times, he eventually sighed loudly and rolled back on the floor, stretching himself out in a gesture of immense relief. "Got it," he whispered exultantly. "Got it."

Amy leaped from the chair and crouched beside him, unable to contain her excitement. "Open it. Open it."

He sat up, reached confidently for the handle, paused for a second then turned the handle and pulled. The door swung open. Amy clapped her hands in delight, then reached into the safe to feel for the soft bags containing the pearls.

In the moonlight the pearls looked fabulously lustrous and large.

"Is that enough capital for you? Am I in?" she demanded with a smile. By way of reply, he lunged at her, pushing her to the floor, pinning her beneath him and as she gasped he put a hand over her mouth. Then she realized his other hand was fumbling beneath her skirt and she could see the gleam of his gap-toothed smile. Giggling, she pulled at his leather belt and coarse cotton trousers.

They rolled on the floor in a frenzy of sexual passion, Amy clutching the bags of pearls with one hand and with the other the tangle of Gunther's oily hair. Oblivious to anything but each other's body they didn't hear the voices and activity down on the wharf until a shout and running footsteps alerted them. Naked, Gunther and Amy peered through the window and Gunther swore.

"That's Ahmed, why is he back?" exclaimed Amy.

"They're carrying someone off, must have been an accident. Get dressed. Let's hope they don't come up here. Does Ahmed have a key?"

"I have no idea."

They dressed in silence and quickly learned from the shouts below as a carriage pulled up, that it was Captain Tyndall who was the patient.

"My God, where will they take him? What will we do about the pearls?"

"Shut the safe door and lock it again. They won't be getting into the safe while Tyndall is sick. Better let me keep them."

"No, I will."

Gunther's eyes were hard. "We're partners. Don't you trust me?"

"No." She was equally tough. "These are my ticket out of here. I'll hand them over when you get us out."

He grinned. They understood each other, they were two of a kind.

"Let's get out of here while all that confusion is going on. We can possibly work this to our advantage. Tyndall mightn't pull through and all your worries will be over. You'll get the lot."

"Let's wait and see. Nothing has changed."

Ahmed arrived at the house early the following morning to break the news to a sleepy-eyed Amy that Tyndall was very ill after being shipwrecked. "He is at his house. Doctor says very bad from the sea and the sun and cuts from the coral. Stay in bed long time."

"I must go to him. Care for him. Oh my." She wrung her hands and looked distraught, but Ahmed's expression didn't change.

"Mem, Doctor send nurse and Rosminah look after him good."

Amy's feigned distress dissolved and she spoke briskly. "Nonsense, Ahmed. I am his wife. I will look after him. Please wait while I dress and take me to him immediately."

"Yes, mem," said Ahmed, sitting on a chair on the verandah.

The minute Amy was out of sight, Yusef appeared at the side of the verandah steps and signaled quickly to Ahmed. The two slipped around the house and Yusef told Ahmed of Amy's clandestine meetings with Gunther.

Amy set herself up in the spare room of Tyndall's house, announcing she was moving in to care for her dear husband. She sent Rosminah back to the house to pack clothes and personal things, for she wouldn't be leaving his side "until my beloved husband is well again."

Tyndall lay in a state of semi-consciousness, only vaguely aware of where he was or what was happening around him. Visions of sharks and swamping waves and the sensation of searing skin haunted him. The pain from his badly infected leg was so bad that the doctor prescribed morphine.

Amy dismissed the nurse, donned a white apron and demure blouse and sat by Tyndall's bed. The doctor saw she was not going to budge and so carefully gave her the directions for the medication he had prescribed. He said he would be back regularly to check on the patient but she was to fetch him if she was at all concerned at his condition.

"Doctor, I will watch over him day and night. Don't you worry about him. He will get all my attention."

She spoke with such concern, such care and compassion that the doctor was slightly taken aback. This was not the glamorous young woman he had observed swishing through the Continental. He recalled conversations between his wife and her friends about Amy Tyndall and pondered briefly on the complexities of women and their relationships. Amy seemed quite the devoted wife, not at all the woman of dubious repute his wife and her friends had described.

In the meantime, Ahmed asked Toby Metta to write to Olivia telling her of Tyndall's accident.

Toby put down the details with copperplate handwriting and then laid the pen aside. Looking up at the distressed Ahmed, he asked, "Was there anything else you wanted to put in the letter, Ahmed?"

"Tell her Ahmed very worried 'bout tuan. While he bin away Mem Amy seen Karl Gunther. Couple of times. Night times, too. Ahmed no like this."

Toby picked up the pen again. "I don't like it

either, Ahmed. But maybe it's best we don't mention Mrs. Tyndall in the letter."

Amy settled herself comfortably beside the sleeping Tyndall, adjusting her skirt over the soft velvet bags of pearls tied to her waist. She smiled at her sleeping husband. "Poor Johnny. Fate works in strange ways indeed, doesn't it, my dear."

CHAPTER NINETEEN

With the approach of the wet, the clan returned to the coast from the desert and made camp. Their diet would also change, to nutritious fish and shellfish.

On a fine morning the small group of women set out toward the mission with the comfortable gait of seasoned walkers. They stopped to greet a young Aboriginal man working in the struggling vegetable garden and asked him where Maya was. He shook his head and told them in their own language that she had been sent away. Far away. To live with white people.

The group sat down to talk this over amongst themselves. It was known that children had been taken away from their people to be trained in missions and sent to work for white people. But they had not expected this to happen to Maya. It was painful for them to accept this news.

Brother Frederick came and sat with them and tried to explain why he had let Maya go with the visiting priest to be taken in by a white family.

How more opportunities and a better life would result. After all she had apparently already had some white upbringing. And she could almost pass for white, he explained. But this meant little to her family. She was what she was. One of them. Maya had been through the ceremonies and given her shell necklace totem. She had her Dreaming and it could never be taken from her.

The women wanted to know when Maya would come back, when her "white business" be over, but the priest could not give them an answer. "Maya has gone to a new home. A new life. It is best for her."

In response to this, the women began wailing as if Maya was dead. Brother Frederick went in to the church to pray. He knew he had done the right thing, she would be brought up in a Christian home and be taught and trained in the morals and beliefs of her new white Catholic family. She would eventually forget the hardships of her nomadic life, and the rituals and beliefs she'd been taught would seem like childhood fairy stories. He tried to block out the wailing cries of the women as he prayed for Maya and those lost souls who called themselves her family.

In her small white room, uncomfortable and unused to the long cotton nightdress and bloomers, Maya dutifully knelt by the bed and repeated the Lord's Prayer aloud as she was bid. Then climbing between sheets and after her new "mother" had blown out the lamp, she sang softly to herself the songs she'd learned by campfires. It gave Maya a small sense of comfort and hope that this part of her life would also change. In her short life she had learned that times of joy and security did not last, but she never gave up hope that somewhere there was a right place for her. And she clung to memories of her mother's arms and soft sweet voice and a laughing man singing loudly as he tickled and teased her.

Gilbert Shaw and Olivia decided to investigate other institutions and set out for the monastery at New Norcia.

It had been a long journey but one Olivia had enjoyed. The train trip from Perth had been comfortable and she and Gilbert had talked undisturbed at length. Olivia's enthusiasm for their modest "halfway house" for girls bubbled over and Gilbert kept smiling at her.

"Why do you look so amused all the time?" asked Olivia. "If I didn't know better I'd think you were treating me like an indulged child."

"I so enjoy your zest for life, Olivia. You tackle everything head on, boots and all. It's bracing and stimulating to be around you." He squeezed her hand. "You make me feel that I still have something to offer."

"But Gilbert, you do! I'm so proud of the work you do. And because you allow me to feel and act the way I do, I feel safe," she paused, "sort of protected, and very lucky to be with you."

"*I* am the lucky one. You amaze me when I stop and think about your life. Such courage, such a will to soldier on despite odds that might have crushed others. You are strong and caring, Olivia, and an inspiration to others."

"I've learned from you that helping others is a balm to your own wounds. Dear Gilbert, you are such a good man." She gave him a tender smile and for a moment Gilbert wanted to sweep her into his arms and smother her face with passionate kisses. But he smiled and stroked her hand.

When they alighted from the train a young monk came forward and asked if they were traveling to the monastery at New Norcia. "I have a carriage. I think you'll find it a pretty ride."

The dirt road wound through lightly timbered and open countryside and the young monk chatted over his shoulder, telling them of many facets of life at the monastery.

"What is Father Torres like?" asked Olivia.

"Very clever, he has degrees in art and science from the University of Barcelona and he teaches maths and science."

"I understood he had some medical knowledge as well," said Gilbert.

"Oh yes, it has been very useful. He is also well versed in philosophy and music."

The first sign of habitation was well-tended vineyards.

"We Benedictines are famous for planting grapes wherever we go," grinned their driver.

They passed orchards and ploughed fields and several barns and farm buildings and soon what looked like a small township came into view. Gilbert and Olivia were effusive with their admiration for the settlement as they drew up before the imposing mellow stone monastery.

The monk led them through a quiet stone corridor to the reception room to meet Father Fulgentius Torres. The handsome Spanish priest greeted them warmly and offered a glass of the monastery wine before luncheon.

"I've heard of the good work your order has done here with the Aborigines, Father. This is far from the bush mission I had expected," said Gilbert.

"Bishop Salvado did great work. Now I have inherited his mantle, I have plans to give the mission a new direction as a center for education for Aborigines. I am also supervising the construction of a boarding school for girls—St. Gertrude's College."

"Who will run it?" asked Olivia.

"The new order of the Sisters of St. Joseph of the Sacred Heart. Now tell me about your plans for a girls' home in Fremantle."

"Many of the foundlings and abandoned girls that we have been sheltering temporarily are sent to the Sisters of Mercy at Subiaco. The boys are well cared for at the orphanage at Clontarf. We are a small operation, a sort of halfway house for girls in emergency situations," explained Olivia.

Father Torres gave them valuable advice, suggestions for fund raising and warned them of the pitfalls of philanthropic endeavor without an institution to back them up. "We have learned a lot from our experience."

"And do your students study Aboriginal culture, too?" asked Olivia.

"I only arrived here in 1901 and have scant knowledge of the native customs," he admitted. "Besides, we want to train the children to fit into society as best they can as well as come to God. Bishop Salvado's ideal was to care for the Aborigines following the Benedictine lines—stability, hard work and faith. We also plan to open a boarding college for boys, St. Ildephonsus' College. French Marist Brothers are coming in to run it."

"We are thinking on a very small scale compared to your plans," said Gilbert.

"Doctor Shaw, any comfort or succor that you can offer these troubled children will be of great benefit. I wish you both well in your endeavors."

Following a simple but bountiful lunch of food grown in the monastery gardens, a monk took them on a tour of the monastery and its grounds.

Gilbert and Olivia settled into the train for the trip back to Perth, talking over their impressions of New Norcia and the advice from Father Torres.

"So, do we pursue the plan for a girls' refuge?"

"Of course we do, Gilbert. That is if you are still willing. While it is a modest enterprise it will be, nonetheless, a big undertaking for us and you do have your surgery as well."

"That is why I am relying on you to run the practical side of things, Olivia. We seem to have the same feelings and thoughts about this project, maybe that is why God intended our paths should cross."

"I want to help very much. It's not just a diversion. I feel very strongly about helping these girls. I'd rather we were just a care and nurturing center without the religious and educational emphasis. Children need a home atmosphere. Somewhere where they can feel safe and loved."

"Well, Olivia, you are embarking on something of a new career, again."

"I will of course keep my interest in Star of the Sea Pearls. It doesn't take a lot of my time but I don't want to lose the connection," she said quietly.

"Before you can make a new life you must let go of the old one."

He spoke gently and Olivia smiled fondly at the kindly man beside her. Although older than Conrad, he reminded her of him in some ways— a trifle conservative, respectful and gentle. She also had profound respect for this good man who had devoted his life to caring for others.

●   ●   ●

After they returned to Perth, Olivia and Gilbert Shaw went to Fremantle and looked again at the large house on Cantonment Street. Partly screened from the street by high trees, it was a stone building with two wings on either side of the main hall and entrance.

"Do you think we should put up a wall, a fence?"

Olivia shook her head. "It would make it too intimidating. I want girls to feel they can come here and just walk in and be part of a family."

"Hmm. Perhaps we need some lights on the outside and in the garden to make it more welcoming."

They went into the house donated by their benefactor, a wealthy spinster, and looked over the changes that were almost complete. Several rooms had been turned into a dormitory, the dining room now had smaller tables and the formal rooms were designated as day recreation rooms. Upstairs, Doctor Shaw had a clinic and Olivia an office. A nurse would be on duty with a cook and cleaner. A housekeeper and her husband lived in.

"The most important thing will be getting the word out that we're here," said Olivia.

"I suppose you're going to walk the streets and go into every hotel and seedy hangout imaginable to tell them about us," said Gilbert with a rueful smile.

"Come on, Gilbert. You need to get out of that stuffy surgery more often."

"This isn't Broome, Olivia."

"Come with me then. Not as my protector, but

to get a feel for what is happening on the streets."
It was a challenge and Gilbert realized he'd be less
of a man in Olivia's eyes if he didn't take it up. It
was a feeling that had troubled him frequently.
He was devoted to Olivia and loved her in his
reserved way. But knowing the wound Tyndall had
inflicted to her heart, esteem and ego, he was
reluctant to show the depth of his feelings. As a
result, he felt Olivia found him unassertive and
emotionally pallid.

"I'll be there. We should start around the
docks. Apparently a lot of girls hang about down
there."

"Good for you, Gilbert."

It took weeks, but through the churches, hospi-
tals, the police, the network of contacts they built
up from back doors of cheap eating houses where
the homeless went for handouts, to the workers
round the docks who knew where girls were sleeping rough, the word of Shaw House spread. Young
girls started turning up to be treated, fed, given
clothing and advice. Some just wanted a bed and
a meal for a night or two, while others were sent
on to the Sisters of Mercy. In some cases, Olivia
tried to find employment for girls who had some
education and were willing to work.

It was tiring, sometimes frustrating and
heartrending, but ultimately rewarding work. It
kept her mind off the past and she only took a
break and made time for herself when Hamish

came home for holidays. He loved his school, was a keen team participant in all sports and in the dramatic society and he looked forward to the Christmas holiday adventure of traveling to a friend's pastoral property. It took his mind off wanting to go back to Broome, which relieved Olivia. Minnie's daughter, Mollie, had made one trip back to Broome since coming to work for Olivia in Fremantle and reported that all was well at Olivia's home in Broome, where Minnie lived with Alf in the servants' quarters as caretakers.

As Shaw House was transformed from a dark and rundown boarding house into the cheerful and welcoming safe haven for "girls in crisis" as Gilbert described it, Olivia and Gilbert spent more time together than ever before. Plans, renovations, furnishing and practical amenities were discussed and the workload shared. When Hamish came home he joined them, doing odd jobs and taking a great interest in the project. The three of them ate meals together and to the childless and widowed Gilbert it was a joy to feel like part of a family.

Olivia, too, was pleased Gilbert and Hamish liked each other. The boy needed a father figure and Gilbert Shaw offered sound advice, took an interest in his sporting activities and discussed world affairs with him. Olivia realized how much Hamish had grown to look like his father. He had something of Conrad's polite reserve and well-drilled school manners but his flashes of teasing humor she recognized as pure Tyndall. At these moments her heart lurched as she realized how much she missed Tyndall's engaging, if sometimes maddening, sense of humor. But Tyndall's down-to-earth manner had been good for Hamish, as had their mixed group of friends like Ahmed and the Mettas, for it had given the boy a balanced perception of people and the world. In one of his letters Tyndall had hoped Hamish wouldn't turn into a snob by going to a posh boarding school.

"Wrong again, Tyndall," Olivia thought. She never wrote to Tyndall about her personal life though she knew Hamish wrote to Tyndall. She kept her correspondence restricted to business matters. She also tried to keep her memories of Tyndall in check. If she allowed herself to think about the beautiful times they'd shared, the joyous future she'd imagined with him, and then the betrayal and invasion of Amy, it caused overwhelming pain and sorrow. If she kept busy, kept distracted, kept her distance, she figured she would get through this tragedy in her life.

Time and again she thanked whatever lucky stars, fate or providence had thrown her together with Gilbert Shaw. He was understanding, gentle and caring. She could see the growing love in his eyes for her and it gave her a warm and supportive feeling. Knowing he was there made her feel less like she was battling on her own. The strength that had helped her through her dark days was still there, but she felt softer, more mellow. She didn't have to fight so hard. She wasn't alone. She liked the companionship, having someone to share things with, and do things together. Their work life now blended with the social and, without anything ever being stated, their lives began to meld.

Gilbert was an attractive man, slim, fit, hair turning silver and the lines in his face spoke of compassion for others and a pleasant nature. He was easy to be with, calm and self-assured. Had Olivia known it, she would have been surprised to learn Gilbert was feeling increasingly uneasy about his feelings for Olivia. He worried that he may seem boring compared with the mysterious Tyndall, that he looked like her father, or uncle, that he aroused no sexual passion in her. Beneath his beautiful manners, quiet nature and easy smile was a desire to behave like a rash impetuous youth. Olivia's energy, enthusiasm and strength stirred feelings he thought had passed for him, and he longed to show her how he really felt; that inside his correct and tailored suit there was a virile young man as swashbuckling and rollicking as he imagined Captain John Tyndall to be.

Contrary to how Gilbert saw himself, Olivia thought him attractive and appealing. In his stillness she saw strength and support, in his shyness she saw cultured manners and a gentleness toward all people. His touch was one of respect and admiration and made her feel glad about herself. They were comfortably compatible and she felt at ease and safe with him. There would never be the wild passion, the unexpected or the boiling emotions generated between herself and Tyndall. No, Gilbert Shaw had come along at a point in her life that was right for both of them.

Amy had quickly become Tyndall's ferocious guardian. She banished the servants from his room and stood watch over him round the clock, sleeping on the chaise longue by the window. The doctor had left a small phial of laudanum which he said contained morphine for the pain from Tyndall's ulcerous legs. With it he gave strict instructions on dosage. Tyndall still had delirious attacks and when not mumbling incoherently, he lay in a fitful sleep.

During the hours she sat in his room Amy thought carefully about her future and her choices.

Ahmed visited the house daily and each time Amy refused him admittance. Concerned, he went to Rosminah and asked her to see or find out how Tyndall really was. She told him that the bedroom was kept locked and when Amy left it to go to the bathroom or wash, she locked it and took the key with her. "I can't see the master. He no eat very good. You get doctor come and check tuan," Rosminah pleaded.

Ahmed looked concerned. "Doctor's gone to Beagle Bay. He say he leave medicine with mem. She giving him medicine?"

Rosminah shrugged.

Ahmed sighed and told her to look for any opportunity to check on Tuan Tyndall.

Several of Tyndall's friends called by, but Amy politely turned them all away, pleading her husband's need of rest. Sergeant O'Leary called as soon as he heard of Tyndall's condition and Amy had allowed him to glimpse the sleeping Tyndall, then ushered him out, promising that she would let him know as soon as she felt Tyndall was well enough to see him. The policeman's visit had shaken her, but he had spoken warmly and wished her well. He said he would take a statement from Ahmed to advise the authorities about the sinking and apparent death of other crew members of the *Shamrock*. The interview with Tyndall could wait, he added sympathetically.

Initially, Amy fled to Tyndall's side out of fear, fear that he was not seriously ill and would soon discover the theft of pearls from his safe. Then when she found he was in such a bad way, there was a flood of relief and a little compassion.

But she became increasingly agitated as the days passed and Tyndall showed slight signs of recovery. He began to eat more and was sleeping better. He tried to make conversation with Amy but quickly tired since she made little effort to contribute to the exchange, doing little more than urging him to rest, and go back to sleep. Several times he called out in his sleep for Olivia, which angered Amy enormously.

Amy soon became aware that an almost permanent confusion of thoughts was sapping her energy. Gunther had told her the boat would be adequately provisioned and ready for sea in a few days, but he needed time to wrap up some unspecified business deals, and to receive telegraph messages from Sydney.

Now that she had the situation under control there was time on her hands, time to think, and time to wonder what she had done and what she had to do. And she knew, too, that she had Tyndall's life in her hands. It was that power, the power of life and death, that at once exhilarated and appalled her, that kept her awake for hours when she desperately wanted to sleep. And in the loneliness and dark one sleepless night she found herself pondering on what advantages would accrue if Tyndall died. She could perhaps have a claim on everything. There would be no need to put to sea with Gunther. But then the robbery bound her to Gunther, didn't it? That could not be undone.

She felt the pearls against her body but her mind wandered elsewhere and images of death filled her mind. But he won't die . . . unless . . . and she found herself thinking of an overdose of medicine. That could kill him . . . morphine . . . an overdose . . . but that would be murder. She pushed the thought from her mind, then was disturbed when it came back, again and again, and haunted her until she fell into a sleep of utter emotional and physical exhaustion.

She awoke shivering in the pre-dawn coolness and pulled a cotton sheet up to her shoulders. She looked over at Tyndall, who was now tossing restlessly. Her eyes drifted to the bedside table and locked onto the bottle of medicine and those terrible thoughts came back, and soon she found herself weeping silently, and praying for daylight in the hope that it would expunge the dark thoughts that festered in the night.

In the early morning came a note from Gunther delivered by one of his crew.

My dear partner,
Everything will be ready in two days. The evening tide will be right and there's a little Jap festival to keep everyone occupied. Have your bags packed.

Karl

Amy collapsed into a chair. But it was not the awareness that there was no turning back now that caused her reaction, but rather the note's reminder of the festival, a festival devoted to the dead. She found herself once again crying uncontrollably while looking at the stirring Tyndall and his medicine by the bed.

Two days later at the edge of town the O-Bon Matsuri festival got under way. This Japanese ceremony to honor their ancestors was a major event in the town and began at twilight at the Japanese section of the cemetery, which was segregated from the white section. In a solemn procession the Japanese community gathered by the graves with offerings of food and sake. Incense sticks burned and the graves were decorated with origami flowers or fresh blooms. A small blue lantern illuminated the name on each headstone. Following prayers, a ceremonial dance, O-Bon Odori, was performed by the Japanese women. These were the night ladies of Sheba Lane who rarely appeared in public, but on this night, dressed in traditional satin kimonos and with lacquered hair, they delicately swayed and turned on their high wooden zori sandals. Hands like white doves fluttered from the long folds of their gilded and colored robes in the movements of an ancient dance. The crowd of spectators watched in silence, the haunting high pitched wailing of the women's voices and strings of the samisens rising into the night air.

The Aborigines watching in the background nodded, recognizing the meaning of ceremonial connection with ancestors being played out on the red pindan dirt beneath the starry sky.

Very much later, after the feast in a park in town, the crowd followed the Japanese community down to the shores of the bay. Here the specially made little boats of mangrove wood laden with food and flowers and a miniature lantern or candle were pushed into the water. These would guide the spirits back to their ancestral home.

As the Japanese mourners knelt on the shore chanting prayers to the slow beat of a drum, the hundreds of small lights glided out across the bay with the tide.

• • •

Further down the bay, the red and black schooner slipped from Dampier Creek and sailed toward the sea.

Amy stood on the deck, watching the receding lights of Broome and the fleet of tiny lights bobbing across the bay and she was seized by a fleeting moment of doubt.

Karl Gunther joined her. "Second thoughts?"

"Bit late for that, isn't it?"

"Yes. It is. But if you don't gamble, you don't win either," shrugged Gunther.

"I prefer sure things when that's possible," answered Amy.

"I thought you'd figured that out by now, Amy. Nothing is sure in this life. It's all a big game . . . so play with the winners."

"Are we going to be winners, Karl?"

"We have the pearls, we have a plan, we have a chance to make big money. Like I said, nothing's sure. But I'd say we are ahead of the game."

Amy didn't respond at once, again thinking through her position. She had more to gain gambling on Karl Gunther than staying in Broome. Besides, she'd burned her bridges there, so she was ready to confront whatever lay ahead.

As the boat picked up a freshening breeze and heeled slightly to port, Amy took hold of a shroud and looked out to sea and the rising moon. She suddenly felt buoyant, excited and tremendously

471

alive. Turning to look at Gunther at the helm, she said brightly, "You're right, Karl. We're ahead of the game."

When Rosminah returned late at night from the Matsuri festival, she found the door to Tyndall's bedroom ajar. She ventured in, it was quite dark— no light was burning and the blinds were drawn. Slowly her eyes adjusted and she became aware of Tyndall slumped across the bed, one arm dangling toward the floor, his breathing shallow and hoarse. The small phial of brown liquid was empty, tipped on its side, as was a glass. There was a small pool of water beside the bed. She rushed for the doctor.

As the sun rose, Tyndall passed the critical period. The doctor rubbed his eyes and smiled at Ahmed, sitting on the other side of the bed. "He'll be all right. Luckily he didn't take the rest of the laudanum. It must have spilled when he reached for the water. Any more would have stopped his breathing."

"You think she give him too much?"

"You'll have to ask Mrs. Tyndall that question. Maybe she didn't understand my directions clearly. I'll arrange for a competent nursing woman to stay with him."

As soon as the doctor had left and Tyndall was settled, Ahmed began searching for Amy.

By mid-morning he had learned she had sailed with Karl Gunther. She'd left the house on the cliff, taking her personal effects with her. From waterfront gossip he learned Gunther was heading to the Far East on an "extended trip."

Ahmed nodded to himself and said a quick prayer of thanks to Allah. This news would no doubt hasten Tyndall's recovery.

Sergeant O'Leary called out to Tyndall as his boots thumped on the verandah.

The Chinese cook appeared, nodding and smiling. "Master in back garden. You likee tea?"

"Something a bit stronger thanks, Ah Sing. Bring the whisky. Two glasses."

He walked through the house and into the garden to find Tyndall stretched out in a hammock under shady trees.

"G'day, Sean," he called cheerfully and gestured to a wicker chair. "Make yourself comfortable. Did you tell Ah Sing to bring drinks?"

"Indeed I did, even though 'tis a bit early in the day. Sun still not over the yardarm as they say in your line of business."

"To hell with the yardarm."

Ah Sing padded up with the bottle, glasses and a jug of cold water. As O'Leary poured, Tyndall slowly hoisted himself out of the hammock and joined the policeman. "I suppose you've come to get a statement."

"Just a formality, John. Coroner will decide if anything else has to be done. Great shame losing the *Shamrock*. All in all you're not having a very good run. Cheers anyway." He raised his glass.

Tyndall drank and sighed in satisfaction. "Damn good medicine."

"And not as dangerous as some," quipped O'Leary. "You still got no idea what happened?"

Tyndall grimaced. "No, it's still a mystery to me. I do have some vague images of Amy giving me medicine, but she did that regularly. And I have images of me reaching out in the night for a drink. But I was going through a bad spot there just before she did a bunk. Fevers, hallucinations, the lot. Ahmed is convinced she gave me an overdose. I don't know . . . it's hard to accept. I can't believe she hated me that much."

O'Leary took his notebook from his shirt pocket, opened it, then took an indelible pencil from its holder and examined the tip carefully before writing the date. "But there is the business of the pearls." He made it more of a question than a statement.

"Ah, now that has the mark of Amy and Gunther about it," remarked Tyndall. Two days after Amy had fled Tyndall had given Ahmed the keys to the safe so that the latest collection of pearls from Toby Metta could be safely deposited. At this point, the robbery had been discovered.

"Of course it is only circumstantial, but who else is suspect?" Tyndall asked.

"Good question. Ahmed?"

"Nonsense."

"I agree. Either Amy found your keys or Gunther

has skills we didn't know of. I'll note the details, but there's really not much I can do about it."

"Know that, mate. But all things considered I don't feel too bad about it. Thanks to Yusef I now have grounds for divorcing Amy. Adultery."

O'Leary leaned back in his chair and grinned. "You don't give up, John, do you?"

"No. Not on this one. Olivia means the world to me, Sean. I've now got a chance for freedom and a chance to win her back."

"Bit complicated getting a divorce when you can't find the wife," observed O'Leary sympathetically.

"There has to be a way," responded Tyndall with some passion. "There just has to be a way."

"Then let's drink to it," said O'Leary, pouring a generous measure into both glasses.

It was Toby Metta who came and broke the news to Tyndall. He arrived at the foreshore camp where Tyndall was getting ready to go back to sea with his fleet.

Tyndall watched from the upper balcony of the shed as Toby puffed his way along the track and up the stairs, his round face aglow with perspiration and some agitation. He waved a copy of the *West Australian* newspaper and collapsed in a chair.

"Read the bottom of the page there," he instructed.

"Toby, what's got you in such a state?"

"Read. I've marked it."

Tyndall looked at the circled story and read it quickly.

SINGAPORE, Friday
British colonial authorities have yet to confirm the identities of two white people found murdered on the schooner SYLPH in the Straits of Malacca but they are believed to be from Australia. The man and woman had both been shot several times. The ransacked vessel was found yesterday and taken in tow by the Royal Navy patrol boat CURLEW in international waters west of the port of Malacca, an area notorious for pirates operating out of islands near Sumatra. The boat's papers indicate that it had been based in Broome in Western Australia before spending time in minor ports in the Sulu Sea. The body of a Japanese crew member was also found on board. The fate of the other crew members is unknown.

"Sounds unmistakably like Gunther. Desperate business by the sound of it. Sorry to bring the news like this, John."

Tyndall was stunned at the coldly reported facts. "I wanted her out of my life. But not like this. Bloody horrible business."

"What are you going to do? Cable Singapore?"

Tyndall looked thoughtful and spoke slowly. "Yes, I will. To get more details. Then . . ." he looked up resolutely. "Then I'm going up there to check on the whole story. I'm her husband, I need to do that."

"She'll have been buried, case closed by the time you get there. Not much point is there, John?"

"I thought she was dead once before. This time I want to be sure." He glanced at Toby's slightly shocked expression. "I have to be sure, Toby. I can't claim Olivia and marry her until I have proof that I am a free man."

Toby rose and refolded the newspaper. "I understand. It's been a hard time for you. Maybe fate has decided to smile on you again. I wish you well, John."

Tyndall didn't make the journey to Singapore. Sergeant O'Leary called in to see him with information sent from the Singapore authorities confirming the identity of Gunther and Amy. Documents, including the death certificates, would be forwarded.

Tyndall was cabled for instructions and he requested that his wife be buried up there and her possessions sent to a charity. There was no mention of any pearls found. He had no idea of the whereabouts of Gunther's next of kin. As to the fate of the *Sylph*, Tyndall told them to burn it.

Tyndall booked his passage to Fremantle, had new clothes made and packed what pearls had been found during the last of the season. He planned to deliver them to Monsieur Barat in Perth.

On the dock before he boarded the steamer, Ahmed pumped Tyndall's hand, a broad grin spread across his face. "You bring back mem. We miss mem."

"Me too, Ahmed. I guess I have to believe in fate after all. You always said things would work out and they have. Tragically as it turned out, but there you are. Life goes on."

"Good luck, tuan."

"Thanks, Ahmed. I still have a lot of talking to do." But Tyndall couldn't help smiling, too. He was convinced Olivia would come round now that matters had been conveniently solved without loss of face or dignity. He anticipated her asking for a discreet waiting period, but marry him she would.

He was nervous, and smoothed his unruly hair, ran his finger round the high collar of his white pearling master's uniform and presented himself at the door of the house in Phillimore Street.

The door was opened by a young Aboriginal woman whom he recognized as Minnie and Alf's daughter, Mollie. He introduced himself as she opened the door wide, smiling and nodding. He passed on greetings from her parents and asked to see Mem Hennessy.

Mollie shook her head. "Not here, boss. She working at the clinic. She go to the office every day."

"Where's that, Mollie?"

"Same place Master work. Shaw Clinic, on Cantonment Street."

"The Master?"

"Doctor Shaw. Mem now Mrs. Shaw. They come back tonight but."

Tyndall was having difficulty taking in the casually thrown out words.

"Mem *married* Gilbert Shaw? The fellow she set up the girls' home, or whatever it is, with?"

Mollie nodded smiling. "You bet boss. Mebbe two month ago. Me was there. Oh, it was lovely. Big cake an' everything."

Tyndall mumbled a good-bye and stumbled into the street, his world falling about him. The pain that burned in his chest made it hard to breathe and he walked toward the port in a daze before turning into the Fremantle Hotel on High Street and ordering a whisky. He sipped it slowly and was tempted to order another but decided he could not put off the ordeal of seeing her any longer. As he trudged to Cantonment Street he prayed Shaw would not be around.

He was ushered upstairs into the small room that served as Olivia's office. She stood in front of her desk, her hands clasped in front of her, biting her lip. They stared across the room at each other as a girl quietly closed the door.

So much passed between them in the space of a second or two; memories of the past they'd shared, of joy and of pain. No matter how hard they tried or how much time had elapsed they could not ignore the threads that united them. The physical chemistry between them was undiminished and it unnerved Olivia to find she was just as drawn to Tyndall as she'd always been. She struggled to compose her face into a neutral expression.

"This is something of a surprise, John. A nice one. Why didn't you tell me you were coming? How are things in Broome?" She gave a hesitant smile.

Her politeness disturbed Tyndall. He'd been more prepared for anger, fierce questioning. He, too, adopted a civil, slightly formal tone. "Er, there have been a few developments. I wanted to come and tell you in person."

Olivia looked immediately concerned. "Is something wrong? Has anyone been hurt? The business . . ."

"No, not exactly," he cut in, paused then started awkwardly. "It's about Amy . . ."

Olivia's face set and her lips tightened.

Tyndall plunged on. "She's dead."

Olivia stared at him in shock, her lips parted, but unable to speak.

"I wanted to tell you in person."

"What happened?" whispered Olivia.

"Murdered. In the Straits of Malacca, by pirates."

"How horrible, John. What was she doing there?"

"She was with Karl Gunther. Ran off with him. He was killed too. I was sick. I'd been wrecked—

lost the *Shamrock*—Ahmed found me. While I was out of it, she took over caring for me. I nearly died in the process, an accident . . . I think."

"I knew that, but I can't believe all this. Why didn't someone contact me . . . ?"

"I haven't finished. She got into the safe and took most of the season's pearls. We've picked up a few more, but she took the best ones. Good haul it was. I'm sorry, Olivia."

"I'm sorry, too, John. For everything. What a shock."

"There is one good thing to come out of this. I'm a free man. So my first thought was to come to you. I've never stopped loving you, Olivia, and I have been utterly faithful to you. I knew you were hurt . . . the whole thing with Amy was painful and embarrassing. I don't want to rehash it all. But I hoped we could start afresh. And now I find out . . . that you . . ." He couldn't go on.

Olivia turned away from him, tears in her eyes, her thoughts jumbled, a wild desire to scream welling in her chest. She took two long, deep breaths and turned back to Tyndall, wincing at his hurt and accusative blue eyes. "Yes, I was deeply hurt. And humiliated. Gilbert is a good and kind man. We worked closely together and he was a great comfort. I was lonely . . ."

"So was I, dammit, Olivia! I never went near Amy. I swore to you I would sort things out. Why didn't you wait for me, Olivia?"

"Please stop shouting, John. Don't forget the circumstances, and how hopeless it looked. You lied to me, Amy was not about to let go of you. What was I supposed to do?" Her voice rose. "I chose to get on with my life. I have a son to think about."

Tyndall was glaring at her and although he lowered his voice, it was filled with seething anger and bewildered pain. "Why didn't you at least tell me you were thinking of marrying? Given me a chance?"

"What good would that have done? You couldn't do anything about it."

"I might have been able to change your mind."

"I couldn't take that chance," said Olivia in a tired, resigned voice. "It all happened rather quickly . . . it seemed the right and logical thing to do. Gilbert proposed, I agreed and we had a small wedding, a few days' honeymoon and back to work. I'm finding the work with Shaw House very rewarding." Her voice trailed off and they stared at each other for a moment.

"You still love me, don't you, Olivia?" he said quietly.

She didn't answer for a moment and closed her eyes in pain. "John, I have a new life. I owe Gilbert a great deal. He has helped me enormously and I owe him that loyalty."

"What about the loyalty you owe me? We were going to spend the rest of our lives together. You're punishing me for something that wasn't my fault."

"Please, John, let's not go over things that can't be changed. It's all too late." She drew a deep breath. "I will always be your friend, we have a responsibility together for Star of the Sea, but it can't be more than that. Not any more." She turned away, knowing her last words had given her away.

He walked slowly to her and sat down on a small bentwood chair by her desk, reaching for her hand. At the touch of his fingers she pulled her hand away.

"Olivia, we only get one chance at real happiness in this world."

"John . . . I beg you. I can change nothing. You know me, I must do what is right. And it's right that I stay beside Gilbert and carry out the work we've started. It is a great satisfaction to help these girls . . ."

"What about me?"

She looked at him, her heart constricting at the love in his eyes, the hopelessness on his face. "I don't know what to say . . ."

"I can't change your mind?"

But she heard the defeat in his voice. Tyndall's fire and wildness had died. She shook her head, not trusting herself to speak.

He rose and turned away from her. "I wish nothing but the best for you, Olivia."

"What will you do?" she whispered.

He turned back at the door. "I'll wait." The door closed behind him.

Olivia dropped her face in her hands and cried softly. Why had she not waited? Her pride and anger had sabotaged their chance of happiness.

Even though fate had stepped in to solve Tyndall's marital dilemma, she'd never given him a chance to free himself and prove his love to her.

But she had made her choice. She would never hurt Gilbert Shaw as she'd been hurt. Her heart ached for Tyndall. She wished he'd shouted, been drunk, or thrown something. She would never forget the sadness and loss he showed, or forgive herself for being the cause.

CHAPTER TWENTY

Tyndall looked down at his white buckskin shoes now coated in red dust. The legs of his white duck trousers were also filmed in red powder. He shrugged and stepped out from under the sparse shade of the pot-bellied baobab tree—dust was a common denominator at the Broome Turf Club. It was still a rough and ready track with limited amenities, but at least all the bush had been cleared from the center of the course so there was an uninterrupted view from the grandstand.

The annual meeting was one of the main social events of the year and a rare chance for the ladies to display the latest fashions. Tussore silk and voile were popular dress choices, topped with large hats with plumes and lace, or neat toques. The women suffered through the dust and blazing sun, wilting as the afternoon wore on. However, at the Race Ball they'd bloom again in different creations.

Tyndall had a fair sum riding on the Broome Cup and he moved to the rail as it got under way.

The favorite, ridden by a well-known station identity, took a comfortable early lead and punters were anticipating cleaning up. But a horse charged from the pack in the home straight and stormed past the leader, winning by a length. The jockey lifted an arm in jubilation and to everyone's surprise, long hair flowed from beneath the jockey's cap.

The crowd roared as they recognized the teenage daughter of one of the leading families. The steward clutched his head and club officials hurriedly conferred.

While someone searched for the club's rules, Tyndall called out, "She won fair and square, let it stand."

The crowd, some of whom had climbed onto the fence by the winning post, and those contemplating their loss, were in good humor and sided with Tyndall. The steward decreed that the win stood. A big cheer went up and there was a stampede to the bar, where everyone declared the tradition of the Broome Cup for providing great entertainment and gossip had been maintained.

Tyndall quietly collected his winnings and headed back to town for a few drinks before changing for the Race Ball.

In recent times he had thrown himself into the social scene of Broome and lived wildly, for times were booming and there was a careless almost desperate atmosphere of gaiety and high living. Talk of the possibility of war in Europe had little impact on this distant outpost of the Empire, despite the headlines in London.

That evening at the Race Ball he danced with mothers and daughters and sent hearts fluttering. Since the departure of both Amy and Olivia, he was considered one of Broome's most eligible bachelors, even in his forties. The roistering young adventurer had become a successful and enterprising master pearler with expanding business interests. His virile looks and charm had increased with the years, as had the mystique of his colorful life.

But for Tyndall, life was far from what he wished. He thought of Olivia every day and sometimes thoughts of his lost daughter Maya came to him, always causing him depression and a deepening sense of loss. He began to think there was a curse on the women who came into his life and subconsciously he kept all women at an emotional distance.

Tyndall kept himself occupied in the wet season working on a project with Yoshi for culturing pearls. At first he had dismissed the idea of an artificial pearl, even though he had learned that "seeded" cultured pearls had appeared on the Japanese market in the late 1890s. Yoshi's interest had been sparked by letters from friends in Japan and the occasional newspaper article. Enthused by the idea, Tyndall decided to investigate further. While he was convinced nothing would replace natural pearls, it was possible the shell beds might not last forever. All that the pearlers had learned over the years was to abandon the overworked banks until stocks replenished themselves. Now Tyndall saw the possibility of a lucrative sideline, an alternative product that met a demand for those who could not afford true pearls. The cultured pearls of Mikimoto in Japan were finally gaining acceptance as legitimate pearls and the canny "pearl king" had established two huge farms, plus a factory in Tokyo where young Japanese were trained in jewelry making. He had also opened his own pearl shops.

It was on their way back to port on the last trip of the season that Tyndall made the decision to look into the Mikimoto success story. The *Bulan* was running easily with the wind almost astern and Tyndall and Yoshi were relaxing by the helm enjoying a smoke.

They hadn't spoken for some time, but were quietly enjoying fair sailing and the peace of a fine day at sea.

"How about a trip home, Yoshi?" Tyndall suddenly asked.

"Home, Cap'n?" queried Yoshi without any visible reaction.

"Yeah. Japan. See your family, friends."

Yoshi had been home only once, and that was from Thursday Island, before he had come to work in Broome. Most of his money, though, went back to Japan. He drew on his cigarette, and Tyndall waited patiently.

"Contract. No time for trip, Cap'n." Yoshi never wasted words and in any case he was bound by his contract for several more years.

"But it's a nice idea?" added Tyndall and Yoshi smiled. He now understood the white boss was teasing him. Western humor still puzzled him. Tyndall turned and caught him grinning.

"Well," Tyndall went on, "I'm thinking of going to Japan in the wet, and I'd like you to come along. The firm will pay. But we'll have to do some work while we're there. What do you reckon?"

There was a sharp intake of breath, a slight hissing, as Yoshi reacted with a rare show of emotion. "Ah," he said softly. "We work in Japan. What work?"

"Pearling, Yoshi. Mikimoto pearling. I think it's time we both took a look at what he's up to." Tyndall waited for Yoshi to say something, then laughed and added, "Mebbe a chance for you to get a missus, Yoshi. Marry a nice girl and bring her back here."

Yoshi smiled briefly, then gave Tyndall a raised thumb signal, which Tyndall acknowledged in style. And both knew the deal was done.

Captain Evans was put in charge of refitting the fleet during the lay up, Toby Metta charged with working up the pearls and dispatching them to Olivia, and the shell take was sold quickly, at a slight discount, so that the trip and wet season activities could be financed. Leaving Ahmed in charge, Tyndall and Yoshi caught a steamer to Darwin, then to Singapore and another to Yokohama.

It hadn't been easy to reach Kokichi Mikimoto, despite the carefully worded letters that Tyndall arranged to be written for him in Japanese. But eventually his persistence paid off, an invitation was issued and Yoshi was summoned from his village. The two traveled to the island of Tatoku in the Bay of Ago where Mikimoto had made his successful experiments in pearl growing.

The small steam service boat nosed close to shore and as it headed toward the landing Tyndall and Yoshi were intrigued to see wooden tubs secured by ropes bobbing on the surface. Yoshi spoke briefly to the helmsman and with a grin he took them closer and idled the engine. Suddenly women divers began popping to the surface, dropping oysters into tubs. They had no equipment to aid their diving. Yoshi questioned the driver and translated. "Women better divers than men. No trouble going down to five fathoms."

Wearing the traditional white loincloth and modest white shirts, their hair tied in a tight bun at the nape of their neck, they plunged and resurfaced like a school of happy porpoises. The men rowed amongst them collecting filled baskets.

Tyndall recalled the Aboriginal women pearl divers in the early days of the Australian industry. "Easier work than the big suit, eh, Yoshi?" said Tyndall.

"Mebbe one make good wife," he grinned back.

Tyndall folded his long legs awkwardly beneath him as he sat on the cushion on the floor opposite Mikimoto. He was a strong-featured man, still young looking in his fifties and wore a simple black cotton kimono. Steaming tea in small bowls sat on the low cherry-wood table between them.

Mikimoto spoke in English. "So, Captain Tyndall, you wish to make pearls grow like turnips, eh?"

"As you do, Mikimoto san!"

The great man threw back his head and laughed heartily. "It is true. I had a dream and I never let it go. It cost me a lot at times . . . my money, my family life, even at one point my good name! My beloved Ume, my late wife, was always beside me and made it possible for me to continue with my experiments. Sadly she was not able to see the day I created a perfect round pearl. But the lesson is, you must not give up what your heart truly desires."

Tyndall thought suddenly of Olivia, but turned his questions to specifics of pearl culture. Mikimoto was generous with information but, as Tyndall had guessed, he did not divulge all his secrets.

Later Tyndall and Yoshi were shown around the tiny family feudal kingdom and came away convinced they should attempt experiments in the sheltered creeks of the north-west. Yoshi returned to his village to make final arrangements for the bride he had chosen to travel to Australia, and rejoined Tyndall in Yokohama to sail home.

But no sooner had they arrived home and settled

into the mundane routine of life than war was declared in Europe. Tyndall's plans for expansion and new horizons were thus put on hold and, as the war dragged on, the bottom dropped out of the pearl shell market.

Olivia stared at her tall young son standing proudly before her in his uniform of the Royal Australian Naval Brigade. How handsome he looked. But how her heart winced.

Hamish read the anguish in his mother's eyes. "Don't worry, Mother. I shan't be off for some months."

"Are you sure about this, darling? I'm proud of you for volunteering so quickly, but you are only twenty years old . . ."

"Mum, it's our duty! You and Dad came from England. We are part of the Empire and we have to do our bit for the home country."

Olivia admired his patriotism but worried about the dangers he faced. For Hamish, joining the navy was not only the chance for adventure and service to his country but also a career opportunity. The sea had called him ever since Tyndall first took him out on the lugger named after his father.

Hamish had joined the Royal Australian Naval Reserves in Fremantle as a cadet while still at school and over the years had continued part-time training, attending weekly drill nights, annual camps and occasional courses. Olivia was pleased he had found his passion and interest early in life.

So, at the outbreak of war, as a trained member of the Reserves he joined up and was posted to the Royal Australian Naval Brigade unit at Albany to work on laying out convoy anchorages and to help set up a naval lookout station.

During this time, Hamish wrote to Tyndall:

Dear Uncle John,

I'm having the time of my life! I am nonetheless aware of the duty that has called us all here and the seriousness of the task ahead, but what a fine bunch of lads are here. You would be proud of my sea skills . . . I realize now you taught me so much and I'm grateful. You would probably have a few blunt remarks to make about the "prissiness" of we sailor boys doing drill in our immaculate uniforms!

I don't imagine life in the navy will be anything like life on board a lugger! However I still look forward to the day I might be a good enough seaman to be taken on board by the Star of the Sea. Keep the home fires burning—or rather the beer cold and the sails set fair. I know you will watch out for my mother no matter what her circumstances. Gilbert is a fine man and what she needs at this time in her life. But you have been very significant and special in both our lives and I think of you often. Please pass on my kind thoughts to Ahmed, Yoshi, Taki and all the rest.

Hamish

A few months later Hamish wrote to his mother:

Albany, October 1914.
I have so enjoyed my time here—I have met a very nice girl. I hope you will meet her one day . . . after the war. But how I yearn to be part of the great military convoy assembled here! It is an impressive sight with so many troop ships and escorts out in the sound. To think they have come from all parts of Australia and New Zealand. Soon they will set out on the great adventure to the other side of the world.

It didn't take long for Hamish to hear of the forming of the Royal Australian Naval Bridging Train, a kind of support service. He wangled a transfer and was drafted to Melbourne to join a unit of the "train" about to be shipped out on the transport, *Port Macquarie*.

On his last leave in June 1915, he traveled to Fremantle by coastal steamer to farewell his mother.

They sat over tea and his favorite cake while he explained to her what his strange unit was all about.

"The Naval Board has offered to send a train of personnel, equipment, vehicles, horses and so on to serve in Europe."

"But what will you do exactly, dear?"

"Build bridges, jetties, piers and pontoons for making harbors and landings on invasion beaches. We're navy but told sometimes we might be under army command."

"And will you be involved in any actual fighting?" asked Olivia apprehensively.

"Officially, no. But if there's a chance, we'll certainly have a go," said Hamish enthusiastically.

"Do be careful, Hamish," said Olivia, taking his hand. She smilingly added, "I suppose it's a silly thing to say."

He patted her hand. "Mum, please don't worry about me. I couldn't bear to think of you going through each day, fretting. Promise me you won't do that. Think of the great things I'll be doing, the places I'll see. Be pleased that I'm glad to be part of it all." His smile softened. "And if, just if, anything happens to me, you must promise me not to be sad. . . ."

"Hamish! You can't say that! Don't even think it."

"Mother, it has to be faced as a possibility. I've thought about it. And you know . . . I'm not afraid of dying. So remember that. And I want to know that you'll go on with your life and be happy. Give me the freedom to go with a light heart knowing you will be all right. I've always admired your strength, don't fall apart, Mum. We all have to do our duty."

She nodded and kissed his cheek, holding his head to her breast for a moment. Then he settled back in his seat, helped himself to more cake and gave her his impressions of Melbourne.

When it came time to say good-bye, Olivia called on all her inner strength to be calm. "Are you sure you don't want me to come to Melbourne and see you off?"

"It's no grand departure . . . not like the convoy leaving Albany. The *Port,* as we call her, will waddle out of Port Phillip Bay without much fanfare. I'd rather remember you here in this lovely room with the smell of cake and tea. Not standing on some windy rainy dock."

"Those poor horses . . . I hope they survive the trip," said Olivia absently.

They held each other tightly. "I'll go and see Gilbert and Mollie and then I'll be off. Stay here. I love you, Mum."

He quietly left the room, turning to blow her a kiss and then shut the door softly behind him.

Tyndall wrote to Olivia that he was staying on in Broome even though many boats had stopped working. Some opportunists were coming down from the Aru Islands up north and applying for the unused licenses in order to build up their own fleets. These men, who had been using cheap labor and working at the Arus just outside the three mile limit, were not welcome in Broome. Tyndall was not going to readily forfeit what he'd fought to build up, but he admitted to Olivia in his letter that the business was doing poorly and it would be hard to keep the fleet in good shape for much longer due to the war.

The pearl shell market was moribund and the buyers in Vienna and Paris were canceling their contracts. Broome had become a ghost town. Some pearlers had gone bankrupt, some left for adventures overseas and down south, putting a brave face on their penniless condition. Others, barely solvent, sold their boats, paid off their crews as best they could and became verandah pearlers.

Tyndall, like many of the master pearlers, was concerned at the rising dominance of the Japanese crews. A powerful band of Japanese proprietors and merchants acted as bankers for the Japanese divers and crews who were engaged in gambling, selling snide pearls or dummying. Officially, a Japanese could not own a lugger, so they set up white "owners" to dummy for them while they controlled and owned the business. Dummying flourished and, although everyone knew, nothing was done about it.

Trying to break the increasing Japanese hold on the industry was regarded as "too hard". The Japanese tightened their grip by refusing to train divers from other races.

Tyndall tried to get the white master pearlers to unite and form a co-operative, but his plan was not well received. Pearling had always attracted an independent breed of man who socialized with others readily enough but played his cards close to his chest when it came to business dealings.

The only matter that the master pearlers agreed upon at this juncture was the appalling loss of life due to paralysis since the recent introduction of engine-driven compressors to replace hand pumps. Although this allowed divers to go to greater depths, the risks were higher. Divers hated the staging required in ascending from extreme depths, preferring to put their faith in a rice paper charm rather than hang suspended at varying depths as they staged their way to the surface. Many lives were saved by the steel decompression chamber presented to Broome hospital by Heinke and Co., the company, along with Seibe Gorman of London, which made the diving suits.

Tyndall decided to take another tack. Sitting in his office he labored over a note pad, occasionally screwing up pages and throwing them with accuracy into the wastebasket across the room. He wished Olivia was there to help him, but finally he was satisfied with what he'd written. In an open letter to all the master pearlers of Broome he set out a proposal or culturing pearls as a secondary industry. He told of his visit to Mikimoto, how cultured pearls could replace the dwindling pearl shell market. He explained that, far from devaluing natural pearls, it actually would increase their value. He told of how Mikimoto set high standards for his pearls, those that didn't meet them were destroyed. He pointed out that the cultivated pearls were produced by the oyster in exactly the same manner as naturally occurring pearls once a "nucleus" was introduced. The use of mother-of-pearl was threatened by the new plastics industry so by creating a middle market for less expensive pearls they would ensure their own survival as pearlers.

"It was as if I'd let off a cannon from Buccaneer Rock," wrote Tyndall to Olivia. *"I scored a direct hit on the Pearlers' Association and also the Japanese Club, so*

help me. They're all dead against it, accusing me of sabotaging the whole industry. I don't mind some chaps tackling me in the Lugger Bar, in some cases I've almost persuaded them. But a few of them just cut me dead. I'm sure you know the ones! Toby and Mabel are my sole supporters at this stage. Ahmed remains loyal but doubtful, however I know he'll be at my side whatever I decide. Yoshi is enthusiastic, having seen the Japanese operation although I was surprised at the lack of interest from the local Jap community. Yoshi tells me it is discussed in their club with downright fear. Where do you stand, my dear partner?"

Fondly, Tyndall

Dear John,

I don't feel well positioned to advise you on the matter of the cultured pearls. It sounds interesting, but I would like to see some of them. Would it be an expensive operation to set up? It's all a bit experimental and perhaps it's early days yet. Plant the seed . . . like a pearl and let them mull about it. In other words, let nature take its course. You tend to be impetuous and rush forth.

I'm sorry I can't be more positive but I am aware of the financial position of Star of the Sea and I'm very taken up with the running of the girls' refuge here. It is rewarding work. There seem to be more girls in need at this time with so many of the young men going away and leaving broken hearts behind!

I hope you are well, give my best to Ahmed and the boys.

Olivia

Tyndall folded her letter and put it carefully in his desk drawer with her other correspondence. Damn you, Olivia, he thought. A polite formal note as always, signed with her neat signature, minus any expression of affection. He was hurt, too, that she didn't want to be more involved with his idea. He just couldn't see Olivia preoccupied with a home for wayward girls.

The local debate about Tyndall's scheme soon came to a head. A meeting was called by the Master Pearlers' Association at the Continental Hotel "for all interested parties".

The dining room was packed with the master pearlers and their wives, leaders in the business community and, sitting in a row at the back, influential members of the Japanese business and pearling community.

There had been some mutterings among the executive about the presence of the Japanese but, after some discussion with Mr. Takahashi who ran several stores in town, it was agreed they should be allowed to stay on the understanding that there might be some remarks which may be disrespectful to their community.

Mr. Takahashi bowed and said he understood.

Once everyone was settled, the chairman of the association, Mr. Bernard, rose behind the small table set at the front of the room, outlined what Tyndall had proposed and opened the subject for discussion. Several men jumped to their feet and speaker after speaker condemned the scheme.

Tyndall sat beside the chairman becoming increasingly angry until he could control himself no longer and leapt to his feet. "Poppycock! Cultured pearls are *real* pearls. They are *no* threat to natural pearls!"

Another pearler stood. "I've seen attempts at making pearls on Thursday Island and it's a jolly tricky business and what they did get was of no value. I have seen some of the Jap pearls and they are of poor quality luster. My concern is that if we use our oysters, which are far superior, then maybe we could produce pearls with a better nacre that would undermine our natural pearls."

Tyndall jumped to his feet again. "That's the point!" he shouted. "We can make good pearls, ones with a decent luster that will meet a market for those who can't afford natural pearl!"

The arguments raged and Tyndall sank in his seat stony faced, disappointed at the little support he was getting and stunned by the lack of vision and understanding among his pearling colleagues. Mabel Metta gave him a smile of encouragement which he acknowledged with a shrug.

Debate moved on to the issue of how to control a cultured pearl industry if it did get started. It wasn't long before someone said what almost everyone was thinking.

"Sooner or later, and probably right from the word go, the Japs will control it," shouted a master pearler and there was a murmur of agreement from practically all the whites present. The speaker went on, "We've had enough trouble with the dummying operations of the Japanese. You can bet your life that they will be running any imitation pearl business, not us. So what's in it for us? Nothing."

There was a burst of applause.

From the back of the hall came a polite call. "Mr. Chairman." It was Mr. Takahashi. All heads swiveled around as the chairman acknowledged the call. Mr. Takahashi bowed slightly to the chairman. "We have conducted our own discussions about this idea of Captain Tyndall and we are against the venture. We feel it will be bad for Broome business. No good for our divers, no good for business people and bring bad feelings between Japanese and Broome peoples. We say no start make pearls. We no let any Japanese start such an enterprise." He sat down to loud applause.

All heads turned to Tyndall. Slowly he stood and spoke calmly. "I understand what you are all saying. I believe you are wrong. You are short-sighted businessmen. Kokichi Mikimoto is a man with a vision, a dream and passion. He can see the future. One day Broome will produce, by deliberate means, large perfect round pearls of a luster and quality that even people like my good friend here, Tobias Metta, will not be able to tell apart from a pearl brought up from the sea bed by a diver."

•   •   •

Tyndall didn't hang around after the meeting but retreated to his office and sat down to pour it all out in a letter to Olivia, but after half a page, he screwed it up, threw it over his shoulder and reached for the whisky bottle.

A few weeks later, Tyndall received a letter from Olivia which gave him no comfort.

> *Dear John,*
> *I read in the paper a report about the meeting over the pearl culture business. How distressing for you. The Mettas wrote me that you put up a spirited defense. Perhaps you are ahead of your time, John. These are hard times with the war getting worse and casualties beginning to add up. Be patient, your time will come I feel sure.*

He added her letter to his stack and spoke aloud to the empty office with some bitterness. "The only time that counts, Olivia, is time with you. And I have precious little of that to look forward to."

Olivia longed for letters from Hamish, which were few and far between. When a fat one arrived from Port Said, she made herself tea and sat alone in the lounge room to savor it.

He explained it was an "illegal" letter in that he was getting a friend to carry it and mail it so it wouldn't be censored. He talked of the great mates he'd made, of the strange places and people he had seen, of how he missed everybody back home . . .

. . . especially you, dearest Mum. It's been a hard trip at sea for the horses . . . we lost seventy-nine of them due to sickness and exhaustion between Australia and Bombay. We were recalled to Colombo and returned to Bombay to land the rest of the horses rather than lose the lot—we need them for haulage. We got our orders to the Dardanelles to help prepare the British Army IX corps for the landing on Suvla Bay. But we had no tugs or lighters so our unit made timber rafts to get men, stores, baggage and equipment ashore. We were all loaded up ready to go when we got word someone had found us a tiny steamer, the Itria, *which meant unloading and dismantling the rafts and reloading the lot onto the steamer. Once ashore we had our only training in building pontoons and piers and the like—five days training, mind you! Now we've loaded pontoons and everything onto the* Itria *for the "proper" landings. What a job it's been but as our CO said, we refuse to be associated with failure!*

On 7 August, the *Itria* anchored off the invasion beach under orders to locate sites for a pier. At dusk Hamish was in the first group to go ashore and build a landing pier of barrels and timber. They'd had no rest for forty-eight hours, were under continuous attack by artillery and shrapnel fire and even had a bombing raid by a Taube aircraft. The anchorage was declared too hot and shifted.

Hamish was then part of a group helping to disembark and land troops and their stores. No thought had been given to water supplies and thousands of troops were suffering thirst.

"It's as bad as being lost in the Nullarbor," muttered one of the men to Hamish.

On August 12, the "train" men were ordered to take over supplying water as well as their other duties. Hamish tried to ignore the sporadic fire from the ridge as they feverishly buried spare pontoons on the beach to use as water tanks, filling them from lighters with borrowed pumps and fire hoses from ships. Men who weren't killed or badly wounded succumbed to paratyphoid, jaundice, pneumonia and blood poisoning from flies and dirt on even minor wounds.

While Hamish was working at the base of the ridge, digging in a post to hold part of a line, a soldier a short way up the hill was shot from above and his body rolled down close to Hamish. Without thinking, in a burst of anger and frustration, Hamish picked up the soldier's rifle and crawled up the ridge. He lay by a boulder for some minutes before spotting movement against the skyline. He fired, and fired again, knowing he'd got the sniper and felt an immense elation and satisfaction as he scrambled back to his duties.

"You navy blokes aren't supposed to fight,"

yelled an army officer, crouching and running past him, adding, "Good bloody shot, by the way."

Feeling quite pleased with himself, Hamish grinned at his mate who gave him the thumbs up and waded toward their lighter which was returning for more equipment. Hamish was about to scramble aboard, when he felt a sharp pain, a searing burning sensation in his back. He cried out, as the world went black and he slipped beneath the bloodstained water.

Everyone at Shaw House had gone into shock over the news of Hamish's death. Gilbert sat by Olivia, who refused any kind of sedative, as she talked and talked. He had no answer to her anguished questioning as to how God could be so cruel. What had she ever done to deserve such punishment? How could she go on?

Gilbert took her hand. "You must and you will. Hamish was so proud of what you are doing here. You're helping others, didn't you say among his last words to you were to look after the girls?"

Olivia nodded, but in a small voice asked, "Who's going to look after me?"

"I am, my dear. We all are. But you must help yourself, too. It's wartime, there is so much suffering. You have been struck a cruel blow, how you deal with this is the measure of where your life will go."

"I don't care what happens anymore."

"Olivia . . . that isn't true. Listen to me. There

is a young girl just arrived. She's pregnant and her husband, lover, I'm not sure, but she apparently adored him, has been killed. Help her. In doing so you will help yourself. Trust me."

"Oh, Gilbert, how can I help her? I feel like telling her not to have the baby. It's not worth the pain of one day losing your child."

Olivia collapsed in his arms and sobbed as he held her and murmured soothing words.

When news reached Tyndall of the death of Hamish, he quietly broke the news to Ahmed and then Yoshi and Taki who spread the word amongst the men who'd known the effervescent youngster. Tyndall's heart broke for Olivia, and he wanted to rush straight to her and comfort her but knew it was not his place. He struggled over a letter to her, trying to find the words to comfort her and make some sense of yet another loss in her life.

> *My dearest Olivia,*
>
> *I loved him too. After losing Maya, and your Conrad, Hamish became like a son to me. His love of the sea I like to think came from our happy days in Broome. How I wish I could ease, no, take on, the pain you must be suffering. So much promise, such hope, I find it hard for God to justify taking him. But so many good young men have been taken in this ghastly mess. Be proud of him, he didn't shirk his duty, and have faith there is some reason for all this.*

It hurts that I can't be more comfort to you. But I am with you, thinking of you, and remembering such happy times . . . hold on to these, Olivia.
You know I will come in an instant should you need me.
Always,
Tyndall

Olivia had read the letter quickly, then stuffed it in the pocket of her skirt. Several times during the day she took it out and re-read it then resolutely put it away. The passion and deep caring that jumped off the page touched her deeply. She realized that others had loved Hamish, too, that he had touched other lives. Memories came . . . of the boy riding on Ahmed's shoulders, trying on Yoshi's copper helmet, standing by the wheel with Tyndall. The shared memories of Hamish somehow helped keep him alive in more than her own heart and made her feel a little better.

Gilbert's patient understanding and wise advice penetrated the shroud of grief that enveloped Olivia and she steeled herself to go back to work and hide her pain, to try to get on with life in the hope that helping others might deflect her anguish and sense of loss. She asked Gilbert to tell everyone not to offer sympathy or pity. She returned to her duties and stoically looked on each minute of each day as a hurdle to be faced, overcome and the cycle repeated.

The staff respected Gilbert's request to avoid any mention of the death of Olivia's son. As Gilbert said, it was war time. Everyone knew someone who had suffered a loss. The best way to deal with life was to put yesterday behind you and go forward.

On her rounds the first morning back at work Olivia met the new girl in the room she shared with three others.

They smiled at each other and Olivia glanced at the medical records. "Well, Maria, I'm glad to say you seem to be very healthy. I'm sure all will turn out well."

Olivia sat by the bed where Maria was hunched in the center, her legs tucked under her, still wearing the simple shift they gave all the girls for the check-up. She looked miserable and tears trickled down her face.

Reaching over, Olivia took her hand. "My dear girl. I know how you must feel . . . truly I do." And as the girl lifted an angry tear-stained face, Olivia managed to say, "I have lost my only child, my son, in this war."

The girl was instantly contrite but she spoke with bitter sadness. "I don't understand why he went. He didn't have to."

"Do you want to talk about him?"

The girl shook her head.

"Then let's make a pact. We can share our grief but we don't have to talk about it and drag it up all the time. It's just something you and I have to bear. They tell us to take it moment by moment, day by day. And it seems the best way. You have your child to think about."

"I don't know what to do. I can't go back to my family . . . the shame of it all. We weren't married yet . . . we were about to be but he was called up to go, so quick . . ."

"Let's wait and see. Maybe after the baby comes, you—and they—will feel differently. It is their grandchild, after all."

The girl looked unconvinced but was somewhat comforted by Olivia's words.

Maria soon slipped into the routine of Shaw House, marveling at the compassion, help and generosity shown to the girls who passed through. Three of them were pregnant—one had been assaulted for running away from a brothel and two were homeless Aboriginal runaways who'd been living on the streets after being taken from their families as young children and farmed out as servants and mistreated.

She made herself useful and Olivia found herself calling on Maria for assistance more and more. Finally she asked Maria if she would be interested in working as her assistant once she was over the birth. Olivia liked the calm and pleasant girl and a bond slowly developed between them. She put it down to their shared loss, but was sensible enough to recognize the girl's abilities.

Gilbert encouraged the friendship, hoping it would help divert her attention. They never spoke of Hamish, Olivia kept all her pain locked up. She had taken down his photos and put them in a drawer by her bed. But once Gilbert had found her sitting in the darkness holding a photo to her chest. Not knowing she was in the bedroom he'd turned on the light and was shocked at the anguish on her pale, still face. He sat beside her and held her silently, wishing with all his heart she would at least cry or share the burden with him.

Maria's baby decided to come in the middle of the night and when Doctor Shaw was summoned Olivia insisted on going with him.

Strange feelings, thoughts and emotions swept over Olivia as she sat beside the panting girl in labor. Memories of the birth of James came back with great intensity and for a moment the awareness that she had lost both sons, her only children, threatened to overwhelm her. She gripped Maria's hand as her child pushed into the world and Olivia fervently hoped Maria would never suffer as a mother the way she had.

Gilbert held up the squalling infant. "A girl," he announced.

She was perfect. Dark hair and eyes like her mother. Olivia weighed and wrapped the baby in a blanket and tucked her into the crook of Maria's arm. Maria lay back and shut her eyes as she held her baby and several tears escaped from under her lashes. "Oh, she's like a little doll."

Olivia patted her head and silently left the room, her heart full, knowing Maria was thinking of the baby's father and how he would never share this joy.

CHAPTER TWENTY-ONE

Over the next two years Maria became firmly entrenched at Shaw House. Olivia had taught her rudimentary bookkeeping and some secretarial skills. Although they'd found her a valuable worker, they knew at some stage she would have to find other work and make a fuller life for herself and her daughter. The impish and mischievous two-year-old ruled the roost at Shaw House and was considered part of the family, bringing great delight to Gilbert and Olivia.

To Maria, the Shaws had become her family as much as her friends. She hadn't been to visit her own family though she sent a note saying she had a baby girl and had chosen to keep her. Her mother had replied with a terse and bitter letter telling her she should have given up the child and then there might have been some chance of her returning to them.

When Maria mentioned her daughter's second birthday was looming, Olivia asked if she would like a little party. It would provide the staff at Shaw

House and other children and their mothers with a happy diversion.

"Oh, Olivia, it would be wonderful," responded Maria with delight. "She's old enough to get some fun out of a birthday party, but it never entered my head to have one. Gosh, we haven't much time to make preparations."

"Time enough, I'm sure. Tomorrow is Sunday so we'll pick you up after church and take you around to our house for lunch and we can sort it all out. The birthday is next Saturday, and will fit in with the routine quite well."

Maria rushed to Olivia and impulsively gave her a hug. "You're a really special person, Olivia. Thanks. We can spend the week making decorations. It'll give everyone something to do. The kids will love it."

Gilbert and Olivia detoured on their way home from church to wait at the Catholic Church until Maria and her little girl came out. They drove home and while Gilbert read the *Bulletin* on the verandah, the two women took tea and biscuits in the garden in the shade of a tree.

It didn't take long to make a list of party items that had to be bought and a menu of cakes, sandwiches, biscuits, jelly, lollies and cordial prepared. It was done with a lot of laughter as both of them recalled funny events they had experienced at parties while growing up.

It was while the two were cleaning up to go

inside that Olivia, without giving it too much thought, remarked sympathetically, "Of course, it must be sad not being with your family for her birthday."

When Maria didn't reply Olivia looked up to see Maria trying hard not to cry. "I'm sorry," Olivia said softly.

"No, it's all right. Truly. It's just that I'm not sure who is family."

"Whatever do you mean?" asked Olivia, sitting down again and motioning Maria to join her.

Maria took a deep breath. "Well, you see, I'm not white. I'm part Aboriginal." Olivia gasped and Maria went on. "Oh yes, I was adopted by a white family living in Albany, but somewhere I know I have another family. I have memories . . ." and her voice trailed away as she tried yet again, as she had for so many years, to make sense of the fragments of images of that other distant life.

Olivia leaned across and took her hands, trying to give emotional support at what she recognized was a cathartic moment in the young woman's life. "You've not talked about your background to anyone?"

"No. Mum and Dad never mentioned it. Not once. The nuns at school never talked about it. It was as if it never existed. I was happy enough to accept it eventually. Seeing how Aboriginal kids were treated made me afraid to mention it, I suppose. I don't know. It's all so confusing. I tried to block things out but those memories just wouldn't go away."

Olivia studied her, seeing the possibility of Aboriginality in her melting brown eyes and olive skin. "What sort of memories?"

"Singing. I hear singing, but not in English. Singing and campfires." She paused and seemed to be almost in a trance.

"Go on," said Olivia in a whisper. "What else is there?"

"I can remember a special night that I was the center of everything. With my mother. But I can't remember clearly what she looked like." Maria's lip trembled.

Olivia waited and squeezed her hands gently.

Maria went on. "It was under the stars. Not a party . . . a ceremony, yes, a ceremony. And I was given something special, like a present, I suppose." Maria broke the clasp with Olivia and lifted her hands to a fine braid around her neck. "I only wear it when I go to Church," she explained. "It seems as if there is some connection between it, the Church and the memories. I just have to put it on for Church." She pulled the pendant from under her blouse and held it out for Olivia to see.

Olivia felt she was going to faint. The blood drained from her face as she swayed slightly and gasped.

"Whatever's wrong?" exclaimed Maria. "Olivia, what's wrong?"

"The pendant . . ." said Olivia in a hoarse whisper. "I can't believe it. I've seen it before. Many times. The pattern, that is." She looked at Maria more closely than ever before, searching for something that would confirm what was swirling through her mind as almost an impossibility. "It's the same as Niah's."

Their eyes met. "Niah," repeated Maria softly. "Niah. I remember that name. It is one of the memories. Who was she?"

Olivia took a deep breath. She was on the point of tears. "Your mother, I think. Yes, your Aboriginal mother."

Maria let the pendant drop and the two women reached out, their hands locking in support of each other. "My mother." Maria could barely say the word. "How can we be sure? It's almost too much to believe. Where? When?"

"I'm having trouble believing it, too, but the story goes back many years to when you were a baby in Broome. At least, it will if we can prove what I suspect. But everything adds up, your memories, your age, your beautiful looks, but above all your pendant. Niah told us that the pattern was special, a family totem."

"Us?" queried Maria.

Olivia took another deep breath, but this time had to reach for her handkerchief and dab her eyes. "Your father, if you are indeed Maya," she said at last. "Your father, John Tyndall. He was a friend of ours when we lived in Broome. When I was there with my previous husband."

"Who was he?"

"He's still alive. A master pearler in Broome. I actually have shares in the pearling company he owns. My husband was a partner with him in getting it all started years ago."

"He's white?"

"Oh, yes. He and Niah . . ." It was too hard for Olivia to go on. "Look, we've got to be sure before we jump to many more conclusions."

Maria closed her eyes. It was too much to take in. The world around her had to be shut out for at least a few seconds so that her racing mind might settle down again and let reason prevail.

"How will we find out for sure?" she asked, her eyes still closed.

"We'll have to go to Albany to see your white parents. There's really no other way that I can see at the moment. And if we're right, you're not Maria but Maya. That was the name of Niah's daughter. Maya."

"And Niah?" The two words said little, but the look in her eyes said everything.

"She's dead, Maria. Died when you would have been quite young. I'm sorry."

"Whatever are you women up to?" came a shout from the verandah and they both looked up to see Gilbert standing by the rail, shading his eyes with the *Bulletin*. "Been chatting on down there like you'd never had anyone to talk to before."

Olivia smiled and called back to him. "In a way, Gilbert, you're right. Wait till you hear what we've discovered."

•   •   •

Shortly after the birthday party Maria and Olivia caught the train to Albany. They'd both written to Maria's adoptive mother and father advising them that they were coming. Olivia had booked them into a hotel by telephone as the trip from Perth took most of the day. They caught a taxi to the modest cottage where the Barstow family lived and arrived in time for afternoon tea.

Mr. Barstow, a schoolteacher, had left class early to be at home and answered the door. He was stern looking, with a clipped silver moustache, thinning hair and tightly buttoned shirt collar. There was a moment of silence as he stiffly acknowledged Maria with a nod. "G'day, Maria," he said a little coolly. "And a good afternoon to you, Mrs. Shaw. Please come in. The wife is in the living room."

"It is good to see you again, Dad." Maria hoisted up the little girl but her father said nothing. He took a really good look at the pretty youngster who reached her hands out to him, but he didn't respond.

A few steps down the hall were double doors that opened into a living room crammed with furniture, little of which matched but looked well used and immensely comfortable. On an old tray mobile with crocheted lace cloth, was an assortment of sandwiches, a sponge cake and lamingtons and a slightly tarnished silverplated tea service.

Maria tried to break the ice as they walked in. "Hello, Mum. Here she is, your granddaughter. And this is Mrs. Shaw."

The small girl spotted the cakes and threw herself forward, knocking Maria off balance. Spontaneously Mrs. Barstow reached for the child and suddenly found herself holding her granddaughter, a little awkwardly and with some embarrassment. The child studied her for a moment, then smiled broadly and planted a big kiss on her cheek. There was laughter, some of it a little forced, but the atmosphere relaxed slightly.

Olivia studied Mrs. Barstow as she poured the tea. She was a bony woman with severely cut short brown hair flecked with gray, dressed in a good green dress with crocheted collar.

Olivia took a sip of her tea and began to spell out more details of the family background she believed to belong to Maria. The Barstows listened in silence.

"I've just got to know, Mum, Dad," said Maria when Olivia finished giving them the facts that she judged to be essential at this point.

"Why, lass?" snapped her father. "You aren't one of them, one of the blacks. You're one of us. It'll only hurt the kid later on, believe me. And it won't do any good digging into what's dead and buried. Bad enough getting into trouble with that young fellow. Can't forgive you for letting us down like that. Hurt terribly. After all we did for you."

"Please Mr. Barstow," pleaded Olivia. "This is painful enough without being so hard on Maria. It hasn't been easy for her, you know."

"Hasn't been easy for us either," interrupted Mrs. Barstow with some feeling. "The shame of it all. The rumors that got around. Was hard to hold our heads up, I can tell you." She smoothed her hair and adjusted the brooch at her collar.

"I'm sorry, Mum. Sorry for the pain it caused you, but there was nothing I could do about it once I knew I was pregnant. There was no way I was going to part with the baby. No way at all."

Olivia tried to dampen emotions. "Let's try to be practical about the current situation. Maria is determined to find out about her past. If you won't tell her, then we will try some other way. But surely you won't deny her right to know, whatever the consequences. That's her choice."

The Barstows exchanged glances but Mr. Barstow was immediately distracted by the little girl trying to climb up on his knee holding a half-eaten biscuit. "Friendly little thing," he said with a hint of softness in his voice, and carefully removed the biscuit and wiped her hand on a serviette. Mrs. Barstow smiled fleetingly then went to a writing desk in the corner, fussed about in the drawers and found a yellowed envelope.

"It's all in there," she said briskly. "Advice from the adoption people. Not much about her background apart from the fact she came from an Aboriginal mission in the north near Broome. Father a white man. Mission people no doubt got records that will confirm everything." She paused while Olivia and Maria read the letter together, then went on, "Really, Maria, I think you're making a big mistake."

"Mum, all my life I've been haunted by these memories. All my life I've been too frightened to even mention them, not even to you. But it's all out in the open now and I can't tell you what a huge relief it is. I don't know if it is a mistake or not. I know I pass for white and Aborigines are regarded as rubbish by most people, but I just can't deny what I am any longer. It's as if something is pulling me, some spirit . . ." Maria slumped back in her chair and put a hand to her forehead and closed her eyes. "I don't know, it's all so confusing. I really can't expect you to understand. I hardly understand it myself."

Olivia reached over and briefly touched her hand, then turned to the Barstows. "I think the next step is to go to Broome. Thank you very much for at least showing us the letter. It tends to confirm everything and that's a big step forward."

By now the little girl was demanding attention and tried to get on Mrs. Barstow's lap. The woman was unable to resist the natural instinct to lift the child up. "Pretty child, isn't she."

"One big bundle of energy and trouble, I can tell you," said Maria quickly, seizing on her mother's softening. "Can't keep still and more adventurous than any tomboy."

"A bit like her mother wouldn't you say, Fred?" said Mrs. Barstow looking briefly at her husband. "You were a handful when you first came to us, Maria, believe me."

Olivia found this reminiscing contagious. "Maya, Maria, was a real tomboy as a little one, I can assure you. She used to play with my boy quite a lot and they were always getting into mischief."

There were a few more exchanges but the Barstows kept a wall of reserve firmly in place and it was clear to Olivia that they had come as far as they could toward accepting the situation. She indicated it was time to get the little one back to the hotel for a nap.

"Before you go, you'd better collect some of the stuff you left behind, Maria," said Mrs. Barstow, hurrying from the room with Maria trailing behind her. In the bedroom wardrobe was a battered school bag stuffed with bits of cheap jewelry, old letters, a favorite rag doll and a few photographs.

The farewells were formal enough, Mr. Barstow extended a hand to both women and nodded, able to do little more than wish them a good trip back to Perth. Mrs. Barstow gave Maria and the sleepy child a fleeting kiss on the cheek. "You might let us know how things turn out," she called from their verandah as the little group reached the gate.

The train next day wasn't crowded and they had a first class compartment to themselves. It gave Olivia plenty of time and opportunity to tell Maya stories of Broome, Tyndall, Star of the Sea, and the story of how she first met the Aborigines of Niah's tribe, the birth of her first son, and many events that gave Maya a better grasp on her other world.

Maya became more and more excited as she learned about the time in Broome when she was a child. "I can't wait to get there. Are we really going, Olivia? It seems such a big thing to do. And I've no money, you know."

"I'm sure Gilbert will be agreeable. Forget about the money. I can't wait to see John's face when he meets you. It will be absolutely wonderful for him. He loved you so much. So much."

They had morning tea then both dozed a little, lulled by the rocking of the train, the hypnotic click-clack of the wheels over the rails and the peacefulness of the passing countryside. They were still about two hours from Perth when Maria took her old school case from the brass rack above her and opened it on the seat opposite Olivia.

"I loved this rag doll. Couldn't let it be thrown away when I grew out of it." She gave it a cuddle and pressed it to her cheek. "Still smells the same." She tried on some junky jewelry which made them both laugh and she handed some jewelry and the doll to her little one to keep her occupied.

Maya then started thumbing through the photographs. "Oh, look at this will you. Me just after finishing high school. Mum and Dad were so proud they insisted on a memorial photograph." She handed the picture to Olivia, who studied the gangly uniformed schoolgirl trying to look scholarly as she clutched a ribboned scroll.

When Olivia looked up to hand it back she

found Maya looking intently at another photograph and was surprised to see tears beginning to form in the corners of her eyes. She said nothing for awhile then, as a big tear rolled down her cheek, asked quietly, "What is it, Maya?"

Maya hesitated. "We promised each other never to talk about our loss."

Olivia nodded in understanding and gave a small comforting smile.

"I'd like to show you. It's the man I loved. Love still. Her father." She looked at the little girl absorbed in her playing. "Everything's different now, isn't it?"

"I'd like that. Yes, I'd like to see him."

Maya handed over the cardboard-backed photograph. She barely had time to notice the look of astonishment before Olivia collapsed to the floor between them. Maya's scream brought a gentleman from the next compartment to the door. He rushed in when he saw Olivia and the two of them lifted her on to a seat.

"What happened, lass?" he asked.

"I'm not sure. We were talking and looking at photographs and she just fainted."

"Odd business. She's starting to come round."

Soon Olivia's face started to get its color back, her eyes opened and she asked for a sip of water. Then she sat up, thanked the man and assured him that she was all right. When he had gone, she looked at Maya and asked for the photograph. Maya handed it over and watched as tears welled in Olivia's eyes. "It's Hamish. My Hamish," Olivia gasped.

"What do you mean?" exclaimed Maya quickly. "It *is* Hamish, but what do you mean, *your* Hamish?"

"He's my son."

The full impact of what she said hit Maya like a body blow. "Your son," she whispered. "Your son. Oh my God." She threw herself across the compartment into Olivia's outstretched arms and they hugged each other and both wept uncontrollably.

Gilbert listened in astonishment as Olivia and Maya told him their story when they alighted from the train in Perth. Oblivious to the bustle of passengers and people meeting them and the clatter of porters' barrows, Olivia and Maya revealed details of what they called "our little miracle."

Later, back at their home, he poured a glass of champagne for them all. "I think a little miracle is worth celebrating in style, don't you? To the future," and they all clinked glasses. "It's really lovely to be able to welcome you to our family, Maria . . . Maya. I think it is going to take some time to adjust to that part of it," he laughed. "And of course, it's great to welcome our newest member. My, it's a little odd suddenly becoming a grandfather. Can't say I've ever seen Olivia looking so happy."

"You're not the only one finding it strange to be a grandparent all of a sudden. But isn't it just so beautiful?" She and Maya wrapped their arms around each other's waists and clinked glasses again.

They settled down immediately to discussing how to tell Tyndall and it was soon agreed that they would catch the next boat to Broome. Chances were he was still at sea and in any case a cable hardly seemed the right way to break the news.

That evening as Olivia kissed Gilbert good night in their bedroom, she whispered her thanks to him for the generous welcome he had given Maya and his immediate support for the trip to Broome. "There's a lot of unfinished business there, Gilbert. I need to go back."

"Of course, I understand."

But despite her joy at the news about Maya, as she lay awake beside the sleeping Gilbert, Olivia was overcome at the loss of Hamish. She cried into her pillow, the lonely grief of a mother who has lost a child. But slowly the tears stopped and she felt comforted that at least she had a link with him—her granddaughter, Georgiana.

The three stood at the railing as the steamer settled its bulk alongside Broome's tidal jetty. Maya took Olivia's hand and squeezed it, her other holding the small hand of the bouncing, excited little girl. All the smells, the sounds, the warm air, the crystal sharp colors of a bright Broome early morning flooded over Olivia with a comforting familiarity that was at once exciting and sadly nostalgic.

Maya, too, was affected and leaned over and murmured to Olivia, "I remember. I remember."

Olivia had not told anyone she was coming. She wanted to be the one to bring Maya and Tyndall together. But looking along the foreshore she realized many of the luggers were still at sea. Others, laid up through the war, remained shrouded in hessian, stranded and neglected along the mangrove creeks. They went to the Continental and as they passed along the familiar streets Olivia noted new buildings, but saw that some were closed. The war had taken its toll. Businesses and families had not recovered from the industry's recession. Olivia knew, too, that the pearl shell stored through the war because of the collapse of the market had just been sold in London and New York for a fraction of its value. She had written to Tyndall suggesting they might have to look to other enterprises, but he had been emphatic that pearling was his life and all would be well after the war.

Despite the recession Olivia couldn't halt her spirits soaring as they walked through the hotel gardens and onto the verandah for morning tea. A few familiar faces nodded and greeted her with surprise but she merely smiled, murmured pleasantries and didn't pause. She'd sent word to Toby and Mabel and hoped they were in town and able to join her as soon as was convenient. She'd been in regular contact with them since she left. Mabel had written to her about Amy's defection and the tragic details and Toby had sent her a valuation of the missing pearls.

Olivia had just settled herself to pouring tea when the Mettas bustled along the verandah, Mabel with arms outstretched exclaiming in delight, "Olivia! Why didn't you tell us! What a wonderful surprise!"

They embraced with affection.

"Are you alone? Where's your wonderful husband?"

"He couldn't come. But I'm not alone." She turned to the beautiful young woman and little girl sitting at the table. "Do you know who this is?" she asked.

Mabel was staring thoughtfully at the young woman who shyly smiled at her, not sure if she should know the plump dark-skinned lady. "She reminds me of . . ."

While she groped for the connection, Toby said quietly, "Niah. She looks like Niah."

The Mettas stared in shock and Olivia triumphantly lifted the young woman's hand. "Yes. This is Maya, Tyndall and Niah's daughter. And this is *her* daughter—Georgiana, or Georgie as we call the little rascal."

The Mettas drew up chairs and they all began talking at once. While Olivia began to tell the story, Maya took the now fidgety Georgiana down to explore the waterfront.

"I noticed some of the fleet is still outside. John

and Ahmed . . . when are they due back?" asked Olivia.

"Any day," answered Tobias.

Olivia hesitated, then asked, "How is John? He hasn't been in touch. I should have told him I was getting married . . . but I just didn't know how to tell him. Things happened quickly. The war took our minds off things . . ." she finished lamely. She didn't have to explain to the Mettas. They understood and knew how hurt and angry Olivia had been over Amy, how anguished over the death of Hamish.

"He's changed a little. Only natural I suppose. Hard times for us all. In so many ways," said Toby softly. "But he remains ever the optimist."

"He has been wrapped up in Star of the Sea and nothing else," added Mabel pointedly. "It's kept him going. This will be wonderful news."

Toby changed the subject. "Are you happy? Is the life you have down there satisfying?" he asked with warm concern. "It seems so different to what you had here. I can't help feeling . . ."

"Now, Tobias, that will do," cut in Mabel swiftly. The kindly couple had been stunned at the news of Olivia's marriage but at the time thought it was probably for the best. How were any of them to know Amy would turn out to be so unpredictable or that she would disappear? The Mettas had found it heartwrenching to see Tyndall return from Fremantle so deflated and depressed at losing Olivia.

"Happy?" answered Olivia thoughtfully. "I am

slowly coming to terms with losing Hamish. So many others have lost sons. I only wish . . . oh, let's not talk about regrets and what ifs. We can't change anything but only press on and try to make our lives meaningful day by day," said Olivia.

"That seems to be John's philosophy as well. You know he took the news about Hamish very badly. He hoped Doctor Shaw was a comfort to you. But like you, he has come to accept what life has dealt him. If you ask me he leads a sort of waiting life. He goes through the motions but it's like he is waiting for something, waiting for his real life to begin," said Mabel.

"This reunion with Maya and his granddaughter will bring him back to life again," enthused Toby. "Will they stay here? Where is her husband?"

Olivia took a deep breath. "There's more to this. Not only have I found Maya, but have just discovered Hamish is the father of her child. They planned to get married after the war. She didn't know she was pregnant when he left. She came to Shaw House and only ever knew me as Mrs. Shaw. Hamish, of course, kept the Hennessy name."

The Mettas stared at her in stunned silence and Olivia went on.

"They met in Albany when he was there in the Naval Brigade for a year. That's where her adopted family are."

"So the little one is your granddaughter, too . . ."

"Naturally Gilbert and I want them to live with

us. But John has to know about it all and the final decision will, of course, be Maya's."

"How sad for her, but God certainly works in mysterious ways. He's brought you all together." Mabel patted her hand. And the three of them sat in silence for a moment, all thinking of Hamish.

Toby spoke first. "The fleet will be back in a day or so. What are your plans, Olivia? Why are you here at the Conti and not in your house? Does Minnie know you're back?"

"No. I'm about to go around. I didn't tell anyone I was coming. I'd have to go into why and it just seemed easier simply to come and bring Maya. Seems a bit strange now I suppose." She gave a small shrug. "And I was thinking I'd sell the house up here. No reason for me to keep it on and what with the setbacks in the business and the cost of setting up in Fremantle, I need the money. I have to cut my ties here, my future is down south now."

"Not a good time to try and sell, Olivia," said Toby. "People are leaving Broome, not moving here. We, too, have thought about leaving. I could get work elsewhere, but this is our home. We'll hang on. Tyndall is convinced things will pick up. He predicts the twenties are going to be great years."

"I certainly hope so," Olivia answered wistfully.

It was sunset when Olivia took Maya and Georgie to her house. Maya had been quiet and said that she was simply feeling "crowded". So many memories were coming back to her. Seeing Georgie rush into the pearl shed and clatter amongst the bags of pearl shells stacked in the dimness of the shed, the light falling through the high open squares that served as windows beneath the tin roof, was like seeing a picture of herself. While the shed was silent and empty, she looked at her daughter running about and heard again the singsong voices, smelled the pungent odors of oysters, and remembered a tall man's laugh.

Olivia glanced at Maya as they stopped outside the gate. She gestured toward the garden and the sweep of the vine-shaded verandah. "Do you remember this place? Your father brought you here almost every evening."

Maya shook her head. "No. But it feels familiar. I feel I have been here before."

At that moment Alf came around the side of the house and stopped in his tracks, then with a smile splitting his face, he hurried forward. "Mem! Strike me down, Minnie didn't tell me yer was coming up."

"She doesn't know. It's a surprise."

A voice rang out. "I see you and I don't believe my old eyes. Them not so good no more. I think mebbe I seein' t'ings. No, by crikey it's mem talkin' to Alf jist like old days." Minnie was stepping stiffly down from the verandah and hurrying to the gate as Olivia stepped into the garden. With her arthritis it was painful to move so hurriedly but Minnie didn't want to risk this apparition slipping away. She wanted to be sure that this was really her beloved Olivia standing there smiling.

The old woman felt a rush of affection and she started to shake as she flustered, "Why you and Mollie no tell us? Never mind, you here, and dat's good news, eh?" But she hugged Olivia tightly and Olivia felt tears rush to her eyes. Minnie had always been a key part of her life in Broome.

"I've brought someone to meet you, Minnie." Georgie ran forward past Minnie and onto the verandah. "That's Georgie," said Olivia with a laugh. Then turning toward Maya started to say, "And this is . . ." but stopped as she saw the expression on Minnie's face change.

"I know who this is. You don't have t'introduce me to my own family. This be Maya growed up." The older woman reached out to the shy young woman. "You still got your totem your mumma get you, eh?"

Maya looked confused for a moment then touched her chest and lifted the pendant that hung around her neck. Minnie glanced at it and nodded with a small murmur of satisfaction. "I better make tea, we got a lotta talkin' to do. Place all locked up, but we fix t'ings up no trouble." She marched ahead catching Georgie and sweeping her into her arms. "Watch you step, Missy. I kin see you gonna have to mind Minnie now."

Maya and Olivia exchanged a smile as they went into the house.

•   •   •

By the following evening, with Rosminah and Yusef helping, they were all settled into the house. It felt strange to Olivia, strange because she felt so at home once more. There were only good memories here, some tinged with sadness true, but it was the happy times she relived . . . her ordered life with Conrad and Hamish, the excitement of setting up Star of the Sea, of Hamish playing with baby Maya, the twilight evenings with Tyndall on the verandah, good friends like the Mettas, and always, the talk of pearls, diving, luggers and adventures. How sedate her life in Fremantle was . . . at this point Olivia forced herself to stop reflecting on the past, and ran through for the umpteenth time how it would be when Tyndall found his daughter was returned to him.

Maya asked no questions about him, so no one pressed facts, anecdotes or information on her. Instead, the demanding, willful Georgie kept everyone occupied.

"She trouble that one," said Minnie privately to Alf. "She like stone in the shoe. Dunno where she come from. I reckon Georgie belong some other tribe. She's a wild one."

"She'll grow up, Minnie. She's only a little one," replied Alf.

Yusef had been detailed to watch for the return of the fleet. And so one morning as the damp mist cleared from across glassy gold water that silently swallowed the mangroves, he saw the shimmering silhouettes of three luggers. Their fat jarrah hulls were low to the water as they headed for Dampier Creek to unload the haul of shell.

Yusef trotted back through town to tell Olivia that Tyndall, Ahmed, Yoshi and Captain Evans were on their way to the foreshore camp.

Now that the occasion had arrived, Olivia was nervous. Glancing at Maya, she realized she was too. They'd decided Minnie would look after Georgie. So Olivia and Maya set off.

How many times Tyndall had looked toward the shore and remembered Olivia standing there, hair blowing about her face, hand shading her eyes as she watched them sail in, desperate to be close to him, anxious for news of their haul. And there she was, just as he'd imagined a hundred times. He shook his head. It was one of those hot mornings where mirages often materialized over the water.

He looked at the shore again. The low line of the sheds of foreshore camps hunched in a smudgy line, a scatter of palm trees sentinel against the morning sky.

She was still there. And walking to her side was the slim figure of another woman. Waist-length dark hair blew around her shoulders and for a second a past image of Niah, hanging over the side of the *Shamrock* with her long hair framing her face, covering her breasts, came back to him.

But these were real people, for now Ahmed came aft and stood next to him as they sailed in.

He spoke almost to himself. "Mem come back. Who she bring, tuan?"

Tyndall shrugged and didn't answer. The sight of Olivia, the knowledge she was watching them come in, that she was here, had stunned him. A faint, excited stirring in his heart gave his skin a tingling sensation.

He busied himself with the moorings and didn't look up again until they were ready to go ashore in the dinghy.

With his pants rolled up his legs, Tyndall stepped over the side of the dinghy and squelched through mud and onto the shore where Olivia, now alone, waited.

It was a walk that seemed a thousand miles. Tyndall locked eyes with Olivia and was drawn to her as if in a trance. She'd had time to prepare for this moment and smiled gently and appeared calm, trying not to show the physical pull this man had over her. He took her hands but didn't embrace her, afraid he'd crush her to his chest and never let her go. "Olivia . . . your turn to surprise me. What are you doing back?"

The years dropped away, each ignoring the small physical changes in the other.

"How are you, John?"

"Good . . . good. All things considered."

"How was the trip?"

"Better, but I'm afraid it's going to take another season—and decent prices—to make up our losses."

They turned away and walked toward the shed and crews' camp.

"Ahmed will be in shortly. He'll be pleased to see you. We all are." He glanced down at her. "So why are you here? Who was with you earlier?"

"She's the reason I came up." Now the moment was here Olivia was at a loss for words. How was she to prepare him, or should she just blurt it out? You never really knew how Tyndall was going to react. "John . . . this might come as a shock . . . well, surprise . . ."

Struck by the serious tone of her voice, he cut in. "Olivia, I tend not to like your surprises . . ." His voice trailed away as they came around the corner of the shed and he saw Maya sitting on an upturned dinghy a little distance away. He frowned slightly, narrowed his eyes against the sunlight trying to see her better.

Olivia linked her arm through his. "John . . ."

Maya stood and walked toward them. Olivia said nothing as the gap narrowed between them. Each studied the other and as Maya drew close, Tyndall stiffened, halted for a moment and then saw Maya's carved pendant worn outside her deep red blouse. Her hair, her eyes, the lithe shape of her body, the small smile . . .

"Niah . . . *Maya* . . ." he whispered.

For Maya, the tall dark man with the teardrop pearl at his ear, was suddenly achingly familiar.

Olivia reached out and took Maya's hand and placed it in Tyndall's. "Yes, John, it's Maya. It's been a long time, a long journey . . . for both of you."

"How . . ." he began, the stunned expression giving way to a broad smile and then suddenly both of them were laughing and weeping and Maya flung her arms about his shoulders, burying her face in his chest. Watching him stroke her hair, a look of such softness, longing and tenderness on his face, Olivia had to turn away. Her eyes were filled with tears and the gladness she felt for both of them was tinged with envy—an envy she didn't want to think about.

Later over cups of tea on the rickety verandah of the office above the shed they pieced the story together. Olivia added the further news about Hamish, and Tyndall gave Olivia such a look of possessive love. "It seems right, doesn't it? That this is how it should be. We are joined, you and I, Olivia, by our children."

Maya looked at them strangely, recognizing there was an interplay of great intensity beneath the surface.

"We also share a granddaughter, John," said Olivia, a smile lurking at her mouth.

"Oh, this is too much." Tyndall laughingly clutched his head.

Olivia stood. "Speaking of that little rascal, I'll go back and see how matters are at home. You two spend a little more time together. You'll come to dinner tonight, John?"

He rose and gave her a quick hug. "Of course. With champagne. It'll be the best dinner ever. How can I ever thank you, Olivia? I thought my world ended when I lost you . . . finding Maya has turned on a light in my life."

They drew apart, both conscious of the comforting familiarity of their touch. Olivia broke the silence. "Maya, enjoy this time with him before Georgie bowls him over."

He took his daughter's hand. "Would you like to come and watch the luggers unload? Do you remember Ahmed?"

"I have so many questions about my mother . . ." said Maya. "I remember little things . . . but I want to know more. About her family, too . . ."

"Minnie can help you there. She's part of Niah's Aboriginal family, they know the Dreamtime story of Niah's family in Macassar."

Olivia slipped away with a light wave. But she didn't go home. She ordered the sulky driver to take her to the house on the headland, the house Tyndall had built for them. She walked around it, the trees they'd planted had grown, but there was no garden. Olivia loved gardens. One day, she decided, one day, she would have the garden of her dreams combining the violent-colored strong native shrubs, trees, vines and blooms with the delicate, perfumed flowers of her English childhood. It would have to be created down south, not in this harsh climate. She'd speak to Gilbert about it one day. With a start Olivia realized it was the first time she'd thought of Gilbert in many days. Venturing onto the verandah, she sat in the heavy wooden settler's chair and looked across the bay where the tide was receding through the mangroves, exposing the wet gray tangle of braided roots.

She closed her eyes. And thought of Tyndall.

She had no doubt Maya would stay here in Broome. Tyndall had a family now.

Suddenly the loss of Hamish hit her once more. He would not be around to watch Georgie grow, to tell her of his little doings and plans. She ached for his soft voice, his warm smile. She again envied Tyndall, but she had Gilbert, she told herself. Tears of self-pity trickled down her face, and Olivia had to admit to herself that life down south was not enough. She sat, lost in gray thoughts until, drawing a deep breath and wiping her cheeks, she looked again at the turquoise water. It was so beautiful—the sweep of the bay, the indigo sky lightly dusted with a swirl of cloud, the soft breeze dancing on top of the wavelets. She lightly lifted a strand of hair away from the coil atop her head and felt her emotional strength returning. Feeling more cheerful, she decided that she would just let life happen and stop worrying about the future. She grinned to herself. Broome had this effect on people. Time took a sidestep and tomorrow could be worried about tomorrow.

CHAPTER TWENTY-TWO

For the rest of the day Georgie attached herself to Minnie who kept the youngster occupied with kitchen activities supposedly contributing to the big dinner that evening, but which simply created an enormous mess all over the floor. Olivia and Minnie stepped over it all with good humor as they cooked and polished glass and silverware and dug out the linen from a camphor-wood box.

Maya arrived home late in the afternoon, excited and exhausted at what the day had brought. "If I don't have a rest and a bath I'll die," she groaned happily as she sipped a cold drink in the kitchen. "It has just been the most glorious day. My father's so wonderful, isn't he?" Olivia smiled and Maya went on, "It's better than the best dream, Olivia."

Soon after sunset Tyndall arrived, dressed in his whites and carrying a brightly wrapped parcel. The two women were relaxing on the verandah and rose when they saw him swing through the gate. Maya ran inside to find Georgiana and Olivia greeted him at the top of the steps.

"Welcome back to the verandah, John," she said warmly. "It's been a long time."

He took her extended hand, then leaned forward and impulsively planted a small kiss on her cheek. "Thanks, Olivia. Thanks for so much. You've no idea what the day has been like. But then, perhaps you do." Before she could respond Maya came through the front door carrying Georgiana, and stopped a few steps from them. No one said a word, and the little girl stared at the stranger in white with big brown questioning eyes, and the stranger stared back, but with eyes that smiled.

"Georgiana, this is your grandfather," said Maya softly.

Georgie said nothing but there was a flicker of a grin and those big eyes went on sizing him up.

"Hello," he said at last. "I'm very pleased to meet you. I hope you'll like the present I've brought. Would you like me to help you open it?" He reached out a hand and with a big smile she leaned forward in her mother's arms toward her grandfather. As he swept her up he gave Maya a big wink over Georgiana's shoulder. Together they unwrapped the gift and Maya's hand flew to her mouth as she recognized the toy lugger she had played with as a little girl.

The dinner was a huge success. Olivia helped with the serving and deliberately let Maya and

Tyndall set the flow of conversation, joining in occasionally with stories of Shaw House or memories of the early days of the pearling venture, a subject Maya found absorbing.

Olivia was pleased when Tyndall offered to take Maya and Georgie for a sail in one of the luggers, but no sooner had she expressed her delight than a sudden surge of guilt made her stiffen. Memories of those distant days at sea with Tyndall and acknowledgment of Gilbert waiting in Fremantle clashed with the violence of a tropical cyclone. It was a struggle to keep her turbulent emotions under control and as soon as the tea was served she picked up her cup and rose from the table. "I think the three of you should have a little time together before Georgie falls asleep, which I don't think is very far off. I have to write to Gilbert and tell him all about the day and I want to catch the mail before the steamer goes. I'll see you before you go, John." She kept up a facade of forced calmness until she closed the door of her room, then leaned against it, shut her eyes and began to weep quietly.

Maya looked after her and back to Tyndall. "Will you get around to telling me about you and Olivia? I sense there is a lot I don't know about you both."

Georgie was almost asleep on Tyndall's lap and he pushed back his chair and hoisted her to his shoulder where she nestled her head and toyed with his pearl earring. "Yes, I will, Maya. It's right you know everything. And I think it will make me feel better, too. It's hard keeping things inside you that you can't share with other people. Now, lead on to the sleeping quarters for the small wretch here."

The news of Tyndall being reunited with his daughter and that he also had a granddaughter gave the town something cheerful to discuss other than the gloom of falling business due to the drop in pearl shell prices. Taki decided to return to Japan when his contract was up and there was a farewell party for him at the Japanese Club where several other divers and tenders announced they were also going back to their villages. Yoshi had made one more trip back to Japan over the years to bury his father-in-law. Now he hoped to eventually retire and run a small business, perhaps a little noodle restaurant, with his wife Sachiko and his son.

There was the inevitable gossip in the white community about Olivia's return and speculation about her relationship with Tyndall. As always, they chose to ignore this and kept to themselves. They did not appear in public together but he resumed his habit of calling by each evening for sundowners and to play with Georgie.

Maya spent almost every day with him and Tyndall had taken great delight in seeing how she enjoyed Ahmed and Yoshi and asked them to teach her about the practical side of diving and the luggers.

"She has a good grasp of figures and book work. The nuns taught her well, though she says she hated the schooling at the time," observed Olivia.

"Poor kid, going from a good home here to barefoot in the bush and then having to knuckle down alone under the nuns. The Barstows should take more pride in her, she's turned out well. But I feel bloody dreadful about the whole thing."

"John, there wasn't a thing you could do about it. I've told her how you tried to find them after Niah went bush. But there's nothing life can throw at Maya that she won't be able to handle. She suffered so much and yet she can still smile her way through the days. She's been an inspiration to me," said Olivia quietly. "I just wish Hamish was here to share in all this. . . ."

"I sometimes feel he is," said Tyndall with understanding. "But Maya will need a man's hand in Georgie's upbringing, that's for sure."

"Gilbert and I have offered Maya a home, but I imagine you have other plans," said Olivia.

"Yeah. I'm working up to asking her to stay here. Would you have any objection to her coming in to help with the business?"

"Not at all, it makes sense. She'll be able to take over my role soon enough."

"Oh no, Olivia! I don't want you to leave Star of the Sea! We need you." Tyndall looked distressed. The business was his link with Olivia.

Olivia was relieved. In her heart she realized she didn't want to sever the ties that linked them. But another voice in her head whispered that perhaps she should cut the mooring ropes. Tyndall now had a new life just as she did. But Olivia was uncomfortable with the thought and pushed it to one side.

The days slid by. Maya and Georgie moved in with Tyndall. Rosminah and Yusef had had another baby and Georgie spent hours playing with the baby girl. Olivia helped Maya settle in and together they decorated rooms for her and Georgie. They spent part of every morning in the office and in the evenings Tyndall continued to ensconce himself on Olivia's verandah with a drink. She was intrigued with his stories of the time with Mikimoto and they discussed at length the feasibility of setting up a cultured pearl farm in or near Broome.

"Why don't we sail up the coast a bit and look for a site in remote river and creek inlets? You haven't been sailing for a time and I know you love it."

"We'll take Maya and Georgie, too," added Olivia hastily. "Oh, yes, we'd all like that."

On the morning they planned to sail, Yusef ran down to the little jetty where Tyndall was helping stow Olivia and the gear. Yusef had been delegated to get Maya and Georgie to the boat after breakfast but arrived with bad news.

"Georgie little bit tummy sick and hot. They no go. Maya say she stay and look out for her. You go. She say to tell you that Georgie not big sick."

Olivia wanted to return home and stay ashore, but once they had seen Maya and were reassured that Georgie was only mildly ill, Tyndall insisted they go ahead with the trip.

"All this preparation. And you were so looking forward to it, Olivia. And it will be useful. If we find the right place, we could think about leasing land."

She reluctantly agreed, concerned at being thrown together with Tyndall and knowing how confusing her emotions had been since she arrived in Broome.

But once they were clear of the bay and heading up the coast in the schooner, *Mist,* which Tyndall had bought to replace the shipwrecked *Shamrock,* all of her reservations fell away. She found the pleasure of being at sea overwhelming. It was as if she was sailing away from her troubles.

"Where are your sailing pajamas?" asked Tyndall with a cheeky grin.

"Threw them overboard years ago," she laughed. "Won't this do?" She indicated the new shorter length cotton skirt, the long loose top with a sailor collar, and plimsolls. A long braid of hair fell from under her hat over one shoulder and Tyndall thought she looked as youthful as the day he'd first met her.

"I guess you pass muster," he said nonchalantly.

• • •

Two days later they found an inlet that opened into a small deepwater bay with a rocky shore and a flat scrubby area suitable for a work base.

Tyndall and Olivia rowed about the bay and wandered through the scrubland, finding a small freshwater creek that had meandered down from the hills that protected the bay.

"It's very remote and private. Could be a smugglers' cove," said Olivia.

"If we set up an experimental pearl farm up here, I doubt anyone would know," said Tyndall. "It's certainly worth an experiment. Our golden-lip pearl shells are much bigger than the Japanese Akoya pearl shell. Our waters are warmer too, so I reckon if we can seed our pearl shell they'll grow pearls that are bigger, fatter and faster," declared a buoyant Tyndall.

"And they're still real pearls?"

"Of course. We're tricking the oyster into making a pearl. It's just trying to get rid of an irritant, same as it would in the ocean."

"You make it sound easy."

"I know it's not. Mikimoto and others have battled for years and still haven't perfected it. Not to say we can't have a go, too." He grinned at her, and she shook her head, amused at his boyish enthusiasm.

The sun was hot and the bay looked inviting. Several of the crew had already dived off the schooner into the clear warm water.

"Want to swim?" asked Tyndall.

"What will the crew think? Though I do have my bathing costume." Olivia lifted her string dilly-bag.

"You think of everything. Well, I don't own one of those new fangled suits."

Olivia disappeared into the scrub to change and Tyndall stripped off to his underwear and dived in.

They splashed and tried to dive to the bottom, though Olivia was not much of a swimmer. Treading water and floating they chatted about trying to find someone in Japan with pearl-seeding experience to come and work with them.

"This is the way to do business, eh?" chuckled Tyndall. "I seem to remember we used to do this quite a bit. But without bathers."

"Things are different now," said Olivia, her ebullience fading.

"Are they? Really?"

She didn't answer for a second then, not looking at him, said quietly, "John, please . . . don't."

"Don't what, Olivia? Don't say what we both know?"

"This isn't fair. Not here, please . . . don't."

"Because you can't run away from it here. Olivia, it's just you and me. Tell me you've never stopped loving me. I know you haven't."

Olivia sank beneath the water to avoid his words. She popped up a few seconds later and began splashing toward the shore. Tyndall was beside her in several easy strokes.

Persistently, he continued, "Tell me you don't love me, Olivia. Look at me and tell me and I won't pester you any more."

Her toes scraped the rocky bottom and she spun around to glare at him. "I don't . . . I don't . . ." She looked away, angry and confused, and stumbled out of the shallows, falling to her knees. Tyndall reached out and gathered her in his arms, and fell back on the water's edge.

"Ouch," he said as his head struck the rough sand, but he didn't relinquish his hold on Olivia. Holding her on top of him, their faces almost touching, he gave her a small grin. "You can't say it, can you, Olivia?"

"I fell over," she said weakly.

"There's nowhere left to run, my darling." Gently he drew her face down to his and, oblivious to the water lapping over their bodies, the rocks scattered through the sand under them, their lips, hearts and bodies came together as one, as if they'd never been two separate beings with all the differences that had kept them apart for so long.

The following day, swept up by love, enthusiasm and *joie de vivre* Tyndall decided they should dive together. The schooner was fitted with two new motorized pumps and divers' suits.

"All right, why not!" answered Olivia, responding to the challenge.

As they were about to lock on the helmet

Tyndall gave her a quick kiss. "Don't be nervous, I'll be right beside you."

She did find her heart beating quickly and the rush of air told her she was breathing heavily from nervous tension. But once settled on the bottom, her air pressure adjusted and with the comforting bulk of Tyndall beside her, she relaxed. He held out a gloved hand and, matching the pace of their footsteps, they set off together.

The magic of the strange world of underwater cast its spell over Olivia once more. The mysterious beauty of the underwater growths, the landscape of reef formations, the oblivious darting quest of colored fish, the activities of shellfish and coral was like looking from space at a miniature planet. They kept pointing things out to each other, exchanging delighted smiles through the glass panels of their helmets. Olivia had the strange sensation that this was the beginning of time, that for her and Tyndall this love of theirs was being born and they were not only connected to the umbilical cord of the real world above them by their air hoses, but they were somehow connected by an invisible glue like the water that surrounded them. Beneath the sea was a world of its own, an escape to a world of different creation where one could leave the everyday human world behind. Tyndall had always understood the lure of underwater for certain kinds of men. Men who could cope with the solitary, intensely personal self-sufficiency required for the loneliness of underwater work.

Fear and claustrophobia affected many who could not take the long hours alone on the sea bed.

A large brightly colored fish with rainbow eyes touched Olivia's helmet, peering in curiously at her, making her smile. Then Tyndall took her hand, put his fingers to his helmet indicating she should be still. A shadow changed the color of the water and Tyndall pointed slowly upward. Passing above them were two devil rays, each almost a ton in weight and close to twenty feet across. They lazed and swayed their bat-like black wings as if balletically choreographed. The flash of white belly, a glimpse of horny mandibles, the trailing whip and razor-sharp tail and they were gone. Tyndall knew the horrors and tales of devil ray attacks where divers were swept up in their powerful wings, lines severed by the tail, the gnashing of a giant mouth. They could breach close to a lugger, landing like a thunderclap when hunting fish and in a pack were a powerful enemy. But to Olivia they were a fascinating sight, just one of many that made her lose track of time. They watched an octopus stalk and devour a shellfish, squirting a cloud of ink as it scuttled away after a kick from Tyndall's boot. They trudged through clouds of weeds whose blades all faced the direction of the tide, and other small plantations of weird sea plants.

When Tyndall indicated they should rise, she was reluctant, but they gently rose in tandem on opposite sides of the boat. Olivia broke the surface and was helped up the ladder. As her helmet was unscrewed and she took her first gasp of fresh air, Olivia felt a strange depression. Which was the real world? Down there, she and Tyndall were safe, together and unobserved. Now reality hit her and she sat quietly on the deck sipping tea as Tyndall changed and regaled the crew with devil fish stories.

When, two days later, they returned to Broome, the time beneath the sea, Olivia's time with Tyndall, seemed a dream. She was prepared to pretend nothing had happened; that the rekindling of their passion was a lapse under bewitching circumstances. However, in the privacy of Olivia's house they shared sunset drinks and fell into each other's arms. She was helpless in the face of this overwhelming love and passion. Her devoted but pedestrian relationship with Gilbert was pushed to the recesses of her mind. Tyndall dominated, swallowed her up, and swept her away.

They talked of the cultured pearl farm experiment, of Maya working in the company, Georgie starting school, traveling to Europe to investigate further sales potential for mother-of-pearl.

"You know they started using it for compass faces in the war. It doesn't have to be just for buttons," said Tyndall.

"Do you really think plastic will take over completely?"

"We're going through a bad patch. Things will get better, you'll see. Broome isn't bust yet." Tyndall leaned over and tweaked her nose and gave her a quick kiss.

How different Tyndall and Gilbert were, Olivia thought. Gilbert was always very balanced, objective, quietly consultative and, in his own way, loving. While she was devoted to their work, Olivia realized how much she'd missed the thrill of pearling. The dangers, the unpredictability, the characters, the challenges, the wild and almost intoxicating lifestyle of the north-west coast. No wonder it attracted the people it did. People like Tyndall.

Weighing up the attitudes and lifestyle of Tyndall and Gilbert was like looking at chalk and cheese. And yet both had good qualities as well as less appealing ones. Subconsciously, Olivia was allocating points for and against both of them. Tyndall certainly had flaws and Gilbert's faults were less irritating, but there was simply no contest if she was honest. Tyndall's physical and emotional pull was magnetic. He was the love of her life and she paradoxically cursed him for it.

Walking along the foreshore after the men had left the camp, Tyndall took Olivia's hand and said simply, "So. What are we going to do?"

"I don't know," she said miserably.

"I do. We have to stay together . . . it's meant to be. You will have to tell him. You can't live a lie."

"Gilbert has been so good to me . . ."

"Olivia, my dearest love . . . if he's the decent

man you say he is, all he would want is your happiness."

She didn't answer, knowing this was true.

Tyndall took her in his arms and said quietly, "Olivia, go and talk to him, then pack up and come back. Come home, my darling."

With Tyndall's strong arms about her, it all seemed so easy.

Tyndall tipped back her face and looked into her eyes. "Olivia, I've said it before, we only get one chance at happiness, and you know I'm right. You might try to cover it up, but you wear your heart on your sleeve. I suspect Gilbert has always known you love me, that there was always a chance you would come back to me. Listen to your heart."

With this, all resistance melted away.

In the dusky mellow twilight Maya held on to Olivia as they said goodbye on the deck of the old steamer. "Dear Olivia, come back soon. I know it will be hard, but you only find a great love once in your life . . ."

Olivia smiled softly into the young woman's hair. "And only if you're lucky. You had it once, I pray you will again, dear girl."

Maya lifted her tear streaked face. "Olivia, all that matters to me now is that I've found my family, thanks to you. I've always felt you were special to me, now you're going to be part of my family too. You and Tyndall belong together . . ."

The loud blast of the steamer's whistle interrupted them and Tyndall suddenly appeared from where he had been chatting to the captain about ensuring Olivia's comfort on the voyage. Olivia looked at him in his white pearling master's suit, the unbuttoned narrow high collar giving him a rakish air, his old skipper's hat tucked under his arm. He was smiling broadly, his face full of love.

He crushed Olivia to him. "Be strong, my precious. If you want me to come down, cable me. I won't be able to sleep, eat, relax until I have you back. I've waited for you, Olivia. I've known since the moment I first saw you that you and I are meant to be."

Olivia swallowed and brushed away the tears. Looking at him she thought her heart would burst. She nodded and bit her lip and Maya took Tyndall's hand. "We'll be thinking of you."

"Every second, my precious one." Tyndall kissed her and he and Maya went down the gangplank.

Olivia kept her eyes on the two of them standing on the end of the jetty until the steamer was far out in the bay and the curtain of a soft night shadowed them from sight. The other passengers moved into the brightly lit lounges and cabins but she took a deep breath and stayed at the railing watching the lights of Broome recede. She felt so loved, so lucky and so hopeful. Sadness touched her, too, but in her heart she knew Tyndall was right, Gilbert only wanted her to be happy. Somehow things would work out.

She finally turned to go inside, and went to her cabin thinking how very different this departure was from the last time she left Broome. She hoped Hamish was watching over her; much as he had liked and respected Gilbert, the boy had worshipped Tyndall. She remembered Hamish saying to her once "He's every boy's hero come to life."

"Mine, too, Hamish darling," she thought.

Olivia knew something was amiss the moment she stepped in the door of the house, yet she couldn't put her finger on why. Maybe she should have gone first to Shaw House. Mollie, a younger plump version of Minnie, rushed downstairs to greet her, clearly distressed and wringing her hands, her words unintelligibly tripping over each other.

Olivia dropped her bag in the hall. "Mollie, what is it? What's happened?"

"Mem, oh mem, we try get you. Doc Shaw at hospital. Something terrible happen. No good, no good . . ."

"What has happened, Mollie, please? Speak slowly and tell me . . . what has happened?"

The young woman swayed from side to side as she continued, her hands wringing. "Mem, it Doc Shaw no good. Him sick. In hospital."

Olivia felt faint for a moment, then drawing

breath she grasped Mollie by the shoulders. "Tell me what is wrong with him. Was there an accident?"

"I dunno, mem. He fall down and no can move. He in hospital."

Olivia turned and headed out the door feeling like she had been winded by a blow from a fist.

She rushed to Fremantle Hospital and a sympathetic matron took her to Gilbert's bedside, explaining that he had suffered a serious stroke. "It happened two days ago and he is still unconscious. At the moment we have no idea how serious the effects will be. He may recover quite adequately . . . or . . ."

"Or he may never come out of his coma," finished Olivia.

It was a shock to her to see Gilbert lying in the hospital bed, his skin grayish white. Suddenly he looked so frail and thin and very old. As she sat by him, taking his hand, the medical superintendent whom they knew well, came into the room. "My dear Mrs. Shaw . . . this is a dreadful state of affairs. Not good at all. So glad you're here, it will surely help."

"Doctor Harrington, please tell me what happened and what's the outlook."

"It's looking a bit grim at the moment. But you never know with these cases. Seen fellows just open their eyes and they're perfectly all right. It seems he got out of bed during the night and was struck down. Your girl found him in the morning in the middle of the floor. Seems he regained consciousness for a moment after they got him here, just briefly. He called for you and lapsed back again."

Olivia tightened her grip on Gilbert's hand and stared at the apparently sleeping man. Although, studying his face, it appeared more that he was floating in some dreamless state. She leaned close to him. "Gilbert, can you hear me? It's me, Olivia. I'm here, dearest."

"I would suggest you stay with him, talk to him, touch him, as much as you can. Just in case he can hear you or sense you're here. It'll help. One of my cases, when he came to, said all the time he seemed to be out of it, he was totally aware of what was going on around him. But he couldn't see, move or speak. Very frustrating."

Olivia looked from the doctor to Gilbert, a feeling of despair, pain and pity enveloping her. "Of course I'll spend as much time as possible with him."

The doctor patted her shoulder. "Don't neglect your other duties, or yourself, my dear. We are doing all we can . . . but, I'm afraid, in these situations we have to let nature take its course."

The hours passed slowly and Olivia began to feel she was caught in a time warp. Her emotions were in turmoil and she tried not to think of Tyndall, but when she did the sight of Gilbert wrenched her heart and caused pangs of guilt.

She read to him, talked to him and gently rubbed his arms, legs and feet. Two days after her return from Broome—which now seemed another world—when she feared Gilbert was going to waste away, she looked up from the book she was reading aloud to find his eyes open and staring intently at her.

Olivia started and gasped, "Gilbert! Can you speak, can you hear me? How do you feel?"

He didn't move. She took his hand and leaned close but the limpness in his grip, the rigid set of his face and unblinking gaze caused her initial joy to quaver. She rushed for a nurse.

They fed him and bathed him and carried out tests but none elicited any physical or emotional response. Olivia let his fingers lie in the palm of her hand hoping for some flicker in answer to her questions. And while he couldn't make any movement, not even to blink, Olivia knew to the depths of her being that behind the intense staring gray eyes, that Gilbert was fully aware of everything about him.

They worked on his shrunken muscles and sat him outside in the sun in a wheelchair. He was able to swallow so they fed him slightly more substantial foods. Olivia now felt free to take breaks from her bedside vigil to spend time at Shaw House overseeing administrative and personal matters.

Then came the hardest task of all—writing to Tyndall.

My darling John,
This is the hardest letter to write . . . we have all been struck a cruel blow. I do not understand how it is that when I have happiness in my grasp it is

snatched away from me. I wonder if I am being punished . . .

> *Gilbert has suffered a dreadful stroke and is totally incapacitated. He needs me and, although he appears as a vegetable, I know inside he is fully conscious. So I cannot turn my back on him. Even if I believed he was not aware I could not abandon him. If I was to do so I believe our own guilt would destroy our love. You have Maya now, and our beautiful shared granddaughter, so it comforts me you aren't alone. I long for your arms, your lips, your laughter, and you know that you are the love and light of my life. But I have a moral responsibility to Gilbert and I don't believe you would ask me to cast this aside. Maybe some day, somehow, you and I will be together. But for now and the unforeseeable future it is not to be.*

> *Always,*
> *Olivia*

Weeks passed. Gilbert settled into a routine and Olivia began to think about taking him home. Tyndall sent a brief broken-hearted note *. . . I wanted to rip the stars from the sky, I wept at the injustice of it, but much as my heart breaks and I, too, long for you, I recognize your predicament and respect your decision. I suppose that is one of the reasons I love you so much—you are good, honest and loyal, my darling. My love will never waver and I am always here. As always, my beloved, if you need me I will come at once . . .*

Maya offered to come back and help nurse

Gilbert but Olivia said it was better if she could help Tyndall with Star of the Sea. Toby and Mabel also sent kind thoughts.

After talking to the doctors, Olivia eventually came to a decision. She would look after Gilbert herself and hope there might come some sort of "re-awakening."

It was a detailed process but Olivia slowly worked her way through the necessary steps. She could not run Shaw House on her own and, while medical colleagues of Gilbert's had been on call, it was his inspiration that had been the driving force. She went to see the hospital board and persuasively argued the case for them to take over Shaw House as a kind of alternative clinic. Church and political leaders agreed to support it. The volunteers would continue, funding was assured thanks to the wise investment money from the original benefactor. Following newspaper stories about the tragedy of Doctor Shaw and the determination of his wife that his work not be lost, even more donations flowed in, assuring the home's future.

Olivia sold her house in Fremantle and also Gilbert's family home. With the proceeds, she bought a large one-storey house on a hill on the outskirts of Perth surrounded by several acres of unkept garden, open ground and a few trees. It had beautiful views over the city to the river which she thought Gilbert would enjoy. She remained convinced that, despite his inanimate appearance, under the surface he could see and feel and think.

• • •

After the weeks of activity she welcomed the quietude that came with settling into the new house. She had a nurse's aide come each day and, with Mollie's help, Olivia was able to move Gilbert from bed to his bath chair. She hired Mollie's boyfriend, Stan, a shy, strong-shouldered Aboriginal, to help in the garden.

Olivia designed a small gazebo which Stan built in the central part of the garden, a shady retreat near the house where Gilbert could enjoy the garden and views. Stan also laid out paths so Olivia could easily push the bathchair.

She tried to stave off occasional bouts of sadness and self-pity when they struck. But she could not ignore the fact that she was still a relatively young woman with desires and needs and that far away was the man she knew could fulfill them and make her happy. But always there was the constant reminder of the man she had married and her loyalty to him.

So what began as a distraction became an absorbing occupation for Olivia. She plunged into gardening and became absolutely fascinated by the wildflowers of the west.

"Gilbert, just look at this extraordinary bush orchid. It's such a lovely blue and this one, it's just like a leopard's coat. Stan has collected some kangaroo paw plants and so many others that I've yet to learn about. Some of them are like little daisies, growing in a carpet over the ground in the spring.

They harmonize with the land, Gilbert. Have to if they're to survive in such inhospitable circumstances. They seem to thrive in the worst possible soil. Mollie doesn't think I can cultivate these bush flowers, but so far we are doing well, don't you think, dear?" She stood beside his bathchair as they looked out at the informal garden beds and terraces Olivia had designed. Arbors sheltered plants and other flowers encircled the base of the shady trees. There were also splashes of color from beds of English flowers, for Olivia loved her memories of English gardens in the spring. Cut and arranged indoors, they made the house seem so much brighter.

Crossing from the laundry, Minnie watched Georgie sitting in the garden playing with the wooden pegs, pushing them into the ground, lining them up in rows and addressing her troops with a frown and a shaking finger.

"Giving back some of the medicine she gets herself," thought Minnie.

She found Maya in the kitchen, put her pile of clean linen to one side, and announced, "Maya, time you went to your mob. You gotta take that girlie, too. Yep, it's time you saw your people. They know you is found, they be very anxious, wondering why you not go t'see them."

"My mob? You mean my mother's people?"

"Our people. We is all one mob, one way and t'other."

Maya pulled out a chair and sat at the kitchen table looking thoughtful. Minnie began making a pot of tea, realizing a talk was coming. "Don' you ever think about your people? Your real people, eh love?"

Maya didn't answer for a moment. She found she was struggling with years of mission education, white culture and lifestyle that forbade this ruminating. She had been trained to forget so much—her language, her culture, her beliefs, even her people, her family. Layers of another life had been papered over her, concealing who she really was. When she spoke, her voice was a whisper. "I've never been allowed to talk about this. And I trained myself not to, it made it easier to deal with things that way. But since I've been back here there's been a lot to deal with—my father, Olivia and Hamish, all of you, trying to help Georgie understand and settle. I've been feeling confused and, while I'm so happy to have found my way back, something has been worrying me." She drew a breath, her voice stronger. "I suppose it's having to come to terms with who I really am. The Barstows hid the fact I was part Aboriginal and I only have vague memories of my early years here and of my mother."

Minnie plonked the teapot on the table with a thump and leaned across and looked into Maya's face. "You ashamed of being black, eh girl?" Minnie demanded.

Maya recoiled slightly at the outburst but didn't turn away from being confronted. "To be honest,

Minnie, I don't know. I don't think so. But it's hard when you've been brought up one way . . ."

"Meaning bein' black is inferior . . ." interjected Minnie.

"Yes, that's how a lot of people thought and I couldn't understand my feelings. At times I felt different to other people the Barstows mixed with, and girls at school. Yet I didn't have any contact with Aboriginal people. Never really thought about it. Whenever memories came up—like dreams—I pushed them away. And now being here and knowing my story, I feel I never knew who I was. And I regret that, and resent the people who took it away from me. But to answer your question, no Minnie, I'm not ashamed of being part of 'your mob' as you say."

"But you gotta learn to be proud. That's the difference, girl. You won't know who you really are till you pick up all them threads that is part of your family. You weave 'em together and you have it all neat." Minnie topped up the cups. "They might've told you this an' that, and you might've lived in a city and worn nice clothes and proper shoes and lived like a white girl, but they can never take away what is in your head and your heart. That's your true one, Maya. And until you find and know who you really are, you can't live happy."

Maya sipped her tea and gave a tremulous smile. "That sounds right to me. I guess it's certainly time to go and see my family again."

Minnie nodded with ·satisfaction. "The little

one should go, too, though she's a bit young for the ceremony, to understand what that means." Minnie pointed to the pendant around Maya's neck. "Your father understands all this. You tell him Minnie said it's time you go south."

Tyndall agreed immediately when Maya told him of her conversation with Minnie. "The old girl is right. These women have played an important part in our life ... they are connected to your great-grandmother, your mother, you. They've played an important role in Olivia's life, too. It's a journey you must make, with Georgie."

"I'm a little nervous, but really looking forward to it."

"Listen to them, Maya. Not everyone does. Re-tie the knot with your family. I let go of mine and when I thought about making contact it was too late. You and Georgie are all the family I have." He dropped his arm about her shoulders and hugged her to him. "Tell you what, I'll sail you down. We'll take Minnie, make it a sort of family pilgrimage."

On the trip south on the *Mist*, Tyndall and Minnie sat on the deck with Georgie and Maya while Ahmed took the wheel. Tyndall told stories about the clan, about how they helped Olivia give birth to little James, the stories Niah had told him of her life and the tales her Macassan grandmother had told her of the family in the land of Marege at the end of the monsoon winds.

As they swung in close to the coast near Cossack, Maya spent a lot of time sitting quietly on deck looking at the shore, taking in the wild semi-arid beauty of it all and feeling for the first time in her life a real sense of belonging. Minnie sat nearby, also content to be with her own thoughts. At first Maya thought this sense of belonging was coming from the sea, for there was something comforting about the steady surging progress of the schooner through the ocean, relying on the wind, on nature. She couldn't help but think about her ancestors who in the distant past had sailed these winds, these waters. Like her, they had been on a journey, a journey with many unknowns. But it was now the land that dominated her thoughts. There was a harshness about it that was uninviting, yet she was increasingly conscious that the land was reaching out to her somehow. She felt a slowly rising excitement and an impatience to get ashore, to feel earth under her feet. It was hard to understand, impossible to explain, so she said nothing.

Minnie broke the silence. "Gettin' close to our country. That one bilong our mob I reckon," she said, indicating a broken spiral of smoke that suddenly rose from a headland.

Maya felt a hand on her shoulder. She looked up and smiled at her father and he smiled back. "We'll be dropping anchor in a bit."

No sooner had the schooner settled into the

anchorage than a group of Aborigines walked out of the scrub and onto the beach, waving and cooeeing.

"How did they know we were here?" asked Maya, puzzled by the unexpected appearance of the welcoming party.

"Bush telegraph," replied Tyndall enigmatically. "Don't ask me to explain it. Just believe it works."

The dinghy was surrounded as soon as some of the men had hauled it up on the beach. There was huge excitement among the women at the sight of Maya, because of the pendant she was wearing outside her blouse. Maya stood beside the boat smiling at everyone as Tyndall went through the formalities of briefly acknowledging the elders in their language and Minnie was emotionally greeted by women and children. Then Tyndall turned and took Maya's hand. "You remember Niah," he announced, raising his voice above the babble. "This is her daughter Maya."

There were astonished gasps and several of the old women wept as they came forward to touch Maya.

Little Georgie, who was still sitting wide-eyed in the dinghy, was suddenly very frightened by the chatter of strange language and a wave of naked black children that fell into the boat all around her. "Mum," she screamed, but it was Minnie who rushed to her rescue and swept her up. She then shouted to the mob that the little girl was Maya's daughter, and there was another outburst of excited cries, and more tears. And as the old women crowded around to touch Georgie's fair skin, and look into her eyes, Georgiana began to howl. Maya pushed through the throng and took her from Minnie and with Tyndall's help quickly quietened her.

Everyone then trekked up the beach, along a winding trail and up a small escarpment to the campsite beside a freshwater stream. Maya and Minnie walked hand in hand with some of the women, Minnie acting as interpreter of the unceasing chat. Georgiana rode on Tyndall's shoulders, her hands tightly clenching his supporting hands.

They all sat under shady trees while a billy was boiled. Tyndall talked to a group of men while Minnie filled in the women with the full details of Maya's life, a story that to Maya seemed to be of epic proportions, for Minnie liked nothing better than telling a good story, and the audience liked nothing better than hearing one.

Several women came forward with shells etched with designs similar to that on the pendant worn by Maya. "Your aunties," said Minnie, leaving the complexities of Aboriginal relationships to be explained later.

All the while Georgiana clung to her mother's arm, but Maya was barely conscious of the child. She was completely overcome by a flood of confusing emotions. It was with relief that she heard Minnie announce that it was "time for a cuppa."

With shouting and laughter several dampers

were produced from the ashes, a tin of treacle that Tyndall had brought ashore in his pack of gifts was opened, and tea ladled into chipped enamel mugs. To Maya it tasted like the best food and drink she had ever had, and across the lip of her mug she caught her father's admiring look and they both winked at each other and smiled. The smile from her father was all that kept back the tears, though her eyes were wet.

After the snack the women took Maya for a walk, leaving the children and men behind. "Gonna see some special place," was all Minnie would tell Tyndall, who knew better than to ask questions. Maya gave him a little over-the-shoulder wave as they set out and Tyndall waved back while Georgiana clung to his leg and began to weep quietly.

Tyndall crouched down. "Now then, Georgie, let's go with the kids to the swimming hole and have some fun."

The rock pool below a small waterfall which was downstream from the camp had a convenient fallen tree for a diving board, and rope hanging from another tree provided a fine swing over the pool. Everyone except Georgie had a great time. She was conscious of her white skin, hated the nudity of everyone and was embarrassed because she couldn't understand any of the language. "I want to go back to the boat, Poppa," was her repeated demand.

As the sun set Maya asked Tyndall to send a swag ashore as she wanted to stay the night in the camp. She was happy to let Georgiana go back to the boat. "It's all too much for her," said Maya as she gave her daughter a big affectionate hug. "You wait for me on the boat with Poppa. I'll see you in the morning. Maybe you can catch a big fish for lunch." It was a prospect that delighted Georgie and she gave her mother a kiss.

That night, after putting Georgiana to sleep with his version of the story of Goldilocks, Tyndall sat on the deck smoking his pipe. He could see the glow of the campfires above the tree line, hear the chant of songs, the haunting drone of the didgeridoo and the throbbing of music sticks. He thought of Niah and once more offered up a prayer of thanks for the gift of Maya.

CHAPTER TWENTY-THREE

Over the next two years Olivia turned their garden into a showplace. On a sunny morning with a hint of autumn crispness, Olivia sat by Gilbert, her head bent over a crewel-work cushion cover as she stitched the formal bouquet of roses. She paused to look about her garden and said to her husband, "I'm thinking maybe I might put in a rose bed. A token gesture to the old country. Cream and pink roses would be nice, don't you think?"

She had become used to the one-sided conversations with Gilbert, but wondered what sort of company she'd be in the social world these days. Olivia rarely went out, and, apart from local shopping expeditions and very occasional trips into the city, she talked only to Mollie and Stan, who were now married.

Mollie and Stan had made a trip back to Broome when Minnie had died suddenly and peacefully.

Mabel Metta had written to Olivia . . . *"she was*

pegging out the washing and fell down, gone, just like that. She had been quite ill with influenza which caused many deaths among the blacks. Alf has gone north to stay at the mission where he has relatives and will be well cared for . . ."

Olivia tucked the blanket around Gilbert's stick-thin legs and adjusted it around his chest saying, "I'm going for a bit of a wander. See if I can settle on a possie for the roses. Wind is getting up, don't want you to get a chill . . ." She was about to turn away but before she lifted her hand it was grasped in a shaking claw grip. Stunned, she looked down to see Gilbert's fingers scratching at her wrist. Then as she stared at him, unable to speak from shock, his head lurched to one side and his mouth twitched.

"Gilbert! You can move! Can you speak? Oh, my dear! You're coming back to us!" She took his hand and felt the faint trembling as he held her hand. His mouth tried to form a word but no sound came and it seemed no other movement was possible. But this was a major breakthrough. Shaking with shock and relief she patted his hand. "Wait, I'll get Stan. We must get the doctor. This is wonderful."

She rushed to the house calling for Mollie and Stan. Panting, she told Stan to ride his bicycle to Doctor MacDonald and ask him to drive up immediately.

"Mollie, please make tea and bring it to the gazebo. Quickly now." Olivia ran excitedly back to Gilbert. All the care, the patience, the prayers had paid off. A full recovery might not be possible but perhaps she would have a companion once again. She hoped Gilbert would regain his speech, there were so many questions she wanted to ask. Now they could communicate if he had movement at least. He could tap once for no, twice for yes with his fingers. Feeling tremendously elated she reached the gazebo and saw from behind that he had moved even further in his bathchair. "Now Gilbert, don't try to do too much . . ." But as she walked in front of him her words froze. Gilbert was slumped slightly to one side, the one arm still outside the blanket, but his eyes were closed and his mouth hung slightly agape.

"Gilbert?" Olivia reached out and took his hand, straightening his head with the other and knew at once he was dead.

Mollie smiled in delight to see Olivia sitting and holding the master's hand as they sat side by side staring into the garden. Olivia took the tea tray and placed it on the small bench and it was then Mollie saw her wet cheeks. Mollie's hand flew to her mouth when she looked over at Gilbert and she took off for the house, frightened and distraught at how the spirits of death could suddenly arrive and take one away on such a fresh and sunny morning.

Doctor MacDonald explained that Gilbert had suffered possibly two strokes as a result of the blood pressure they could not control or treat. "That might account for the sudden movement, a minor stroke triggering a muscular response before the fatal one."

Olivia shook her head. "No, Gilbert wanted to say good-bye. It was sheer willpower or God's intervention that made him reach out to me," she said firmly.

The kindly doctor, who had known Gilbert since their medical student days, didn't argue. "You have been devoted and inspirational, Olivia. I'm sure you're right."

A large memorial service was held for Doctor Gilbert Shaw in Perth. Pale light from an overcast morning filtered down from high, leadlight windows and in the front row Olivia looked by her feet at a patch of light that ran like spilt milk across the stone floor. She became lost in the pattern of light, her mind drifting back to the light of other times. Walking in a cold London night with Conrad and seeing the comforting glow of lights in shops and pubs. Her first glimpse of Australia through a shimmer of dawn light from a ship's rail, morning light in Broome, fresh-washed blue sky, deep clear aqua sea and a golden light that touched mangroves, mudflats, leaftips and glaring tin roofs with a magical glow. She was hypnotized by the diffused pattern of light on the floor for most of the service, hardly conscious of what was going on around her, and was surprised when

Doctor MacDonald took her by the elbow and stood up. The service was over. The tributes had been paid and Gilbert Shaw laid to rest.

In the following weeks Mollie and Stan silently watched Olivia wistfully drift through her garden. Then, one day, when she was kneeling by a flowerbed, lost in plucking out weeds, a shadow fell across her and a strong hand helped her up.

The world was no longer held at bay. It now intruded in her garden. Tyndall stood before her. She expressed no surprise, made no move, but stood there, gazing into the face that was imprinted on her soul.

He, too, looked into her eyes. "Come home, Olivia. It's time."

They returned quietly to Broome on a sunset tide on a balmy evening refreshed by an afternoon thunderstorm that left the sky cloudless velvet against which the rising moon shone in the mirror of the sea. The lavender and rose sunset melted as the lights of Broome sparkled to life and Tyndall and Olivia went ashore without fanfare. They hadn't alerted anyone about their arrival, not wanting any fuss. Maya had stayed in Fremantle after the funeral to take Georgie around the city sights and visit the Barstows in Albany.

At Tyndall's house, all was quiet. They could

smell the curry Rosminah was cooking for Yusef in their quarters, but the house was empty. Tyndall grinned and dropped the bag he was carrying and gathered Olivia in his arms, sweeping her off the ground. "This might be a little premature, but it means a lot to me." He carried her up the steps, across the verandah, nudged the door with his shoulder and strode down to the bedroom. He kissed her and dropped her on the bed. "I'll get Yusef to fetch the rest of the bags."

She laughed at him as she struggled to sit up. "You've got style, John Tyndall, I must say."

Late in the evening they sat in contemplative and companionable silence on the darkened verandah looking at the moon shining across the bay. He kissed her fingertips. "Now we can plan our wedding."

"I want nothing more, my darling. I think we've waited long enough. I doubt there's anyone in town who won't be glad to see us together at last," said Olivia with a small smile.

That night, wrapped in each other's arms as they drifted to sleep, Olivia gazed at Tyndall's face beside hers and knew, with great peace and certainty, that they would spend the rest of their days together.

In the following days there was a busy round of catching up with old friends. The Mettas held a luncheon at the Conti, and for Olivia it was a return to the good old days of high spirits, talk of pearling trips, snide sales and prospects for the shell market. It was acknowledged and accepted among the white community that the partnership between Tyndall and Olivia had become a personal commitment.

Ahmed couldn't stop beaming and had grasped Tyndall's hand, pumping it enthusiastically, when Tyndall told him he and Olivia would marry.

And when Olivia arrived at the foreshore camp there was an enthusiastic reception from the shell openers, tenders, divers and other workmen. It was seen as a good omen, a closing of a circle, for they knew the story of Olivia's long association with Star of the Sea.

The luggers returned to sea and Olivia began decorating and setting up their home while also planning their wedding. "Just a simple ceremony, I mean at our age and after all this time . . ." she began, but couldn't hide from Mabel her bubbling joy.

"What nonsense! You're in the prime of life. The town will expect a big event, Olivia. John is a popular man with all races and they love you, too."

"We'll see. I'll talk it over with John when he gets back."

Olivia walked along the track at the edge of the bay. With the luggers outside on a last run over the beds, the town dozed in the salty air heavily humid with the threat of the first rain of the wet season.

She paused to watch an old Malay fisherman unload silvery barramundi, thread them along an oar and, hoisting it to one shoulder, lift a bucket of cockle oysters and set off for town. His faded batik sarong was knotted firmly around his sinewy frame, his black topi set at a jaunty angle, his sandals scuffing the orange dust. Memories of fish dinners Minnie had prepared from Alf's catches came back to Olivia. Or times Alf had caught a couple of big mangrove crabs which Minnie declared "were sweeter even than dugong."

A puff of the last of the south-east trade winds skipped across the bay, lifting a lock of her hair, and she could smell the sea, the mangroves, the mudflats, tar from a repaired boat and mock orange blossom in the front yard of a small wooden shuttered house. And it came to Olivia that this was indeed home. Broome was in her blood.

Every morning here held promise . . . promise of excitement, adventure, achievement, a feeling that in this remote spot on the north-west coast of the continent almost anything could happen, that it was unlike anywhere else on earth. One was part of a rough, roistering community of many races, ordinary folk doing their ordinary jobs on shore, adventurers, wild and funny misfits, and that great mixed band of men who lived for the sea and its treasures which were sought by the rich and the famous in the great cities of the world who couldn't possibly imagine places like Broome. The realization that this odd little town and the great emptiness around it had become so much part of her inner self excited Olivia. She recognized how artificial her life in the city had been, that her apparent satisfaction with work at the refuge and life with Gilbert before his stroke was indeed superficial. This was where she really belonged, in the outback where life was still quite raw, the land untamed, the sea magnificently challenging. It was where she had first discarded the emotional baggage she brought from England and discovered within herself new emotions, new aspirations, new abilities beyond her imagination. In Broome she had been reborn, and here she belonged.

She confided these feelings to Tyndall, who understood perfectly. He shared her love of the place, but had to acknowledge in turn that it was his finding of her love in Broome, rather than more physical aspects of his life here, that made his attachment to the place so strong. "It's like we belong to this place because we belong to each other," he whispered to her one evening. "I always felt that if I left here I would never get you back. Do you understand, or am I talking nonsense?"

She laughed a little. "Nonsense? Of course not, darling. It's beautiful sense. Although I'm quite sure there are a lot of people who think we're crazy staying here, that we're missing out so much on what the world has to offer." She snuggled up close to him. "I'm quite happy to let the rest of the world go by so long as you're around." They were treasuring every moment together, for too well they both knew how joy could be snatched away.

Olivia had asked Yusef to find a small poinciana tree and when she had decided on the right spot in the garden, he dug the hole and Olivia spread the soil around its roots and patted it firmly in place. She stood back and shut her eyes and could see it in the years ahead, rising upward, its sweeping soft green branches smothered in brilliant gold and orange blossoms, silhouetted against the turquoise waters of the bay.

Later when she was alone, Olivia returned to the freshly planted little tree. Kneeling down, she unwrapped a small jar filled with powdery red soil. She unscrewed the lid and sprinkled the soil from James's first grave around the tree. Then, digging a small hole, she reached into a pocket and took out Hamish's war medal and buried it.

"Now my sons are home at last," she whispered. "Be at peace, my boys. Grow strong, little tree." She lightly touched the feathery leaves and turned to go indoors with tears in her eyes.

Olivia slowly withdrew from her role in the office at Star of the Sea as Maya became increasingly competent. It pleased her that Maya was so committed to the business and that her father got such joy from having her involved. One day as they were getting letters and parcels together for the mail south, Olivia remarked how much Maya seemed to enjoy the business and life in Broome generally.

"I thought you might find it all a little dull after living in the south with so many amenities, so many attractions," said Olivia.

"But I was white then," responded Maya almost casually, tightening a knot in the string around a parcel.

Olivia was stunned. "Whatever do you mean?"

Maya looked up, slightly puzzled at her reaction. "Well, life down south isn't that great if you're an Aborigine."

"But you're . . ." paused Olivia, searching for the right word.

"Different?" suggested Maya with a raised eyebrow.

Olivia paced a little nervously around the office. "No, I don't want to say that. It's just that, well, I really hadn't thought about it much since we came here. You just fitted in so well. Everything seems so . . . normal."

"Ah yes, but that's because this is Broome and Broome is not normal, is it? Being part Aboriginal here isn't much of a problem, is it? Nobody really makes a big issue of it, do they? You can see it every day in the streets, Aboriginal blood mixed with God knows how many races." She flipped a rubber band around a pile of letters, then went on. "I hid from my real self for most of my life. Now I am being me, and that means being

Aboriginal as well. It's pretty easy to do that here, I couldn't do it in Perth, or Fremantle. Down there hardly anyone wants to know an Aborigine, even a white-looking one," and she laughed, breaking the tension she knew the issue had created between them. "I can never go back down there, not to live anyway."

Olivia took Maya's hand in hers. "Maya, I'm sorry I haven't talked about this with you before. I really took too much for granted. I just haven't thought about how you were adjusting to your Aboriginality."

"There's nothing for you to be sorry about, Olivia. But I do feel sorry for Georgie. How she has reacted to Minnie's tribe, how she doesn't want anything to do with our people. It saddens me a lot, but I don't think she wants to know. She listens to you more than she listens to me. But I can't change, Olivia. What I've found is too valuable to give up."

"I know what you're saying, my dear Maya. I know," said Olivia softly and they embraced.

Maya then hoisted herself up on the desk and motioned Olivia to sit in the swingback chair. "Sit down and I'll tell you something I've not talked about much to anyone, except Dad." She paused, looked down for a moment in contemplation, then gave a little sigh. "Remember after you left here and I wrote to you saying that I had been down the coast to see my family." Olivia nodded and Maya went on. "My family," she repeated thoughtfully. "Sounds odd doesn't it when you know them—still bush blacks mostly. Anyway, it was fun, it was exciting and they were beautiful and warm and wonderful. But there was much I didn't write because I just couldn't find the right words, and, well, it seemed to be a very private thing. Something very spiritual happened that has changed me forever. It will help you understand why I feel like I do now."

Maya leaned back, hands on the desk behind her. "It was the most magical experience, Olivia. Magical." She then told briefly of the welcome on the beach, the damper and treacle lunch, the walk in the bush with the women. "Imagine the scene, Olivia. Me in a big straw hat and feeling almost dressed well enough for shopping in Perth, taking off with a band of black women wearing not much more than their old skirts, and I had absolutely no idea of why or where we were going. I was completely unconscious of the outward difference between us. We were family, but I think they felt it more than me at that point. Well, they took me into another world without leaving this one. It was like Alice through the Looking Glass."

Maya then told Olivia of how she learned, with Minnie interpreting, that she had a special relationship with certain rocks and trees along the way. She learned about features in the landscape that had significance for all women, sacred places. And then there was a rock overhang, not quite a cave, where there were some ocher paintings on the rock wall, paintings of strange figures. "It was the most special place, Olivia. I could feel it, right into my heart, my soul. Even before Minnie explained it to me I knew it was special, to them and to me. I can't tell you everything that happened because it's secret." Maya watched for Olivia's reaction.

"I understand, Maya, truly I do. I know why you must keep it secret. Over the years, Minnie taught me quite a lot about her culture. Remember, I, too, had a special relationship with the same people."

"Goodness, it must have been a really amazing experience. I mean you were fresh out from England, alone in what must have seemed like the end of the world. I really find it hard to imagine you sitting in that scrub, pregnant, waving a gun at Dad."

They both laughed, then Maya went on to vaguely describe some of the ceremonies that took place at the sacred site of the women, choosing her words carefully and avoiding detail. "It was all for me, Olivia, all to make me totally one of them, one of the family, and with every hour memories of my childhood with them came flooding back. Those dreams I used to have in Albany as a kid, they weren't dreams, but reality. I remembered places, words, names, recognized relatives and even some of the children I played with. They remembered me, too. It was just so strange and exciting. And that night, back at the camp we danced in the light of the campfire."

Olivia couldn't conceal her astonishment. "You danced!"

"Yes. I just *had* to. Something in me just took over and I had to dance. I was one of them. It was the proper thing to do."

Olivia recalled the times she had seen the Aboriginal women dancing at missions and the occasional events staged for visiting government officials, but she had some difficulty putting Maya in the same picture. "You danced . . . in bare feet and . . ."

"Yes."

Olivia gasped. "Maya, I can't believe it. Weren't you embarrassed?"

"No. Can't you see, Olivia? I was one of them. I *am* one of them. It just seemed so right, so natural to let them paint my breasts and shoulders and face, so natural to get up with them and dance. They understand that I live in another world so removed from theirs, but they know and I know, that we share a spiritual world and this is something really important. I can never deny it, Olivia, never."

Olivia rose and they hugged. "I know what you're saying, my dear Maya. I know. Thank you so much for telling me. I'm so proud of you."

The next day the mailboat arrived and on the same tide many of the luggers returned to port, now towed in line behind a small steam tug. Maya and Olivia were there to welcome them back and Tyndall boldly jumped down from the gunwale onto the wharf even before the first mooring line had been thrown to envelop them both in a big hug. "My dear girls! I can't tell you how my heart feels to see you both!"

"How was the trip? Any pearls?" asked Maya.

"All in good time." Tyndall winked at Olivia. "And, my beauty, what news do you have? How is that scallywag granddaughter of ours?"

"Raising merry cain at school. The Sisters say they've never had such a handful."

Maya raised her hands. "I give up. Trouble is her middle name."

"We have to bribe her with threats of not being a flower girl at the wedding," added Olivia with a loving smile.

"*Our* wedding? *The* wedding? At long last?" Tyndall clutched his brow. "How can I wait?"

"You'll wait. Now tell us, John, how was the trip?"

Stepping between them, Tyndall linked arms and together they almost danced along the jetty. "Tremendous. Hit a great patch of old shell. And, if I'm any judge, Toby is going to be very busy and Monsieur Barat very pleased."

The postwar years were living up to expectations as a time of profit, progress and fun. There was an intensity of living that made everyone buoyant. The industry was booming again after the wartime slump, mechanical advances had brought engines for boats, cars to town and even a truck for the bush mailman, though anyone traveling north or south overland was considered a bit mad. The Bristols now flying an air service were faster, although their schedule was unpredictable. All this and the joy of having Tyndall back in port made Olivia feel like a young girl again, and with an enthusiastic Maya at her side she threw herself into the wedding preparations.

She was working on the invitation list on the verandah one morning when Stan announced that there was a "bloke from Alf" at the back door. The "bloke" was a young black from the mission at Beagle Bay, in town with one of the Brothers helping with shopping for supplies. "Me Tommy, missus. Alf told me t'give ya message."

"Thank you, Tommy," acknowledged Olivia.

"Alf says he found grave bilong Niah. Says ya would understand."

Olivia was stunned. Her hand went to her mouth to control her shock. "Tommy, can you tell me anything else? How does Alf know this?"

"Me an' Alf cuttin' in old cemetery and he see some shell on a stone an' ask the Brother. He lookit up in some book." The boy bobbed his head to reinforce his words. "Alf sure. Said youse were t'tell everyone."

"Yes, of course. I understand. Please give my thanks to Alf. Does he need anything up there, Tommy?"

"Nope. He doin' good, missus. For an old fella."

Olivia broke the news to Tyndall and Maya when they came in laughing and exhilarated, after a day at the foreshore camp.

Tyndall took Maya's hand. "I've always wanted to know . . . what happened . . ."

"I must go to her," whispered Maya, looking at her father.

"Of course. We both must. We'll go together. The weather is good. We'll sail up to Beagle Bay. Olivia . . ."

"Of course you two must go as soon as possible. Just the two of you," urged Olivia.

Although they didn't say it out loud, both Tyndall and Olivia realized the circle was closing, the loose ends being tied up before making their own commitment to each other.

Tyndall and Maya rowed to the rocky shore and walked through the scrub along a sandy track to the mission. Alf was sitting on an old chair on the verandah of a small shack. He greeted them with a cheerful wave, pushing himself stiffly to his feet.

"I figured you'd be along any day. Good to see you, boss. Hey there, missy Maya."

Maya gave him a hug. "How're you managing up here, Alf?"

"Good. Real good. Plenty t'do, they serve up decent meals in the mess hut over there. Lotsa friends."

"Mem sends her best. We'll be getting married in a couple of weeks. Want to come down to the big day, Alf? Come with us and we'll get you back here somehow."

Alf rubbed his thinning, but still shiny, black

hair. "I dunno 'bout that. But I'm real pleased t'hear. Minnie would've been there with bells on."

"She'll be there in spirit, we don't doubt that." Tyndall took the old man's arm. "Now how about we find the Brother and get him to tell us about Niah. Your young mate said you found the grave?"

"Yeah." Alf pointed to Maya's pendant. "Recognized that thing. The carving. It's the same. I remembered Niah had one same as Maya. It's all written down in the book the Brother's got."

They followed Alf to the whitewashed church. "Is it the same Brother who was here then?" asked Maya. "I remember a Brother with a bald head. I'd never seen a man with no hair before."

"No. He went back to some country or other. Spain, I think. This is a new fella. Nice bloke."

Brother Jean, followed by a group of young children, appeared and introduced himself. He took them into the long room where simple wooden tables and benches were set out in rows. A young Aboriginal woman brought tea, smiling shyly to them all, but eyed Maya with special interest.

Excusing himself for a few moments, Brother Jean returned with a dark brown journal and turned to an entry which briefly told the story of the arrival of the wounded girl, Brother Frederick's attempt to nurse her to health, her deep attachment to the interior of the church with its shells, and her sad death. He believed her name to be "Neea." Having no clue to her identity or family he placed the carved pendant she wore on

the headstone. He passed the journal to them. "I
will take you and your daughter there directly we
have had tea."

Brother Jean left them alone before the simple
stone that marked the resting place of Niah.
Tyndall stood gazing at the embedded carved
shell, remembering how it had been so much a
part of Niah. Maya stood beside him, one hand
holding his, the other pressed to her own pendant resting close to her heart. Waves of sadness,
joy, relief, and a sense of finality and strength
swept over her. All the feelings she had locked
away for so many years broke free and with a sob
she fell to her knees and wrapped her arms about
the headstone, pressing her forehead against its
cold rough surface.

Tyndall crouched beside her and gathered her
in his arms. "Maya," he whispered in an effort to
comfort her.

"It's all right, Father, really it is." She lifted her
tear-stained face to him and smiled. "It's such a
relief to find her. To know . . . so much is coming
back. I can hear her voice, singing, I remember
her laugh, her holding me . . ."

She cried again and Tyndall wept, too, with joy
and sadness. "Let those memories free, my dearest, listen to her voice. That way you will never
lose her again."

When they returned to Broome, Maya hugged Olivia. "I feel a whole person again. I know who I am. My story is complete and I can pass it on to Georgie. We're family at last. I hope Hamish is watching all this."

Olivia smoothed her hair. "I feel he is. I know his spirit is here, back in Broome. It's where you and he first came together as little children. God, fate, the journey of life, it's all planned, I feel."

Olivia opened her eyes on the morning of her wedding to Tyndall and clasped her hands together and whispered, "Dear God, thank you for this day, for the life we will share together. After all that has gone before, let this be my time of joy. I promise to love and care for my beloved man."

Rosminah brought in a cup of tea and opened the shutters. "Look, mem, sunshine. Goin' to be perfect day."

Maya soon joined her, sitting up in bed beside her. "Your new life starts today."

"New? Perhaps . . ." she mused. "It feels so inevitable. John always insisted you only get one great love in a lifetime. Conrad and Gilbert were dear to me, but great passion, great overwhelming love . . . that's rare."

"I know," said Maya softly. "I'll never find another Hamish. And you know, Olivia, I don't even want to look or think about anyone else."

"Maya dearest, you are a young woman . . . it

might never be the same but you shouldn't resign yourself to a life alone . . ."

Maya took Olivia's hand. "You just *know* some things. And I know there will never be anyone for me but Hamish. Don't feel sad for me. I feel so lucky to have loved him, to have Georgie and to have you."

Olivia didn't press the subject. She was so consumed with her own feelings of love for Tyndall. She wished every woman could feel this surging power of love and of being loved in return. "It's been worth everything," she said and Maya, understanding, nodded and smiled.

It was a sunset wedding in the white Church of England corrugated iron church near the dunes bordering Roebuck Bay.

The bridal party walked through a huge crowd of friends and onlookers overflowing onto the struggling lawn. Japanese, Chinese, Malay, Koepangers, Aboriginals and blends of all of them, gave a small cheer and tossed hearty comments at Captain John Tyndall, resplendent in his pearling master's whites as he strode to the church, did a small sprint up the three wooden steps onto the portico, turned, lifted his hat in salute and took a bow.

Inside, his exuberance was more subdued and he took his place next to Ahmed at the front of the church, nervously fingering his high buttoned collar. Spotting Mollie and Stan with their little girl, he gave them a broad wink. The interior of the church was plain but Maya and Mabel had festooned it with candles and masses of flowers and branches of flowering trees. Floor to ceiling windows along the sides, normally shuttered, were thrown open to flood the church with golden light and dappled shadows of the nearby palm trees. Above the quiet murmur of the wedding guests drifted in the croak of frogs and call of a curlew.

Olivia arrived in Toby's shiny Ford motor car which he pulled up with a flourish and opened the door to help Olivia step down.

Maya moved forward to fuss about her. "Olivia, you look a dream."

She wore an ankle-length ivory guipure lace dress over mother-of-pearl silk. Matching silk roses were pinned to the side of her head and she carried a bouquet of native orchids. But what caught the eye of the crowd was the strand of pearls that gleamed against the lace. This was Tyndall's "collection", strung by Toby, who was astonished that Tyndall had managed to keep these to himself for so many years.

"I started it for Niah and continued for Olivia in the hope I might one day give it to her as a wedding gift," he told Toby.

Maya, in a turquoise dress that matched the clear brightness of the waters of the bay, followed Olivia as she walked the final steps to be united with the man she'd always loved.

The romantic atmosphere of the wedding changed to jovial exuberance at the Continental

Hotel. There was a champagne reception in the gardens for what appeared to be most of Broome. Then the guests were ushered into the dining room for the official dinner. Toby, dressed in formal suit, his dark skin glistening from the heat, a smile constantly in place, made the toasts. Mabel, glittering in a red and gold sari, leaned across to Olivia. "I have a feeling my usually staid and sensible husband is going to overindulge tonight."

"Most of the master pearlers are already well away," sighed Olivia.

"There'll be a lot of sore heads about tomorrow. But, goodness me, we all do have something to celebrate, yes?" Mabel lifted her glass of lemonade and clinked glasses with Olivia and Maya. "Here's to you and John. I am so happy to see my dearest wish come true."

"Thank you dear Mabel for being such a good and true friend."

"To new beginnings," added Maya. "For all of us."

As Olivia and Mabel had foreseen, the night turned into a spree of uproarious drinking and outrageous storytelling once the master pearlers dragged Tyndall into the Lugger Bar and began challenging and betting each other on who could kick the ceiling fan from standing on top of the bar. Tyndall with his height and long legs won, but at the cost of crashing into several chairs and breaking them.

The women had deserted the festivities as soon as "nightcaps in the Lugger Bar" was suggested. Olivia, Maya and Mabel sat in Olivia's kitchen, brewing tea and laughing over their stories of the evening's events. Maya had won the attention of several pearlers and the Inspector of Pearl Fisheries himself had requested two dances.

"This is not how you should be spending your wedding night, Olivia," said Mabel. "I thought you had the best room at the Conti set aside."

"We do, and I hope someone pours John into it. When they started singing and talking of going round for drinks at the Star and the Roebuck . . ."

"And the Governor Broome . . ."

"Yes, I thought I'd rather sleep in my own bed. John and I have the rest of our lives together," she answered.

"You're not mad at him?" asked Maya.

"How can you be. He's so happy, he's just a silly kid at times. Leave them to it. He'll make it up to me."

Mabel left and Maya and Olivia got ready for bed.

Maya slipped down the hall and tapped at Olivia's door. "Good night. Sweet dreams, Olivia."

"Maya, come in for a minute." Olivia was standing in her nightgown brushing her long hair, still wearing the pearls. She put down the brush and lifted the pearls over her head. "Maya, these are to be yours one day. And I trust you will pass them on to Georgiana."

"Oh, Olivia . . . I don't know what to say. They're so beautiful."

Together they fingered the perfect spheres the color of moonlight.

"You and I know, maybe better than most women, at what cost these come. The price men pay is not in money."

"It's like these cast a spell," said Maya softly.

"Men have always searched for some prize, a reward, but secretly I think it's the adventure of the search that lures them. I often think that pearls hold the souls of men. See how they come to life against your skin. Don't put them away in a box, wear them."

"I'll remember that."

They hugged and Maya went to her room.

And while Tyndall and his pearling mates began a game of bowls using tennis balls and bottles of champagne in the grounds of the Conti, his daughter and his wife slept peacefully.

There followed years Olivia always remembered as the Happy Years. She and Tyndall were blissfully content, enjoying every moment they spent together, whether working over details of the business or simply watching the sunset from the verandah. He made her laugh, they still found each other's company exhilarating and their lovemaking continued as passionate as ever. Occasionally Tyndall swept a willing Olivia away from their bed to make love under the stars or on one of the boats they motored to a far reach of the bay. They built a tiny one-room shack further along the coast past Cable Beach where they sometimes camped for days at a stretch. "Shipwreck House" they called it. They cooked over an open fire, swam naked in rock pools and slept in hammocks between palm trees.

Olivia described these days of simple fun in detail in her diary . . . watching the big circus that came up by coastal steamer and performed in the grounds of the Conti . . . an evening at Sun Pictures sitting in the canvas deck chairs in the open air, a length of lattice dividing the whites from the "coloreds" who sat on benches on the other side . . . cold lemon shaved ices on a hot afternoon . . . wild turkey and duck hunting trips to Lake Eda, Stan's young relatives acting as retrievers . . . and watching at sunset hundreds of brolgas performing mating dances around the fringes of Roebuck Plains. On these trips Olivia collected flower and grass specimens which she pressed in her flower book.

The Depression knocked the bottom out of the pearling business once again. By the mid-thirties the sliding price for shell had forced many pearlers out of business and others had to sell off some of their luggers. The Star of the Sea fleet was down to the schooner, *Mist,* and four boats, six having been sold off for very poor prices. The situation was made worse by new incursions by foreign vessels into Australian waters as well as the deep sea beds. The development of small engines for the luggers had given fleets a much greater mobility and the Australian pearlers were faced with a virtual invasion of mainly Japanese operated craft, particularly in the northern waters.

The pearlers, including Tyndall, were furious but there seemed to be nothing they could do.

Olivia tried to be philosophical about the changing world. "John, you're in your sixties and we've had a good run. There's still money to be made and we're comfortable."

"It's just not right though . . . Sure, a lot of the pearling is done in international waters, but the foreigners are coming into territorial waters as well. You know, the police tell me they've heard of lubras being sold to Japanese and Malay crews for liquor, tobacco, and flour. But they haven't caught anyone. And the customs people are bloody hopeless, too. Haven't any decent boats."

Tyndall was not in a good mood at all and he stomped off inside, found a bottle of beer in the ice chest, filled a pewter mug and returned to Olivia on the verandah. "Another thing. I'm not going to become a bloody verandah pearler, so don't bring up that age business again."

Olivia looked up from her diary and smiled as she dipped her pen in the inkpot. She loved the way her husband always bridled whenever reference was made to his age. "No darling, of course not. It wouldn't suit you at all."

The only shadow over their life was the rebellious Georgiana. Years ago, after long and often tearful discussions, they had capitulated and agreed to send her to high school in Perth where she boarded with old friends of Olivia's. Georgiana had never settled into Broome life, nor taken to its people. It saddened Maya deeply that her daughter seemed so determined to turn her back on their Aboriginal heritage.

"You can't force it on her, Maya dear," said Olivia sympathetically. "She may come to it in her own time but that has to be her decision. It must be very difficult for her."

It had been Olivia, not Maya, that Georgiana had turned to for help when she graduated from high school. Olivia had gone to Perth specifically to help her get settled in a secretarial school and now she was working in the office of one of the coastal shipping companies. Georgiana no longer came back to Broome for holidays, and her letters were becoming less frequent.

It came as quite a shock to them all when a letter arrived from Georgiana announcing that she had been offered a job in the head office of the company in Sydney and she was sailing east in a couple of weeks.

Maya immediately went to the post office and sent a telegram to her daughter. *Good luck God bless you love Mother.*

As she walked slowly and sadly back home, Maya knew in her heart that the move east was designed to put even more distance between her daughter and a heritage that she couldn't live with.

CHAPTER TWENTY-FOUR

Maya glanced up as the MacRobertson Miller de Havilland mail plane circled over Broome before landing. She must have had a premonition, for the following morning Olivia handed her a letter. It was from Georgie in Sydney.

Dear Mother,

I'm well settled here in Sydney, I just didn't think there were enough opportunities in Perth—and how right I was! I have a wonderful job with David Jones department store in Elizabeth Street. I'm secretary to the fashion buyer—all those boring practice sessions on the old Remington have paid off—and I'm enjoying it. Through friends at work I have found a teeny flat in Kings Cross, a very bohemian sort of area where a lot of artists, writers and musicians and "characters" live—right up my street! I really feel I'm in the hub of things here and have a proper career path lined up. Those years as an office junior, then secretary, in the shipping company in

*Perth have proved valuable even though I found it
so deadly dull at the time. When I was boarding
with Olivia and Gilbert's friends there, they thought
I was such an independent modern woman to be
out in the world supporting myself. I think they'd be
quite shocked if they could see the career girls about
in Sydney. Everyone dresses so nicely and the social
life is outstanding. I'm glad I get my fashions at a
discount! I am considering saving what money I
can to travel abroad in a year or so. I've met a lot of
sophisticated foreigners here and I can't wait to see
London. Give my love to Olivia and Tyndall.*

Love,
Georgie

Maya folded the letter. It was written in
Georgie's large flowing hand and had the same
breathless quality as the way she spoke. Probably
dashed the letter off on the tram on the way to
work, thought Maya. She was pleased at her
daughter's capacity to look after herself and get
on in the world. Georgie was a survivor and an
adventurer, she certainly wasn't looking over her
shoulder toward Broome. Georgie had shown her
independence from a very early age but it made
Maya sad that in so doing she had turned away
from the family. Georgie had never felt connected
to her family and Maya didn't really understand
why. Perhaps she should have persisted in trying
to instill more knowledge of her Aboriginal heritage to give her more of a sense of belonging.
Minnie always said Georgie should have got the

knowledge and done the ceremonies but the girl had rebelled at anything to do with "Minnie's mob." There was not the emotional closeness Maya would have liked and sometimes she felt Georgiana was closer to Olivia than to her.

She shared these thoughts with Olivia after giving her Georgie's letter to read.

"She is something of a free spirit, Maya, that's for sure. But I think it's how she was born. You can't have any regrets about how you brought her up. Let's hope that one day Georgie stops rushing at the world and finds her true self. Maybe when she marries she will come to realize how important family is," said Olivia, trying to comfort Maya.

Maya nodded but didn't answer. Deep down she had her doubts about Georgiana returning to the fold as a loving and devoted daughter and it felt like a rejection. Some people don't need that closeness and never face up to who they really are and what's important in their lives. Minnie used to say such people died as "lost souls" and Maya fervently hoped Georgie wouldn't be one of them.

Tyndall walked along the almost deserted verandah of the Continental. In the old days it would have been crowded and noisy just before lunch. He spotted the rotund shape of Toby Metta talking to the slim man in a formal gray suit sitting next to Olivia, and headed toward them. The man rose to his feet as Tyndall joined them.

Toby did the introductions. "Ah, John, please meet Claude Barat ... Claude, this is Captain John Tyndall."

"I'm pleased to make your acquaintance, sir. I've heard a lot about you."

Tyndall smiled as he shook hands with the handsome young European on his first trip to Australia to buy pearls. "How is your father? We will miss him, he has been such a good friend as well as business associate over the years. Men of his quality rarely find their way to Broome."

"Thank you so much for your kind words. He remembers you all with affection. It's a pity that he now finds the trip a bit much, but he's still active in the business. I'm looking forward to being a regular visitor to Broome. When things settle down, of course."

"Drink, John?" asked Toby.

"I have one on the way, thanks. So you and Olivia have finalized your transactions?" He smiled at his wife. "You've probably discovered Olivia drives a hard bargain."

"Ah, my father told me Mrs. Tyndall is always fair ... and ... charming." Monsieur Barat's son lifted his glass to Olivia with a courtly nod.

Tyndall sipped his drink. "The shell market has been poor but we still manage to find a decent pearl or two. But what do you mean 'when things settle down'? The market you mean?"

"I was thinking more particularly of the political events in Europe, especially in Germany. The Jewish people are being persecuted terribly. Hitler is getting ready for war, there's no doubt about it. The repercussions will hit Broome, believe me."

Olivia gave a small gasp of surprise and turned to Tyndall who looked unfazed. "Well, if there's one place unlikely to find itself involved in an international conflict, it's Broome. Though we've had our share of our own little wars right here over the years. Isn't that so, Toby?" said Tyndall with a laconic grin.

"Indeed we have. But the rumblings in Europe are sounding ominous," said Toby, lighting a cigarette.

"So much so that my father is moving the family and the business from Europe to New York."

Tyndall raised his eyebrows. "That is a big step. Especially when times are so grim. The recovery from the Depression has been very slow. War in Europe could have disastrous effects . . . kill off the industry for good. And we can't have that. Plastic is no comparison for pearl shell."

"Well, times change, Captain Tyndall . . ."

"They do indeed," Toby agreed. "It's hard to imagine pearling not being Broome's lifeblood."

"You wouldn't consider retiring, Captain Tyndall? This seems the time to bow out," said Claude Barat delicately.

"No bloody way. Never," said Tyndall firmly.

That night he talked to Olivia. This was not verandah sunset drink chat, but lying in bed holding each other in the warm darkness.

"Young Barat's remark hit home, I have to

confess," Tyndall admitted, "I don't feel any different . . . do you?"

"Older, you mean? No. I sometimes get a surprise when I look in the mirror and see this 'woman of a certain age' and wonder where the young Olivia disappeared to."

"She hasn't gone anywhere. She's right here." Tyndall tightened his grip around her. "I always see you as the windswept fresh-faced young woman in those mad sailing pyjamas."

Olivia smiled in the darkness and snuggled close to him. "But the fact remains, my darling—we aren't as young as we were, and sailing and all the physical work involved in pearling takes their toll."

"Olivia . . . I'm still fit and I'm still a pearler. I'm not about to sit on the verandah."

"I know, John. But what Claude was pointing out is the bad state of the industry. And this talk of war is very worrying. It will devastate the business."

"Young Barat reckoning a war could hit us here seems a bit far-fetched. I doubt Hitler is eyeing the north-west of Australia, but I think the Barats are probably smart to move their headquarters to New York. Don't worry, we'll keep pearling as long as we're able."

Tyndall's dismissal of the events in Europe was contradicted in a matter of months as they all began to follow the deteriorating situation in Europe with mounting tension.

It was Maya, making a cup of tea one morning,

who came running to Tyndall and Olivia, tapping urgently on their bedroom door. "We're at war! The news just came over the wireless. Because Britain is at war with Germany . . . something to do with Poland. Oh dear . . ." Maya went in and sat tearfully on the edge of the bed.

Olivia took her hand. "It seems incredible . . . two wars in our lifetime. When will they learn? When I think of Hamish and all those brave boys who died . . ." The two women sat quietly for a moment, then Tyndall broke the silence.

"I'd better go find out if the RM knows any more details."

Later that morning small groups gathered about the town to discuss the news. The RM's aide was dispatched on his bicycle to the homes and offices of the leading citizens in the town, calling them to a meeting at the Residence.

Tyndall, the Senior Customs Officer, the Inspector of Pearl Fisheries, the new Sergeant of Police, the Bishop, the doctor, the postmaster, two other pearling masters and several other leading citizens gathered in the front garden of the Residence while a Malay houseboy in white uniform served cool drinks. The men talked quietly amongst themselves, digesting the latest news that had been picked up in a shortwave broadcast from London. The group fell silent when the Resident Magistrate appeared, stood next to the flagpole and cleared his throat.

"Gentlemen. It is my unhappy duty to tell you that I have received official advice from the Government that Australia is now at war. It is our duty as citizens of the British Empire to support her. I know that I have your wholehearted backing to do whatever is necessary for the defense of the Empire in the dark days ahead. I am sure that I can telegraph our Prime Minister, Mr. Menzies, that we are all behind the Government and the King."

The short speech was greeted with a hearty, "hear, hear," followed by three loud cheers, then everyone took up the lead of the Church of England minister and sang. This was immediately followed by an enthusiastic burst of "God save the King."

Several Malay and Japanese crew members passing by glanced at the small crowd around the flagpole, but when the anthem was sung they stood still, at attention, as was the custom they had learned.

At its conclusion they continued on their way, shaking their heads at the prospect of war. There were few enough luggers working as it was because of the effects of the Depression. A war would mean the bottom falling out of the pearl shell market.

Maya was very withdrawn and preoccupied and it seemed to Olivia there was something bothering her apart from the war news. Maya looked pale and was racked by a persistent cough. Olivia was about to mention this to Tyndall one evening as they sat on the verandah but, at that moment, Maya quietly came along and asked if she could join them.

"What's up my love?" asked Tyndall. "I haven't seen a smile in weeks."

"There isn't much to smile about, is there?" she said with a sigh.

"That depends now," said Tyndall. "You could smile because you live in a safe little backwater, it's a terrific sunset out there, and you have a family who loves you."

"You're right, Dad, but the war is worrying. What's going to happen to us? The business isn't doing well." She sighed heavily and leaned back in the deckchair as if very tired. "There's another thing. For some reason, I feel I want to go down the coast to see the mob. Maybe that's what I need to brighten things up. It's ages since I last went bush."

Tyndall gave her a penetrating glance and Olivia jumped in quickly. "That's a good idea, Maya, it's nearly the end of the wet. The weather is calm, the sea trip will do you a world of good."

"Then why don't we all go," announced Tyndall. He was about to add that he had a feeling it might be their last opportunity for some time, but decided against it.

It was a "family expedition" down the coast. Olivia, Maya, Tyndall and Ahmed laughed and reminisced as they sailed south in smooth seas and sunny weather. A little color returned to Maya's cheeks and Olivia was happy to be at sea again. Tyndall declared they all looked as young as when they'd first started sailing down to Cossack and, looking at him, legs braced on the deck, long brown fingers delicately guiding the wheel, the wind in his hair, his back straight, Olivia had to agree. And looking at his beloved Olivia, Tyndall still saw the defiant chin, the bright eyes, the soft curves of the body he adored, her hair falling in a thick loose braid down her back in shades of pepper and salt. Olivia moved a little more cautiously on the boat than in the past, but she, too, still held herself firmly, her grace and poise unbent.

"What a marvelous pair you are," said Maya.

"I agree," said Tyndall. "The only old fella in this crew is Ahmed there."

Ahmed, slightly stooped and wizen-faced, his bright black eyes still merry, gave a nicotine-stained, gap-toothed grin and raised his cigarette. "You right there, tuan. Ahmed old fella now." But his sure movements on the boat and agility in the little galley proved he was not as ancient as Tyndall's teasing hinted.

They moored and, as expected, there were members of the black community there to greet them. The numbers had decreased and they traveled less these days. Some had chosen to settle permanently at the mission on the coast. So the arrival of the schooner was greeted with much excitement, a welcome diversion and reunion.

After greetings were exchanged on the beach, almost all talking at once, they walked through the well-worn track over the dunes to the camp.

Olivia fell silent and the chatter became background noise as she was transported back to the first time she had landed here—frightened, exhausted, pregnant. This place and its inhabitants might as well have been an alien planet. Now she knew almost everyone and the women still told the story of her arrival and the birth of baby James. It had become folklore. What might have happened to her had they not befriended her? She had Tyndall to thank for that. She had found that there was a kinship between these people and Minnie and Niah. Now she better understood and appreciated the intertwining relationships. Maya had lost her identity then rediscovered it here. Olivia had helped bring Maya into the world and always felt a bond with her, little knowing she would one day give birth to Olivia's granddaughter. Momentary regrets drifted through her mind, that Hamish had died in the war, and his child Georgie chose not to know these special people, but she dismissed them and concentrated on the conversation around her.

Later, settled round the campfire, passing damper and treacle, Tyndall glanced across at Olivia and felt such pride and love as he watched her, so at ease and genuinely fond of these people. She was as gracious and relaxed as if in a drawing room.

What a delight it had been sharing these past fourteen years with her. He smiled to himself, recalling the first moment he'd seen her here—alone and defiantly brandishing a gun, so strong, yet so vulnerable. What an incredible journey her life had been, yet despite the tragedies there was no hint of bitterness, no hardness in her face or heart. He had loved her from that very moment and the intensity of his feelings for her had never wavered. Niah had been a special brief light in his life that, if he was honest, filled the space reserved for Olivia. He fervently hoped he had made Olivia as joyous as he had felt all this time.

As if sensing his thought she glanced over at him and they exchanged a loving smile.

Ahmed caught the swift look between them and it warmed his heart. Tyndall was his family and he had silently watched the trials of Olivia and Tyndall as they stumbled along their separate paths. He knew the great pull between them was like the moon and the tides and had prayed that fate would bring them together.

Maya, too, was moved by the feelings of love and friendship amongst them all. How she wished Georgiana was here to share this. But Maya had now accepted that her daughter was not one of them, that she had chosen to go her own way in life—her independent streak would see her survive and achieve whatever she set her mind to. Maya felt at great peace here with her people. And to share this time with Olivia and

Tyndall made it doubly so. She was conscious of her links, secure in her identity. The childhood years, even if not fully remembered, were imprinted in her psyche and added to her spiritual sense of belonging. The wisdom these women passed on to her, as they had passed on to each other for generations, gave Maya strength and peace.

That evening as everyone gathered around the big fire, they feasted and sang and told stories. It was a jewel-bright time that would glitter in the memories of each of them.

The early wartime complacency of Australia was shattered with the bombing of Pearl Harbor. The shock waves rippled to the shores of the town sleeping in the sun on Australia's remote northwest coast.

"It's hard to take in. I just keep thinking of Yoshi and Taki and their families back there and all the wonderful times we had here," said Olivia with tears in her eyes.

"It's going to be bloody difficult for our Japs here. Think I'll pop down to the Conti and see what's going on."

Olivia gave him a fond look. "That pub is going to be busier than the War Cabinet."

Knowing where to find the key men in town, the Resident Magistrate arrived at the Continental looking grim. He joined the group on the verandah with Tyndall. "Bad business this. Just got the news we have to round up the Japs."

"Our fellows? Half of them are still at sea on the luggers."

"They could be halfway to Japan by now," joked one of the men, who then quickly lapsed into silence at his faux pas.

"What are you supposed to do with them? Send them back? I don't reckon they'll want to go," said Tyndall.

"They have to be arrested." The RM sighed. "Seems damned silly. I doubt these fellows are a threat to the country. Besides, there's not enough room in the gaol."

"Who's going to tell them?" asked Tyndall quietly.

The RM looked at Tyndall, the most senior and most respected of the pearling masters. "I was rather hoping you would."

Tyndall dressed in his whites with care, buttoning up his collar, tightly tying the laces on his freshly whitened shoes, pulled on his skipper's hat, and with a heavy heart joined the Police Sergeant at the main wharf. Word had been sent from the RM that all Japanese nationals should assemble.

There were close to one hundred and fifty men gathered about the waterfront.

"Good afternoon, Sergeant MacIntyre. What's the procedure here?" asked Tyndall.

"I understand the RM has briefed you. So if you want to make the announcement, we'll take it from there."

Tyndall nodded and walked slowly toward the front of the group. The son of Takahashi, who had been elected spokesman, detached himself and came forward.

Tyndall removed his hat and put it under his arm. "Good-day Takahashi san. You have heard the news, I take it?"

"Yes, captain. We no like. No good for anybody."

Tyndall looked around at the earnest, concerned faces watching him.

"What we do now, captain?"

Tyndall took a deep breath and slowly explained the situation as the Australian Government saw it—that they were now considered enemy aliens and they would have to be arrested and sit out the war in gaol and internment camps.

There was a soft murmur but no one stirred. Tyndall looked around at the faces of the men he had known for so many years. They, too, had chased the same dreams, fought the same battles against the dangers of the ocean, above and below the sea, celebrated each other's good fortune and festivals. They were as much a part of this tightly knit community as anyone else in Broome.

Takahashi bowed to Tyndall. "We understand, captain. Tell Mr. Magistrate and the Sergeant we go as he say." Straightening up, he gave a rueful half-smile. "Too bad. Good shell now."

The gaol and adjoining ground were crowded with Japanese divers, crews, workers and business-men—some with families. Their children had been born in Australia and in the sweltering humid summer heat, conditions in the small gaol were harsh. The Japanese overflowed into flimsy temporary dwellings next to the makeshift compound that they helped to erect.

The rest of the townsfolk rallied and the women set up a roster system to take homecooked meals and small practical gifts to the prison to make them comfortable.

The RM, formally attired even to his plumed hat, had addressed the assembled "prisoners" and had come away humbled at their patience and tolerance. He allowed regular shopping trips into town and assured them they would be looked after as well as possible until they were sent to the internment camps.

As the luggers returned, groups were let out of prison to help pull them up on the beach and bed them down for the wet season.

Ahmed shook his head in dismay as he and Tyndall sat on the small deck of the foreshore camp quarters. "Broome going to sleep till war over I think, tuan."

•   •   •

In Olivia and Tyndall's world, the war was over-shadowed by their concern for Maya, who had caught influenza. Olivia cared for her, while the doctor made calls each day. Tyndall sat by her bed, but found Maya's breathing difficulties, persistent cough and obvious discomfort distressing.

"Isn't there something more that can be done for her?" he asked Doctor Haynes.

"She isn't responding well. I think we should put her in the hospital for some tests," he suggested.

Maya lay in the hospital bed staring at the lush greenery outside the window. She felt as if a great boulder was crushing her chest, it was painful to take a breath and her energy simply seemed to melt away moment by moment. She turned toward the door as Doctor Haynes came in. One glance at his face and she briefly closed her eyes, knowing the worst. Opening her eyes, Maya gave him a comforting smile. "Cheer up, Doctor Haynes."

"I should be the one cheering you up."

"I don't think you have good news for me." It was a calm statement, not a question.

"No, Maya. We've got the results of the chest X-ray. You have tuberculosis." He took her hand and went on. "That means careful nursing, good food and plenty of rest."

"I don't have to go away?"

"Not for the moment. It's complicated by the

influenza. Let's just take matters one day at a time. But it's best you stay here."

Tyndall and Olivia were devastated by the news. "Would she be better off in a sanatorium? Though I couldn't bear her to be far away from us," said Tyndall.

"She's too sick, John."

They spent every possible moment they could at her bedside, but despite the care, Maya seemed to fade before their eyes, day by day. Finally she whispered to them that she wanted to be moved home.

Maya seemed much happier in her own room but her health continued to deteriorate. Olivia suggested they send Georgie a cable.

One evening Olivia went in to sit with Maya, who had been picking at her supper. Maya opened her eyes to see Olivia sitting by the bed doing her embroidery. "Olivia . . . ?"

Olivia put down her needle and took off her glasses. "Yes, pet?"

Maya's thin arms lifted and she pulled the shell pendant necklace over her head. The effort tired her and Olivia leaned over and smoothed Maya's face. "What is it, Maya dear?"

Maya spoke in a soft but firm voice. "I want you to have this. Keep it safe. Pass it on to Georgie." Maya pressed the shell pendant on the twine necklace into her hand.

"Keep it safe, Olivia," Maya repeated.

Olivia was about to protest that Maya keep it on, but realized the gesture obviously meant a lot to her. "I'll hang it on my pearl necklace." She fingered the carved shell. "'Tears of the Moon' Minnie called the pearls . . . sounds so sad, but so beautiful."

Maya gave a little smile. "I always think of them as tears of joy. Pearls are so beautiful and so special. They symbolize much to our people . . ." her voice faded and she closed her eyes.

Later Olivia showed Tyndall the pendant. "She wants me to pass it on to Georgie . . ."

"That seems a very final sort of gesture. Have we heard from Georgie?"

"No. She appears to have moved and hasn't left a forwarding address."

Soon Maya developed pneumonia. Tyndall sat beside her, holding her fine small hand, telling her stories of the old days, though she seemed unaware, drifting into a nether world where her rasping breath, gurgling lungs and cough dominated.

The decision of whether to move her or not was a difficult one. But in brief lucid moments Maya shook her head and pointed to the view of the bay, indicating she wished to stay.

"We couldn't do much more for her in the hospital," said Doctor Haynes. "If she wishes to stay here, then I think it best. Call me, however, if she experiences any severe difficulties. We're doing all we can."

It was a bright, sunny morning, with a breeze from
the bay drifting damply, softly, into Maya's room.
Tyndall had taken his tea and toast to eat with
Maya. Olivia stood on the verandah, lost in time
and thought. Times when life was bright, cheerful
and hopeful seemed lost in a fog. The war was
closing in but still seemed far away and far
removed from the small battle being waged by
Maya.

Sighing she turned and walked into Maya's
room.

Tyndall sat on the bed tenderly smoothing his
daughter's hair, murmuring quietly as he cradled
her in his arms. He looked at Olivia with stricken
eyes. "She's gone, Olivia. My girl . . . just slipped
away."

The fall of Singapore brought the war to
Australia's doorstep. There was much activity as
the Navy requisitioned luggers and there was talk
of the white families being evacuated.

Orders came to move the Japanese south to the
internment camp.

They assembled at the wharf, a casual gathering,
the Japanese milling about amongst their families
and Broome residents. Olivia and Tyndall joined
the Mettas for the departure, helping hand out
packets of home-baked biscuits and small memen-
tos to the men who had been such a vital part of

Broome's life. When the ship sailed, the Japanese hanging over the railing waved energetically to the crowd who waved back, and tears were shed on both sides.

Tyndall called into the Customs House where the officer commanding the naval unit had set up base. Tyndall, smartly turned out in his pearling master's uniform, stood before the young officer. "Just wanted to offer my services, coastal patrol work perhaps. I know these waters very well."

The lieutenant took in the tall, suntanned older man before him. "We appreciate the offer, Captain Tyndall, but the navy has matters in hand, I believe. However should something come up where we can call on your expertise . . ." he was polite but dismissive.

But Tyndall was not so easily rejected. Late the following evening he returned from the Lugger Bar looking pleased with himself.

"I've got an assignment . . . going bush for a bit. Going to train a band of warriors."

"Whatever do you mean, warriors!" Olivia couldn't keep the amusement out of her voice.

"Sergeant MacIntyre and a bloke from 'native affairs' as he calls it have come up with a scheme to save us should the Japs land on this strip of coast."

"Go on." Olivia was noncommittal.

"Well, it's a plan to train the natives in coastal surveillance and dealing with the enemy."

He began undressing as Olivia sat up in bed. "Do they seriously believe we might be invaded?"

"The Government thinks a Jap invasion is possible. They aren't that far to the north of us, Olivia. And just how are we going to protect all our uninhabited coastline? They can't patrol it adequately. So some smart bureaucrat has suggested we train the Aborigines. Just the top warriors. They've got two dozen hand-picked from round this area. I'm to help train them in how to handle a gun, hand-to-hand combat, that sort of thing. Though they know that better than us. Basically, we're to spread the word among the tribal people so if by chance the Japanese came ashore they'd be tracked and attacked."

"Are the Aborigines willing to do this?"

"Well, the mob from Blue Mud Bay in Arnhem are already at it up the top end. The brass think the nor'-west coast should set up the same thing." Tyndall lay back on the pillows and folded his arms under his head. "They have bush knowledge, skill with spears, can appear out of the night like a shadow and you'd never hear them. With proper weapons they'll be ace soldiers."

Olivia felt everything closing in on her. Why did men find such stimulation in the call of war? Hadn't they learned from the last deadly fiasco?

She turned on her side and Tyndall, sensing her melancholy, took her in his arms. "Don't worry, it probably won't happen. We just have to be prepared, that's all."

CHAPTER TWENTY-FIVE

Tyndall and Olivia stood in the narrow hallway outside their respective offices. "Two small rooms upstairs in town and a bunch of ramshackle sheds down the foreshore. All that remains of Star of the Sea. Not much to show for what was a pretty hot enterprise in its day, eh?" remarked Tyndall. There was a tinge of bitterness in his voice.

"John, we have a lot to show for it and you know it. Think of the friends, the adventures, the money we've made—and lost. Admit it, you wouldn't change it."

"Some things I'd change," he said sadly, taking Olivia's hand.

"We can't bring them back, darling." Olivia squeezed beside him as they went down the tiny staircase. "Maybe it's time we turned our backs on it all. Went back to my place in Perth."

"I'm not a gardener," he snapped.

"Well, you could plot out your next move for after the war. Look at cultured pearls again." They stepped out into the street where Ahmed waited.

The three of them gazed up at the window where the sign STAR OF THE SEA PEARL CO., so faded now, could barely be read.

"I feel like putting a match to the whole place," said Tyndall.

"No luggers, just the schooner; no work, no luck. What we do now, tuan?"

"Let's go home and have a Star of the Sea wake," said Olivia. "Mollie's granddaughter cooks up a great curry. Let's round up Mabel and Toby."

Ahmed looked pleased at the idea and Tyndall somewhat mollified.

They drove to the Mettas' house and as they got to the verandah Mabel came bustling out looking distressed. "Oh, my dears, isn't it dreadful. What is going to happen to us all?"

"Mabel, what's wrong?"

She dabbed at her face with the edge of her sari. "Haven't you heard, it's on the wireless . . . Darwin . . . it's been bombed!"

"My God! How bad is it?" gasped Olivia.

Tyndall tensed. "Olivia, forget lunch. I'd better go see what's afoot. We could be next."

"Broome too far for Jap planes, tuan," said Ahmed, looking worried nonetheless.

"Come inside, Olivia. John, Toby has gone to the Conti."

Ahmed trotted through the garden beside Tyndall, who called over his shoulder, "I'll be at the Residence, then the Conti."

•   •   •

Later, settled in the Lugger Bar, the conversation humming like a swarm of bees, Tyndall told Toby of the latest plans. "White families here are to be evacuated. The pearling masters will have to club together and pay off the Malay and Asian crews. The Aborigines in town are going to Beagle Bay mission along with the Sisters from the St. John of God Convent."

"What will happen to Ahmed?" asked Toby. "Where's his home?"

"With me," said Tyndall. "He can move into the back of the house."

Fearing an invasion, the Government purchased all the luggers, those deemed unseaworthy were destroyed. The aerodrome had been upgraded and was already a refueling station for the RAAF and planes on the run to the Dutch East Indies.

By the end of February 1942, Broome was a shell of its former self.

When the Mettas announced they were leaving Broome for Perth, Olivia's heart sank. Toby put on a brave face, his stout frame quivering with emotion as he embraced Olivia. Mabel seemed less composed, indeed as Olivia hugged her dear Ceylonese friend she felt that Mabel had shrunk. She seemed lost in her somber maroon sari, and her long hair coiled at the nape of her neck was streaked with gray, but her smile was as dazzling as ever.

"Don't leave it too long before you join us," begged Mabel. "Get John out of here. You must."

Several state ships already had left with families on board, and this would be the last. A few people were leaving by aircraft.

"It's not first class travel, we're jammed in and it's so hot, but we'll have to make the best of it," sighed Mabel.

A lot of the men stayed behind, knowing they might be needed in Broome and it was heartbreaking to Olivia to see them waving farewell to their wives and children. As the ship pulled away, Olivia burst into tears against Tyndall's chest. "I have this feeling I'm never going to see them again."

"Nonsense. You can go back to Perth any time. You still have a house there remember. Just say the word."

"I will not leave you, or Broome."

"Then dry your tears. You've made up your mind, my darling."

The streets of Broome were silent, buildings deserted, Sheba Lane abandoned. And as evacuation ships headed out to sea, the men left behind got royally drunk in the pubs.

With the Japanese push through the Philippines and the Dutch East Indies, Broome suddenly became the transit center for refugee families. Allied servicemen, and civilians and their families, American service personnel from the Philippines and desperate Dutch families from the Indies, were evacuated to Australia through Broome, mainly by air.

The Institute Hall was turned into a medical and care center and Olivia worked tirelessly helping the refugee families. There were few women in the town, a nurse, the lady at the telephone exchange and several of the Sisters at the St. John of God Convent. The hotels were full and the remaining families threw open their homes to cope with the thousands coming through.

Tyndall also poured his efforts into helping out at the harbor where there was little provision for the flying boats. The spring tides stranded many of the flying boats a mile from shore. It was a long walk through the mud to the jetty and then to the shore and many of the older people and mothers with children chose to stay on board the flying boats despite the cramped conditions. Ahmed worked beside Tyndall helping to put down moorings for the flying boats and running a stripped-down lugger as a fuel barge.

"The aerodrome is badly cut up. Those Flying Fortresses and the Liberators are so big, they have to make repairs after every landing," said Tyndall.

"All the Malay and Koepanger boys out there fixin' it up," said Ahmed. "They dig up gravel. Hard work for them livin' out at the 'drome."

"Those pilots must be exhausted, refueling and straight back for another load. I heard there were over fifty planes out there today. Those poor people. Its sounds awful up in the East," said Olivia. "They're shuttling them out just ahead of the Japanese."

• • •

That evening Tyndall called Olivia to come out on the verandah. But instead of the tranquil sunset view they generally enjoyed, the bay was full of activity. As they watched, two Dutch Navy Dornier flying boats skimmed in and landed, skidding across the water like great silver sea birds.

After their supper Tyndall and Olivia returned to the verandah. The wet was almost over, a soft fuzz ringed the moon. The calm waters were dotted with Qantas Catalinas and Short Sunderland flying boats. "They look like great big birds bobbing out there in the bay," said Olivia. "It looks so peaceful."

"For the moment. There's still a lot of activity down there. They have to get out on the tides. Makes it tricky."

"What's going to happen to us, John?" whispered Olivia.

"Who knows? All we can do is our best, as we've always done. Do you want to leave? Maybe you should. Maybe we both should."

"Do you want to go?"

"No. A captain doesn't leave his ship. Don't worry, my precious." He kissed the top of her head.

"I'm with you, Captain." Olivia felt comforted as Tyndall put an arm around her.

Two days later in the afternoon as the lighter *Nicol Bay,* carrying drums of aviation fuel, ploughed across the bay to one of the three flying boats,

Tyndall and Ahmed paused while working near the jetty and looked up. A distant buzz high above them materialized into a small aircraft turning in a lazy arc and circling several times before heading north-west.

Tyndall hurried along to an engineer working nearby who was also gazing skyward. "What do you make of that?" asked Tyndall.

"Jap reconnaissance plane, I reckon."

"I don't like it. The brass think we're out of flying range for the Japanese, but at the rate they're moving their bases this way, I don't think we are."

"Good thing only a couple of planes in."

"There'll be more tonight. They're damned sitting ducks," said Tyndall ominously.

"See, I knew there'd be more arrivals," declared Tyndall the next morning as he stood on his front verandah with a mug of tea. "There's sixteen aircraft out there."

"They're all Dutch by the look of it," said Olivia, joining him.

"I'd better get down there and help with the refueling, they should get them out as soon as the tide is right." He kissed Olivia and handed her his empty mug. "See you later on, my darling."

While the aircraft were being refueled, some of the air crews were celebrating the success of the last refugee run down in the bar of the Conti.

Most of the Dutch women and children were waiting in the flying boats. At the aerodrome the first of the half dozen aircraft was preparing to leave. A Liberator had arrived at dawn from Jogjakarta with wounded men and was given first priority out.

On the spur of the moment, Olivia had decided to go down to the wharf to watch the aircraft take off. She joined the small crowd of remaining locals and a group of evacuated women and children waiting for a launch to take them to their flying boat.

The crews in the Conti looked at their watches and tipped back the last of their drinks. It was a bright clear morning approaching 9.30 A.M.

From the north came the drone of aircraft which no one took any notice of until, seconds later, from Cable Beach came nine silver specks swooping low and fast over Roebuck Bay.

Olivia glanced up, then screamed at the sight of the deadly little Zeros with the brilliant red circle of the rising sun on their fuselage. She watched in horror as the planes struck with surprise and accuracy.

At the sound of machine gun fire, men raced from the Continental and watched helplessly as one after another of the flying boats was hit and burst into flames.

Olivia's first instinct was to dive flat on the wharf, putting her hands over her ears trying to block out the screams of the women and children in the sinking and burning aircraft.

The Zeros turned for another attacking run and their tracer bullets ripped through other boats and planes that had survived the first onslaught.

Suddenly, everyone sprang into action as clouds of black smoke rolled around the brilliant waters of the bay.

"John!" screamed Olivia, starting to run down the long wharf to find him and Ahmed.

The captain of the refueling lighter cast off and the crew frantically began picking up burned survivors. Some women and children not trapped in the belly of the aircraft were in the water. Few could swim and through the noise and gunfire came a scream, "Sharks!"

Other small craft were pushing out into the burning sea, heedless of danger, looking for survivors. All the flying boats sank within minutes.

Tyndall and Ahmed had grabbed a dinghy pulled up on the shore and pushed out into the pall of smoke and fumes. Ahmed rowed with all his strength as Tyndall shouted instructions. They dragged two women and a young girl into the dinghy. Then another woman was dragged over the side, coughing and still clinging onto her drowned baby. A badly injured man was next.

"There's a head to starboard, Ahmed."

"No can take more, tuan. We sink. We come back."

Willing hands helped pull survivors from the boat and Ahmed and Tyndall turned back into the nightmare on the bay.

Despairingly they heard the Zeros turning for another attack. They only attacked the aircraft, ignoring the rescuers, the spectators on the wharf and the town. But tracer bullets were slicing in every direction. Ahmed pulled as hard as he could at the oars. He caught Tyndall's eye and Tyndall gave him a swift smile of encouragement.

"Want me to take over, Ahmed?"

Ahmed shook his head and returned the smile, then suddenly he slumped forward with a cry.

"My god, Ahmed. You're hit!" Tyndall reached for him, seeing the blood already seeping across his white shirt. He lay him down and took over the oars, turning for shore, stroking as powerfully as he could. He kept his eyes on Ahmed's face, willing his loyal companion not to die. "Hang on, old friend, we're getting there. It's not going to bloody well end like this. It can't."

An oar struck the muddy bottom and Tyndall leaped over the side and reached for Ahmed.

Olivia was frantically running along the shore trying to see into the fumes and pall of smoke that blurred the sun. The noise of the gunfire, cracking and burning, the shouts and screams, had seared into her soul. "John . . . Ahmed . . ." she cried. It seemed an eternity had passed since she was standing in the sun on the wharf but it had been less than fifteen minutes.

Then, miraculously, like some apparition, through the drifting smoke she saw the tall figure of her beloved Tyndall wading from the bay, with Ahmed in his arms.

A pain stabbed at Olivia. "Oh, Ahmed . . ." In the next second her world spun and in slow motion she saw Tyndall's head jerk upwards, his knees bend, and he sank down into the mud. His body made one effort to rise, to lift Ahmed, but then he pitched forward and both of them lay in the mud at the water's edge.

By the time she got to them, they were both dead.

Olivia sat in the mud, Tyndall's head on her lap, stroking his hair with one hand, her other hand resting on Ahmed's shoulder, oblivious to the chaos about her.

The Zeros swooped from the bay to the aerodrome and destroyed what planes remained on the ground. The opposing force from the Volunteer Defense Corps fired their .303 rifles in anger and frustration but were no match for the Zeros which now jettisoned their long-range fuel tanks. But a Dutch submachine gunner who had been repairing his gun at the aerodrome workshop emptied his ammunition at the departing Japanese and scored a hit.

Glancing over his shoulder, the Japanese pilot saw the disabled Zero spin out of control and reflected that one loss was a small price to pay for the honor they had done the Emperor.

Their mission accomplished, the Zeros turned and set a course for Timor and their base at the town of Koepang, where divers had been recruited for the Broome pearling industry since the late 1800s.

But Takeo Yoshikuri was uncharacteristically slow in joining the formation. Instead he took a long curving sweep over Broome and looked with intense curiosity at the rather shabby and sprawling little town. He had heard so much about it but couldn't see anything that helped him understand the attraction it still had for his father, who had worked there for so much of his life as a diver.

As he adjusted the throttle to catch up with his colleagues he remembered a photograph his father had on display all the time at home. It was a photograph of him as a young man in his diving suit on the deck of a lugger and beside him was the tall, smiling Australian captain. What was his name? Father was always talking about him. Suddenly it came to him. Ah yes, Captain Tyndall. And as he took his position in the formation, Takeo wondered what Captain Tyndall was doing on this day.

Broome 1995

In the reading room of the Broome Historical Society, Lily came to the last entry in Olivia's diary.

June 24, 1953
It is now a week since Georgiana and Lily flew back to Sydney and I am missing them so much. Their

*visit was as bright as Broome sunlight in the dry
season. Georgie is as flighty as ever, gushing with
enthusiasm for everything and full of schemes and
plans now she has settled there from America after
the divorce. Lily is a beautiful child and has quite
a serious streak and an intelligence that I think will
take her far. She reminds me so much of Hamish.
We had some lovely moments together, particularly
in the garden. When I was with her, I felt so much
younger and found an energy that I didn't know I
could still muster. Now all that energy has gone
again and I'm left with only the memories . . .*

Beneath it someone had printed *"Died July
15, 1953."*

Lily closed the journal she had been reading
for the past few days and rested her chin in her
hands. The diary had told her much about the
lives of people who were now a meaningful part of
her life.

She felt utterly exhausted, yet at the same time
exhilarated. So many thoughts, such emotion, an
overflowing of love, pride and awe for the people
whose journey through life she now shared. These
women of her past were part of her but some of
the knowledge was overwhelming.

About two-thirds of the way through the journal had come the first startling clue that she had
Aboriginal blood. Confirmation of her link with
Niah, through Maya, the grandmother she never
knew, was a shock. The link was something that

she still had not come to terms with. It was put in a holding zone in her mind until she had finished the compelling story the diary told.

That her name was mentioned with such affection in the final entry swamped all thoughts as she sat quietly amid the furniture and memorabilia of another era, the time of John and Olivia Tyndall. She was struggling to hold back a tear when someone bustled in.

"I've shut the museum for the day and brought you in a cuppa. Just couldn't wait till I was home for a boost." It was Muriel, the elderly and effervescent archivist.

Lily quickly dabbed an eye and forced a smile as she took the cup. "You're a darling, Muriel. You've no idea how much I need this."

Muriel sat down in one of the exhibition chairs. "Finished the big read?" she asked, taking a sip.

"Yes. It's almost a bit much, I'm afraid."

With a slight murmur Muriel signaled that she wasn't surprised.

"A lot of people often discover more than they anticipate. Not all good news at that. How about you? Something seemed a little sad, I rather think."

Lily nodded.

"Want to talk about it?"

"Not now, Muriel, but thanks. I've just got to do a lot of thinking."

Although bursting with curiosity, Muriel had a fine appreciation of the impact personal history could have on people when they delved into the past. She tactfully changed the subject. "I s'pose you'll be rushing off back south now that you've finished the read. One thing, you've had lovely weather for it."

Lily was grateful. "Every day has been a gem," and she chuckled at the double meaning of her response. "No, I think I'll spend another couple of days here. One or two little things to clear up yet."

Muriel rose and put Olivia's journal on a bookshelf. "I'll have a read of the diaries myself one day. Never got past the first couple of pages. There's always too much work to do and not enough time to fully appreciate what we've got in here." She picked up the cups. "See you at the door in a couple of minutes, luv."

Lily looked around the room then moved about lightly running her hands over pieces of furniture and imagining them as they once were in the house of Olivia and John. They had sat in these chairs, relaxed on this chaise, used this china, watched that clock. And finally, as she had ended each day since she came into the room, she stood in front of a large portrait of John Tyndall. His eyes smiled at her, though this time she imagined she saw more affection and a little amusement. "Well, great-grandfather," she said softly. "I guess you're wondering how I'm going to deal with all of this?" She gave him a rueful smile. "So am I."

She picked up her bag and notebook but turned back to the portrait when she reached the door and spoke again. "I'll start by having a strong drink at the Lugger Bar." She winked and quietly closed the door.

The next morning Lily telephoned the Aboriginal artist Rosie Wallangou, whom she'd met at her exhibition at the Cable Beach Club soon after arriving.

"Rosie, it's Lily Barton. We met at the exhibition. I'm from Sydney, remember?"

"Of course. You came here searching for something. Any luck?"

"Yes, quite a bit. 'Tears of the Moon' now has a lot of meaning for me."

There was silence at the other end of the line.

"Rosie . . . ?"

"Sorry. You took me aback a bit. Want to come round for a chat?"

"I'd like that very much."

Rosie gave directions which Lily scribbled in her notebook. "Might as well walk, Lily. Not far enough to warrant a taxi."

Lily walked through the town looking at the buildings, the streets and the foreshore with new eyes. Everywhere she could see the lively past. Beyond the clean streets, modern shops and strolling tourists, Lily visualized the Broome of her great-grandfather's day. Remnants remained, some lovingly restored and recreated. Some things were frozen now in rust-coated time—the horse-drawn train carriage, the decompression cylinder, the cracked iron railing around graves. Others were freshly painted—Sun Pictures, Sheba Lane, the old sheds now housing pearl shops. And everywhere, the painted Asian signs, the multicultural faces in the streets, the smells, the colors, were as they'd always been.

Following Rosie's instructions she found herself climbing along the foreshore to the point that rose above the bay. A big old house faced the emerald waters, its surrounding verandah looking shady and cool. She felt a surge of recognition as she went toward the house, and her heart skipped a beat when she saw the massive poinciana tree in the garden. She remembered the poignant notation in the diary of Olivia scattering James' burial soil there. Lily knew this was the home of Olivia and Tyndall. She paused as she reached the front gate, almost afraid to walk to the verandah. As she hesitated, Rosie came to the front steps and hailed her cheerfully. "Hi Lily. You're at the right place."

Right place, thought Lily as she walked up the path almost in a trance. Right place? She stopped at the top of the stairs and looked at Rosie, who was now standing by a cane chair on the verandah. For a moment neither said a word, both looking each other in the eye.

It was Rosie who broke the silence. "Yep, I can see it now. You're one of us all right. Felt it a bit that night at the exhibition when we talked about the painting but figured I was just imagining things. Just goes to show, we should always listen to the spirit. How did you find out?"

"From my great-grandmother's diaries in the Historical Society. I've been reading them for days." Lily paused and took off her straw hat. "It's a bit difficult to take in. Hardly slept at all last night."

"Then you'd better sit down," urged Rosie with a laugh. "I've just brewed the coffee, so your timing is perfect." She poured some and passed a mug to Lily. "So you think the 'Tears of the Moon' means something, eh. Like what?"

Lily told the whole story as briefly as she could, concentrating on the relationship with Maya and Niah and then showing Rosie the pendant which she had in her shoulder bag. Rosie handled the pendant with reverence, then gave it back. "It's proper. So, you're one of Minnie's mob, eh?"

Lily took a breath. "Looks like it, doesn't it?"

"That makes you and me relatives, same mob." She looked keenly at Lily.

"Yes, I guess it does," acknowledged Lily in a whisper. Rosie settled back in her chair and just looked at Lily, who went on, "You'll have to bear with me. It's hard . . ." she faltered, searching for the right words.

Rosie's solemn face fractured into a big smile. "It's a real blast, Lily. Really it is, when you think about it. You don't have to make any big decisions right away. Geez, people like you are popping up all over the place these days. Come and have a look around the house. You probably have a mind full of images of what it's like from Olivia's diary."

Lily felt a huge weight lift from her shoulders as Rosie grabbed her by the hand. They were still holding hands when they went into the living room where a beautiful oval, framed photograph of Olivia was hanging.

"There she is," said Rosie with admiration. "Magnificent isn't she. So strong, so beautiful. There's nothing like it in the shots down at the museum. It was taken by a touring Japanese photographer just before the war." Olivia gazed out from the picture with a bemused expression as though about to break into laughter. Her thick hair was pulled neatly back from her face in a complicated loop, a soft chiffon print dress was draped across her torso and around her neck hung the strand of magnificent pearls.

"You must have become very close to her somehow," said Lily, acknowledging the warmth with which Rosie talked about Olivia. "I only ever met her once, in Perth when I was very little. Mum had come back from America after her divorce. I remember walking with Olivia in the garden. And I remember the pendant. She must have given it to Georgie then."

"Probably," said Rosie brightly. "Yes, she was wonderful to me. Although I was very little, too. I was brought up by my grandmother, who worked for Olivia and John in their last years. Olivia helped keep me in school and then set up a trust fund to send me to art school. 'Tears of the Moon' was one of the first paintings I did at the art school. The teachers loved it and that helped make me proud of my heritage and I knew I had to paint it. 'Tears' is still special to me, but I told you that the other night."

"How did you get the house? Did you buy it?"

"Yes. It got sold up when Olivia died, just like the house in Perth. I guess your Mum put it on the market. Several people owned it before I bought it . . . thanks to the art punters in New York."

They reached the verandah that overlooked the bay. "Great view, isn't it? said Rosie.

"Wonderful. It must have been a sight in the old days when the luggers were putting to sea under sail." They stood in silence, taking in the view, then Lily turned to the attractive woman beside her in smart cotton slacks and a T-shirt emblazoned with the Aboriginal flag and the word MABO. "You're living in two worlds, Rosie. How do you cope?"

"It's easy. I've always lived in two worlds, but I know why you're asking. You want to know if you can live in two worlds like me. Well that's something only you can answer. It depends on the spirit in you, I guess. You see Lily, it's one thing to acknowledge you've got Aboriginal blood. It's another thing altogether for you to really know in your soul if you are one of us." There was the noise of someone in the kitchen and Rosie called out, "Out here, Gran. Come on out and meet a special visitor."

Lily turned and gasped in surprise when the old woman came through the door. Gran was Biddy, the wizened old woman she had found fishing on the sand spit the day she arrived in Broome.

"Catch enough for dinner again, Gran?"

"Yeah. Done orright." She eyed Lily thoroughly. "G'day."

"Hello, Biddy," said Lily softly.

The old lady peered at her, then broke into a gap-toothed grin. "We talked down on the spit. You brung in me line."

"That's right," explained Lily to Rosie, "I was wandering around when I first got in and we chatted for a bit."

"Grandma Biddy is a bit of a fixture down there when the tide allows. Doing well for her age, pushing eighty." Rosie turned to Biddy, took her hand and brought her closer to Lily. "Gran, this is Lily. She's the great-granddaughter of both John and Olivia. Maya's granddaughter."

There was a sparkle in the old woman's eyes that delighted Lily. "Ah, you're one of our mob then. I f'git your mumma's name. She went south, never came back."

"Georgiana," prompted Lily.

"Yeah, that right. Georgie we called 'er. Yeah, Georgie. Wild one she was." Biddy plopped into a canvas director's chair and began unlacing her well-worn sandshoes.

"Grandma is Mollie's granddaughter or Minnie's great-granddaughter. Gran worked with

Olivia right up to the time she left town to live in Perth after the war. Show Gran the pendant."

Lily again took the pendant from her bag and gave it to Biddy.

The old woman examined it carefully, but said nothing, giving Lily only a slight nod of acknowledgment as she handed it back. Lily was putting it in her bag when Biddy asked, "Yer got kids?"

"Yes. Only one. Samantha."

"Well, bring 'er up 'ere t'meet family. Proper t'ing t'do that."

Lily was speechless. That simple statement by Biddy, the invoking of family ties and responsibilities hit Lily like a blow to the body. Her mind whirled. How would Samantha react to all of this? She could barely cope with the reality herself. Biddy, that old black woman, was family—at least in Aboriginal culture she was family. The enormity of it all made her feel faint.

Rosie came to the rescue. "Now, Gran, Lily hasn't had time to think about this family business. She only just found out in the last couple of days. Her mother never told her about us."

Biddy hauled herself out of the chair. "Betta put them fish in the fridge. Yer comin' for a feed t'night?"

"Thanks, Biddy, I'd like that," said Lily, then exchanged a grin with Rosie.

That night, after dinner, Lily lay on the bed staring at the slowly revolving fan. Like the fan going round and round, her mind replayed the events of the day. The meeting with Rosie and Gran, the dinner, then the long talk with Rosie on the verandah about Aboriginal concepts of family and the complexity of kinship relations as they watched the moon swing over the bay. She also replayed the agonizing emotional confusion that had been compounded by the meeting with Biddy. The old lady's words echoed in her mind. *You're one of our mob then.* She found herself pondering on Rosie's comment about the difference between having Aboriginal blood and being Aboriginal. Did she really belong to Biddy's mob? Was she really one of the family in spirit? Lily didn't know the answers.

She looked at the telephone beside the bed and for a moment considered phoning her daughter, then her lover, then her best girlfriend, but dismissed each option as it presented itself. None of them could possibly understand what she was going through. It was her struggle, she realized, one she had to resolve alone. She had almost fallen into an exhausted sleep when a thought surfaced from the mists of her mind. Tomorrow she would go to Niah. Then she lapsed into a deep sleep.

In the morning Lily rang the car rental company and asked them to bring a good four-wheel drive around to the Continental. She took off along the red sand road with confidence. Unlike the first time she drove down this road, she was comfortable with the brightness of the sky, the softness of the orange talcum-like dust beneath the wheels, and the hot breeze that blew into the car.

As she headed north, Lily ran through the scenario of her life story once more, occasionally fingering the pendant that hung around her neck. How easy it was to accept her white Broome antecedents. How fascinating was the story of the history of their lives. They had struggled and won. But within that struggle lay a story of mixed races and entwined histories that had brought her to where she was today. Lily now understood why her mother had turned her back on her family, choosing to reject her heritage. In those times, a hint of mixed or black blood was socially devastating in white society. It meant being a person without rights.

She could adopt her mother's attitude and do as Georgie did—turn her back and ignore the knowledge. But the more Lily thought about her mother's attitude the more she realized Georgiana was a product of her times. Yet deep down it must have affected her, because she hadn't turned her back completely. After all, it was Georgiana who had sent Olivia's diaries, letters and photos to the Broome museum. She must have surmised if Lily was really interested in her roots she would set out to find her history and what Lily chose to do with the knowledge would be her decision.

And how would her friends in Sydney react? Rosie they would embrace. But Biddy? In Broome and the north it was accepted and understood. But in city heartlands it was all very well to be politically correct provided it didn't encroach on one's personal life. Lily knew some of her more snobby friends would be appalled at finding she had Aboriginal family connections.

She drove into the mission at Beagle Bay late in the day to find Brother William sitting on a chair outside the church reading a small prayer book.

"Hello again, Brother William."

"Hello there. You were here before. The lady asking all the questions."

"That's right." She held up a plastic bag, "Look, I've brought you some black bread and liverwurst from the delicatessen in Broome."

The old man's eyes lit up. "So kind of you. Come, we'll make tea."

They went into the dining area and the young Aboriginal mother set out the cups and plates as Lily sliced the bread. They exchanged a smile and it immediately struck Lily that she was now looking at Aboriginal people differently. Even so, could she go back to Sydney and never return to Broome, never tell anyone about her family history, and pretend it didn't exist?

She talked with Brother William about the old days, dwelling mainly on the life of Olivia and Tyndall after they were married, and avoiding any reference to the Aboriginal side of the story. Then she changed the subject. "I gave the Bishop's journal to the Historical Society. They were very grateful. It's a valuable addition to their archives."

Brother William was pleased. "We have been able to help each other, and that is the way it should be. Now, what is the purpose of your visit? More questions?"

"In a way yes, Father, but I don't think you have the answer. I've got to find it myself. I'm sorry if that sounds a little mysterious."

Brother William threw his hands up and laughed. "In our business we live with that sort of mystery all the time. Is there any way I can help?"

"Not really. I just need a little time to walk around on my own. Do you mind?"

"Of course not. Please go ahead, take your time. The church is open if you want to pray. It might help."

He watched from the verandah as Lily walked slowly across the settlement to the cemetery, paused at the gate, then went in and began studying the headstones. Absent-mindedly, he scratched his head a little, nodded slowly several times as if he suddenly understood something, then walked briskly to the church to pray for this unexpected visitor.

The headstone was in a rather neglected part of the cemetery, a spot where the weeds had grown out of control in the last wet. It was without any markings and adorned only by the carved pearl shell, exactly as described in Olivia's diary.

Lily kneeled down and ran her fingers over the carving, now almost worn smooth by nine decades of wind-driven dust in the dry and lashing rain in the wet. But there was no mistaking the design, the symbols of journeys across the sea and circles that represented pearls. She sat back on her heels and just looked at the simple headstone, which was devoid of any words yet said so much to her.

All the knowledge gained and the emotions experienced in an extraordinary few days flooded over her yet again. Despite the confusion in her mind she realized, more than at any time this week, that she was now center stage in the ongoing drama that Olivia's diary had recorded. It was being here at the grave, close to one who was yet so distant in her family line, that made the continuity of it all so clear, and at the same time so awesome in all its implications. This was no longer a story in a diary. It was reality, and a reality that posed a huge challenge to her.

Picking absently at some of the long stems of grass, she recalled Rosie's words of the night before. *Being Aboriginal isn't a hat you can put on and take off, Lily. It's a commitment, a spiritual thing. Without that, you don't belong. If you've got the spirit, Lily, then you've got something. That mightn't always be easy to carry, but believe me, it's something really special, really worth hanging on to. And you won't want to hide it from anyone.*

Lily had a choice—to reveal this truth to the world or keep it to herself. It would not be easy to walk back into her own world in Sydney and proclaim her new identity. And it would not be easy to reject it, for the knowledge was now part of her and could not be erased. The facts of her links were indisputable; whether she was going to be fully accepted by her Aboriginal family was a very different issue and dependent on her own honesty. Was she really one of the family in spirit?

It had all seemed much clearer last night sitting on the moonlit verandah with Rosie. But now . . . ?

Lily dropped the stems of grass and reached out again to lightly touch the shell on the stone. "Do I have the spirit in me, Niah? Do I?"

Make Your Own Beautiful
Memories Down Under

WIN A FABULOUS TRIP FOR
TWO TO AUSTRALIA!

Enter The
TEARS OF THE MOON
Sweepstakes!

No purchase necessary. Details on back.

Offer expires May 29, 1998.

Name: _____

Address: _____

City: _____ State: _____ Zip: _____

Mail to:
TEARS OF THE MOON S/S
P.O. Box 9139
Bridgeport, NJ 08014

OFFICIAL RULES

No purchase necessary to enter. This sweepstakes is open to U.S. residents 18 years or older, except employees and families of HarperCollins Publishers, Tristar Fulfillment Services, and their agencies, affiliates, and subsidiaries. To enter, fill out this official entry form (original or facsimile), or print your name and address on a 3" x 5" piece of paper. Mail your entry to: TEARS OF THE MOON S/S, P.O. Box 9139, Bridgeport, NJ, 08014. Enter as often as you wish, but mail each entry in a separate envelope. All entries must be received by May 29, 1998, in order to be eligible. HarperCollins is not responsible for late, lost, incomplete, or misdirected mail. All entries will become the property of HarperCollins and will not be returned or acknowledged. Entry constitutes permission to use the winner's name, hometown, and likeness for promotional purposes on behalf of HarperCollins unless prohibited by law. Winner will be selected from all eligible entries on or about June 15, 1998, in a random drawing conducted by Tristar Fulfillment Services, an independent judging organization whose decision shall be final and binding. Odds of winning are dependent on the number of entries received. Winner will be notified by mail. To claim prize, winner must sign an Affidavit of Eligibility, Assignment, and Release within 10 days of notification. One (1) Grand Prize winner will receive a 7-day, 6-night trip for two to Australia. Trip for winner and his/her adult companion will consist of round trip airfare from major international airport nearest winner and hotel accommodations. Any other expenses, including taxes, are the sole responsiblity of the winner. (Approximate retail value: $4,000.00) All travel arrangements will be made by sponsor. Trip must be taken within one year from the date prize is awarded. Prize is not transferable. No substitutions of prize will be offered. Void where prohibited. For the name of Grand Prize winner, send a self-addressed, stamped envelope after July 1, 1998, to: TEARS OF THE MOON S/S, P.O. Box 9298, Bridgeport, NJ, 08014.